LOVE

Now it [obscured by label] ignore a binding. It grows tighter and heavier until your body fails and your spirit is broken." She took his hand in hers. "That's why I know I must break your binding, why I don't beg you simply to leave the caves. I would stay if I could. You are the only friend I have ever had, Kabeiros . . . and I'm afraid to go alone, Mother knows where . . . I'm afraid." Her voice died to a whimper.

He didn't answer, but tears streaked his face.

"How are you bound?" Hekate pleaded. "I beg you to tell me. I will find a way to break the binding. I swear it. I swear that if you must drink babies' blood if you leave the caves, I'll find some way to supply you. I will not turn from you. I will protect you no matter how horrible your secret."

"Will you?"

He laughed wildly, jumped up, and rushed out of the cave into the pale pinky-blue light of first dawn. And the man Kabeiros was gone! A huge black dog staggered a few steps, shaking himself free of Kabeiros' tunic, then threw up his head and howled pathetically.

BAEN BOOKS by ROBERTA GELLIS

Bull God
Thrice Bound

THRICE BOUND

ROBERTA GELLIS

THRICE BOUND

A Baen Books Original

Baen Publishing Enterprises
P.O. Box 1403
Riverdale, NY 10471
www.baen.com

ISBN: 0-671-31834-9

Cover art by Carol Heyer
Interior map by Charles Gellis

First printing, August 2001

Distributed by Simon & Schuster
1230 Avenue of the Americas
New York, NY 10020

Production by Windhaven Press, Auburn, NH
Printed in the United States of America

To my most excellent agent, Lucienne Diver, and to her charming husband Peter and the adorable Tynan.

Pontus Euxinus
COLCHIS
Colchis
Trapezus
carusa
Sinope
Heraclea
Cyaneae
Symplegades
Lysamachia
Propontis
THRACE
Heraclea
Olympus
Plutos
GREECE
Mare Aegaeum
LUD
MESHECH
JOGARMAH
Satala
Kanish
TUBAL
Miletus
Aleppo
Quatna
Hamath
Caves of the Dead
SHEM
CRETE
CYPRUS
Byblos
Urkabas
DAMASCUS
KAANAN
Mare Internum
Canopus
Nile delta
Memphis
EGYPT

PART ONE:

THE BINDINGS

CHAPTER 1

In the instant that she became aware of the tug of her father's will, she felt the change sweep over her. She didn't need to look down at her hands to know they were now twisted and knobby, the knuckles swollen, the skin spotted with the brown patches of old age. Her tunic hung loose on her, sagging over flat, fleshless dugs where a moment before proud young breasts had lifted it. Her head felt oddly light because the luxuriant growth of blue-sheened black hair that hung to her hips had transmuted into scanty white locks. Hekate looked down instinctively to hide her eyes, where a flicker of triumph might be exposed.

That change of form had originally been a punishment for some forgotten misdeed in her first blossoming of adolescent rebellion, but the punishment had been far more valuable to her than simply teaching her that obedience to her father was the easiest path. Some instinct had wakened in her when her father's spell touched her, and when he tried to change her back, she resisted him and remained a withered crone.

Even now as she turned to leave her portion of her father's house—the building that housed the entrance, the slaves . . . and her—drawn by his will to his underground lair, even now a smile twitched at her lips. Perses had been frightened, the first and only time Hekate could remember doing anything that frightened her father.

The impulse to smile faded. It was sheer good fortune, or perhaps owing to the protection of the Great Mother, whom Perses laughed to scorn, that he hadn't perceived the resistance to be deliberate. Possibly he'd been so shocked by the failure of his restoration spell that he hadn't understood it was by Hekate's own will that she retained the form of the crone. He had struck her, and to conceal his failure had screamed at her that she should wear her disgusting form until the spell wore thin and she could find a way to dismiss it herself.

She had fled, as if terrified—and some part of her was—across the fields that her father's slaves worked and into the forest where she had willed herself back to her natural form and then back to the image of the crone. She had spent a happy day in the woods, calling the small, shy, wild things to her, touching their soft fur, their long ears, even their dainty paws, offering them nuts and berries she had found. When she returned, still in the form of the crone so that her father should not learn how easy it was for her to change, her mother wept with horror . . . but as ever Asterie could do nothing for her daughter.

Hekate crossed the long reception chamber and turned left past a heavy wooden door into a small chamber in which another door—surfaced with modeled clay to match exactly the sun-baked brick of the back wall—opened at her touch. The opening revealed a covered walk leading to another building, somewhat larger than that a visitor would see at first. The entryway led to a courtyard lavishly planted with bushes and flowers. To the left was an arch open onto an opulently furnished reception chamber. Behind that, Hekate knew, were the bedchambers. Her skin, coarse and leathery as it was, prickled at the thought, but she turned right where a narrow door, again painted to match the surroundings walls, now stood open onto a dark corridor.

To her right was a solid wall. Hekate stared at it. She was either losing her mind or that was the way she had gone the last time she had been summoned. However, since she had no choice, she turned left and began to walk. Within ten steps a part of the corridor wall suddenly disappeared showing the head of the stairs. Hekate shivered. He–or something he had summoned–was watching and knew where she was. She could have sworn she had walked much farther when the corridor had opened to the right. She looked down the stairs. They were unlit, steep, uneven . . . dangerous.

As she looked, the door behind her swung shut and she was in darkness. The temptation to form a mage light flicked at her, but because of the watcher, she fixed her mind on regret, thinking "too weak," stretched a hand to the wall and began to feel her way from step to step. She had long been aware that her father could scry her, or summon some otherworld creature to watch her, but she was not certain how deep that scrying or the creature's seeing went. She had never been able to discover whether it could read her surface thoughts as well as her position and expression.

At least neither scrying or summoned slave could read below the surface; her mother had assured her of that, but Asterie was not sure whether he or his creature could read thoughts at all. She feared he could but knew he couldn't reach into the back of the mind; Hekate had proved to herself that she could safely bury her satisfaction there.

Slowly, step by step, she felt her way down the stairway that curved steeply along the side of a natural sinkhole. From far below came a faint echo—moving water? her own steps? As far as Hekate knew, no light had ever exposed those black depths.

Under her hand the smooth baked brick of the wall changed to rough-dressed stone. Hekate hesitated. The pull of her father's will intensified. Soon it might become pain. Fear made her heart clench. Hatred and a despairing resistance kept her still, clinging to the wall, panting for breath. The pull grew no stronger. Hekate waited, letting her breathing ease, clutching her tiny triumph to her.

The crone's pretense of weakness had a second advantage in addition to reminding Perses of his failure; it increased the time before she had to face him. And a third. Hekate swallowed. Before she'd worn the guise of the crone, Hekate had begun to dislike the way her father looked at her. She tried to assure herself that he wouldn't violate his own daughter, and truly she had never believed he lusted after her. What he wanted was almost more foul. Coupling was a doorway to binding a person close enough to enslave her or suck out her power.

A stab of rage almost tore through the fear and submission Hekate kept in the forefront of her mind. It was through coupling that Perses had seized and subdued her mother. Asterie hadn't always been the near-mindless shadow she now was. Bit by bit, from a whisper here, a word from there, a sad sigh and headshake, Hekate had learned that before she married Perses, her mother had been a strong sorceress with an unequaled ability to create spells.

Asterie could still create spells, although she could no longer cast them, and in secret, when Perses was busy with his own sorceries or when they could escape to the mysterious shelter of the shrine in the forest, she had taught her daughter all she knew. But that was in years past. As Hekate matured, Asterie faded until she scarcely seemed to know her daughter and would pass her when they met in a chamber without a word or a sign of recognition. At first Hekate had stopped her, spoken to her, embraced her, but of late she had given up trying.

The stair ended. A corridor darker, if possible, than the stairway was an emptiness before Hekate's extended hand. She hobbled forward slowly, favoring the aches in her knees and back. A few steps brought her outstretched hand into bruising contact with a wall. Hekate hissed with pain and frustration. Doubtless Perses was laughing. No matter how careful she was, she met that wall too hard. Perhaps he had some way of moving it.

She wondered, feeling her way along the wall to the right, whether he hoped she would break a bone. The form of the crone was no illusion; in it she was truly old and had all the ills great age brought with it. Unfortunately, since she had not lived the years the shape betokened, she had garnered no wisdom to go with the appearance. Her mind was her own; it held no more and no less whatever her form.

If that was a disadvantage while she was the crone, it was advantageous when she took on the third form natural to her and didn't reduce her to a childish fool. Hekate paused, leaning on the wall and breathing hard, keeping the fore of her mind filled with fear and her awareness of a pounding heart. That should please Perses and divert him if some image of the blonde, barely nubile maiden she could also be had been exposed.

She had discovered that form by accident. Staring into a still pool that reflected her image, she had wondered what she would look like with blonde, curling hair instead of the shining black curtain that hung to each side of her face. And the image was there. Hekate had sat, blinking at it, wondering how it had formed without a spell of illusion being cast. And then she'd touched the hair, and it *did* curl. Her new form was no illusion.

Shape-shifter. She had realized then she was a shape-shifter, that her father's spell might have decided the form the crone took, but the change into that form was her own doing—and that was why Perses' restoration spell could not dismiss it. Remembered terror over that knowledge pulsed through her again and she did not fight it. Let Perses feed on the fear. As long as her panic bound his attention and his vanity accredited that fear to himself, he would not learn the secret.

Magic was accepted, if grudgingly, by the rulers and people of Ka'anan. Magic was useful; spells could make building bricks light, could heal, could ward against thieves—if one could afford the price. Moreover it took training and study to learn magic, and most spells were not quickly or easily cast, the sorcerer being vulnerable and thus controllable before that casting was complete.

Gifts like shape-shifting were another matter entirely. They benefitted only the person Gifted and required no preparation. A man who could change into a wolf could tear out your throat before you could find a defense; a woman who could change her form could steal, cheat on her husband, do gods knew what. The Gifted were anathema, an abomination; if discovered they were sacrificed to the king of the dead.

Hekate shuddered. Slow pace or not, she had

reached the door. Before she could touch it, it swung open.

"Come in, Hekate."

Here there was light enough, in some places too much light for Hekate's comfort–light that deliberately picked out the twisted, tortured forms her father had bound in some kind of stasis–but for the moment she was blinded, unable to see anything. She hobbled forward, hand outstretched, shuffling her feet, bent a little crooked, until Perses bade her stand still. By then she could see.

Perses scowled. "I know you weren't a wizened old hag a quarter candlemark ago. Why did you change yourself?"

"I didn't do it apurpose, Father," Hekate answered in a thin, meek voice. "As soon as your will touches me, I become what your spell put on me, long ago. You can't think I would choose to look this way or feel so weak and full of pain."

He stared at her. "That will complicate matters."

What matters? Hekate wondered. What does he want now?

"Will yourself to be a beautiful woman!" Perses ordered. "Will it, I say!"

Be the woman. Hekate thought, outwardly obedient, while deep within her will clenched tighter around the old, fragile body she wore. Pain lashed her; her skin burned; a bone snapped in one finger, then another. She screamed, tried to writhe away from the pain, but darkness washed over her and she felt herself falling. "Old, old, old," her heart drummed. Somewhere far away she heard Perses cursing, but she lay crumpled on the floor, clinging to the darkness, and inside it listened to the drumming, "Old, old, old."

A blow, another. Hekate was aware of them but felt no pain inside the black blanket. Then nothing.

"Old, old, old," the drumming was softer, slower, but steady, perhaps for a long time, but she was not sure. Then the blackness began to soften into gray. She tried to cling to it, but it raveled away like mist rising from a meadow. She allowed herself to twitch, to stir.

"Get up," Perses ordered.

Hekate tried twice. A stick skidded across the floor and hit her shoulder. She put her hand on it, realizing as she reached out that the pain was gone. Perses had not been able truly to break the bone, only to inflict pain. To hide the relief she felt, Hekate concentrated on the stick he had thrown at her.

It was all twisted and knobby, the wood so old that wear had smoothed it like oil, but without grease. One end was pointed, sharp enough to prick her hand, but the knob at the other end had an odd shape that fitted into her palm. What was more, the twists and bends could be used as handholds. Setting the pointed end into a crack in the stone-paved floor, Hekate climbed the stick to an upright position.

"Very well," Perses snarled. "You can't break the spell when my will touches yours so you will have to accomplish my purpose on your own without my help. This is important to me. I want you to understand that if you cannot or will not perform what I desire, you will be of no use to me and I'll find a way to be rid of you. Do you understand?"

"Yes, Father," Hekate whispered. "Why do you threaten me? Haven't I always been obedient?"

He made no reply to that, just staring with a very faint upcurve of his lips. Hekate clung to the staff that supported her, heart pounding again. No, he couldn't read her deepest thoughts, but he didn't trust her either. He felt something, sensed her resistance enough to make him uneasy.

Then suddenly he smiled. Hekate could hear it in his voice as he said, "You'll enjoy this obedience. It will make you a queen."

Hekate kept her eyes down. The last thing she wanted was to be a queen, particularly under her father's direction. She didn't wish to imagine what he would require her to do to and demand from the people she was supposed to rule. Studying the floor by her toes, her eye was attracted by a dull sheen. It was the tip of the staff, well dug in between the stones of the floor, and it seemed to her that the mortar, stained black with years of wear and spilled effluvia, was lighter where it rested.

"Every woman wishes to be a queen," Perses insisted. "Isn't that so, Hekate?"

"I don't desire power," she murmured.

Perses laughed aloud. "Then what I have planned for you is perfect," he crowed. "You'll have the trappings, the gowns and jewels and the fawning of many subjects, but you won't need to make decisions. I'll make those."

"Yes, Father," Hekate said. Since it had been her experience all her life that Perses tried to make all her decisions, this was nothing new, and Hekate's toneless voice carried no resentment.

"The queen of Byblos must die," Perses said sharply. "And *you* will take her place."

For a long, breath-held moment, Hekate made no response. Her tongue had frozen as solid as her heart. The queen of Byblos! She had thought her father had designs on the ruler of the town near their homestead, Ur-Kabos, but apparently he intended to start at the top. And then her brows knitted.

"But there is a king," she said. "The queen of Byblos does not rule."

"Oh, did you think that you would hold a

kingdom in your own hand?" Perses' sneer was as audible as his smile had been; Hekate had no need to raise her eyes to see it. "Your role will be far less exacting. You need only arrange for me to have access to the king in the queen's bedchamber—your bedchamber—where we can be private so I can instruct him whenever I wish."

"You mean you wish me to become the king's concubine . . . after you kill the queen?"

"You will become the king's wife, after *you* kill the queen," Perses said. "Being a woman you would have far easier access to her than I would. I don't care how you do it. I would suggest that you go in as the old woman and poison her, but it would be even better if you could arrange for an accident to befall her."

Hekate stood silent, leaning on the staff. She was tempted and allowed that sensation to come to the fore of her mind. The queen of Byblos certainly needed killing. The latest little frolic rumor had brought to Ur-Kabos was that she had beat her puppy to death for treading on her gown, but that had only been an excuse to have the maidservants who cared for the dog similarly treated.

That was nothing compared with her more serious escapades, like having executed every living being—including newborns, cattle, and caged singing birds—in a village that because of a drought drew water from a pond in which she had once swum. And that was not to count the hundreds or thousands who had died from other causes owing to her cruelty and extravagance. The death of the dog happened to annoy Hekate particularly because she was very fond of dogs.

"So you agree," Perses said. "I thought you would. I'll give you three days to decide on a method."

"I'll try for an accident," Hekate whispered,

looking up at last, "but I'll need to go to the woods to gather special plants."

"We have enough in the garden," Perses said.

Hekate shrugged. "If that is your will, I will use the plants from the garden, but if poisoning is suspected and the king's mages use a spell of concurrence . . ."

Perses stared at her.

"In the woods I'll touch nothing with my bare flesh, and I'll burn the gathering basket."

Her father's stare grew more intense as if he were trying to penetrate the simple puzzlement she was presenting. Why should he stare? she wondered. He knows I have studied some magic, enough to know about spells of concurrence. Does he want me to be caught as a murderer? The last idea, fearful and resentful, seemed to have put Perses' doubts, whatever they were, to rest.

"Very well," he said smoothly, "you may go, but don't take your mother with you."

Hekate lowered her gaze to the floor again. Take her mother? she repeated to herself. But her mother didn't seem to know her or want anything to do with her. She made no effort to hide that thought, but below it lay a muted pang of hope. Did Perses suspect there were depths in Asterie where he couldn't reach and somewhere in those depths a concern for her daughter?

"She knows the plants better than I," Hekate murmured.

"That's as it may be," Perses said, and Hekate could hear him smiling again, "but she is my warranty that you will return, for if you do not . . ."

"Where have I to go?" Hekate whispered.

He laughed aloud at that and bade her take herself out of his sight. She turned at once, stumbled, caught herself on the staff—and then carefully put her foot over the bleached bit of mortar between the stones where the staff had rested. Leaning heavily on the wooden support, Hekate ground dirt into the lighter spot before she hobbled toward the darkness of the passage, but it was no longer dark. Mage lights bobbed along the wall and up the stair. A reward for being compliant? Hekate allowed herself to feel gratitude, but didn't move any faster; nor did she allow herself to slip back into the woman until she was safe in her own chamber.

Not that her father could not scry her there, he could, but what she would do would be natural in her own chamber and he would assume, she hoped, that because he was no longer willing her to act, his spell would release her. The change swept over her, bringing a sensation that was almost erotic. Her skin, now smooth and soft, could feel the caress of her silk gown. Of course, her tenderer flesh also felt the bruises Perses' blows had inflicted. Nonetheless, Hekate could see better, hear better, and despite an awareness of draining and exhaustion, the well-being of youth sang in her veins. She smiled, stretched, not hiding her pleasure in her most natural shape, reinforcing the notion that she wouldn't willingly exchange it for the hag if she could avoid the change.

Now she dropped the staff carelessly in a corner, as if no longer needing its support, she dismissed it. Then she sat down and thought about the queen of Byblos, dredging up her dislike of all she had heard of the woman. She thought of what an old woman could do to murder a young one without a weapon. Without a weapon? Her gaze went to the staff. There was a weapon and most appropriate for an aged crone.

She let her mind play with this plan and that,

seeking reasons for an old woman to appeal for an audience with the queen, reasons good enough to obtain such an audience. The mental exercise kept her busy and hid any other thoughts until the worst of her exhaustion passed. She didn't question why she was exhausted; whenever she was near her father she lost strength as if she were ill.

Twice she rose from her chair, once to wash carefully and to change her dress for a gown of rougher fabric with long, loose sleeves, and once again to take a handful of sugared dates from a bowl on a low table. Both times she had felt cautiously for a watcher, but the presence had faded some time during her ruminations on how to gain access to the queen and did not return.

Even so Hekate did not relax completely, thinking carefully of what herbs she would need and how to gather them. First, however, she would need a new basket, not one that belonged to the household, and she must not touch anything. Hekate took a long shawl from a chest near the wall, keeping in mind that it could be used to hold the basket and to cover her hands while she culled the plants she needed.

She must buy the basket. Hekate went to a shelf built out from the wall by setting in several wider bricks. A softly murmured word changed a statue of the sacred bull to a small metal-bound box. A second word caused the lid to spring open. From the box Hekate scooped a large handful of metal wire and a few pieces of metal. Most of it slid imperceptibly into her wide sleeve. She picked over what she still held, choosing five twists of copper wire of varying weight and length. The remainder she returned to the box, which again appeared like a winged bull as she replaced it on the shelf. On her way out, she picked up the staff.

Throwing the shawl over her head so that one end was longer than the other and could be drawn across her face, Hekate again crossed the reception chamber. This time she went directly out through it into the courtyard and then passed through a room that held several benches and stools upon which messengers could wait under the eye of the doorkeeper. One bench now held two young slave boys, who would carry messages within the house. Pulling her shawl aside, Hekate winked at them and then passed close enough to drop several of the sweetmeats in each slyly extended hand. One giggled, the other looked down to hide a smile.

The doorkeeper was something else again. The old man turned his dead eyes to her when she entered the chamber in which he was chained, but Hekate didn't bother to speak to him. Whatever lived in that body no longer responded to kindness even though the body was still quite human enough to require food and drink and sleep. It knew her and that no order had been given to keep her within; whether it had the power of thought beyond dealing with such matters and with visitors and messengers, she could not guess.

Down three broad steps to the wide path that passed through the garden and out to the road. To right and left were other paths through the garden, which led to the fields her father's slaves tilled. Beyond those the dark groves of cedars rose up the slope of the hills and whispered and murmured to each other in the dawn and the evening.

As she stepped out of the house, Hekate felt the watcher descend on her almost like a muffling cloak. She had expected that. Ordinarily her father didn't bother to set a watcher on her, but having spoken to her about the murder of the queen of Byblos, this time he would want to know if she met any person in particular or dealt with anyone he might construe as an enemy. Fortunately she saw no one who was even a nodding acquaintance on her walk to the town.

The road was steep, Ur-Kabos having been built on a small plateau where a substantial stream, almost a river, poured down through the foothills of the mountains that rose behind the town. Hekate leaned on her staff and paused briefly to glance at the mountains. That was the best place for herbs, she thought, then brought her attention to the open gate in the walls, behind which the market spread right and left and then along the road that led deeper into the town, to the palace and the temples. The watcher seemed to close around her; in one way its touch was feather light—had she herself not been Gifted, doubtless she would never have noticed its presence—but knowing it was there stifled her.

Sometimes the press of people and the noise—merchants shouting to attract customers, customers chaffering, children squealing, women gossiping—also stifled her, accustomed as she was to quiet and being alone, but this time one pressure negated the other. The watcher—not Perses scrying; this must be one of his otherplanar slaves—seemingly had no experience with noise and crowding; it was bewildered or diverted by the confusion. Its grip on Hekate grew tenuous, but she was careful to suppress any feeling of relief.

Baskets were plentiful. Hekate went from stall to stall, apparently seeking the cheapest product—logical if the basket was to be destroyed. Each time someone spoke to her or bumped her Hekate could feel the watcher's attention waver and sometimes even fix on someone else. Nor did it cling so heavily around her when it returned. It seemed to be pulled this way and that, attracted to all the minds and souls moving around her. Shielded by others, she at last allowed her true thoughts to surface.

As she looked and asked prices of baskets, she thought that killing the queen was not the problem. The queen of Byblos deserved to die and Hekate knew herself capable of stopping the woman's life without need of poison. Not that she would ever do such a thing at her father's bidding or allow him to know she was capable of it. But marry and bed the king? Hekate's lips turned down as bile rose in her throat. Never! He and his queen deserved each other.

How to *avoid* killing the queen and marrying the king was a far greater problem than killing them. Hekate began to turn away from a stall that showed beautifully designed and woven baskets. The merchant called to her, drew her back; she shook her head, saying regretfully that she had not the money for such fine work and showing in her hand three of the five small pieces of copper wire she had taken with her.

"Ah, but I have just what will suit us both," the merchant said, drawing from the bottom of the stall a long basket that was of coarser weave and less perfect ornament. "Apprentice work," he said. "I am sure you can find about you something else that I could use. Another piece of copper, that handsome shawl you are wearing. Come, come, you have a purse. Look into it. Perhaps there is a hairpin or comb?"

Hekate shook her head. "Why should I give up my shawl or comb? I am only looking for a coarse basket to carry unwashed roots and such matters. What you show me is pretty, but not suitable for my purpose."

"Oh, you must have an old basket in the house that you could use to carry your roots. This one . . ."

He continued talking, lifting and twisting the basket so that Hekate could see it inside and out. The words became meaningless to her because a strip of light-colored material tucked into the coarsely woven withies had caught her eye. A scrap of parchment? She felt no change in the watcher, but she fixed her gaze on the merchant's face and for a little while continued to argue price, finally allowing herself to be convinced and to seek in her purse for a fourth piece of copper wire, which she handed over grudgingly. Equally grudgingly the merchant accepted the additional metal, whining about how she was cheating him.

At last, Hekate took the basket, carefully dropping her long sleeve over her hand so her flesh would not touch the handle. With it in hand, she continued to wander about the market for a time, looking idly at a tray of knives. A long poniard with a blade so thin it was more like a flat needle than a knife attracted her attention and she picked it up with her hand shielded by her long shawl. Put in just where the head meets the neck, under the hair, it would kill and likely no one would ever find the small wound. She put it down, saying "Perhaps tomorrow, I do not have the price now," to the merchant who had hurried over.

Then she went to look at the herb-sellers' wares, but over those, she mostly shook her head. However, there were some strange bundles that came, the seller said, from far west, over the sea. She expended the fifth twist of copper wire on a handful of each type she did not recognize and had the merchant drop the sprigs, tied with a thread of bright wool, into the new basket. When she looked in as if to check that what she had bought was all there, the slip of parchment was covered.

Finally she walked slowly out of the market,

looking from side to side at the stalls. After she passed under the gate, she quickened her pace and when she was past most of the crowd and obviously headed toward Perses' house, the touch of the watcher was suddenly gone.

CHAPTER 2

Hekate continued to walk toward her father's house with an unvarying pace after the watcher left her until she reached a tongue of the forest of cedars that bordered his lands. Here she stopped and sat down in the shade with her back against the trunk of a tree, resting the staff across her lap. After a few minutes she allowed her eyes to close. After a few more minutes she carefully thought of nothing, of utter blackness. She waited, but there came to her no sense of the watcher probing for her and, still thinking of utter blackness, she rose and sidled off between the trees.

Although she had never before sought the silent shrine from the direction of the road, she had no trouble finding it. A thin thread of light? warmth?—not something she could truly see or feel but very real to her—led her onward through the trees. Sooner than she expected, she found the place where, for no reason at all, there was a space in which nothing except a soft odd-smelling moss grew. The odor was not unpleasant, being sharp and spicy, but it was not like anything else and the moss would grow nowhere else.

In the center of the open area was a very tall stump. Perhaps in the very distant past it had been carven; if so, time had smoothed away the marks so that the barest suggestion of a rounded head sat atop narrow, sloping shoulders. Possibly some of the irregularities over the front and back of the figure had been meant to show the folds of a gown. Perhaps not. The stump could have been a natural formation and she was imagining that the marks were the work of ancient worshipers.

Natural or carved by hands, what could not be mistaken was the sense of welcome, of protection, that enveloped the moss-grown clearing. Whether or not the stump was a made image of the Mother, She was here. Hekate breathed a long sigh of relief, crossed the clearing quickly, and rested her staff against the image. There was a quiver in the power around her and then it steadied.

She stared at the staff and the stump, but there was no change in either—and a question that had lingered in the back of her mind had been answered. If the staff had been some device of her father's, bespelled to record what she did, drain power from her, or mark her for her father's scrying or his creatures' finding, it was so no longer. Now it was either a simple wooden staff or a vessel for her filling.

Sighing again, Hekate crouched down at the foot of the stele, the bands of muscle that had held her shoulders rigid since her father laid his will upon her relaxing. She then emptied the bundles of herbs out of the basket and carefully pulled the scrap of parchment free of the withies.

The writing, so small that Hekate had to lift the scrap closer to her eyes, was undoubtedly her mother's. However, each symbol was formed painfully, clearly made with terrible effort. Asterie must have fought with all her strength against both physical weakness and magical coercion to write the message. And how had she gotten it into the basket?

Hekate knew that Asterie often went to the market. Apparently Perses did not bother to scry her or set a watcher on her because he was so confident (more confident than he should have been it seemed) of his control over her. Even so, how had she ever managed to bespell the merchant to get the basket into her daughter's hands? Now she thought of it, Hekate realized that the merchant's behavior had not been natural.

She blinked back tears. Asterie must have been hoarding tiny scraps of power, saving them in some artifact she could hide from Perses . . . perhaps for years. All the time Hekate had believed her mother no longer knew her, no longer cared, Asterie had been gathering strength and will for one final effort to save her daughter. The tears welled over Hekate's lower lids and streaked her cheeks. Why had she been so cruel as to abandon her mother? She had not even continued to greet Asterie, to kiss her even if she did not respond.

Hekate read the message again. "Coercion spell. Suck power. Flee or die."

Hekate stared at the little scrap. So Perses had decided to use a coercion spell on her even if she did his will. She shivered. She had really known that but had been unwilling to acknowledge it. Flee? Where? Where could she go, alone and on foot, that her father's creatures, paid human or otherplanar, could not reach her and drag her back?

She was safe here . . . No, she was not. The otherplanar things would not dare this clearing—

Hekate had learned all her magic here, how to cast spells, how to build new spells, and Perses and his creatures had never sensed the magic or pierced the protections—but the armed men would care nothing for the Mother's protection. Or even if they did, there was nothing here to eat or drink; they would surround the clearing and take her when she was forced out by thirst and hunger.

Suddenly there were two other marks on the parchment. Hekate swallowed. More magic from her mother's tiny store, for those symbols had not been there when she first looked. The spell that released them would have been set to respond to some sign of her distress, perhaps the rhythm of her breathing or the damp of her fingers reacting to her fear.

The first was an odd mark at which she stared for a while before she remembered that her mother had made her memorize it, although it accorded with no word or sound in their language; it was a symbol of where her father's enemies lived: Olympus. The other Hekate recognized easily. She shivered again. It was the priests' mark for the caves of the dead.

For a moment a dreadful suspicion seized her. Could this message be a trap laid by her father? The caves of the dead were not a burial ground; they were the places where the Gifted or scapegoats or condemned folk were sacrificed to the king of the dead at the spring and autumn equinoxes. The sacrifices were bound and delivered to the caves on the last day of the two great festivals together with rich offerings of metal and cloth and sometimes food and wine. Had Perses forced her poor mother to write that message? Did he intend to be rid of his daughter by having her dragged into the underworld?

A moment later, the fingers that had tensed to

tear the message to shreds, touched it gently instead. No, he would never have included the symbol for Olympus, if he even knew it. He was truly terrified of the dwellers in that city. Nor was it the time of either equinox festival, and it was long established that the king of the dead or his minions accepted human sacrifice at no other times. No, Perses would not risk offending the king of the dead by a mistimed sacrifice; he was possibly more afraid of the god of the underworld than of the Olympians. Besides, she would not be bound by sacrificial cords and could escape the caves.

Hekate frowned. Even if no ill was meant her, the caves of the dead were no place to seek sanctuary. But as the thought came, her black brows lifted. That was everyone's reaction . . . did not that make it the best place for her to go? Yes, of course it did. She nodded and took her bottom lip between her teeth. Had not her mother once said it was another place they could go if the protection of the silent shrine failed? Because . . . yes, because Perses was convinced that the emanations in the caves would interfere with his magic.

Was that true? Or was it another of her father's false notions. It must be or her mother would not have said she and Hekate could go there to work. But they never had gone to the caves of the dead; Asterie had said there was a reason why that must be a last resort . . . but she had never told Hekate why. Possibly there was something in the caves that damped magic. That might conceal her presence from her father or his creatures.

There was still the problem of food and drink. Hekate reached for the staff and began to get to her feet then sank back. Offerings other than human sacrifice were welcome in the caves at any time during the year and were made daily. Those offerings were mostly food and drink. If she had food and drink, she could hide in the caves until Perses gave her up and then she could find a way west to Olympus. Perhaps her father's enemies would protect her.

Then in doubt she twisted around to look up at the stele. Would it be safe to steal from the king of the dead? But did the offerings go to the king of the dead? Why should he bother to collect mostly worthless offerings of food and cheap date wine when he would not take men and women? But then what happened to the offerings? They disappeared, yes; they were always gone before the next sunrise.

Well, there were plenty of hungry folk about. What was more likely, that the king of the dead came to collect a few rounds of bread, a few platters of vegetables, and a jar or two of cheap wine or that a group of semi-outlaws kept a watch on the caves and helped themselves to the offerings. Hekate giggled faintly.

That made sense, even explaining why Asterie preferred not to go there. Folk who made their living by robbing the king of the dead were unlikely to be timid about ridding themselves of intruders. And they could not afford to have intruders. At best, betrayal would dry up their source of income; at worst, it would set the ruler of Ur-Kabos into a vengeful search to exterminate them.

The smile that had lingered on her lips disappeared. Such people would be no more welcoming to her than to any other. She could use a "look-by-me" spell, but if she had escaped Perses' notice that far, the spell would certainly betray her. That thought made her bite her lips. If she fled, how long would her absence be overlooked? Sometimes she might not see or hear from her father for weeks at a time, but now the most she would have would be two days and what was left of this one. Perses had said he would expect to hear her plans for killing the queen of Byblos in three days.

Byblos! Yes, her father *expected* her to go to Byblos and kill the queen. Well, why shouldn't she go to Byblos? If he set a watcher upon her, it would seem as if she were doing his will. But Byblos was a great seaport. She could find a ship going west. She could . . .

Suddenly the clearing was cold, all sense of welcome gone. Hekate leapt to her feet and faced the stump she associated with the Mother. Before she could even wonder what the withdrawal meant, a face formed in her mind. It was very young, very beautiful, with hair as golden as a sunrise, crisply curled, a straight, handsome nose, a wide, generous mouth, and the largest, bluest eyes. A face completely foreign to the people of Ka'anan.

"Dionysos," Hekate breathed.

How could she have forgotten? She had refused to try to save the mother and, like a fool, bound herself to protect the son, who had been exposed to die when Semele was sacrificed to the king of the dead. She could not leave Dionysos without explaining to him. He was so strongly Gifted and so unable to control his Gifts that he was half mad already. He depended on her to assure him that he was not mad, that he would learn to manage the power within him, to make clear to him what was real and what was Vision.

Whatever the danger to her, she must go to the dwelling of the Nymphae, who had nutured the babe she had rescued, and speak to Dionysos. Sure now of her object, she stooped to pick up the bundles of herbs she had cast out of the basket, and her glance caught the scrap of parchment she had let fall when the Mother withdrew. She picked up the parchment and in the same moment became aware that the warmth, the welcome, had been restored.

So, the Mother had been reminding her of her binding to Dionysos . . . or was She warning against the attempt to escape Perses by pretending to go to Byblos? In either case, Hekate realized, when she was about to wander, she had been slapped by a motherly hand to return her to the best and safest path. Hekate smiled, placed the slip of parchment on a flat rock, and whispered, "Burn," knowing she need not fear any magic she performed here would echo back to Perses.

When the scrap was gone to ash, she scraped the ashes tenderly into her hand and let them sift into one of the many cracks in the stele. The Mother would hide whatever faint traces of Asterie might cling to the ash. As she bowed to the power that dwelt in the stump, she remembered the symbols her mother had so painfully inscribed and her conclusion that her father meant to use the coercion spell on her whether or not she did as he had ordered. He would not have been fooled by her starting on the road to Byblos without first telling him . . . and telling him would not have been safe either.

She hoped that he planned to use the spell either when she returned to the house or when she described her plan to kill the queen of Byblos and would not seek her sooner. It was a reasonable hope, for the coercion spell could then be used to reinforce what she had herself planned, and her behavior would be more natural. Hekate took a deep breath. She had said she would gather herbs and that is what she would seem to do while she made her way to the house of the Nymphae. Fortunately they had some protection against magic; for a little while it might mask her presence.

Although she tried to ward herself against the touch of a watcher by again fixing her mind on utter blackness, when she stepped from the Mother's clearing into the cedar trees she felt nothing. Relieved, she set as fast a pace as would not exhaust her, hurrying uphill and somewhat northward through the trees. They were dense enough here to have lost many of their lower branches and to cast so deep a shade that little grew between them and she was not hindered by underbrush. Eventually the trees thinned and to the left she saw the road that curved around Ur-Kabos. She followed the curve but stayed within the shelter of the cedars.

The sun had passed its zenith by the time she worked her way around the town. Hekate turned more sharply north, feeling a renewed touch of anxiety because the many spirits and auras of the town dwellers would no longer mask hers; however, there was still no sense of an otherplanar watcher or even the fainter foulness that was her father's personal scrying. She increased her pace, not bothering to pretend to search for herbs, moving swiftly through the cedars and cypresses that were now interspersed with other growth, oak and ash, the trees just beginning to leaf. Little by little the cedars and cypress gave way entirely to ash and oak.

She was tiring, the westering sun beginning to trouble her eyes, when she reached the barren ridge. Hekate paused under the last of the trees and looked around carefully. She could see no sign of shepherds or the flocks of goats and sheep that sometimes grazed on the undergrowth that rimmed the edge of the forest. Then she scanned the ridge until she saw the cleft that looked so much like an upper lip. After a last glance to be sure the area was clear, she ran as fast as she could for the cleft.

On the other side was a sheer cliff, dropping away

into a naked, rock-strewn ravine, but Hekate did not hesitate. She ran boldly ahead into what seemed thin air, gasped as a brief spate of dizziness made her slow, and stumbled slightly because here the true slope, gentle and covered with grass and bright flowers, was somewhat less precipitous than she expected.

Beyond the illusion that she had fashioned for the Nymphae as part of the price for raising Dionysos was a small but lush valley. At the bottom of the gentle hill, a clear stream ran. The air was warmer and much more moist than on the other side of the ridge, and the trees that dotted the hillside were as full-leafed as in summer. The stream, Hekate knew, came out of the truly unscalable cliffs that surrounded the valley elsewhere.

Straight ahead, across the stream which was well-furnished with stepping stones, there seemed to be a patch of dense woods. It was only when Hekate entered the grove that she could see—what she knew was in the inner cluster—a house whose walls and roof were created out of living trees sealed with thick vines with broad, flat leaves.

The Nymphae—even after knowing them intimately and visiting them at least once a month for years, Hekate could not tell them apart—waited for her outside the hanging vines that could be pushed aside to form a door. They were beautiful, if not quite human, with faintly green skin and long, yellow-green hair, which was really closer to very fine root tendrils. Their large, almond-shaped eyes were green, too, the bright yet soft green of new foliage, but their ears were very long and pointed, standing well above the crowns of their heads, and, as if to make up for that, they barely had noses at all, just delicate nostrils protected by slightly protuberant flaps of skin.

"Greetings, O Nymphae—" Hekate began formally.

She got no further. The free-hanging vines flew this way and that as a boy exploded outward barely avoiding careening into the Nymphae. As one they turned their heads in his direction and smiled fondly, showing small, but very sharp pointed teeth behind their darker green lips.

"You must go away," the boy cried. "You must go to that dark place, that deep dark place, where I may not go with you now but I will meet you, oh, sometime, sometime, I don't know when."

His naturally fair skin was pale to near transparency. Sweat beaded on his forehead and streaked his cheeks. His hands trembled, and his eyes, already too large, looked as if they might fall out of his head.

Hekate stepped forward and took the boy's hands. "You have been Seeing *me*, Dionysos?"

"Not at first," he said and suddenly shuddered. "That was terrible. Evil. Evil. I didn't want to See it. And I will See it over and over. Not that. I can't bear it."

He uttered a stifled sob, and the Nymphae rushed to him; one embraced him, another stroked his hair, the third stroked his back. He clung to them for a moment, unmarked by their long, brown nails that looked much like very sharp thorns, and then drew himself together, shuddering again.

"If I was in your Seeing, Dionysos," Hekate said, "I will know what it means. You will have told the Vision to the right person, and it will leave you."

As she spoke, she drew him out of the embrace of the Nymphae, who let him go without protest and then all waited together, watching him. Ignoring them, although she knew them to be capable of killing her or, for that matter, a full troop of armed men, Hekate led Dionysos to a raised bank of turf where she sat down beside him.

"Oh, yes." He seemed relieved by what she had said for a moment but then swallowed hard. "But what I Saw wasn't good. An evil one brought more evil into the world and . . . and set it on *you*. What will happen when you go into the dark place? I couldn't See any more, but I was afraid! I have never been so afraid in my life."

"No, I don't suspect you've had much cause to fear. The Nymphae have protected you well. But don't worry about me, Dionysos," she added, her lips tightening into a thin line. "I'm well versed in dealing with terror. Now tell me what you Saw."

He nodded and took a deep, calming breath. "I was braiding vine for a new sandal strap, and it seemed to me that the vine grew longer and longer and that I was forced to follow it. I came out of the valley and down the hill past two herds of goats . . ." For a moment his face lost the pinching that made it old and lightened into that of a delighted child. "I like goats. The kids are adorable. Can we have goats here?"

"No, I'm afraid not. Goats eat shrubbery and they might be tempted to dine on the Nymphae's hair or on their house. Sheep maybe, but not goats."

"There are goats on the estate of Lady Io," one of the Nymphae said; her voice was like the sighing of a breeze in tall grass.

Hekate turned to look at her. The Nymphae spoke seldom and only when what they said was essential. "We will speak of Lady Io later," Hekate said, nodding to acknowledge the importance of the remark. "First I must hear Dionysos' Vision." She turned to the boy. "Go on, Dionysos."

"Well, I'm not certain how far I walked or, rather, floated or flew. You know how it is when I See. Anyway it was beyond a place where the houses were all of mud brick and built almost atop one another.

Then I came to a very large house–two houses really. I felt you there, but you weren't there. Is that your home, Hekate?"

"It was. No more, I think."

The boy nodded again. "Good. It's a bad place, very bad. I went into the second house, down through the roof and then down into a very deep place. It was very dark. I know I can't fall when I am Seeing, but if one fell there . . . I don't know what was at the bottom because I didn't go all the way. The plait of grass drew me through a passage–"

"A straight passage?" Hekate asked.

Dionysos shrugged. "So it seemed, but Seeing isn't all that clear."

So the twists and turns, even the wall she bumped into, to get to her father's workroom were all illusion. Hekate bit her lips. She thought she was good at illusion; apparently there was much she still had to learn.

"Go on," she said to Dionysos.

"I heard shouting, a man screaming about the wrong kind of spell–"

"The wrong kind of spell," Hekate interrupted. "Wait, Dionysos. Can you remember the exact words? This is important to me."

The boy closed his eyes. "He said, 'You stupid bitch, how could you build a spell that cannot be cast but must be passed by touch? Do you think she'll let me lay my staff on her, or even a hand? Change it!' But there was no answer, just the sound of something soft but heavy falling."

Hekate's teeth set hard over a gasp of consternation and an expletive of bitter rage. But there was nothing she could do. She was no match for her father's magic. Her return would only put her totally in Perses' power or mean her death. That couldn't help her mother. If she could escape, she would have the chance to grow in knowledge and power. Then if she returned she might have a chance to free poor Asterie. Caught up in his Vision, Dionysos hadn't noticed her distress and had continued speaking.

"And then the plait of grass pulled me into a strange chamber. There was no one on the floor, so I suppose some time had passed, but time is strange in my Seeing. A horrible room, all lit by mage lights, and dead things were somehow fastened to the walls . . . Poor creatures. They didn't die an easy death. And a man, tall and heavy, soft-looking, as if his body was not used enough or older than his face. I didn't like his face, although it was handsome in the Ka'ananite style—long dark hair, much curled, black brows, large black eyes, a long, hooked nose, and a full beard, also black and curled. There was something about it—"

"Never mind, Dionysos, I know the face all too well. Then what did you See?"

For the first time, the boy hesitated, then reached for her hand. Hekate clasped his and found the fingers cold. "The words won't be right," Dionysos said. "They'll sound silly, but inside . . . inside me there was such sickness and loathing . . . my throat was thick with bile, and I couldn't breathe because of the stench." His grip on her hand tightened. "You know, I'm not often aware of warmth or cold or smell in my Seeing, but this time I was so cold that if I had teeth they would have chattered loud enough for the man to hear. I was sorry he couldn't hear. I wanted to stop him."

"I have told you many times that a Seeing is not a real thing, Dionysos. It might become real in the future or might have been real in the past, but . . ."

"I know that, but this felt real and it felt . . . soon." Dionysos shuddered, but didn't stop speaking. "The man got a basin from a table near the wall. Then he went behind a screen and carried out a boy who was bound and gagged but lay limp in his arms. He carried the boy to the basin, turned him over, and—and cut his throat."

"Mother have mercy," Hekate whispered.

"I screamed and I pulled at the plait of rope, but it was tight around me and wouldn't let me move, not even reach out. The man looked up and around, as if he might have heard some echo of my cry, but by then I was still for the boy was dead already or as good as dead. And the man looked younger, stronger."

Blood magic, Hekate thought, and her hand turned as cold as the fingers she gripped. But then she frowned. If the purpose of killing the boy had been to absorb his life-force, the victim should have been conscious and terrified, and he should have been killed in the longest and most painful way possible. Cutting the throat of an unconscious victim . . . Caught up in his Vision and unaware of Hekate's thoughts, Dionysos nonetheless reminded her that Perses' purpose was not essentially to gain power.

"When the basin was near full of blood, the man began drawing forms on the floor, first a very large pentagram with the bowl in the empty space in the middle."

Hekate's lips twisted with disgust. "You don't need to tell me more about the forms. I'll never do such a summoning and don't care what Perses drew."

There was another silence, brief but pregnant. "It appeared," Dionysos said, seeming to force a thin voice through a constricted throat. "Right in the center of the pentagram, this . . . thing . . . appeared and began to lap up the blood from the basin. I was cold before. Now I was freezing and . . . I told you how sick I was."

An otherplanar creature but in true physical manifestation! Hekate almost smiled. That must have cost her father high in power and life-force, more than he got from the death of the boy. Good. But then she put together her father's rage over needing physically to touch the spell—almost certainly the coercion spell—to its victim and the summoning of a physical outdweller, and there was nothing to smile about.

"I'm sorry, Dionysos, but I must ask you to tell me what the creature looked like. If it was summoned to put a spell on me—"

"It was." Dionysos swallowed hard. "I Saw that later. I know I must tell you so you will know what to watch for. And if I don't say what I Saw aloud, I'll See it again and again." He sighed. "But it sounds so . . . so . . . nothing! And I . . . it terrified me!"

Hekate reached out with her free hand and touched the boy's cheek. "There is nothing to be ashamed of in fearing otherplanar creatures. I have been terrified by some I could not see at all. Their touch on the soul is foul."

Dionysos nodded eagerly. "Yes. Yes. The whole room was full of filth although the thing itself was little, about the size of a large cat. It looked more like a rat, only the naked tail was short and thick, except for the very end, which was like a stinger, only curved, and the face was flatter, without whiskers. It was all gray and its private parts were huge. I could see them clearly because when it had lapped up all the blood, it stood on two legs, like a man."

Hekate became aware that the Nymphae had come closer. "Very bad," one said, not the one who had spoken before, Hekate thought, but the voice was identical. "Guhrt. Fifth or sixth plane. All hunters there."

"Hunters," Hekate repeated, her voice flat. Then she looked at Dionysos again. "Was that the end of the Vision?"

"Nearly." Dionysos looked relieved, and his grip on her hand loosened. "Then the man picked up a long staff and made the end of it start to glow. Even that was disgusting, like yellow-green snot. He reached over the edge of the pentagram and touched the thing. It screamed and tried to seize the staff but failed, and the end of the staff stopped glowing."

The third Nymph spoke. "It has the spell now. The guhrt hunt by sight and scent and are relentless. They do not need to sleep and with a bowl of blood in it, it can go without food and water for a long time."

"I don't think it will go into the deep black place," Dionysos said. "That was the end of my Seeing in that place. After the man's staff touched the . . . the thing, the grass plait pulled me swiftly into the mountains. I Saw you go in to the dark place and I felt the fear come out. The fear was so great that the grass rope let me go, but I didn't See the creature follow you in."

"But that *was* the end of the Vision, wasn't it?"

"When you went into the black place and the fear came out, yes."

"Dionysos, this is very important. Do you have any idea when the man gave the spell to the guhrt?"

He frowned. "There's no time in my Seeing. It could have been hours or days or weeks between when I heard him complain about the spell and when I saw him summon the guhrt. And more weeks before you went into the dark place."

"No, that's not what I meant. I know the summoning of the guhrt must be within three days. What I need to know is whether the summoning was done after I left the house today or whether it will be done in the morning tomorrow or even the next day. If it's here already and has traced me . . ."

Dionysos shook his head. "The chamber where the man worked was deep underground and lit with mage lights. I couldn't tell whether it was day or night or even whether days and nights passed while he did the summoning. I'm sorry. This Seeing is the most useless Gift! Oh, wait. When I was drawn out of the man's chamber, the rising sun near blinded me. Is that a help?"

"I–" Hekate began and then took a deep breath. "Yes. Yes, it is! Perses set a watcher on me when I left the house this morning, but it was no hunter and was not material. So if you saw the rising sun after the summoning, then the creature cannot set out to hunt me until tomorrow morning. I need not run this moment. The caves of the dead are no more than two or three candlemarks' walk. From here to Perses' house is at least four."

"They are swift," a Nymph said; Hekate thought it was the first one who had spoken, "but it is not in this world yet. We will warn you."

"However it will follow you here," the second remarked.

"I'm so sorry," Hekate cried. "Is there some way I can hide my trace?"

"Do not fear for us," the third of the Nymphae said, baring her pointed teeth. "We cannot attack it; we are forbidden. But we can defend ourselves. However, the child should not be here."

"Can I take him to the caves of the dead with me?" Hekate asked.

"I can't go there now," Dionysos said. "I must meet you there some other time."

"Was that part of the Seeing?"

"No. It's something I just know. And I know that

you will go away and I won't see you for a long time." His voice shook a little, but then he smiled suddenly. "But there will be lambs and kids and—and a vine, a vine I must carry with me when I, too, go. East and south."

"His mother's sister, the Lady Io has returned to her homeplace from Thebes." The sighing voice of the first of the Nymphae followed as Dionysos' faded on his final words. "The Lady Io, like the Lady Semele, quarrelled with her father. We learned that she made inquiry about her sister and arranged for her to be told the tale of Dionysos' birth and Semele's sacrifice. The Lady Io then communicated to us her desire to nuture her sister's son, she being childless."

"But will he be safe?" Hekate asked anxiously. "I am bound to protect him."

"You will do that best by going away," the second Nymph said.

And the third added, "Dionysos can protect himself from any ordinary magic and Lady Io has good defenses."

"Are you willing to go to your aunt, Dionysos?" Hekate asked.

He blinked his huge eyes slowly and shrugged. "Since I know I do go, I must be willing." Then he smiled. "Yes. There will be people to talk to. The Nymphae are very good to me, but . . ." He shrugged. "I have been lonely, and I will be more lonely when you no longer come. And it is time to see to the planting of my vines."

CHAPTER 3

Under the pale-streaked sky of false dawn, Hekate set out for the caves of the dead. She was well fed, although the Nymphae's cuisine was strange—all made up of nuts, dried berries and mushrooms, bulbs, and roots that Hekate, no mean botanist, had never seen before. Still, it was all delicious, covered with delicate sauces of honey and spices, sweet and sour, hot and tangy. She was well rested also, for the Nymphae had showed her to a sweet-smelling couch of boughs and grasses and told her it was safe to sleep. But it was still dark when one of them came and touched her.

"The other planes are troubled. You must go."

A second said, "Hekate, will your protections go with you or fade with time now that the child will leave us?"

"No," Hekate said. She made a mage light and smiled at them. "The illusions are linked into the power of the earth. Only if there is a shaking so bad that the roots of the spell are shifted from the power source will the illusion fade. As long as the land lies still–as long as the bond between the spell and the boiling below is unbroken–the spells will protect this place."

"Then you have overpaid us for our care of the child," the third said. "Especially since he has given us great pleasure. He is attuned, as no other human child we have known, to growing things."

And then all spoke together. "If he needs more protections than Lady Io can furnish, he will have them."

That promise eased a tight band that had circled Hekate's heart ever since the Mother reminded her of her binding to Dionysos. In truth, although she never failed to visit him, that had been less because of the binding than for a reason to escape Perses' house and eyes and to some extent for the pleasure of watching him grow. Now she was still conscious of a light tether to the boy, but nothing that would impede her.

She washed in the warm pool behind the house of the Nymphae, dressed in the garments she had shed the night before, and ate the strange but satisfying morning meal that appeared at the side of the pool. When she was ready she took up her staff and stood for a moment looking around, but the Nymphae did not appear and Hekate knew enough not to seek them. They had given their promise; they had said all they had to say.

Dionysos did not appear either, for which Hekate was actually grateful. Now that she was leaving him, she discovered that she was more fond of the child than she had realized. A final parting would be unnecessarily painful; there was no more they had to say to each other. Still, Hekate fashioned a tiny spell that would be triggered by Dionysos' presence. "Farewell," it would say in her voice. "Be safe. Take joy in living."

Beyond the pool was a garden and where the garden ended, a gate guarded by a tall figure shrouded in vines. Hekate stopped before it for a moment. Here was hard scrutiny, and although a shield covered the dwelling of the Nymphae, there was none of the warmth and welcome she enjoyed in the forest shrine. Still, Hekate knew she was seen and recognized.

"Am I free to go?" she asked.

The binding around her heart twitched, tightening for one moment and then relaxing again. I am free, but I carry the binding with me, she thought, and bowed slightly, and passed the gate.

Hekate had made her way back to Ur-Kabos and about halfway around it; in fact she was just about to step onto the road that began at the east gate of the city and went across the mountains to Kadesh when a sense of unease, of unsteadiness, of hot, foul windless buffeting passed over, around, and through her. Although not a leaf stirred on any tree nor was the smallest puff of dust raised on the road, Hekate almost fell and needed to put out a hand to the nearest tree to steady herself. This was more than a troubling of the other planes. She had no doubt what she felt was a violent rending of the immaterial walls between this world and others.

The Nymphae had said the hunter was swift. Hekate took a deep breath and began to run down the road toward the footpath that angled north to the caves of the dead. She would not allow terror to close her throat because she needed to breathe in order to run. Nor would she allow herself to be pushed into running at top speed; that would only exhaust her too soon. Over and over she told herself it was not far now, no more than a half candlemark at the pace of a procession. Surely,

surely she would reach her haven before Perses had completed his instruction and transferred the spell.

For a while the panic receded. Hekate did recognize a few landmarks; Perses had insisted she travel this path a few times in her life when he forced her to witness the sacrifice of a Gifted. It was an object lesson that she must only ever appear to use magic as a learned tool, not draw it from within her. Still the path was clear and without branches. She was making good progress when suddenly she felt as if a cold and filthy hand were groping for her.

Blackness! Nothingness! I am nothing and no one, she thought. But it was very hard to keep the blankness in her mind and at the same time watch the path under her feet. She ran doggedly, her strength renewed momentarily when another blind groping passed over her. That gave her hope that the hunter hadn't yet found her and, indeed, the seeking seemed to come from another quarter. If the thing had diverted, following her trail to the dwelling of the Nymphae, it would give her a little longer.

Although the illusion that kept curious humans from the valley of the Nymphae would not affect the otherplanar creature, she didn't fear for the plant maidens. First, the ghurt was not hunting them and second, they had thirty poisoned thorn-talons and an untold number of near-sentient root-fibers that could bind or strangle to oppose the ghurt's one stinger. For a brief moment of bright hope, Hekate thought that they could destroy the creature if it would only attack them, but she didn't slow her pace and the hope didn't last long.

She could feel the brief burst of rage when the guhrt understood that she was not to be found in the Nymphae's valley and two questions jostled together in her mind. Was it by the Mother's favor that the creature had not scented or sensed her exit at the Nymphae's gate? How could her father have been so careless as to allow the guhrt's aura to spread abroad without hindrance? Again she had a very brief spurt of hope that Perses had been too drained by the summoning to work a spell of concealment, but again the hope didn't last long.

Hekate would have shaken her head if she hadn't been running and feared it would unbalance her. Two other, much stronger, possibilities existed than Perses' exhaustion. The likeliest was that he didn't know she could sense the guhrt's aura; she doubted he knew that she was aware of the watchers he set on her. Another likely explanation was that he *wanted* her to sense the creature to increase her terror.

She found it was no use to tell herself she would not yield and give him the satisfaction. She *was* terrified, more and more terrified as the foulness that was part of the guhrt grew stronger and stronger. Despite knowing that the creature could leap upon her from any side, even from ahead of her on the path, she was constantly tempted to look behind her. She could no longer control her breath, which came shorter than it should, nor could she keep her pace to what she could sustain.

Gasping and sobbing, with a spear of pain lancing through her side and her lungs burning, Hekate drove her failing body forward. She burst out of the trees into a clearing. Ahead was a huge arch of utter blackness, from which protruded an ugly tongue of gravel and raw, red earth that was bare of any growth, any softening touch of living green. To go into that blackness . . . But it was here! Hekate flung herself over that raw, red tongue and fell sprawling.

At first she could do nothing except breathe. Behind her the clearing was full of foulness, but the guhrt hadn't followed her into the cave. Hekate felt its aura pulse forward as if it were about to do so, and she struggled upright, desperately creating a spell of warding. But the pulse of evil retreated more swiftly than it had come forward, as if something in the cave repelled it. Still it pulsed forward again. Hekate rose to her feet, murmuring another protective spell and gripping her staff like a club, but the aura withdrew again even more suddenly.

Safe! The idea had barely formed, however, when Hekate became aware of a thread of the immaterial filth of the guhrt sliding along the ground toward the entrance of the cave right along the wall. There was a thin space where the grass of the clearing edged the earth and gravel apron at the cave's mouth and grew almost into the dark. Like the slimy track of a snail, the evil crept into the cave. A second thread stole around the other side, and both squirmed forward toward Hekate.

Hardly realizing what she was doing, she backed away. Inside the cave the threads engorged, grew finger thick, took on a slimy sheen. Hekate stepped back again, and again . . . and one foot found nothing. With a small shriek, she fell backward, but she was not swallowed by a deep abyss; she had only tripped into the trough that collected the blood of the sacrificial animals.

Disgusted, brushing frantically at her clothing, Hekate got to her feet on the far side of the trough only to be struck by such an overwhelming sensation of fear and despair that she barely remained upright by clinging to her staff. Wave after wave of the emotions poured into her. She choked on sobs. Tears coursed down her cheeks. Never had she felt such terror, not even when she ran before the guhrt; never had she been so utterly bereft, so despairing, not even in the worst moments of her father's domination when she was a child and had no defenses.

Hekate turned and prepared to leap back over the trough, but the questing ribbons of the guhrt's evil had run together so that there was no way to avoid them. They did not carry the full force of her father's spell, she was sure; the guhrt had to touch her physically to transfer that. However, she was equally sure that the creature had some power of its own, some way of entrapping its prey. If she stepped over the blood trough, she would be little more than dead meat for her father's consuming.

Unable to endure the panic and horror eroding her soul, Hekate gathered them into a tight spear, added the hatred that was now nearly consuming her and flung them out of the cave mouth at the creature that was pursuing her. In the "no place" between the planes, usually lit to Hekate's mind's eye with a soft gray luminescence there was now a dull red aura. When the spear she had cast struck, the red exploded into writhing convulsions followed by a wash of utter blackness; from outside the cave came the squall of a creature surprised by pain. And then the aura of the guhrt was gone.

The sense of slimy ribbons laid out to entrap her was also gone as was the mental stench of the guhrt. Hekate stepped across the trough into the outer section of the cave. The burden of fear and despair that had oppressed her lifted at once. She could still sense the emotions, but they hung in the dark behind her as a threat or a warning now rather than being an active torment. Hekate shivered. She could not remain in the caves of the dead with that sense of coming doom surrounding her.

Perhaps she would not have to do so. Turning her inner sight inward and outward at once, she looked cautiously into the "no place." It was still black and empty. So far so good. She knew she had hurt the guhrt when she rid herself of the building terrors of the caves of the dead. Perhaps she had really harmed it. Killed it or driven it away?

Cautiously, Hekate approached the cave opening. Nothing was in sight to her mortal eyes, but very faintly she sensed the guhrt. It had withdrawn beyond the clearing and well back into the surrounding forest, drawn its power back into itself, too, she thought, but it was still there. She tried to gather her fear and hatred and launch them again, but the emotions were dissipating, unraveling like a weakening spell.

A weakening spell. Hekate turned sharply and looked into the blackness of the cave. If it was a spell, she thought . . . but before the idea could form fully the sense of the guhrt grew stronger. Hekate spun on her heel to face the woods beyond the clearing and sent a blast of hatred at the creature. It came no closer, but it did not squall or retreat. The hatred that was her own was not enough; she needed the terror and despair that came from the caves of the dead to drive it back. And even so, she realized, she could not drive it away. It would wait. And sooner or later she must sleep. As soon as she did, it would send out its slimy excresences. Once they touched her, she would be lost.

She saw again those loathesome ribbons, saw how they crept toward her but stopped at the edge of the blood trough. So she could not find shelter in the outer section of the cave. The only place she would be safe from the guhrt was on the other side of the trough–but could she survive the agony of terror and hopelessness induced by intruding into the domain of the king of the dead?

The guhrt was moving again. Hekate again cast out a shaft of hatred mixed with her own fear and terror, but she did not even know if it struck the creature for she was now close to exhaustion. She retreated inside the cave, creating a mage light; since her father already knew where she was, the small magic could not betray her and it took very little power.

She stood teetering on the edge of the trough. She could feel the looming threat of unbearable anguish, but extending her senses did not find an overall aura like that in the secret shrine in the forest. What she felt was more like a thin curtain rising above a knotted cord of magic. But that was a trigger spell she knew—a spell designed and set by a human mage. No trigger spell surrounded the clearing in the forest where the Mother dwelt. And Hekate could not imagine the Mother hoarding Her power and releasing Her aura only when it was needed.

Would the equally powerful king of the dead need to hoard power? For that matter, could a mortal seize feelings generated by the king of the dead and use them as a weapon, as she had done? The thought of trying to mold and wield the Mother's power turned her cold inside.

Curiosity woke in Hekate. If it was a spell and not a protection placed by the king of the dead, could she follow the spell to the spell-caster? Could she induce or force that spell-caster to stop using the spell or to give her protection against it?

For one moment she gave all her attention to that fascinating thought, letting her awareness of the guhrt ebb. The creature reacted at once, coming as close to the cave entrance as it could. Through it, Perses launched a powerful psychic assault. The blow struck at her should have rendered her unconscious, but the wards she had built and put in place as a protection against the guhrt held. Even so, Hekate's mage light flickered out and she staggered forward, stumbling across the blood trough and several steps on into the depth of the cave.

Again the spell of fear and despair fell on her, but the weight that descended upon her was not enough to crush out a rising tide of rage that beat against the oppression. The cruelty and unfairness of an assault from every side when she had done nothing to deserve such treatment now aroused in Hekate such a fury that it lifted the burden of terror, replacing it with a rage so great she felt she would burst. And it was all Perses' fault! All!

"Perses, I will destroy you!" she screamed into the hollow void and then turned to face outward. "I swear I will somehow make you more helpless than the many who have died as your victims." Tears poured down her face. "Witness my oath, Mother!" She spun back to look into the blackness of the inner cave. "Witness my oath, king of the dead, in whose realm I now stand."

"*DONE!*"

The wordless, soundless acknowledgement echoed through Hekate's being, shaking her to her core. The staff, to which she had been clinging to keep herself upright, came loose from the ground as she started in surprise. She felt the binding take hold of her, and the realization of what she had done sapped away what little strength remained in her. Misery, dread, and desperation fastened on her. She slipped to the ground, feeling her body shrink into the fragile, bent form of extreme age. A last pang of fear that her father had somehow managed to touch her with his will sent her over the edge into the emptiness of unconsciousness.

"Thief!" The voice creaked rustily as if long unused.

Hekate blinked up at a young man, who stood over her, his mouth tight with disapproval. Except for his pallid complexion and his severe expression, he would have been a pleasant sight. He was somewhat fairer than the ordinary Ka'ananite, with long, light brown hair, large eyes of a brown so pale as to be nearly golden, a straight nose, and a mouth that was meant to be generous but was pinched back in displeasure.

She put an arm behind her to lever herself to a sitting position, realizing as she did so that she must have been lying on the ground for some time. She was terribly cold.

"I am not a thief," Hekate said indignantly. "You must see that my hands are empty. You may take my cloak and examine it, and I will show you that my gown conceals nothing."

The young man looked contemptuous. "Don't take me for a fool. I realize that the protection over this cave felled you before you could seize any of the treasures left for the king of the dead. That doesn't make you any less a thief for you intended to take what you could."

"I intended no such thing!" she exclaimed. "I fled here for protection."

"A liar as well as a thief, then. No one comes to the caves of the dead for protection. That offered by the king of the dead is not the kind a sane person seeks, especially those of your ripe years, who seem to cling all the tighter to life."

"It depends on what one is fleeing from," Hekate said, fighting to make sense against the terror and hopelessness that filled her. "I have heard that the king of the dead is a merciful god and does not torment the innocent."

The young man began to look uncertain. "You were threatened with torture?" he asked. "For what?"

Hekate suddenly realized that she could see him because there were several mage lights, but of a slightly more golden hue than her own, which was a pale silvery blue, hovering around them. Hers must have gone out when she . . . fainted. With that memory came another, of the oath she had sworn to render her father powerless. She uttered a small gasp, and put her hand to her mouth. The young man's mouth twisted with pity.

"Nothing," she cried, angry all over again. "I had done nothing to deserve such treatment."

The lips firmed again into displeasure. "Of course. No one ever does anything to deserve punishment."

All the while the terror and remorse, the despair, permeated Hekate's soul. She turned her head to look out over the blood trough. No ribbons of entrapment stained the floor, but she knew the guhrt was not gone. It had withdrawn again, perhaps even farther into the forest, but it was waiting. This time, likely, it would let her get well away from the caves of the dead, too far for her to seek shelter again, before it revealed itself and seized on her.

"I was threatened with worse than torment of the body," she snarled. "I was threatened with a binding of the spirit that would reduce me to an automaton, and that automaton would be used for terrible purposes . . . for murder and entrapment. The binding would be forever, for the whole length of my life, and worse yet, even death wouldn't release me. What more awful could happen to me here?"

"Who could set such a binding on you?" Doubt showed again in the small creases around the golden eyes. "That is no small spell."

"My father," Hekate replied bitterly, forgetting she wore the guise of the crone.

Doubt vanished. The young man burst out laughing. "He'd be a mighty sorcerer indeed to still be living and be your father." And then he said more gently, "I think you're a little mad, old woman, and that you did come here to steal. I'll have pity on you, though, and ignore your lies since you haven't stolen anything yet. Go home. You'll find nothing in these caves that could make worthwhile what you'll suffer in seeking for it."

The laughter nearly stunned Hekate. She could feel sweat cold on her body and she was shuddering continually, whereas he could laugh. She could fight the pain inflicted on her, but to laugh . . . No, he must be protected against the torment she was suffering.

"I can't go," she cried. "I tell you there's something terrible waiting outside for me. I can't even go across the blood trough. The creature is called a guhrt and it carries the coercion spell. If it touches me, I'm lost. I cannot and will not leave the cave, not even if I die of this agony."

As she spoke, Hekate righted her staff, set it firmly in the ground, and pulled herself upright with its help. The young man opened his mouth to answer her, but his gaze, which had flicked over the staff, fixed on it.

"Where did you get that staff?" he asked sharply.

His urgency drove the lesson she had just learned from Hekate's mind. "My father threw it at me when I couldn't obey him. I had fallen and I couldn't get up."

But this time the young man did not laugh. His eyes still fixed on the staff, he asked, "How old is your father?"

"I have no idea," Hekate answered slowly, remembering now that she looked very ancient herself. "But he doesn't look as old as I."

She was not paying terribly much attention to what they were saying. If the young man questioning her had protection against the spell designed to drive invaders out of the caves of the dead, perhaps she could also build such a spell. The wards would need to be inside, rather than outide.

"Feel under the handgrip of the staff. Is there a hard knot protruding from the wood? Push it upward."

Concentrating more on the spell she was trying to form, than on the young man, Hekate simply did what she was told. She was amazed and nearly lost the thread of her spell when the grip parted from the body of the staff. Hurriedly she initiated the spell, before it could fall apart and lash back at her, but it was not really complete. Still it sealed off some of the anguish, enough for her to focus on the grip of the staff, which was loose in her hand. Instinctively, she pulled on it, and a long, thin knife came out of the shaft. She stood looking at it and then at the man who continued to stare at what she held.

"Then it is my staff," he muttered.

"You want proof I am no thief?" Hekate thrust both pieces of the staff at him. "Here, take it back."

He shook his head. "I didn't say you stole the staff. A long, long time ago I dropped it in a back street of Ur-Kabos. I never knew what became of it."

"It couldn't be so very long ago," Hekate said. "You are a young man—" She stopped abruptly and then continued, "That is, you look to be a young man. Sorcerers are long lived."

For perhaps a dozen heartbeats he didn't answer and then he said, "It takes one to know one, I suppose."

Hekate nodded. She saw no point in lying about that. As soon as he began to *think* about what she had said about the guhrt and the spell of coercion instead of concentrating on driving her out, he would realize she must know magic. And she needed the spell of protection he had. He would be more likely to give it to a fellow sorcerer, she hoped.

"Is that how you are able to withstand the punishment of the king of the dead for entering his realm?" he continued.

Hekate slammed the thin knife back into the shaft of the staff and the parts joined invisibly. Then she snorted lightly. "You mean how am I able to withstand the spell *you* use to frighten people away from the cave?"

As she said it, Hekate realized that that was the answer. The young man had no protection. It was his spell, so of course it did not affect him. His slight wince told her she had hit her mark and she continued, "What *you* inflict on invaders of the caves of the dead has nothing to do with the king of the dead. I know what the aura of a god is, and it is not turned on by a trip spell. Oh, no, I know you. We are of the same kind, you and I, and it is more likely that you are a thief and one of long standing than that I am." She shrugged. "As to how I am able to withstand it, I am accustomed to pain. I endure."

He raised a hand, defensively or apologetically, then sighed and whispered, "*Thialuo trouos, panikos, phobos.*"

The weight of fear and despair was gone as suddenly as it had fallen upon her when she crossed the blood trough. Hekate sagged against the support of the staff, no longer needing to stiffen herself against screaming and beating her breast or writhing helplessly on the ground.

"Since you know the truth, and I can't drive you out, I suppose there's no need to make you suffer needlessly," he said. Oddly, there was a kind of eagerness in his voice and stance, but then he seemed to recognize what he had exposed. His body stiffened, and he added, "But don't think I believe you and trust you. I'll watch you to make sure you steal nothing."

Hekate laughed aloud in the euphoria of relief. "What is there here to steal? I haven't seen—"

She stopped abruptly as one of the mage lights whisked away toward the wall. Immediately glitterings of silver and gold answered to the light. Hekate saw that there were urns and cups and bowls, goblets and gold-inlaid boxes, and other things standing on shelves.

She shrugged, still smiling. "So there are treasures. Well, watch all you like. I'll take none of those. However, I fled with nothing, only what I am wearing. If offerings of food and drink are made, I will take those. If you call that stealing, then I will be a thief, but I can't leave and I don't intend to die of thirst and starvation. I'll settle my score with the king of the dead when he demands payment from me."

Free of agony and able to be aware of subtleties, Hekate noticed a relaxation in the young man. She had seen him make himself rigid, but now understood it was not to resist pain but to hold back from something he desired. Her? An ancient crone? Nonsense. But he was now smiling at her.

"I can't argue with that. I take the offerings of prepared food and drink myself, but not the dried grain, fruit, or meat or the sealed flasks of date wine or preserved cheeses. Those are stored separately and someone or something gathers them up on the equinoxes and takes them away with the treasure. The food and open pitchers of beer or wine I use."

Feeling as light and silly as a thistledown now that she had a sanctuary—and possibly even a companion—Hekate said, "Aha, then you are, as I said, a thief of long standing. Do you take the food to feed your hungry wife and children? Would you not be better off doing some work instead of taking the offerings to the king of the dead?"

"I have no wife and children," the young man said, his voice suddenly flat, his face expressionless. "I can never leave the caves. I am bound here."

CHAPTER 4

"Bound?" Hekate echoed. "Who are you? How did such a dreadful fate befall you?"

He smiled again, but his lips were pulled awry into a grimace. "I remember that I sneered when you said you had done nothing to merit punishment. Now I'm about to say the same thing. I—I was, I think, only in the wrong place at the wrong time and saw something I shouldn't have seen . . ." He shook himself suddenly, oddly like a dog shaking water from his fur. "Come," he added, "there's no need for us to stand here in the cold and dark. My fate isn't quite so dreadful as it appears here."

Hekate followed readily, although she wondered at the phrasing. How could the fate of being bound to the caves of the dead appear more dreadful in one place than another? However, the answer to that became partly apparent as they crossed the depth of the cave. The ceiling dropped and the cave narrowed as they moved toward the back wall, which permitted the mage lights to wake myriad gleams and glitters in the rock. The oppression caused by the utter blackness beyond the area lit by the mage lights was relieved by the sparks. It was like being surrounded by a starry sky. Hekate was so fascinated that she nearly walked into a wall.

"Hi! Have a care!" her companion exclaimed, laughing.

He caught hold of her arm and steered her toward one of what she now saw were several dark passages. Immediately aware that he could be drawing her into a maze of caves in which she could be lost, Hekate fixed a marker spell above head height on the wall of the passage.

The opening was dark, without any of the crystal glow that had enlivened the walls and ceiling of the larger cave, and Hekate saw with considerable surprise that that was no accident. The walls and ceiling had been coated with some black substance, perhaps tar or pitch. Then the passsage turned sharply to the right, and Hekate realized the crystal that lit the walls had been deliberately covered. Ahead of her the passage was bright with fixed mage lights, which would have been visible as light from the front of the cave.

The passage turned right again, opening into an irregularly shaped chamber, not as large or high as the first cave, but of a comfortable size and lit as bright as day. Hekate stood in the doorway, gaping. Opposite her, a wall of golden brown water near the ceiling broke up into myriad cascades and poured down the back wall. Instinctively she looked at the floor, expecting it to be awash, but only a shallow trough carried away the runoff. The young man, who had turned to see why she was not following, laughed.

Then Hekate saw that the streams were frozen in stone with no more than a sheen of water on the surface. That gave an even greater realism to what appeared to be a lace of foam at the foot of the cascade. She shook her head in amazement.

"Beautiful, isn't it?" The smile on the young man's lips grew wry. "Thank you. I've been here so long, I don't see it any more. You've given it back to me."

"All of it is beautiful," Hekate said, glancing up and all around, awe in her voice.

To the right and the left, on either side of the cascade, the walls of the chamber were patterned with what seemed to be tightly pleated flows of different colored stone. These too showed a sheen of wet on the surface, which gleamed in the light of arcs of mage light. From the ceiling hung delicate flower-like projections; at first Hekate thought they were very strange flowers with thin, sharp-pointed petals growing from small cracks in the roof without stems or leaves. Then she realized the "flowers" were also of stone, translucent and delicate as feathers. Those too glowed brightly from mage lights caught inside.

Hekate was deeply impressed. She had power, but such an extravagant use was beyond even what Perses could expend. However, the slightly envious awe changed to solid appreciation when her mage-sense told her that the power was not coming from the young man himself. As she had bound the illusion disguising the valley of the Nymphae to the power in the earth, so had he done with the mage lights. The floor and walls of the place were threaded with lines of power and each mage light had its own source. But not many could see or use that earth power.

"That is a very clever use of the veins of the earth," she said. "Not many sorcerers can even sense the blood running through them."

He lifted a brow. "But you can, and you have cleverly told me so. The power warms the room too." He gestured for Hekate to enter. "If you've seen all you want to see, come in. But there are caverns far more beautiful than this chamber. This is only convenient because it's so close to the entrance. If you'd like to see the deeper caverns, I'll gladly show them to you."

He had started to speak in a tone he wanted to be indifferent, but as he mentioned the other caverns an eagerness came into his voice and manner that he struggled to keep in check. Hekate was aware of the painful intensity in that eagerness. Although she couldn't help feeling suspicious of so great a desire of a rather handsome young man for the company of an aged crone, she couldn't help smiling either.

"I would indeed like to see them," she assured him—and it was true. If the caverns were more beautiful than this chamber, they would be a great experience, a thing to remember all her life. "But not at this moment," she added, still smiling. "I have come a very long way today and at a much faster pace than is good for me."

"Of course." He damped down his flickering excitement and smiled ruefully. "Forgive me. I forgot you said you were fleeing some magical threat. Sit down and rest."

He gestured toward a grouping of what must be called furniture. Hekate stared, again impressed. Thick pillars of stone had either grown up from the floor or been carved out of it. Three surrounded a stone table, and that had clearly been worked from a huge boulder, the top broken off to provide a flat surface and the sides chipped away so that one could sit on the flat stones with one's legs comfortably under the table.

"Thank you. I will," Hekate said. When she reached the table and stools, she touched a cushion made of a folded blanket and laughed. "Earth power does many things, but I've never known it to provide cushions and blankets."

He shrugged. "No. I suppose I am a thief. But . . . Never mind. Come, sit down. Are you hungry?"

"Very!" Hekate exclaimed, coming forward eagerly and seating herself. "Who carved the stone?" she asked, touching the edge of the table, which had clearly been ground smooth.

"I did," the young man replied, his voice again flat.

He moved away toward an opening in one wall of the chamber. Now that Hekate's attention had been drawn to it, she could hear water running. A mage light sprang into existence as he entered, and a moment later he came out carrying a crude wooden platter, plainly meant to be left behind with the offering it bore. Hekate's mouth watered; the platter held some slices of meat and some rounds of flatbread, but even her hunger could not distract her from the stone table and stools. One man alone? How many years would that work have taken, unless it was done by magic?

"Did you use the earth power to form the table and stools?" she asked as he came and set the platter on the table before her. "How—"

His laugh was so bitter that she left the question unasked. "I am not the king of the dead, who can shape stone with his hands," he said. "No, I did it the usual way, hammering one stone upon another." His mouth twisted. "There are stones aplenty here and time enough too."

She had reached a hand toward the meat and bread, but did not take them. "Time enough for you to carve these? You alone? Who are you?"

"Who are you?" he countered.

She took a slice of meat, put it on a round of flatbread and bit into it. "My name is Hekate," she answered promptly, if somewhat indistinctly.

The offer of her name without hesitation should reduce his suspicion of her; however, it was more ingenuous than truthful because Hekate knew he could not use that name against her. As soon as she was old enough to speak distinctly and follow instructions—at least some of the time—Asterie had brought her to the Mother's shrine and bade her choose a soul-name, a name that she wanted for herself alone and that she and the Mother would hold secret between them. Then, Asterie said, no man, woman, or god could enslave her by that personal tie.

Since Hekate had already suffered her father laying his will upon her, she was more intent and serious to have the protection Asterie offered than an ordinary child of three might have been. Even so she had no memory of why she uttered the word she did—perhaps it was the Mother's doing rather than her own—but she called herself Pheraea and sealed that into her deepest being.

"I am the daughter of the mage Perses and the Lady Asterie," she continued between swallowing one bite and taking another. "I don't know whether you are acquainted with them."

He shook his head and sat down on another of the padded stone stools. "I don't really know anyone from Ur-Kabos. I'm not from these parts." He shrugged. "I come from the west by way of the north." His mouth twisted again. "The Gifted are not welcome there."

"The Gifted are not welcome anywhere," Hekate said, her lips thinning.

He stared at her, then said, "My name is Kabeiros."

"Kabeiros!" she echoed, again failing to take a

bite of the bread and meat she had started to lift to her mouth. "How do you come by–" She stopped abruptly. "No, that's none of my business. If you wish to be called Kabeiros, that's what I'll call you."

Kabeiros was staring at her in astonishment. "Want to be called? It is my name." Then he grinned. "Oh surely, my pranks could not be remembered for so long."

"*Your* pranks? There is a fountain called 'the water of Kabeiros' in the poorest quarter of Ur-Kabos. It has the best and purest water–only it is pouring from the penis of a bronze dog seemingly urinating on a post. The legend is that the god Kabeiros struck the ground there and brought up the water. Are you telling me you are *that* Kabeiros?"

"Legend?" he said, his voice rather faint. "Has it been so long as that? To make a prank into a legend?" His eyes were full of tears. "When it is always black, one loses count of day and night. When nothing grows, one loses count even of the seasons." His lips trembled and he firmed them.

"You have been here in the caves of the dead since the water of Kabeiros began to flow?" Hekate whispered.

She was in no doubt that the young man–no, the man far older than she, and had her life span been as that of others, she would have been older than the crone looked–had spoken the truth. His emotion was too raw, and it was all turned inward. It was clear he hardly knew she was there.

What troubled her was that Kabeiros was a local god–a trickster god who plagued people with all kinds of mischief, some good some bad. Kabeiros was far more likely to grant a prayer than the gods worshiped in the temples but to grant it in such a way as to sometimes make it worthless, sometimes make it a curse, and sometimes bring ten times the blessing for which one had prayed.

If one were wise, one prayed to Kabeiros to be ignored, or did not pray to him at all and hoped for the best. And certainly no one had ever named a child after *that* god, so this young man was not likely to be a distant descendant of one of Kabeiros' naughty tricks. Unless some poor woman driven to the point of madness had cursed the unwelcome fruit of her womb with that name. Poor woman. Poor child.

Hekate examined Kabeiros with care. This being was a sorcerer; she had felt the power of his spell of fear and despair. He was also Gifted by his own admission, although he had not named his Gift. She studied his face, blind-looking, though the eyes seemed to be fixed on the table. Although it was a dangerous thing to do, making her terribly vulnerable, she opened herself as she did in the secret shrine; a moment later she shook her head infinitesimally. Whatever else he was, this Kabeiros was no god.

He was staring downward, one hand moving gently over the table's smooth surface, the other clenched tight. Hekate put her hand over his fist and patted it gently. When he did not respond, she went on with her meal, finishing the bread and meat and drinking the beer. She was not fond of beer, but the date wine was too sweet. Dionysos had told her there was a better fruit for making wine than dates; it grew on the vines of which he dreamed.

Thinking of Dionysos reminded her that Kabeiros wasn't the only one trapped in the caves of the dead. The guhrt, the Nymphae had said, fed full on blood could wait and watch for her for weeks, perhaps months. Would Perses' summoning hold the creature that long? She shrugged. It didn't matter. She glanced at Kabeiros again. He was still lost inside himself; however, she was now reasonably confident that she would be welcome to stay as long as she was willing.

She was also able to dismiss any ideas about such ulterior motives as secret sacrifice as the cause of Kabeiros' suppressed eagerness to show her the other caverns. He would be eager to show her anything that would hold her attention and keep her with him. If he had been alone so long, naturally he would be eager for company, even that of an old hag.

Hekate's lips tightened. She didn't welcome the thought of keeping the form of the crone for any extended time. Not only was it unattractive to others, but it was uncomfortable. However, even less welcome was the idea of letting a total stranger, and a sorcerer at that, know that she could shift her form. And yet she was very tempted to become the woman and to be completely honest with Kabeiros. She snorted gently. Completely honest. She doubted after the many years she had lived with Perses she could ever be completely honest with anyone. Still, the temptation to tell Kabeiros the truth persisted. She had no idea why; there was just something open and childlike about him.

Childlike! Hekate suppressed a chuckle. If he was who he claimed to be, he was hundreds of years old, perhaps as much as a thousand. No, it could not be. He must be the offspring of a woman who truly hated him, or hated herself and his father–and he was a sorcerer. A sorcerer was, if she judged by herself and Perses, a practiced deceiver, far better at playing a role than the best of storytellers. She did not know this man at all and must be cautious.

And yet . . . and yet . . . Cocking her head to see his face better, she felt her heart contract with pity.

The yellow eyes were staring wide, searching with the pathetic intensity of a lost child for something on the top of the table or in his own hands, which were now lying open.

"Kabeiros," she said softly.

The eyes lifted to her, but they saw nothing. Hekate sighed. She hoped she had not jolted him into madness by reminding him how long he had been in the caves of the dead. There was nothing she could do, however. She had the feeling that to try to draw him back to the present would do more harm than good, so she swept the few crumbs she had left onto the platter, took it and the empty wooden cup, the two crude pottery pitchers to the opening she had seen him enter.

The chamber behind it was now dark, but the mage light she generated showed her a narrow room, little more than a passage, but with a lively stream falling down the far wall. It sprayed over a thin rock shelf, tilted slightly backward and down toward the entryway, so that the water ran along it and over the back before draining off into some hidden opening. Hekate shivered slightly. The room was very damp and chilly. Cured hides hung over the front of the shelf, protecting whatever was behind them from any direct wetting. Meat and cheese and the beer and wine could be stored there, but the bread would spoil.

A breath of warmth from behind her drew her attention to another hide-covered opening. Hekate went through and found, as she expected, another small chamber, this one dry and heated by the power of the earth. Stone shelves, some seemingly natural and others bearing the marks of work, lined the walls. On them were more crude wooden and pottery cups, more pottery pitchers, more wooden platters and some rough, carelessly woven baskets.

Contesting with the warmth from the walls and floor was a cold draught, coming from the back of the chamber. Hekate went to look and saw a wide crack, its edges partly smoothed as if water had run into it for some time and then stopped. Listening, Hekate could hear the chuckle of water running down below, and at the edge of the crack was one piece of moldy bread, apparently caught there when garbage had been carelessly scraped off a platter. She smiled and kicked the crust in following it with the crumbs she scraped off the platter. Then, with some maneuvering, she managed to relieve herself down the crack without soiling the edges. That was a relief.

She had nothing with which to wipe or wash the platter she still held, so she left it separate from the others on a bottom shelf, squinting a little in the dimming light. Dimming? Hekate found it surprisingly hard to lift her head to look at her mage light, but in a moment realized that she was so tired even that small drain of power was too much for her to maintain. There would be time enough tomorrow and for, she thought, many tomorrows to examine how Kabeiros had lived. Now she must sleep.

In the main living chamber, the young man still sat at the table. Now his eyes were closed and tears marked his face. Hekate uttered a soft sigh and resisted the urge to smooth back his tumbled hair, a lock of which was plastered to his cheek. If he was grieving over his lost years, he was not mad. Although if he were truly Kabeiros, a few hundred years could not matter much.

She smiled tiredly at the thought and stepped softly to the table where she took the blankets from the two unoccupied stools. Then she found a sort of niche in the irregular walls, an indentation that was dry instead of gleaming with a trickle of water, laid one doubled blanket on the ground and drew the other over her. She had much to think about, not least the question of whether it was safe to sleep unwarded in Kabeiros' presence, but whether because she was exhausted or for some other reason, she could feel no fear and was asleep almost before she had settled down on her hard bed.

"Hekate?"

The call rang though the cave, startling Hekate awake but leaving her totally bewildered. She felt bruised all over from sleeping on a stone floor and she had no memory at all of her surroundings until her wildly roving glance caught the frozen-in-stone fall of water. By then, the call had come again, louder, anguished.

"Oh Mother, help," the voice cried, breaking on a sob. "I am alone again."

"No, no. I am here," Hekate called, struggling to sit up, her stiff muscles protesting both yesterday's run and the night's accommodation.

Kabeiros appeared before her, sighing, "Mother, thank you." But then his eyes widened in astonishment. "Why are you lying on the floor?" he asked. "Did you think I would be angry if you took at least part of my bed?"

He had twice called on the Mother. Although Hekate only laughed amidst her groans, her feeling of confidence in the young–well, he looked young–man increased to a near certainty that he was someone she could trust.

"I had no idea where your bed was or if you even had one," she said, still smiling. "You do not look to have slept in it last night."

"No. I slept on the table, I think."

Hekate thought so too, since one cheek was marked with a slightly pebbled look, but she did not interrupt him.

"I was trying to remember . . . to remember . . ." His eyes lost their focus.

"Help me up!" Hekate said sharply, and extended a rather imperious hand toward him. She understood that it would be better for him not to think too much about the missing years. "And you had better show me your privy," she added. "I confess I used the one in the drying room–the warm room–of your kitchen last night. I'm sorry if I did wrong, but I could wait no longer. I was careful not to soil the floor."

While she spoke, he had taken her hand and raised her to her feet. "It doesn't matter. That all goes down the same stream, but the privy is more comfortable. This way."

He guided her to another of the openings on the back wall, this one to the far right, again calling a mage light into being as they stepped into the dark. The arrangement was somewhat like the kitchen, the short passage leading to one chamber, which opened into another.

The first had water running vigorously somewhere below an opening. Here, however, stones had been assembled and fitted together to form a stool with a central opening. Hekate made directly for it, her need too urgent for her to be troubled about modesty, but Kabeiros backed out into an opening on the left wall, entering another chamber so she had privacy.

When she called his name, he came to the doorway but only to invite her in. "This is my bedchamber," he said. "As you can see, there are more furs than one person needs to be comfortable. If you would not feel easy sharing the room with me, I will carry some out to your chosen spot, but it is warmer here because it is a small room and easier to heat."

"Thank you," Hekate said politely, but she didn't try to hide the fact that she was choking on laughter. "I'm not afraid to share your room. I know you've been alone for a long time, but even so I can't believe you would be overcome with lust for *me*."

Kabeiros was now smiling, which was what Hekate had intended, but what she had said woke a stirring in her. She would not mind sharing not only his room but his bed, she realized, then choked back another laugh. No one would willingly share a bed with the crone, but if she changed to the woman . . . It would be a good test of Kabeiros. She jerked her mind back from that enticing notion. She liked Kabeiros and even trusted him . . . but not enough to expose to him that she was a shape-shifter.

CHAPTER 5

Two ten-days later, Hekate was beginning to rethink that doubt. She was very tired of the crone with her aching joints and physical feebleness, particularly when her magical power seemed to be increasing until she was almost bursting with it. Still, every time she came to the point of telling Kabeiros, she drew back—less because she feared she could not trust him than because she didn't want to see his disgust and withdrawal.

He had, as he promised, shown her the beauties of his underground domain, and they were many, some truly breathtaking. She would never forget the chamber where more than half the floor was a pool, so clear and so still that the rock below seemed dry and the roof above reflected as a perfect mirror. She would never have known it was water or how deep it was if Kabeiros had not caught her arm to prevent her from falling in. A moment later she saw very large fish swimming lazily around what looked like huge, perfect pearls.

"They are only stone," Kabeiros assured her when

she pointed to them. "I don't know why they form like that, but they aren't as smooth as they look when one takes them out of the water."

"Too bad," Hekate said. "If they were real, neither you nor I would ever have to do a day's work again."

They caught several of the fish for dinner, so easily tempted with leftovers from the food they had carried that Hekate felt slightly guilty. However, after Kabeiros showed her how to bake them, wrapped in a jacket of clay dredged from the side of the pool, and laid in a bed of rocks heated by the blood of the earth, she put guilt aside and enjoyed her meal heartily.

Another chamber frightened Hekate half out of her wits. From the roof hung hundreds or perhaps thousands of huge needles of rock formed by water that dripped very slowly along each needle's surface, leaving more rock behind. Sharp pillars grew up from the floor to meet those needles. Near the entrance, the needles above and pillars below had fused together leaving a central opening. The formation looked exactly like a gigantic mouth surrounded by jagged teeth. It took some force of will to step through the opening. Hekate could not help but envision those jaws closing on them.

Beyond that in some places the needles dropping from the roof met the pillars growing up from the ground so that the way was blocked and they were forced to weave this way and that. Kabeiros had once tried to clear a path by knocking the needles from the roof, but he had not got far. What he had done exposed what seemed an unending vista of jagged needles, but he told Hekate he didn't dare try to clean more away because the reverberations of his hammering had caused other needles than those he struck to fall. He was afraid if he continued, the ceiling would come down and kill him.

Despite the uneasiness it caused her, even that chamber had its strange beauty. Many of the needles were of different colors and the moving mage lights caused them to flicker and glow. Still, neither of them liked the place, fearing that sound or movement or some touch during their passage would begin a collapse. And once, a needle did come down not far from them when they were walking through.

Unfortunately, they had to pass through that place every day to bathe in a wonderful cavern full of pools and geysers of hot water. One could choose there a bath of exactly the right size and temperature and some of the geysers had produced a sand as fine as powder from wearing away the rock that surrounded them.

"I wish I could go out," Hekate had sighed when she had finished washing with the fine sand. "This mixed with a little oil and some ash from the bones of the meat would make a paste that leaves one feeling truly fresh and clean."

For a long time Kabeiros did not respond, and Hekate looked at him in surprise. "I wish so too" might have been an expected answer. But by the time she had finished drying herself on cloths used to wrap offerings—the offerings having been tidily stored on the shelves—he said, "I can take you to an opening on the east side of the mountain, but I wish you would tell me honestly if you plan to leave. I will not try to stop you."

Perhaps not physically, Hekate thought, but I suspect you would reason and plead, and I am so comfortable here. . . . "No, I wouldn't leave without warning you," she said. "I promise not to do that. I trust you, Kabeiros. I don't feel I will need to escape. Perhaps—" She didn't finish what she had started to say, which was to ask him to come with her. That was something he couldn't do if he were magically bound to the caves of the dead. Or could he?

As she swallowed the invitation, she wondered why she had done so. If she could break the spell that tied Kabeiros to the caves of the dead, he would be an ideal companion to accompany her to some safer and more comfortable refuge where she could work out the problem of dealing with her father. And the combination of the friendship between them and his gratitude for her breaking his bondage would doubtless make him grateful enough to accept her as a shape-changer. She would be able to take the form of the woman again.

She finished dressing and came around the spur of rock that gave her some privacy. Kabeiros was sitting on a boulder, his sandals still unlaced, his head in his hands. Recognizing the blow she had dealt him by confirming she intended to leave, she went to him and touched his shoulder.

"Tell me how you are bound," she urged. "For my own protection, I have studied bindings and the ways to loose them. Perhaps I could find a key to free you."

"It is useless." Kabeiros shook his head. "Mother knows I have tried myself in every way I know, even drawing on the earth to enlarge my power. Moreover, when I first was imprisoned here, I called and some of my friends heard me and came. But none of them could loose my bonds either."

"Perhaps none was as strong as I."

Hekate spoke without false modesty. She had always been powerful, although warned by her mother she had kept as much of her strength hidden as she could. Still she had never come near Perses in her command of leashed energy, which was why he could fell her and control her. Now, however, her power grew every day and the steady increase puzzled her. When she had spoken, she suddenly wondered whether the power came from the caves, and she asked Kabeiros.

"Not to me, anyway," he said. "As far as I can tell, I am what I always was. But for many, it is the opposite. The caves drain them or make their magic go awry. That was why my most powerful friends couldn't even try to help me."

So Perses was not merely superstitious, Hekate thought. What he feared was true, and he was one of those whose power was drained or damaged by the caves. Even if he were not, his fear would shake his concentration and make his magic less effective. Hekate drew a deep breath. Would there be some way to draw him into the caves? Even as the idea came to her she knew it was hopeless. If anything could have drawn Perses there, it would have been his determination to retrieve her and use her.

Perses was out of her reach, and just as well. Strong as she had grown, she still feared him too much to challenge him. She winced away from that honest if shameful admission and brought her attention back to Kabeiros. Once again he had not told her what bound him to the caves of the dead. She sighed. He had a right to keep it to himself if that was what he wished, but that secrecy would prevent her from helping him and deprive her of a valuable companion. Perhaps she could come at the answer sideways. Hekate brought the conversation back to power.

"You have power enough, if that spell of terror and despair was any example and if you still claim to be the Kabeiros who made the fountain." She laughed suddenly. "I remember how I laughed when I first saw it. But why? Why choose such a . . . I mean, if you wanted the poor to have good water, that is estimable, but why that form?"

He shrugged. "I'm sorry to say that I don't believe I even thought of the need of the poor for good water. I was not given to serious thought in those days. They were both there, the water and the dog, that's all. I told you it was a prank. I was very young . . . so very young . . ."

"So was I, once," Hekate said. "You still haven't explained why a dog peeing."

He had begun to look lost when he spoke of his youth–it still happened once in a while, though not as frequently as at first–but she knew a sharp question or remark would bring him out of it. Now he smiled at her sharp tone and answered.

"I saw the water under the ground–as I see the blood of the earth in the veins–and I think I had just stepped in a puddle of filth or there was garbage all over the road or something of that kind. Anyway, I thought what was needed was a fountain and that it was ridiculous that someone hadn't paid a sorcerer to bring the water up."

"Not everyone can see what you see. I told you that before. And the people who live there probably can't afford to pay a sorcerer and would be too frightened to approach one anyway."

"Either I didn't know it then or just didn't think of it. I could have been drunk. Then farther along the street I came across the statue of the dog . . . ah . . . watering the pole. Of course the two things came together in my mind at once, so I moved the statue to the water and brought it up." He grinned. "I suppose I could have made it come out of the dog's mouth, but that would have been so ordinary. I've seen ten thousand fish spitting water and nymphs pouring it out of pithoi and–"

Hekate laughed. "And a dog peeing it was a little different. Yes, I can see that."

Kabeiros smiled, laced his sandals, and stood up. Both fell silent as they entered the chamber of the needles and stepped as gently as possible. However when they were safely through, Kabeiros said, "I wish all my pranks had been so innocent. Sometimes people got hurt." He frowned. "A child . . . I remember grieving over that. A child died because of my carelessness and stupidity. The father had annoyed me, raving about some heavy chest that was either at just the perfect height or too low or something of the sort. It was so long ago, I don't remember the cause, but I do remember bespelling the chest some two handspans above the floor and going off. I suppose I meant to come back and tease the man, or make him admit his work of art wasn't perfect or something, but I forgot. And eventually the spell wore out and the chest fell—and the child was beneath it and was crushed."

Hekate looked at him sidelong. His eyes were fixed straight ahead, his mouth downturned with remembered sorrow or possibly even with new pain. A better nature than mine, she thought. She would have cursed the man and his woman for carelessness, not blamed herself.

She said soothingly, "I'm sorry about the child, but you couldn't have known. Usually a spell fades a bit at a time, so the chest would have settled down very slowly over several days. And it was a pure accident that the child should be there at the particular moment the spell failed all at once. It *was* only a prank, not meant to harm."

He smiled at her doubtfully. "At least that was the worst," he admitted, "but so often I meant to do good and caused harm, like when I dropped a merchant's purse to a poor whore with a sick child. She took the money, took the child, and ran. Naturally, she left the purse behind, and a thief who came to buy her body found it and was blamed for the crime."

Hekate laughed aloud. "That seems more like a fated justice than a prank that went wrong. I suspect he well deserved the punishment he received."

"That's true enough, but if the woman had been slower to flee . . ." Kabeiros went on to relate a dozen or so adventures, most of which ended far differently than he expected. Hekate had only been listening to what he said with half an ear, and finally she frowned.

"Are those the only spells you can use?" she asked in the first pause.

He shrugged. "Well, I can make mage lights and fire and send terror abroad. I know most of the basics, what is pounded into a child who shows promise in magic. Later . . . As I've implied, I was a fool when I was young, only wanting to play with my power, not really use it. I never even learned properly how to make wards. Later, ah, later I regretted that. I had cause to regret it bitterly, but it was too late."

"What do you mean it was too late? One can learn spells at any time in one's life, or even learn to make them. It isn't necessary to start from childhood. Well, many sorcerers only come into their power at puberty or even later."

Kabeiros' lips twitched. "True enough, but I don't see a long line of sorcerers willing to teach me. And I have nothing with which to pay . . . and don't look toward the outer chamber. The minions of the king of the dead do come at the equinoxes to gather up the offerings. I don't know whether they have some way of knowing what was left for them, but–to speak the truth–I'm not brave enough to discover whether they do by stealing from them."

"But I am here," Hekate said, laughing again. "And if I say so myself, I am no mean spell-caster. I can teach you wards of any kind and any power. I am a specialist in wards from trying to protect myself from my father." She grimaced. "Not that I ever found one that would completely protect me, but . . . but I had less power then, and simply being in my father's presence exhausted me more than casting ten spells."

She stopped speaking abruptly. That was how she had always felt in her father's presence, as if she had been pouring out power into spells. Was there some way he could have been draining her all these years? Not draining her completely, as he drained Asterie because he had never had any intimate contact with her, but . . .

Holy Mother, that added another layer of impossibility to the binding she had accepted to make Perses powerless. If he had some way of draining her without coupling, as soon as she came near him, even if he could not touch her with the coercion spell, he could drink her power until any spell she cast at him would be too weakened to do him any harm.

"You will teach me spells?" Kabeiros' voice broke into her unhappy musing.

Hekate smiled at him, glad to be diverted from her unpleasant thoughts. "And I won't charge you. After all, haven't you lodged me without charge? I can teach you spell-making, too. What kind of spells would you like to have?"

His face lit with eagerness. "Is there some way to make me invisible? Sometimes when they bring one of the Gifted to the caves, they don't obey the rule of the king of the dead that the person not be molested. If I could go among them unseen, I could give back a shrewd blow or two or blast a few with my spell of terror while not touching those who do the victim no harm. I would like that!"

"Invisibility is *very* hard. I know the spell but it takes a practiced sorcerer to put together the commands and the mental images. The backlash from such a spell can be dangerous. I could build it myself and give it to you, but then it could only be used once or perhaps a few times, and each use would take more power." She shook her head. "However, there's an easy spell I call 'look-by-me.' That would permit you to walk among the worshipers and not be noticed, but it wouldn't serve if you struck someone. That would be too strong an attention provoker for the spell to cover."

"That will do," he said eagerly.

So Hekate taught him the look-by-me spell and then a spell for stasis, so he could keep the food brought as offerings for a much longer time and in more perfect condition than the cool room. And then she began to teach him how to create spells of his own. That was much slower work and took considerable practice.

Another ten-day passed. Hekate was growing very tired of her confinement. She was beginning to miss the sun and the wind, the sounds of birds and beasts and the activities of people. The caves were not silent, but the many noises made by water were not enough. There was no doubt that Kabeiros sensed her restlessness. His face was always sad now at any time when it was not animated by his interest in what he was learning or by their conversation.

Despite that restlessness and longing for the outer world, Hekate was not quite ready to leave. She and Kabeiros were good friends now, and she had never had a friend before. It would be very, very hard to part with him. Also, somewhere, like a faint aftertaste of something foul, she still sensed the guhrt.

Then one day when she had been sitting for a long time explaining how a trap spell could be used to delay the magical attack of a stronger sorcerer until a more effective spell could be made ready, she found she could not get to her feet when she was done. Suddenly despite the light of the mage lamps, the sparkle of the crystal in the ceiling, the image of rushing waters on the walls, Hekate could bear the cave and her ancient body no longer.

"A pox on these ancient bones," she cried. "I must take them out into the sun."

Kabeiros said nothing for a moment, then got to his feet. "Well," he sighed, "I knew I couldn't keep you forever. I will pack all the food we have in stasis. It will take us two days to reach the other way out of the cave. I hope there will be enough dried meat and flatbread left after that to feed you for several days, until you reach some settlements and can buy or trade spells for food. On the way, you will be able to gather some fruits and berries that ripen in early summer."

There was no expression at all on his face. Hekate limped over and took his hand before he could turn away. "Come with me, Kabeiros."

"I cannot," he said.

"Why not? You have never told me what binds you to this place. Did you anger the king of the dead?"

"No. Not him. Only another sorcerer, but he . . . Half the spell was my own. He just twisted it so that . . . I cannot leave here."

"Let me try," Hekate begged. "Let me see the binding and try to break it. You will not die, will you?"

"No," he said softly. "I will not die." But he would not meet her eyes nor agree that she should examine what bound him to the caves.

She argued with him and pleaded with him all

that day and night while they made ready to leave. The next day, Kabeiros spent some time in the outer cave, rearranging the tribute to the king of the dead and writing a letter, which he left plainly visible in one of the vases, stating that he would be gone for some time. Someone should be told to collect the offerings.

"Who collected them before you came?" Hekate asked curiously, distracted for the moment from the hope that had roused in her. If he only intended to show her the mouth of the cave he should only be gone for four days and return well before the autumn equinox.

"One of the dead," Kabeiros answered. "I would have gone mad in the beginning if he had not been here. He had a funny Gift. When he got angry, his hair would burst into fire. I think he could cause fires, too; but there's nothing much in the caves that would burn, so it was safe enough."

"Except you," Hekate remarked dryly. "I can see why his Gift was not widely appreciated."

"Oh, I was in no danger. He was very glad of my company and was careful not to let his fire touch me."

"What happened to him?"

"I have no idea. He went to take the tribute to wherever the king of the dead accepts offerings and he never returned. I had been helping him gather the sacrifices and . . . and I just went on doing it . . . but I had no idea for how long."

"Long enough," Hekate snapped. "I need you more than the king of the dead."

"Do you?"

He looked at her with such longing in his eyes that Hekate thought he would surely tell his secret, but he did not. Nor did he agree to let her try to undo the binding, although she argued with him and pleaded with him all the way through the passages and chambers they traversed to find the hidden way out. She begged him for reasons; she railed at him for stubbornness, but all he would say was "I cannot."

When they arrived at the cave mouth, it was almost as dark outside as in. Only the faintest gleam of promised dawn showed on the eastern horizon. They had lost the rhythm of day and night while traveling and had walked through the night. Kabeiros set down the pack of food and other necessities he carried, keeping only the roll of furs and blankets he had been using as a bedroll. He touched her gently, then turned away.

Hekate caught at him, crying, "Wait! Wait! You can't leave me without a word, without trying to plan to meet again. We have been friends. I care for you. You can't simply turn away from me."

"I must," he muttered. "I can't bear it. I can't bear parting from you, knowing that I will again be all alone . . . all alone . . . all alone . . ."

"And I will be alone too," she cried, "an old woman alone in the wilderness. Have you no affection for me at all? Don't you care what will happen to me? I need you Kabeiros."

He turned on her a look of bitter reproach. "You could stay in the caves and be safe. We could be together. Some time the creature that watches for you will grow weary or be summoned back to where it belongs. Your father will give you up. Then you could go out. I can't, but you could go out to gather in the forest even to visit the Nymphae and the boy Dionysos you have spoken of to me."

Hekate dropped her bedroll to the floor and sat down on it, pulling Kabeiros down beside her. "Now it's my turn to say 'I cannot,' " she sighed. "I'm not bound to the caves but to an unwise oath. When I was trapped between the guhrt outside and your spell of fear and despair inside, I flew into a terrible rage and swore that I would render my father, who had placed me in that position, powerless. I have no idea how to fulfill that oath. If he weren't my father, I could simply kill him . . . but to shed kin blood would bring on me a worse fate. . . ."

Kabeiros shuddered. "No, you can't kill him. The 'Kindly Ones,' unlike demons, do not fear the caves of the dead. What are you going to do?"

"Drain his power somehow. He has a way to suck power from my mother, but that involves his coupling with her."

"She allows it?" Kabeiros asked, mouth twisted with revulsion. "I know lust, but when she knows–"

"There is no lust involved–at least not on my mother's part, I assure you. She hates him–" Hekate drew a shuddering breath "–with whatever of herself is left within her, she hates him. But she is bespelled to obey . . . just such a spell as the guhrt carries to set upon me. For all I know she is even bespelled to enjoy their coupling."

"That–that's disgusting." Kabeiros swallowed. "If only the 'Kindly Ones' were more reasonable. Surely Perses deserves killing."

"Yes, but not by one of his blood. Asterie could do it, if we could free her from her compulsions, but I don't even know how to reach her."

Kabeiros frowned. "But what if you don't fulfill the oath? You can stay here and never see or hear from your father again."

Now it was Hekate's turn to sigh. "You can't ignore a binding. It grows tighter and heavier until your body fails and your spirit is broken." She took his hand in hers. "That's why I know I must break your binding, why I don't beg you simply to leave the caves. I would stay if I could. You are the only friend I have ever had, Kabeiros . . . and I'm afraid to go alone, Mother knows where . . . I'm afraid." Her voice died to a whisper.

He didn't answer, but tears streaked his face.

"How are you bound?" Hekate pleaded. "I beg you to tell me. I will find a way to break the binding, I swear it."

"You won't want to know me if I tell you."

"Kabeiros, nothing you tell me or show me can change what has grown between us. I swear that if you must drink babies' blood if you leave the caves, I'll find some way to supply you. I will *not* turn from you. I will protect you no matter how horrible your secret."

"Will you?"

He laughed wildly, jumped up, and rushed out of the cave into the pale pinky-blue light of first dawn. And the man Kabeiros was gone! A huge black dog staggered a few steps, shaking himself free of Kabeiros' tunic, then threw up its head and howled pathetically.

CHAPTER 6

Hekate had leapt to her feet moments after Kabeiros and rushed after him to the cave mouth, fearing that he was about to throw himself off a cliff or do something equally fatal. When she saw the dog, she stopped short, her mouth open. In the next instant she had cried out faintly in horror and pity. Snuffling for her scent, the dog had turned toward her. Its eyes were blank and white. It was blind!

"Kabeiros! Kabeiros!" she cried, snatching up the discarded tunic and bending to throw her arms around the dog's neck. "Come, come with me," she urged, drawing him back into the cave that, blind as he was, she thought he could not find.

Inside, he became a man almost instantly, with that same sensous shudder she felt herself when she shifted form. She pushed the tunic into his hands, and began to laugh, hugging him tightly as soon as he had pulled on his garment.

"I suppose it's better to be laughed at than cast aside with loathing," he said.

"No, no," Hekate gasped. "The reason I'm

laughing, dear, dearling, perfect Kabeiros is . . . Look!" And she shifted form into the woman.

He stared at her, open-mouthed, then with some effort, swallowed and said, "How beautiful you are! Which form is the illusion?"

"Neither. . . . None." She became the girl as she spoke. "I can do others too, a deer, a leopard. But those take thought and effort; they aren't natural to me. Now you can laugh, too. You've been trying to hide your shame at being a shape-shifter from me, and I've been enduring the greatest misery of aching bones and tired flesh to keep my shameful secret from you. Isn't it laughable?"

"I suppose so," he agreed, disengaging himself from her embrace, but he wasn't laughing. "I suppose we were foolish not to confess to each other, but unfortunately knowing changes nothing. You can change any time from one form to another. I'm bound to the form of the blind hound everywhere except the caves of the dead."

"You're fixed in the form of the hound outside the caves? But . . . but that's impossible if you are truly a shape-shifter. Changing form is as natural to us as breathing. How could this have happened to you?"

"A long story."

"I have time and more than time for the longest story in the world. I'll make us some tea and we can break our fast while you tell me. Is there water out there?"

"I don't know." Kabeiros smiled sadly. "I've never been out. But the dog can find water. He has a very good nose."

"But blind . . . You won't be able to get back to the cave."

"I'll find the cave. I can smell that, too. But I'm afraid I have no way to carry water if I find it."

"Hmmm." Hekate made a thoughtful noise. "Yes you could. You could carry the pannikin by the handle and dip it in the stream and carry it back in your mouth."

"So I could," Kabeiros agreed rather dryly. "And carry a pack across my back, too. I'm a *big* dog. What a shame that I'm also blind and would trip in a hole or over a stick. Or that I couldn't tell whether the water I dipped up was clear or muddy." He frowned at her. "You don't seem to be taking this very seriously."

"Of course not," Hekate exclaimed, throwing her arms around him again and hugging him. "Why should I? All I care about is that you can come with me. I don't mind that you'll be a dog, and we can search for a way to disrupt the spell that's interfering with your ability to change."

Kabeiros shook his head. "I can't come. Hekate . . . your name is Hekate isn't it?" When she nodded, he continued. "I–I can't tell you how sorry I am. I want to go. I want to go with all my heart. If it were only that I knew being a dog for a long time would kill me, I wouldn't care. I would go anyway. I would do anything to be free of these caves, but after a few weeks, all you would have would be a big, blind dog. There would be no Kabeiros."

"What?" Hekate relaxed her grip on him so she could step back to study his face. "The maiden, the woman, and the crone all have Hekate's mind. That doesn't change with the changing."

"But a dog's mind is small and it's filled with many things that a man doesn't notice–scents, urges . . . Little by little, day by day, the things a man thinks about become overlaid by the stronger, more urgent desires of the dog. I know. It happened to me. I was . . . truly a dog, all dog, when I wandered into the cave because it was raining very hard and even a dog has sense enough to seek shelter from such a storm. The binding spell was disrupted and I became a man again."

"Mother help us." Hekate bit her lip. "This isn't as simple as I thought it would be, but I will *not* lose you nor go without you, Kabeiros." She bent down to undo the pack of supplies and took from it a pan with a handle and a leather bottle. "Come," she said, "let's find that water. We must discover a way around this problem, but there's no sense in being hungry and thirsty while we think."

The water, a small clear stream in a stony bed, was not far and Kabeiros did find it without difficulty. Generally his blindness was not much of a problem–dogs seeing more with their noses than with their eyes–but he did blunder into a bush and trip over a fallen log that a sighted animal would have easily avoided. Hekate shook her head and began to run over spells in her mind.

As soon as they had returned to the cave, she asked whether Kabeiros could change to the dog in the cave. He looked surprised and anxious and admitted he didn't know. He had never tried, having conceived a horror of the dog form when he became a man again.

"To know you've been an animal–only an animal. To have lost all sense, all memory of humanity . . ." He shook his head. "And there was no purpose to being a dog in the caves. Once, it was a thrill to run in that form, to experience so many new sensations, but I never ran as a dog for more than a few hours and never lost myself."

"But you must be the dog for me to try out the spells, and if the easy one doesn't work, you must be a man to build and invoke the spells."

He was silent, staring at her. Then he asked softly,

"What if I cannot change back to the man?"

"I won't let you be a dog forever," Hekate said, taking his hands and holding them hard. "I swear it! I swear that my first purpose, even before finding a way to diminish Perses to nothing, will be to break the binding that fixes you in the form of a dog."

"THRICE BOUND!"

The words echoed through Hekate's mind. Kabeiros started and cried softly, "No, don't take another burden," but Hekate looked all around and smiled.

"Thrice bound!" she agreed. "This last I take gladly, willingly, even joyfully."

And the dog was before her, his great forepaws still in her hands, his fear showing in his wrinkled lips and flattened ears. She released his paws and he stood there, pushing his head against one hand in his need for comfort. She stroked the smooth fur while he lifted his head, his blind eyes staring just a little past her.

"Do you understand me, Kabeiros?"

The dog nodded. Hekate breathed out a sigh of relief, placed her other hand on his head also, and said, "*Thialuo tuphlox tha ommata.*" The dog's eyes remained white. Hekate made a small irritated sound. "You are still blind?"

The dog nodded again.

Hekate sighed. "That sorcerer was *very* angry. I'm afraid he wound them all together, the binding to the hound form and the blindness." She sighed again and said calmly, although icy chills were running up and down her spine. "We will think better when we're fed and rested. Be a man again, Kabeiros."

The man appeared, uttered a small gasp of relief, and sank down to the floor as if his knees wouldn't hold him upright. He began to laugh weakly when he saw that Hekate's legs had also given way. They sat together on the floor of the cave breathing heavily as fear released them.

"We were neither of us very sure, were we?" he asked.

"Of course not." Hekate's shoulders slumped and she allowed her head to fall forward for a moment before she straightened. "How can one be sure with a spell like that? But you had to believe I was sure so you wouldn't lose confidence. Do you know who did this to you, Kabeiros? I'm all ready to add a fourth binding so that I can wring his neck with my bare hands or maybe turn him into a toad."

"Three is quite enough," Kabeiros said. "I can fight my own battles." He gritted his teeth, then shrugged. "If I had known who it was, the black dog would have torn out his throat. When it happened, I only thought to run so he couldn't call any witnesses to my change of shape. By the time I realized that I couldn't change back to a man, he was long gone. I tried to track him by scent, but it happened in an inn yard and there were so many scents. I wasn't sure which was his."

Hekate smiled grimly. "I imagine if you ever come across it again, you'll recognize it. But I urge restraint. Don't tear out his throat. Maim him, mangle him, and I will bespell him never to heal! He'll regret his cruelty." She snorted lightly. "He reminds me of Perses."

"I doubt I'll find him. It was very long ago. Sorcerers are long-lived, but . . . Well, I'm still alive."

"And still young."

He smiled at her. "In a way I am, since no matter how many years have passed, I never truly lived between the time I was bespelled and now. But I won't bother seeking the devil. I never knew him at all and only saw him twice in my life."

"You only saw him twice in your life!" Hekate echoed. "How did you manage to infuriate him so much?"

"I have no idea, but I can tell you what happened and even what the man looked like—*that* is stamped firmly into my brain."

"Food first," Hekate said firmly.

Kabeiros gathered a pile of stones that he could heat while Hekate filled the pan with water from the bottle and went through the supplies. While the tea brewed he told her that he had been running as a dog when he had smelled magic and out of curiosity trotted over to see who had such a strong Talent. He had found an old man—it was from him that the powerful smell of magic oozed—and a young one, who was surely Talented but not so strongly. They were sitting in an inn yard and talking earnestly.

Since he didn't recognize either man and those with magical abilities always interested him, Kabeiros decided to introduce himself. He had gone behind the privy and changed to a man. He had then entered the inn through the back door, bought a tankard of beer and gone out into the yard, but the men were gone. He returned to the inn and asked the tapster what had become of them and had learned they had gone into a private chamber.

"That was disappointing. I was ready to introduce myself to men sitting in an inn yard, but not to intrude on sorcerers who had made it clear that their business was private. I was a bold fool in those days." Kabeiros swirled the herb tea in his cup until he managed to swallow a bite of flatbread smeared with honey, then he sipped to help the bread and honey down. "But not bold enough for that. I finished my beer, and since they had not come out, left the inn."

"But you went back."

Kabeiros looked a trifle shamefaced. "I went to find some friends to ask if they knew of new sorcerers in the city, but before I found anyone I became aware of strong and terrible magical energies. I ran back to the inn."

Hekate shook her head. "Young and foolish, yes. Brave, too. I think I would have run the other way."

"Brave? I don't know. I didn't have time to think, and anyway, I don't think I could have resisted." Kabeiros frowned. "There was a drawing in of magical power . . . a–a swallowing. It stopped before I was pulled into the inn and sucked dry myself."

"And you didn't run then?"

Kabeiros grimaced. "Neither would you have done. I was so curious . . . The remnants of the spell drew me to the window of the place where whatever happened happened, and I looked in. There must have been a duel. To my surprise, the old sorcerer lay across the table. I think he was dead. The young one was just releasing his grip on the old one's hands. He turned his head and saw me at the window. His face was terrible. He said, 'The curious dog. Well, you will never see what you should not again, and you will tell no one.' And I was the dog--and blind."

"He had recognized you?"

"Perhaps from my aura. For those who can see such things, it is strong for shape-shifters. I'm not sure. All I knew was that I was in an inn yard and I hadn't noticed whether others were there too. If so, they had seen a young man approach the window and now a dog stood beneath it. It would be enough, I was sure, to bring me bound as a sacrifice to the caves of the dead. I ran."

Hekate munched a date in silence then took a last bite of her bread and honey and washed it down with tea. She poured herself another cup and while waiting for it to cool enough to drink, asked, "What did the young sorcerer look like?"

"He was tall and broad-shouldered, handsome in a hawk-nosed, full-lipped way. To me he looked more like those who come from Ur or Urik, with a mixture of the black Egyptian in the blood. What surprised me most was that the magical smell was that of the old man. I must have been mistaken when I first thought the young one was the weaker. Somehow he had stolen the old man's magic."

"Or had the old man stolen the young one's body?" Hekate muttered. "I have heard of such things among the priests of Egypt, those favored with the ability living on and on . . ."

"I never thought of that," Kabeiros admitted. "That might have been the drawing I had felt. But how had he magic enough left to bespell me so deeply if he had expended the power it would take to pull a man's soul out of his body and thrust himself in?"

At first Hekate made no reply, mutely offering the dates to Kabeiros and, when he shook his head, folding them into a packet. Still silent, she gestured at the bread and honey to restore the spell of stasis, then packed all away. When she was done, she looked at Kabeiros and sighed.

"I don't think he did bespell you. That's why I couldn't find a spell when I looked. I think he tried to kill you by sucking out your life, but you were something he had never touched before, Gifted rather than Talented, and all he managed to do was to somehow tangle the threads of your Gift with his magic." She sighed again. "It will be no mean feat to unwind that drawing spell from your Gift. I admit I don't know how to do it . . . but the world is wide. There are great sorcerers, great mages. We'll seek them out."

"The greatest mages I know of live in the enchanted city of Olympus, far to the west."

"Olympus," Hekate repeated. "Olympus. Why do I know that name? Good Mother! That's the place my father hates and fears. Years upon years ago my mother told me that his enemies lived there."

Their glances met and held, then Kabeiros nodded. "We have a goal," he said, "but I must warn you that I fled the west because they were even less accepting of the Gifted than those here in Ka'anan. It is not only the shape-shifters they sacrifice to the king of the dead."

"But you said that there were great mages in Olympus."

"Those of the west call them 'gods.' Mostly they've forgotten the Mother and some wage war on those who still worship Her. My village was destroyed." His lips twisted. "Not that I was any favorite there either. Fortunately it happened after I had been driven out for being the black dog. I had actually started going north and east to look for Olympus, but I could never find it."

"Are you sure it exists?" Hekate asked.

"Yes. That's how I know the 'gods' are great mages. I came across two of them in one of their temples. I smelled magic–" he smiled. "As the black dog, I smell all magic; as the man I see some things, like the blood of the earth in its veins and auras, but not most magic."

"You smelled magic, so you went to see." Hekate shook her head and sighed. "As the black dog, you manage to get into more trouble than ten mischievous children. When we travel together I will have to leash you! How come you escaped with your skin whole?"

"They weren't fierce or evil. The girl was so . . . so . . . I can't even tell you what she was like. I loved her. No one could help loving her. And the man . . . Holy Mother, he aroused lust in *me*, and I am no man lover; my taste was always for women." He sighed. "I don't know how long ago that was, but I'll never forget them."

"But have they forgotten you? Did they notice you?"

"Oh, yes. They were gathering up the offerings on the altar and when I first saw them I thought they were thieves and was about to bark, but the girl turned and put her finger to her lips, and the man smiled at me and mouthed 'Hush, brother'–and they both disappeared with the offerings."

"Disappeared?"

"Vanished. Without a sound. They transported themselves elsewhere."

"Transported *themselves*?" Hekate scowled. "I feel like an echo valley. All I do is repeat what you say, but I can hardly believe my ears and need to hear the words again. I can transport things with a spell–if they aren't too heavy–but how can one transport oneself?"

"I have no idea, but it was a spell. I could smell the magic, but the magic was . . . was inside themselves, not pulling them away from outside. And they weren't thieves. They were the 'gods' that were worshipped in that temple. I saw them drawn in the frescoes and carved into statues. Of course, the images couldn't really reproduce the beauty of the originals, but they were close enough to prove that the artist had seen the girl and the man."

"Then why do you say they are mages and not

gods? The Mother is over all, but there are other gods."

"Like Kabeiros?" Kabeiros laughed. "What true god comes to take away the sacrifices? Does a god need to eat food like you and I? Does the Mother? Even the king of the dead isn't a god. Doesn't he send his people to gather up the grain and dried meat and fruit? So he eats too."

"But the caves? They can undo the damage that sorcerer did to your Gift."

"The caves are something else. I don't think what they do is owing to the king of the dead. I didn't smell any magic . . . except yours . . . when I changed to the black dog."

Hekate nodded slowly, thoughtfully. "You may be right after all. As soon as your spell of terror and despair was gone, I felt comfortable here. Warm inside. Safe. To me that's a sign of the Mother. There's never any feeling of 'magic' with her, only power . . . endless power. But the feeling was different from that of the secret shrine in the forest so I assumed it was owing to a kindly king of the dead. Still, the Mother has many forms."

"If only the Mother can help me in the aspect that is manifested in these caves–"

"We won't know, will we, until we look for another answer," she interrupted, then sighed impatiently. "Well, if those who live in Olympus are mages and not gods, so much the better for us; perhaps one has a Gift that will solve your problem and mages are easier to bargain with than gods. But if we can't find the place–"

"I think I could find it as the dog. I was ages younger when I first sought Olympus and didn't think of changing to the dog and smelling for magic. Then the hound form was for play, to enjoy. Also I know better where to look, now. After I had come here to Ka'anan, I learned that Olympus is in a cup among the mountains between Hestiaeotis or Perrhoebia and Pieria. But by then I was enjoying my life here and I had no special reason to go back."

"But now you do, and it's certainly worth trying to find such powerful mages. It's as good a place to go as any other, and if we can't find it or if no one there can help you, we can always come back here."

Kabeiros looked away, ashamed. "Except that it's a very long way, and by the time we get to the lands of the west, I won't have enough mind left to remember what I'm seeking."

"Yes, you will," Hekate said. "The reason you lost yourself to the dog was that you lost contact with humans. Few knew you were a dog and even those feared to show they knew you were also a man and didn't try to speak to you or make you think. If we talked together constantly—well, as much as we spoke in the caves, for example—neither of us would welcome constant chatter—you would never forget your humanity and the dog would never dominate the man."

"You would extend my time, I'm sure, but without the power to reply to you and to present my own thoughts, I'm afraid my interest in what you said to me would fade."

"But you *would* be able to reply! I meant we would speak together mind-to-mind."

"I know that Gift exists," Kabeiros said, sighing, "but I don't have it."

"Neither did I," Hekate replied with a grimace, "but that is not always a natural Gift. It seems it is also a skill that anyone's mind—perhaps only those who can use power, but you can do that—can be taught. My father forced it on me when I was a child the better to control me. It wasn't a pleasant experience. He might as well have raped my body."

Kabeiros stared at her, appalled. "Have you known what I was thinking all the time we've been together?"

"Of course not! Holy Mother, always knowing what everyone else was thinking would drive a person mad." She stopped speaking abruptly and her glance went past Kabeiros, her brow suddenly creased with thought. "Hmmm," she muttered, "I wonder if those who hear voices and are said to be mad have some kind of uncontrolled Gift . . ." She shook her head impatiently and waved away the idea with a quick gesture. "I wish I wasn't so easily distracted by this and that idea."

"I am not so easily distracted," Kabeiros said, his voice harsh. "You did know what I was thinking."

"Sometimes." Hekate raised her brows. "But that was from how you looked or held your body, not from listening to your thoughts. Nor will I be able to know what you wish to keep private after I show you how to hear me and send thoughts to me." She laughed bitterly. "Do you think my father would have taken any chance that I would learn what was in his mind? This is a skill, just like talking. You must think at me what you wish to say—and only I will 'hear' you, no one else."

"Truly? It will be like talking to you? That's all?"

"Truly, but I'll tell you that giving you this skill will be very unpleasant, like having hot needles stuck through your skull—at least, that was how it affected me. I think I screamed for a week straight." She frowned. "Should I put a sleep spell on you?"

"Will the teaching—or whatever it is you do—work through a sleep spell?"

"Why not?"

"Your father didn't use one."

Hekate laughed again, a single bark of sound without mirth. "My father enjoys others' screaming. He may even have some way of gathering power from another's pain."

Kabeiros wrinkled his nose, lifting his upper lip; if he had been a dog, his tearing fangs would have been exposed. "I am not of Perses' blood," he growled. "The 'Kindly Ones' would not trouble me if I killed him."

"He is not so easy to kill," Hekate said with a shudder. "Worse than the tangling of your Gift might befall you if you tried to attack him."

"What worse? He could kill me. That's all."

"He could enslave you, turn you against me." She shuddered again and then her mouth thinned until only the sharp tips of her teeth showed; her eyes shone with a blue glitter. "And I'm not sure I want him dead so easily as a torn-out throat," she added in so sweet a voice that Kabeiros recoiled. "That would be too easy for him." Her eyes looked like polished metal, nor was their expression any softer. "He should live, utterly without power, utterly helpless under the control of one who *really* hates him, and knowing he will die a drooling nothing. No, I do not want him so easily or quickly dead."

Kabeiros took a deep breath. "You know how to hate, Hekate."

"I have learned, over long and painful years." She stood quiet a moment, breathing deeply, then shivered. "No, I am not yet ready to try my strength against Perses, and I won't risk you, my only friend, before I'm sure we have a good chance at winning. Let my power grow. Let me learn from other mages. When I'm ready, we will return."

PART TWO:

THE SEEKING

CHAPTER 7

Hekate discovered over the next ten-day that she had been a bit overconfident in her estimate of how easy it would be to give Kabeiros vision and mind speech. The problem for the vision spell was that, although Kabeiros had plenty of power, he couldn't use it while he was the hound. Hekate didn't know whether there was some lack in the mind of the dog or whether it was simply that a dog has no way of pronouncing spells and no way of gesturing. Perhaps either would have been sufficient–the spell spoken silently in the mind with the gesture to invoke it or the words spoken aloud with or without gestures–but the dog could manage neither. Once the spell was invoked, it could feed off Kabeiros' power and would not fade, but getting it invoked was tricky.

Nonetheless, after a few false starts on the afternoon of the first day, the spell that was to provide vision went very well. The initial failures made Hekate understand that Kabeiros must invoke the spell just as he changed form. The next morning, she drew the lines of power on a flat rock with the dregs of their tea just after they broke their fast.

Kabeiros watched, nodding as the designs became fixed in his mind and then repeating the words without the mental images so he would not invoke the spell. Then they tested how close to the edge of the cave he could come without changing. Finally he stood with one foot raised to take the final step, invoked the spell, and walked forward into the sunlight outside the cave.

The hound Kabeiros took two steps, swayed dizzily, and fell over. Hekate rushed to his side. The white eyes were closed and the dog was panting hard.

"Come. Come," she begged, trying to pull him to his feet without success—the hound weighed as much as the man Kabeiros. "Keep your eyes closed. I will take you to the cave so you can tell me what is wrong."

He shook his head for no and after another few moments climbed to a sitting position in which he carefully opened his eyes. She saw him swallow convulsively and then begin to drool—a sure sign of nausea.

"Is the spell hurting you?" she asked. "Come back with me to the cave. You can dismiss the spell and I will make a new one."

He closed his eyes. Shook his head again. Climbed unsteadily to his feet and turned toward the cave. He lost his balance as he turned and fell, but recovered quickly and this time began to walk back and forth along the length of the cave mouth. Hekate stood by, watching him as the signs of nausea and unsteadiness slowly diminished. Then he walked into the small area of open land by the cave mouth and down to the stream. When he lowered his head to drink, he almost fell into the water.

Hekate hauled him back, but he went forward again, bent, and lapped at the water. Finally he turned toward her, barked twice, and ran off into the wood.

"Wait," she called, but her voice was cracked with anxiety and he was a huge dog, well away, and could not hear her.

She stood by the stream for some time, wringing her hands and trying to think of a way to call him back, but she had no idea where he had gone and the aura by which she knew Kabeiros the man was gone. By midday she realized that standing or pacing by the stream or sitting on damp moss or wet rocks would not help in getting him back. She remembered he had told her he could smell the caves and the hound had gone there once for shelter. Perhaps he would return. Dusk had fallen and Hekate had nearly given up hope by the time he came loping out of the wood with two dead rabbits hanging from his jaws. These he dropped at Hekate's feet, looking up and wagging his tail.

"Oh dear Mother," she breathed, "have you turned all dog again, so soon?"

At that the hound's mouth opened and his tongue lolled out, lips drawing back. Even through her anxiety, Hekate could see that he was laughing.

She rolled her eyes. "Don't tell me worse has befallen me and you have reverted to playing tricks and japes!"

The hound laughed harder, but he also bent his head to seize the rabbits again and ran back into the cave. "I am very tired of dried meat," Kabeiros the man said, grinning at her when she followed him in. "So I thought I would just get us some fresh rabbit."

"I'd like to *murder* you!" Hekate exclaimed. "I thought you'd gone mad or totally lost yourself and run off for good. I was frightened to death! What went wrong with the spell?"

Kabeiros looked surprised. "But I sent my thoughts to you to say what I was about to do, and you didn't object."

"Kabeiros!" Hekate exclaimed, quite exasperated. "We haven't got to the mind speech part yet. That isn't a simple spell—I told you that. All I heard was two barks." She breathed deeply, suspecting from the gleam in Kabeiros' golden eyes that the trickster *was* back, that some effect of the change woke a dangerously mischievous streak in the dog and that traveling with him might be a livelier experience than she expected.

"Anyhow," she continued, "that wasn't what I meant. Why did you fall over and feel sick after the vision spell took hold?"

Kabeiros laughed aloud. "Because you gave me the vision of a man, and dogs see differently. Dogs don't see much color and their depth perception is different from a man's. Dogs don't see well at all—that is, most don't. Maybe the sight hounds see better, but I think they mostly are able to catch movement. I'm not sure, and anyhow my form is more fighting mastiff than sight hound. I never saw any detail and now I see more perfectly than I do as a man. Well, the dog's mind couldn't cope at first." He smiled at her. "But I *am* a man, not a dog—whatever I look like—so I adjusted."

"Maybe we should have worked on the mind speech first, so you could have told me what was going on," Hekate said, sitting down rather limply.

"If you want to do the next spell now," Kabeiros said, "just let me skin and cut up these rabbits first so you can cook a meal for us."

"The next step can wait until tomorrow," Hekate replied. "It isn't a spell. I'll have to invade your mind, and it will hurt." She hesitated, then frowned. "If I must work on the dog directly, will the dog attack me?"

Kabeiros looked troubled. "I want to say 'no.' But the hound's reactions are so much faster than a man's that the body could act before my mind could stop it."

"Then let's hope what the man learns the dog will know also."

While they talked about what sort of sleep spell to use, Kabeiros disjointed the rabbits and Hekate went through her pouches to find suitable spices. Then they went out to gather firewood; the rabbit could have been roasted over hot stones, but Hekate had a yen for meat that had felt the touch of flames.

It gave Kabeiros another chance to adjust to his strange vision and to renew his acquaintance with the dog's body. He confessed to Hekate, when they were back in the cave and the rabbit parts impaled on spits and cooking over the fire, that he had forgotten some of the things he could do as a dog.

"Some instincts are so strong that you follow them without planning–which was how I caught the first rabbit. It leapt away almost under my feet, and I seized it and broke its neck before I really knew what I was doing. The second I had to hunt for, using the scent of the first as a guide. This last time we were out, I began to remember how to tell an old trail from a new one and how to set my feet and sense brush about me so that I can move in silence."

"I begin to see how a man could forget he was a man," Hekate said thoughtfully. "I've never remained in an animal form long enough to learn about the body or of what it is capable. I only wanted to discover if I could choose such a form. There are intriguing puzzles an animal must solve. One could become so interested in honing the skills of the form that the doings of mankind became dull."

She leaned forward and prodded one cooking haunch with a sharp stick, but it sank in only a little way and the fluid that oozed out was too bloody. Kabeiros turned the spit a quarter turn. They fell companionably silent and may have dozed. Eventually the meat was cooked and they ate, drinking fresh water from the stream. They had several skins of wine, but by mutual consent they left those for the journey ahead, at least that night, because they thought they would be on their way in a day or two.

In the end, they drank the wine before they started. Both needed the support it offered because opening the mind of Kabeiros the dog to mind speech went very slowly, very painfully. At first Hekate thought it would be as easy as the vision spell. She induced sleep in Kabeiros and did to his mind what her father had done to hers. Kabeiros had a horrible headache when he woke, but a tisane of willow bark and other herbs helped, and by afternoon she and Kabeiros were having short conversations.

Since using the skill renewed the pain, they left it there for that day and busied themselves with preparing for the journey. Kabeiros went hunting and the game he brought back was mostly cut into strips for drying, the gut carefully cleaned and conditioned for use in binding and tieing. The dog was large enough to carry a pack, but it would need to be secured to his body. Later if Hekate could earn some metal trading pieces, they might be able to get a small cart that the dog could pull.

They went to bed in a very cheerful humor. Kabeiros' headache was gone by the time they sought their bedrolls, and the dog had had no trace of the man's headache right from the beginning.

That should have warned them, but neither thought much of it. The dog had no headache, and it also had no mind speech. Worse yet, no sleep spell that Hekate tried had any effect on the dog.

Opening the mind of the animal was horrible. Not that the animal tried to attack her nor even tried to run away; instead it whined and cringed and begged, crawling to her feet and licking them while whimpering with pain. Hekate broke down in tears and stopped what she was doing, patting and hugging the hound, whispering reassurance to it.

However, when it could stand and return to the cave, Kabeiros the man was utterly exasperated. He dried Hekate's tears and silenced her apologies with a gesture.

"I *know* you don't mean to hurt me. I *know* what you are trying to do and that it is necessary. I am quite ready to bear the pain, but the body of the dog doesn't respond to what I know. The body of the dog only 'knows' that you are its master and you are hurting it. To the dog that can only be a punishment so it tries to show it is sorry for what it has done."

"But what am I to do?" Hekate wailed. "I *like* dogs, and your hound form is a particularly attractive one. I can't bear it when the poor creature begs not to be hurt. And if I continue to hurt it, won't it become shy of me and be unwilling to travel with me or protect me?"

"I don't know," Kabeiros sighed. "Some of those reactions are so deep within the animal that I cannot control them. Let's try again and I'll try to make the man dominate the dog enough to suppress its reaction to pain."

More effort gained some success, but not much. Hekate pried here, bored there. She tried to hurry when the dog grew restless, but that made it worse.

In the end they found a compromise by making the sessions short, achieving one small goal at a time, and rewarding the hound lavishly with praise and tidbits of food and the kind of play a dog enjoys.

Hekate shook her head at herself one evening when she and Kabeiros were sitting on their bedrolls near a small fire—lit for comfort not for warmth; Kabeiros could generate warmth by drawing enough earth energy through the rock to heat it slightly—sipping some of their wine.

"I have no idea why I feel the need to hurry," she said. "We are just at the beginning of summer. We have plenty of time to get through the mountains before the cold weather. We could easily take another ten-day or a month even before there is a *need* for us to go."

Kabeiros shrugged. "I know the source of my impatience. I want to be free of this place and the sooner the better. I think you can push the dog harder now. It has learned, I think, that the pain is for some purpose other than punishment for wrongdoing and that it will be rewarded for patience."

He had eaten well that day, but not the cooked food Hekate had prepared for herself. He had gone hunting as the dog—a reward to that body for bearing so much discomfort and a bribe to reduce the faint unwillingness he had felt that morning when he slipped into the dog form. He was surprised—and a little disgusted when he became a man again—at the intense pleasure he had felt when he tore out the throat of a small deer he had found and the hot blood flowed into his mouth; he had lapped it eagerly. It was delicious, and the red, bleeding meat of the abdomen had a savour even Hekate's skillful spicing of cooked meet could not match. And the entrails . . .

Now a man, his gorge rose slightly as he recalled how he had torn and gobbled the intestines and their contents, the liver and heart. But he felt the need, a desperate need, and the flavor was exquisite. Moreover he felt replete, sated, as he had not felt no matter how much he ate of good wholesome food in the caves. He could only guess that he had been missing something in the food that the hound needed and the hound, even if not visible, was a part of the man Kabeiros. Now he wanted only to sleep.

That caused no questions. Hekate was as tired as he. They finished their wine, washed the cups, and curled up in the bedrolls they had stretched out where each could see the low, yellow flames of the fire flickering as they died.

On the tenth day, success was complete. The hound sat patiently through a much longer session than usual and at the end the white eyes sought hers and the dog said, *I am the hound, Kabeiros, but with me is the man. Do you wish to speak to him?*

"Yes, I do," Hekate answered aloud, then silently, *Kabeiros, how is it between you and the dog? Will he be able to control you, or you him?"*

I think we will work out a compromise. I will be happy to let him rule when you throw a stick for us or in the hunt. There was a hesitation and then the soundless words continued. *I hope Kabeiros the man does not yield completely to the joys of the hunt. I seem to remember from long, long ago that it was the hunt and the taste of flowing blood and hot red meat that seduced me into—* And then he showed that the man was all there by picking up her subtle change of expression and asking sharply, *What is wrong, Hekate? Do the desires and joys of the hound disgust you?*

"No, not that," she replied aloud, smiling, but not for long. "I have had dogs."

The answer was perfectly true, but Kaberios proved that the man could remember what he had said and thought as the hound. When they were back in the cave setting up a cradle of stones for Kabeiros to heat so they could warm the remains of yesterday's stew, he said, "When I asked what was wrong you answered what I said about the hound, but you didn't really answer my question. Something is making you uneasy."

"I wish I knew what it was," she replied, adding a little water to the pan to thin the stew, stirring it, and then setting it on the stones. "I don't feel anything in here, but just for a moment when we were outside and I was talking to the dog, I felt . . . well, just what you said . . . uneasy, as if someone might be listening."

"The bindings?" Kabeiros asked. "Have you neglected them too long?"

"No, I think not. I know that feeling well because I kept forgetting poor Dionysos when he was a baby. Of course, he didn't care then. As long as he was fed and cleaned and hugged and held–and the Nymphae did that–he was content, but the binding didn't know that, and I felt it if I was away from him too long. No, the bindings won't trouble me unless I forget them, and Mother knows they are clear in my mind and heart. I don't know what it is . . . possibly my father still watching for me?"

"Could it be the guhrt?"

Kabeiros' nose and lips wrinkled; if he were the hound then, he would have been snarling. Hekate was so interested in the fact that the man showed many characteristics of the dog now that he was changing form often that what he had said did not make a deep impression and she answered almost absently.

"The flavor of the watching . . . Perhaps. But I've

never known a summoning to keep an otherplanar creature more than a ten-day. My father is very strong and fed it well—on human blood, too—but we were in the caves invisible to it for nearly two months."

"We could stay within longer." Kabeiros sighed and then shook himself. "I'm eager to go out into the world, but not eager enough to risk your safety. I can wait."

Nervously, because she had finally focused on what they were saying, Hekate shook her head. "I have the urge to be gone, to be elsewhere. If you think the dog is fluent in mind talk, I would like to go as soon as possible . . . even tomorrow."

"Tommorrow it is then," Kabeiros assented heartily, taking the bowl of warmed stew she handed him and beginning to spoon it into his mouth hastily. He swallowed so fast he almost choked in his eagerness. "We have little enough to take and I can hunt and you gather on the way." Then he laughed. "The only thing we have never talked about was how we are to go."

Hekate shrugged and laughed also. "On foot. How else?" And when Kabeiros, his mouth full, glared at her, she added more soberly, "Olympus is west—so that is the way we must go—but we must not pass near Ur-Kabos. There is too great a chance that my father will sense my aura if we are close."

"Then perhaps the safest path, the farthest from your father, is to go east across the mountains. It will be longer, but I have heard that there is a river to the east that comes from the north and we can follow that until you feel safe. In these lands a sure source of water is not to be despised."

Hekate nodded eagerly and hastily swallowed a mouthful. "I've heard of that river also. It's called the Orontes. And there will be villages and towns along the river where I can do some healing, which will provide us with bread and vegetables to go with the meat you bring in. I have some metal." Hekate set down her dish and got off the bedroll to rummage in her pack. She found the twist of cloth that held the bits of silver and wire she had taken from her sleeve soon after settling into the caves with Kabeiros and held it out for his inspection.

"Good enough," he said, pouring a little water into his empty bowl and wiping it clean. "We won't starve then even if I can't hunt or there is no healing to be done. But it's not nearly enough to take us to Olympus."

Hekate's brow furrowed. "Something is tickling my memory. Wait, let me think. Yes, it seems to me there is another place where magic, even the Gifted, are welcome. Once when my father did something that annoyed the ruler of Ur-Kabos, he said he would leave here and go to . . . to . . . Colchis!"

"Colchis," Kabeiros repeated. "I've heard of that place also. Someone . . . yes, a friend who was also Gifted with shape-shifting and could change into a bear . . . said he wished to go to Colchis. I never knew whether he did or not because soon after that the sorcerer damaged my Gift, but he said it was on the east coast of the Pontus Euxinus. He said the king there was a young man who was already a mighty sorcerer and welcomed any who could spellcast; in particular those who could build spells."

"I hope that king is not long dead . . . No, he couldn't be, or if he is, his heir must be of much the same mind because it can't be more than two or three years since Perses spoke of going there." She nodded. "Maybe it was only last year. I'm sure it was the quarrel with the ruler of Ur-Kabos that made my father decide to rule the king of Byblos so he need never again fear the use of force against him."

Kabeiros' eyes were alight. "Colchis—that will be a place utterly new to me and the lands between here and there also."

"Every place will be new to me." Hekate smiled at Kabeiros' eagerness, finished her meal and wiped out her bowl. "Still, the place sounds almost as promising as Olympus and it may be much nearer. If we can find an answer to the tangling of your Gift and I can learn what I need from the sorcerers there, we could come back to free my mother and end my father's power much sooner. And if we don't find our answers in Colchis, since it's on the coast, we could take a ship to reach Olympus."

Kabeiros was almost quivering with excitement and eagerness. He got off his bedroll to unfold it for sleeping. Hekate laughed silently, watching him unbind his sandals, pull off his tunic, turn twice around (much like a dog settling himself, she thought), and lie down. Still smiling, she followed his lead, thinking the sooner asleep, the sooner awake, and the sooner on their way.

Suddenly she was so eager to start that she would have urged Kabeiros to begin their journey right then, except that she knew they couldn't go far at night. Neither of them knew the ground and picking their way through the forest would be much quicker in daylight. Unless she used magic . . . She began to sit up, then remembered that bare hint of watching. To use magic would be like lighting a beacon fire for that watcher, if there was one.

Then she remembered that the pressing desire to leave the cave had come upon her only after she had been out of the cave. Well, that might be natural after being confined, never seeing the sun or the stars or feeling the wind, for so many ten-days . . . but it might not. If her father were still watching for her—he did, after all, know she was in the cave—it was by no means impossible that he would set into that watching an urge to leave the place of safety.

Hecate bit her lip. Her first instinct was to do the opposite of the compulsion, but it was equally likely that the feeling was genuine, particularly since the urgency to go didn't leave her when she was inside and she was sure the caves were Mother-protected. Besides, they must go. If they didn't, she couldn't loosen the bindings that held her and they would grow stronger and tighter the longer she resisted. Go, yes, but no magic. She would do no magic until she was sure she was well beyond her father's scrying.

She woke in the morning feeling the same urgency, although now the desire to leave was mixed with caution. Still, she was impatient about relieving herself, reluctant to take the time to wash even though she knew there might be few opportunities once they left the stream. Although they would be following a river, the water might be highly prized and guarded against use by casual strangers. Fortunately Kabeiros was as eager to leave as she and was content to wait to break his fast until they were on their way. He said he could eat strips of dried meat and she some dried fruit as they walked.

Hekate took the bedroll into which Kabeiros had tucked his cloak, the pan for cooking, and one change of garments for himself and Hekate. When he had changed to the dog, she laid that across his back and fastened it by loops of deer and rabbit gut to a harness he had contrived from the same materials. The harness was closed with a slipknot on his chest that the dog could reach with his teeth. One pull on the correct line and the whole thing, harness and pack, would tumble off leaving the hound free to fight or run.

When Kabeiros said he was comfortable and that

they would need to go some distance before he would know what adjustments he wanted made, she rolled her bedroll over the greatly diminished pack of supplies, tucked her cloak on top, and strapped the whole closed. Another pair of straps was fastened to the first and she slid her arms into the empty loops, grateful to the worshiper who had left the support in which he carried his offering to the caves of the dead.

Finally she slung her pouch, with her herbs for both curing and magic, over one shoulder, the last, half-emptied, wineskin over the other, picked up her staff, and looked down at the hound. He wagged his tail and lolled out his tongue; Hekate patted his head and ruffled the fur around his ears. Together they stepped out of the cave into the bright morning sunshine. With the dog slightly in the lead, they crossed the open land, crossed the stream, and headed for the forest.

Just before they entered the shade of the trees, Hekate turned suddenly and faced west, swinging her head from side to side and closing her eyes the better to "see" and to "listen." Kabeiros went a few steps back, almost to the bank of the stream, and sniffed the air. He came back a few moments later.

What did you sense? he asked. *I got no smell of magic, only a little whiff of something rotten . . . * The dog could not shrug, but there was a feeling as of a mixture of puzzlement and dismissal about the words.

I don't know that I sensed anything, just a . . . a flicker of unease. Then it was gone. One thing I thought of last night just before I fell asleep was that if there is a watcher, I mustn't do any magic.

I hope our talking this way will not betray you.

Oh, no. I know there are some who have the Gift to speak over great distances, but I never learned the paths to make that possible, if it is possible for those who are not so Gifted by nature. We can talk side by side and perhaps several rooms apart, say from the loft to the main room of a sleeping house, but I doubt you or I can reach farther than that.

And this close to Perses, it would not be safe to try. When we have reached the river, you can try to call me when I am hunting and see if I can hear.

Hekate laughed as they turned their backs on the small open area and the stream and set off under the trees. *If I can make you hear when you are hunting, I will have a far more powerful call than I ever believed.*

CHAPTER 8

Although Kabeiros and Hekate had been concerned about the possibility of encountering high mountains and difficult terrain, they discovered that the traverse of the caves from the west entrance to that on the east had brought them through the worst of the heights. Before them lay only rugged foothills. There were several steep climbs and more precipitous descents—those were more dangerous for the hound than for Hekate aided by her staff and once they spent half a day wandering the edge of such a drop because she would not allow Kabeiros to take a chance and jump.

"You'll break a leg," she protested.

The dog looked up at her. She remembered that her father had once told her dogs had no expressions and began to laugh. Anyone who wasn't blind could have read the irritation and impatience on the hound's face.

So what if I do break a leg? Even the mental voice was sharp. *I'm not a horse. You won't have to cut my throat. I can limp along on three legs until the leg heals.*

"Which will delay us a lot longer than finding a safe place to get down."

Since that was probably true, Kabeiros was reduced to uttering a snort, which made Hekate laugh and ignore him when he turned suddenly and trotted back the way they had come, sniffing. She continued her search for a way down and had found a marginally possible spot when the hound came trotting back.

"Do you think you could get down here?" she asked.

I'd better try. The back trail is worse. There's a waterfall there, and I can see that the ground is rising again ahead. If we take off the pack and drop it, I should be all right.

"Shall I climb down and try to catch you?"

The dog laughed soundlessly. *Do you know what I weigh? If I came down on you, you might suffer worse than a broken leg. Just throw the pack down and stay out of my way.*

At first it looked as if all were well. Having leapt and stumbled, the dog rose to his feet and looked back at Hekate, who was climbing down with relative ease. When she reached the floor of the descent, however, she saw that Kabeiros was holding a forepaw off the ground.

"Did you break it?" she asked anxiously.

No, it's only twisted. I can walk on it, but it hurts.

"Then we'd better camp. How far back is that waterfall you saw? It would be nice to camp near water."

The dog put his sore foot to the ground and took a step or two, but he whined before he put the foot down a third time and sat. The smooth black brow between the white eyes furrowed.

*There was a nice pool, but I'm not sure we should go back there. I smelled something . . . *

"Magic?"

No . . . well, maybe . . . no, no, not what I think of as magic. But like magic gone bad? Only magic can't go bad like meat kept too long, can it?

Hekate, who had knelt down to rearrange the cords on the dog's pack so she could carry it to their campsite, stood up abruptly, clutching her staff. Magic gone bad! That was what the foulness had been. Magic gone bad.

"The guhrt," Hekate breathed.

The dog snarled, then said, *It was not near, but still we are too far from the caves to try to go back. Can you outrun it? It doesn't want me, so you can leave me behind.*

She shook her head. "No chance. It covered in a few candlemarks what had taken me two days running–and part of that time was taken up by its going to the valley of the Nymphae. Perhaps they delayed it also. But otherplanar things don't like running water. If we could get to the waterfall before it arrives, there would be one place from which it couldn't attack me."

Go ahead, the dog said. *Leave the pack. I can drag it. You can't miss the place. Just follow the base of the cliff. I'll come as quick as I can.*

"The pack won't slow me," she said, thrusting the staff through the straps and snatching it up in her arms. "Don't come too close, Kabeiros. If my father hasn't fed it since he laid his commands on it, it will be very hungry."

Go, Kabeiros urged.

Actually, although she set off running, Hekate had no expectation of reaching the waterfall before the guhrt caught up with her. All she wanted to do was to put as much space between her and Kabeiros as she could, hoping the creature's attention would be fixed on her and it would leave Kabeiros alone. However, the guhrt was much slower than she remembered. She not only reached the waterfall but was able to open her pouch and pick out a handful of herbs to crush between her hands and sprinkle on the ground around her. What good they would do, she didn't know, but at least their scent battled against the increasing foulness that was beginning to drown her senses.

She had time, too, to tighten her wards, to seek in the cliff behind the waterfall for a vein of the life of the earth. She noticed that on the other side of the stream the cliff beetled outward and wondered whether that could be used in some way, but she found a vein of earthblood just then and concentrated on tapping into it. Unfortunately, she wasn't able to drink full of what she found, but her wards were high and strong when the mind-stench of magic gone bad nearly choked her. She had just time to sense not only the foulness of evil, of twisted wrongness, but of true decay when the guhrt was there, almost on top of the circle of herbs.

Hekate had been standing with her back to the stream that ran out of the small pool formed by the waterfall. Now she turned, leapt across the stream, and turned back to face the guhrt. The move put the pool and waterfall to her right and the bulging cliff face almost behind her but increased the distance between her and the guhrt and kept the half-moon of herbs and the stream itself between them. Her terror eased just a trifle when she saw that the guhrt did not step past or scatter the herbs.

It stood for a moment and stared at her. Fear and horror rose from it like a miasma of fog, but behind the strong shields she had erected, the emanation was nothing like what Hekate had felt when it was pursuing her the day she fled to the caves of the dead. The creature's hesitation gave her time really to see it and she was surprised. Dionysos had said it was the size of a large cat but naked and gray. Now it was closer to the size of the rat that it resembled—and it was more translucent than gray. Its skin hung in folds, mute evidence of how it had shrunk, and the enormous penis and testicles flapped emptily between its thighs almost down to the ground.

A blow struck Hekate's wards and a seeking tendril tried to force a way into her mind. The wards held; the tendril found no opening, and she sent a thread of fire back along it. The guhrt whined—a thin, high sound that pierced her ears—and another blow struck her wards. She reached to the vein of earth-blood, but something glutinous and putrid seized on the questing ribbon of power she had extended and began to run back along it to her. Without a moment's hesitation, she cut the ribbon loose, feeling the drain on her power that cost her but unwilling to take within herself anything tainted by the guhrt's foulness.

Had the creature swelled a trifle? Was it more solid? Hekate couldn't be sure, but she knew she dared not try again to tap the earth's blood. Quickly now another blow and still another battered her wards. She couldn't relax those shields even to open herself to seek the Mother's strength. That left her with no reserves, with nothing but whatever power she had within herself, and how long could that last?

"Come here! Come here to me at once!"

Hekate started. That was her father's voice. She almost reached out to sense if he was there, but saw the trap in time and tightened her wards all the more as thin slivers of force pried at her protection. Again she touched magical fire to the intrusions and they were withdrawn, the guhrt again whining.

"Obey me at once! You will regret it bitterly if you resist."

That time in the face of her fear Hekate laughed. It was most unlikely that she could regret anything more than *not* resisting, but she was beginning to suspect that the voice was simply another spell the guhrt carried. If her father could see or sense the confrontation, surely he would have said something more pertinent.

Suddenly the guhrt screamed, an amazing volume of sound for the size of the creature. Likely the scream was meant to distract a victim, to break that victim's concentration so the guhrt could shatter or invade its shields. But Hekate had learned the trick of distraction by bitter experience as a child. When startled, she instinctively tightened her innermost wards. Her instinct served her well. The guhrt struck at her mentally once more—and then it was gone!

She stared around, terrified that it could make itself invisible, but the crack and slither of falling stone made her look up. She was just in time to see the creature reach the top of the cliff. Her breath caught. It would not cross the water, but it could climb the cliff and come down those overhanging rocks on the other side where what little protection the herbs had provided was lacking.

She leapt the stream again, just in time because the guhrt had launched itself from the cliff and landed just where she had been standing. She turned to face it again, but only its voice remained, screeching in rage as it climbed the cliff once more. Hekate glanced up nervously, but on this side of the waterfall raw rock showed there had been a landslip not long ago and the earth sloped backward. The guhrt would have to jump far out as well as down, and it was unlikely that it could manage to land on her or be sure of not landing in the water.

Perhaps *she* should be in the water. Why had she not thought of that? But she had no time to find a place to enter the pool; the guhrt was crouching just on the other side of the ring of herbs. It snuffled and snorted, clearly repelled by the scent but desperate enough now to ignore the discomfort. The creature looked utterly ridiculous, but Hekate did not laugh. Indeed, she nearly choked on terror when she realized she could neither move nor attack.

She knew too well that to fear was to invite defeat and she grappled with her panic, gathering her diminishing strength to defend herself against the near-paralysis that afflicted her. The struggle brought a flashing memory of how Dionysos had been afraid she would laugh when he described the creature that engendered so much horror in him. She had not laughed then, more out of consideration for the boy than because she understood. Now she understood. The fragile, rat-sized nothing looked as if she could crush it to jelly, had it not been carrying her father's coercion spell and had she dared to touch it at all. But it exuded a sickness that bred so strong an abhorrence it froze her soul despite her shields.

Likely it could read her because *it* laughed, and one of its arms began to lengthen. The hand hesitated at the ring of herbs and the guhrt whined, but as if compelled, in less than a heartbeat the arm began to grow again, even faster. Hekate watched, her mind caught in a kind of abject fascination, as the hand at the end of the arm started to glow with a sickly greenish-yellow light. Simultaneously the body of the guhrt shrank even more.

Somehow the process bound her; instead of gathering her forces and reviewing the key words for a spell of dismissal, Hekate found herself wondering what would happen if the guhrt disappeared completely before the arm could reach her. Would the hand crawl by itself along the ground dragging the lengthening arm behind it . . .

Before the thought was complete, a black missile flew from behind the nearest tree. A red maw gaped wide. Long white teeth clamped on the guhrt's arm and dragged it back, away from Hekate. The guhrt screamed so loud the waterfall seemed to sway; the hand twisted as if the arm were boneless and gripped the neck of the black dog. The greenish-yellow glow ran out of the tips of the clawing fingers and enveloped the hound.

Hekate's scream echoed that of the guhrt, but she screamed words that tore at her throat with their intensity. "*Guhrt, exelthein plateia eautou. Anagkazo stigme pheuge! Metakino! Metatheto! Pheuge! Pheuge! Pheuge!*"

She emptied herself into the spell and then, throwing caution to the winds, reached out for the power of the earth-blood and poured that into her willing that the guhrt be gone into its own plane. The yellow-green glow brightened until her eyes teared, brightened even more, until the light was unbearable–and winked out. Very far away she felt a shriek of pain that was echoed in some dark place in her soul. Her hand flew to her breast to ease a peculiar, distant agony, but at the same time the darkness within her lightened. She thrust that problem away to attend to more urgent needs.

Nothing remained where the guhrt had stood except the black dog lying on the ground. Heedless of leaving her refuge and of the danger that the compulsion spell might drive him to attack her or have been transferred to him and still be able to infect her, Hekate rushed to take his head onto her lap.

"Kabeiros! Kabeiros! Can you hear me?"

The hound's head twitched away. *Hear you? You are like to deafen me. Stop shouting in my ear.* The dog struggled to peer around her and rise. *Where is the guhrt?*

Hekate clung to him. "Answer me! Are you hurt? What did that spell do to you?"

It knocked me down. The big body in her arms shuddered. *I felt as if someone had poured the contents of a huge chamber pot–one that hadn't been emptied in years–over me and hit me with the pot too.*

The mental voice had been growing fainter; suddenly the dog wrenched itself free and crawled a little way from her, choking and retching. Hekate followed on her knees to stroke his head and his heaving body. Then she reached behind her and scooped up some of the herbs from the ground which she used to smooth over the dog's head and shoulders. He stopped retching and sat up, sniffing eagerly at her hands. Then the black forehead furrowed and he began to sniff the air.

Gone, he said with strong satisfaction. *The stink is all gone. How can such an all-pervading stench disappear so completely? Does that mean the guhrt is gone?*

Wrapped tight in her shields, Hekate had no very strong awareness of what was beyond them unless it was overpowering, as had been the guhrt's near presence. "Are you sure the foulness is all gone?" she asked.

The hound shook himself, shivering his skin to shed the bits of herbs, and limped farther from their protective scent. He continued to sniff lustily.

Gone, he repeated. *Nothing in the air now but wet earth, a rabbit or two–* he paused to lick his swollen paw with an expression of regret *–you, and the herbs, of course. No bad magic stink. The place is clean.*

Hekate sighed and sank down to sit on the ground. "Then I think the guhrt is gone. I hope I bespelled it back to its own plane, and since it was no longer carrying my father's spell, it's possible I was successful." She shuddered as the dog had done. "I've never dealt with otherplanar creatures if I could avoid it, so I had to make the spell myself." She shrugged. "I can't be sure it was effective."

Speaking of spells reminded her of her father's foul coercion cascading over the black dog and she wondered if she could trust him. Cascading over. She didn't think the spell had been absorbed. But why? Then she remembered that her sleep spell, instantly effective on the man Kabeiros, had not touched the dog. Could it be that the dog, a magical construct itself, was immune to magic?

Then what had happened to the coercion spell? It had run out of the guhrt–she had seen it flow from the fingers. Then it had grown brighter, as if some power was feeding it . . . or fighting it. And then it had disappeared, and there had been that distant sense of violent pain . . . as if the spell had backlashed . . . echoed by the pain within her.

Hekate shuddered. Was that because her father had set some link into her–a link to protect him from her if she ever grew strong enough to oppose him? Anything that caused him pain would hurt her . . . Would she die if he died? But she didn't plan his death. So if he were drained of all power as she planned, would she lose her power also?

That was a horrible thought. If she did not oppose and defeat Perses, the binding would somehow destroy her; if she did, the hook he had on her soul might accomplish the same thing. She stared unseeingly into the wood that bordered the pond. But the effect of the unwelcome bond was not certain, and now, at least, she knew it was there. She would seek it out and try to undo it before she began to worry about what it could do to her.

Now there was the more immediate problem of making sure the coercion spell had backlashed and not disappeared into Kabeiros. The trouble was she could not sense it if she maintained her wards. Cautiously Hekate relaxed the shields until she could feel the ambience of the place. No magic. Not even a distant sense of anything beyond the threads of earth-blood. It was very pleasant. She directed her senses at the hound, her wards ready to snap shut at the first flicker of any spell. Nothing. She rose and walked closer to him.

"Kabeiros, do you feel any different? Are you fighting any urge to . . . to hurt me?"

He swung his head toward her. *Hurt you? Of course not. Why should you ask me that?*

"Do you have any special urge to touch me?"

There was a blankness, as if Kabeiros the man had withdrawn somehow; then he thought slowly, *I am a dog. You are a woman. You should have asked that question while we were still in the caves of the dead.*

Hekate smiled ruefully. She was recalling Kabeiros' face and body. She sighed. "If I had, you would have been disgusted. Don't you remember that I wore the body of the crone all the while we were together in the caves? I didn't dare change before I knew you were a shape-shifter too."

*Then it's too late to ask whether I wish to touch you. Why should I? Except as a dog seeks warmth and comfort from his master . . . *

"You feel no urge to transfer the spell that my father gave to the guhrt with which to enslave me.

I wondered whether it could have gone from the guhrt to you . . ."

But you've already touched me, you silly woman. If the spell was meant to be transferred, wouldn't I have done it then?

Hekate breathed a long sigh of relief and nodded. Amidst all the stresses, she had forgotten her unguarded rush to help Kabeiros when she first saw him lying on the ground. Aside from that, she wondered what made her suspect him of resisting an urge to touch her, and her eyes widened a bit as she bent to spread her crushed herbs more evenly over a larger piece of ground. She suspected him because she felt that desire to touch . . . but not the hound.

The image of Kabeiros the man was always there for her, strongest when the dog did something compatible with a man's shape, like sitting on his haunches. Then she saw the dog almost like a shadow, darkening but not obscuring the face and body of the man. But she also saw the man totally separate from the dog, almost palpably there, striding along beside and melded with the hound shape even when the dog was walking on all fours.

She wondered if that could also be true for Kabeiros. Did he see the bent old woman with her bony hips and flat dugs obscuring the lithe and full-breasted body she now wore? Fretfully, she shook the image from her mind, recalling that Kabeiros had never said "If only you were younger," to the crone when they were in the caves. Then she recalled something even more discomforting; he didn't seem to take any special interest in the women who brought offerings to the caves of the dead. True, he was pledged not to show himself to those who came to make sacrifice, but there were places from which he could have watched.

A stupid thing to waste time on, Hekate told herself, and went off into the woods beyond the pool to find firewood. As she gathered, she wondered whether lighting a fire would be safe, then shrugged. If it drew the attention of local people, so much the better. She and Kabeiros surely needed directions to the nearest road and a day or two in a town would be most welcome. Her clothing had been nothing much to begin with; now it was approaching rags. She had metal; in a town she could buy clothing.

On the other hand, there might be outlaws in the foothills of the mountains. She shrugged again and piled several small dead branches into the crook of her arm. No one had gathered wood here in a long time—if ever. As to outlaws, she and the black dog could defend themselves. She smiled. She was not afraid to use magic now, and even so soon after the battle with the guhrt, she felt strong and ready.

Blocking her direct passage forward was a large branch of deadfall. If she dragged that back to the camp, they would have wood enough for the whole night. She wrinkled her nose as she broke off a few of the smaller branches. They had no way to deal with the whole branch. A small ax was another purchase she would make as soon as they found a town.

A slight scrabbling in a nearby hedge made her freeze, except for one hand that stealthily sought a rock. She waited, bent and uncomfortable but unwilling to display herself as a large and possibly dangerous creature, and her patience was rewarded. A long-eared, long-legged hare slipped through the hedge to sample the softer, sweeter grass where the deadfall had cleared a small open space. As it bent to nibble the grass, Hekate rose and flung her stone in one movement. She crowed with pleasure, leaping after the rock to seize the hare, which lay half stunned, kicking feebly, and wrung its neck.

She tied the limp body to her belt with some of the loose bits of Kabeiros' harness and went on gathering firewood, hoping for another small animal to come her way. She was not fortunate enough to make another kill, but she returned to the campsite in good spirits and became even more cheerful when she found that the dog had been busy too. Both packs, which she had cast away rather hastily, had been dragged to the side of the stream where she had spread the herbs. One had been opened and a modest sheet of oiled leather drawn out and spread. Beyond that a place had been pawed free of growth and a circle of stones set around the raw earth. Now how had he managed to clear the tough grass with one forepaw badly strained?

More stones were nearby, as if the dog had intended to make the circle either higher or wider but had been defeated by the lack of dexterity of his mouth. Hekate set down the firewood and spent some time fitting the readied stones into a second row. While she was bracing a slightly rounded rock with some pebbles, the hound came into sight past a group of bushes at the side of the stream. He carried another rock in his mouth.

Is your paw better? she sent to him. *How did you get across the stream?*

I intended to wade, but when I stepped in, my foot felt so much better that I just stayed until the pain was gone. I thought maybe it was just numb, but the swelling was down. Maybe the stream has healing qualities, or all that magic you were throwing around dissolved in it.

He jumped across, landing more heavily on one side, but when he came toward her he was hardly limping. Hekate smiled at him, took the rock, and found a place for it.

Unfortunately I don't think it's healed enough for me to hunt, the dog remarked, sitting down across the fireplace from her. *Too bad. The banks of the stream are full of the smell of rabbits and wild goat, too. If I could run, I could bring down a kid.*

No kids or lambs, Hekate said sharply. *We don't know how the people on this side of the mountains graze their animals. One look at you in the first town we come to–unless it's farther away than I hope it is–and they'll start pointing at you and yelling 'cattle-killer.' Stick to deer and hare. I don't want you blamed for domestic rabbits that disappear either.*

As you say. But the dog uttered a deep sigh. *I am not that fond of dry meat.*

"And tonight you will not need to eat it," Hekate said aloud, having satisfied herself that she could send to and hear the dog at twenty or thirty arm lengths. She gestured toward the hare lying atop the firewood. "I will gut it and skin it in a few minutes, but I want to start the fire first."

The dog snorted. *That will take more than a few minutes, but I can wait.*

"I have only to break up the sticks." She did so as she spoke, casting several onto the patch of raw earth surrounded by stones, gestured–and they burst into flame. "The guhrt is gone–I hope for good, but if not, at least out of this plane–and my father is too far away to reach me in such a way he can force me to obey." She hesitated, then nodded decisively. "Yes, it would be to my benefit if he could sense that I was getting farther and farther away from him. I hope he will be confident that I am too afraid of him to come back. That will work to my advantage, so I am free to use magic again."

While we are away from humankind. That thought was all from Kabeiros the man, no tinge of the dog in it. *When we come to a village or a road, you will need to be more careful. We don't need a village full of superstitious peasants after us because they fear your powers—or an army, if magic is forbidden in the lands through which we must travel. I know nothing about them. When I first came to Ur-Kabos, I meant to travel on eastward to the fabled lands of the Indies and the Chin, but I found drinking and playing companions and I put off my going from day to day, and then . . . *

"Colchis first," Hekate said, busily breaking more wood and laying some branches on the fire, others nearby. "Then Olympus if necessary. I can't go *too* far from my father until I deal with him and there are times when I would like to have the man Kabeiros near so we must solve that problem also. But after that . . . why not the Indies and Chin? We are two together—"

She stopped abruptly and shrugged, got up to fetch the dead hare from the diminished woodpile. The dog needed her because she was the only one who could talk to him and keep his humanity alive. But what if, after they discovered the way to bring back Kabeiros' control over his shifting ability, he found he preferred other company?

Having cut off the head and legs and gutted the carcass, Hekate brought the offal to the dog and laid it near him. She then turned away slightly and began to skin what remained of the hare; it was the one time she found it disgusting to see the man Kabeiros melded with the dog. She hated to connect the sound of cracking bone and liquid gulping as the skull was broken and the brain devoured with the handsome young man she knew.

Skinned and quartered, pieces of the hare were

impaled on peeled sticks of green wood that Hekate got from the brush around the stream. She then piled the two packs one atop the other and leaned back against them. The dog was finished, licking his whiskers clean.

When the meat was cooked—or mostly cooked—Hekate ate two of the quarters with some waybread. She was too tired to bother seeking bulbs or edible plants by the stream. The other two quarters she gave to the dog, silencing his protests by pointing out that he was larger and heavier than she and that he would have the more arduous task the next day, specially if they found a village and he had to bring in several animals to buy them a welcome.

However, no such demand was made on the hunting skill of the hound the next day, since they saw no sign of habitation in the rough terrain they scrambled through. It was just as well because, although his foot continued to mend, they did need to stop to rest it from time to time. The slowed pace produced a nice compensation; Hekate found a number of medicinal herbs that she culled, tied in bunches, and hung from her belt and pack to dry in the sun as they walked. And, before the light failed, they came down out of the most precipitous portion of the foothills into still steep but more fertile ground.

When they had negotiated their way down one last steep drop they came to an area where grass and low bushes grew in abundance though there weren't many trees. They camped there even though there were no deadfalls and they had to make do with brush for their fire.

Hekate thought that the land had been grazed over earlier in the year and then left to grow again. If the same patterns prevailed here as in the foothills around Ur-Kabos, it would be several ten-days, or even months, before the shepherds brought their herds back. Still, that shepherds had been there at all meant that there must be villages not too far distant.

They found clear signs of human habitation the next day. Not long after midday, the hound stopped and began to sniff. Leaning on her staff, Hekate watched him but did not extend her senses. If Kabeiros could indeed smell magic in the dog form and, in addition, was immune to it, she would be ten times a fool to open herself to what might be great danger.

What is it? she asked.

I'm not sure, but domesticated beasts–asses or goats, I think, not cattle or sheep. They're too far away for me to pick out the smell, but if it is asses, then we may be near a road.

"Good. A road means a village sooner or later."

And you are hungry for human company?

Hekate had begun to stride on down the hillside, but something in the mental quality of the dog's statement made her stop and look at him. *What do you mean, human company?* She pointed at him with her staff. *I *have* human company, which I don't doubt is more interesting than shepherds and village idiots. What I do not have is a decent garment and an ax, and perhaps a pallet to lay between my tired bones and the hard earth and beer or wine to drink and fresh bread and–*

The hound laughed, and Hekate's spirits lifted. She had managed to soothe whatever had caused that thread of bitterness she had detected. And then she thought remorsefully that it could not be easy to look and feel like a dog when, perhaps, you wanted to be a man. As they began to walk forward again, she glanced sidelong at Kabeiros. Could he want to be a man because she was a woman?

CHAPTER 9

Hekate fought the temptation to raise again the question of how Kabeiros felt about their relationship. She did not know whether she would be relieved or disappointed if he answered once more as he had in the past that he was a dog and felt to her as a dog to its master. She never thought of him as a dog, feeling bereft when he only offered a warm back as a comfort if the night was cold. Although she knew how ridiculous it was, Hekate inwardly blamed him for being unable to put his arms around her. She *knew* he was there . . . and yet, he wasn't.

"Kabeiros–" she said.

Quiet! he replied. *I smell dust. That means a road close by and likely animals or people that have walked along it to stir the dust.*

Why quiet? Don't we want to find people?

Not until we can give good reasons for why we are here, from where we came, and why. Hasn't it occurred to you that a young woman traveling alone is very unusual?

*Mother save me, I'm an idiot. It's so unusual that

I'm sure anyone we met would take me for a runaway slave.* She laughed softly. *In a way I am, but at least my father never branded my outward flesh.* Then she laughed again, a bit louder. *Thank the Mother for your brains, Kabeiros. Even as a dog, you are cleverer than I.*

I wouldn't say that, but before my misfortune I did travel a long way and I know how suspicious people are of strangers and the kinds of questions they ask. Also, in all that traveling I don't believe I ever saw a woman alone.

Hmmm. That will take some thinking. She was mentally silent for a while, one hand on her staff, the other automatically splaying the herbs fixed to her belt and the two packs to open the interior of the bunch to the sun. *A healer. Healers do travel.*

Yes. You should claim healing as your craft, but we need a reason for you to be . . . Wait. A childless widow with no family of her own, put out by her husband's family. But why? You're a beautiful woman. Surely one of your husband's brothers would have married you.

No brothers and no sons. Hekate thought back promptly. *Aha, an old man. A rich old man who purchased me from his old friend, my father, to warm his declining years. Then he outlived them all. His brothers and my father are now dead and he had no sons, only daughters. And the daughters were all jealous of me, unwilling to have me taken as a concubine by their husbands.* She tousled the dog's ears roughly. *And that will account both for my rough gown–doubtless they put me out in the coarsest clothes they could find–and for the silver I have, too. That would be my tirhatu–the gifts and money the old man gave me upon betrothal to make me willing to be married to him.*

*Yes, and the reason you still have it is that he

never told the daughters he had given it to you lest they nag at him.* The dog, who had sat down while they were talking, got to his feet and pulled open the knot of his harness. *Stay here,* he said, shaking free of the pack and straps. *I'll go scout out how far the road is and how heavy the traffic is. If I can find a good patch of brush or trees by the road, we can stop there until the road is empty, then come out as if we had been resting in the shade. From where are we coming?*

Damascus, I think. I don't want to admit coming from anywhere too close to Ur-Kabos, like Byblos, lest my father has alerted other sorcerers about my escape. I hope Damascus is far enough away that no one will know any more than the little I've heard about the city from traders who visited Perses.

And you wouldn't know much anyway if you were wife to a sickly, jealous, old man. He'd keep you close in the house and not let you wander about to see the city.

True enough. Hekate grinned and scratched the dog's head again. *But you be careful. You're a valuable dog. If anyone sees you, he might try to catch you for his own.*

The dog loped off and Hekate shed her pack, pulled the dog's close to her, and went about spreading the herbs, picking out any well-dried swatches and exposing those still damp. After a while she closed her eyes.

A gentle lick on her temple and a cold, wet nose pressed to her hand woke her. She drew in her breath sharply when she saw the hound; that touch on her temple had felt like a man's lips.

I have a good place for us to wait by the road. Even if someone comes upon us there, which is not impossible because it's near a camping place, our being there will seem natural. There is water at the camping ground, so we could have stayed more than one day. It's empty now.

They moved along quickly, since it was already past noon and some groups stopped early, especially if they had women and children with them. Although the road was empty when they reached it, dust was still settling and it appeared that their anxiety was justified. By the time they came to their goal, people were already in the camping place. Hekate and Kabeiros crossed the road and went into the brush and tall grass that bordered it until they were clear of the camp, noting from the sounds and the shouted orders that the group was newly arrived; however, the area that Kabeiros had picked for them, some hundred paces down the road, was still empty.

It was a much smaller open area and had no water; the entrance to it was narrow and less inviting than the main campsite, and the brush concealing it from the road was thick. Once behind the screen of bushes, Hekate chose an area close to a thinner spot in the brush farthest from the road that she wished to mark as her own. If they were seriously threatened, she thought, she and Kabeiros could push through the somewhat scraggly growth there and escape into the open countryside where she could make herself disappear and Kabeiros could hide.

When Kabeiros agreed with her choice and her reasons, she decided to make it seem they had been there for some time. She undid the packs, laying out her blankets and spreading the culled herbs on the piece of oiled leather she usually used between the blanket and the earth. All the while she had been listening to the sounds coming from the camping place. When she was sure the party was settling in, rather than stopping to rest and water their animals, she sighed.

They aren't going to leave, she said to Kabeiros. *So, do we try to hide and take the chance they will come on us by accident, or do we try to act like ordinary travelers?*

I think we'll have to let them know we're here. They don't sound like thieves or outlaws, the hound said slowly, thinking hard. *You'll have to get water, and we have to cook the hares I caught and that bird you brought down, but there's no wood here for a fire. Maybe they'll trade some charcoal for one of the hares.*

Do you smell any magic?

Not the tiniest whiff. I'd have told you right away if anyone smelled of spells. But that doesn't mean there isn't someone who can do magic. If a person isn't casting or carrying working spells and isn't strongly Gifted, it's possible I wouldn't sense him.

I wanted to use the look-by-me spell so I could see what kind of people they are without showing myself. It's not strong magic. Would it be safe?

The hound wrinkled his muzzle. *How can I tell? Not everyone who can do magic can sense it. We can try. Cast the spell and I'll see how much it affects me and from how far away.* And when she had done as he suggested and he had retreated first to the edge of the clearing farthest away and then right across the road, he returned and said, *I can smell you from anywhere. It isn't strong or unpleasant, but it isn't anything natural either. So, if they have someone with them who can detect magic, he or she will probably sense the spell.*

Hekate sighed. *The question then is whether I want to take the chance that they're just traders and will ignore us or leave us in peace or take the chance that I'll be exposed as using magic.*

I think it more dangerous that you be exposed as spying on them using magic. The hound panted for a moment in mental silence and then continued. *Veil yourself–I think there's a piece of cloth that you can use to cover your head and hold across your face–and take one of the hares and some of the herbs. Offer to trade for charcoal. If you are threatened or in danger, call, and I'll come. I'm sure a sudden attack from a hound as large as me will cause shock and free you. Then if you want, cast your spell and we can go our way. I doubt anyone will wish to meddle further with you when you are known to be a sorcerer.*

While she sought out and covered her head with a cloth from the dog's pack–it was meant to serve as a kilt if Kabeiros should recover his human form–Hekate considered the few other options they had, such as continuing on down the road or slipping back up the hills. To retreat to the hills would only delay, not alter, the problem of meeting other people, and continuing down the road could be as dangerous or more dangerous than taking their chances with this group of travelers.

I can't think of a better plan, Hekate agreed finally. *I'll take the waterskin and see if I can refill it before I'm noticed. Then I can reveal myself and ask about trade.*

The hound lay down near the herbs and Hekate took the waterskin, emptied what little it held into the brush, and then picked up one hare and two bundles of herbs in her other hand. She went out on the back side of the clearing, through the thin section of brush and found, as she had hoped, a rear opening into the camping place. From the odor, she guessed that that exit led to the privy ditches.

The stench made her glad that she and Kabeiros had taken care of their needs, neatly burying the debris, before they reached the place. Still, it was an advantage to come in from that exit. If no one looked closely at her, she might be taken as a member of the party returning from a trip to the necessary.

She paused to one side of the entrance and glanced quickly around. Her dress would not betray her. Men and women wore very similar garments—the men's being only somewhat shorter, and Hekate's was ragged enough that the original length was not too easy to determine. No one was veiled, and many of the men had long hair; however, they wore hats of some kind or turbans, and all of them were heavily bearded. She shrugged mentally, stepped back a couple of paces, and quickly wound the cloth around her head into the semblance of a turban.

From what she could see, although there were no women and children in the group, Kabeiros' reasoning about the sounds he heard were correct. These people did not look like outlaws. They were well fed, and even those who were doing the hardest and least respected work were not in rags.

She came forward again, slowly but not pausing. Using the waterskin to cover the hare and the herbs, she made her way to the well. No one seemed to notice her as she dropped the bucket and drew it up. Undoing a plug from the opening, she poured water from the bucket into the skin, rinsed it thorougly, drew another bucket, and began to fill it. When water gurgled in the neck of the skin, she replaced the plug carefully and slung the bag over her shoulder. She was wondering as she turned away from the well, whom she should approach, but the matter was taken out of her hands.

"Who are you?"

Hekate jumped, almost bumping into a bearded man who had come up behind her close enough to grab her. She bowed very slightly, relieved that she had understood him. The people of Ka'anan spoke the same language as those of Lud, Mesheck, and Togarmah, but with many variations. She knew that the speech of Ka'anan was heavily salted with words of the traders of the west and of Egypt; Mesheck was even more Egyptian. This man spoke what seemed like an old form of Ka'anan, without the many embellishments the language had absorbed from its neighbors and trading partners. However, the three words had been comprehensible.

"By your leave, good sir," Hekate spoke slowly, hoping he would understand. "I am a fellow traveler on the road."

"Are you?" he asked, his voice hard. "I didn't see you come into the campsite and neither did my guards."

"I came in the back, from the path to the necessary."

"Secretly? To spy on us?"

The swift angry questions proved to Hekate that Kabeiros had been right about dangers in traveling on the road. It would be wise to join a caravan. But Hekate didn't allow her thoughts to slow her response. She shook her head at once.

"Oh, no, sir. I did come in quietly. You are many; we are few. I admit I wished to escape notice. All I wanted was to fill my waterskin and . . . and we have come to the end of our fuel. I hoped you were peaceful folk and I could make a trade for some charcoal. See–" she raised the hare and the bundles of herbs "–I have this hare–it was fresh killed today–and these herbs–these are strips of willow bark, which steeped in water or wine is good to soothe pain and fever, and this mullein, which when crushed is good to lay on bruises."

She met his eyes hopefully, then looked away as if out of shyness, but quick sidelong glances under lowered lashes revealed several men quietly leaving the camp by both exits. Hekate suspected that they had gone to check on where the rest of her party was and discover if they were peaceful or dangerous. She was a little annoyed; they would find nothing but her drying herbs—she had already warned Kabeiros to hide with a quick mental thrust—however, she realized that she wouldn't be able to conceal the fact that she was traveling alone. She had just time enough for a grateful thought about Kabeiros insisting she prepare a credible story when the moment of revelation drew closer.

"You are a woman!" the trader exclaimed, having examined her features with more care. "Why is your hair bound up in a turban like a man?"

Hekate hitched the waterskin higher on her shoulder, using that movement to disguise a step toward the rear exit from the campsite. "When I saw you were all men here," she said, "I was afraid to come among you as a woman."

He snorted and took a half step toward her to which Hekate responded by taking another long backward step toward the exit. The trader shook his head, but did not argue the point she had made nor her keeping her distance from him. Indeed, he looked thoughtful and was silent, biting his lip, and giving Hekate time to examine him more closely.

Both beard and hair, long and bound back by a leather thong, were black, and the beard, although neatly trimmed, curled, and combed, covered so much of his face that his features were not easy to make out. However they were dominated by a great beak of a nose, and what she could see of his lips were full and neither drawn tight nor loose with overindulgence in pleasure. The eyes, very dark and shaded under beetling brows, looked kind . . . and worried.

"How do I know what you have here is willow bark?" he snapped. "For all I know it could be poison."

Hekate felt a stirring of interest. The worried expression and the interest in willow bark implied that someone was ill. "I'll steep some and drink it, sir. Although it's very bitter, willow has little or no effect on a person in good health so it is perfectly safe for anyone to take. Those who have pain or fever are often soothed."

"And why should I take your word?"

"For that I have no answer except the offer I made to prove to you that the potion I will make is harmless to me. I can't swear that it will help anyone who is ill without knowing what ails that person, but I am a healer—at least, I am an herb-wife—"

"Are you?" he asked, interrupting almost eagerly. "And will your husband allow you to help a sick child?"

"I am sure he would have," Hekate replied, her heart clenching at the thought of a sick child. "He was a most kindly person, but I have no husband now."

"I am sorry, for your loss." Absorbed in his own problem, the statement was perfunctory. "What of your new lord? Would he be willing to lend your service? We have no healer with our group and . . . and my daughter . . . ails."

At that moment, one of the men who had left the clearing hurried to the trader's side. This one's clothing was as fine as the trader's own and he wore a sword. He spoke briefly into the trader's ear, too low for her to hear, but the trader, who had turned partly away, turned back and stared at her—but not before Hekate had moved even closer to the way out.

This time he noticed. "Where are your people?" he asked, following and grasping her arm.

Be ready, Hekate mind-shouted to Kabeiros.

I'm at the back opening.

Not yet, Hekate added quickly, as the man released her arm when she winced away. *He has a sick child. If he will let me treat it, we will be able to join the caravan.* Then, to the trader, she said aloud. "I have no party. I am alone."

"A woman? Alone?" His lips tightened. "Where is your home? I'll take you back to the husband you have shamelessly abandoned."

Hekate laughed. "You will have a long journey and no welcome at the end. I come from near Damascus. And I have no husband. I didn't lie to you. My husband is dead."

"Damascus? Alone? I don't believe you!"

She shrugged. "You've already sent men to look for anyone else and found no one. I've no doubt your men saw my little camp with my drying herbs." The thought of the sick child pulled at her. "I'm a good herb-wife," she said, hoping he would take the hint. "I have cured many and had gratitude as well as my keep, so I have traveled safely alone. And often I wasn't alone. From one village to the next, a man or a family would let me accompany them when they went to visit married children or neighbors or to trade. Sometimes I joined a trader's caravan."

"But you didn't stay with them. Why?"

"Because they turned back on their tracks and I wished to continue onward."

"Onward? Where?"

Hekate had known the question must come and had thought about it. She didn't think it wise to say she wished to go to Colchis. Too many knew it as a place of magic, but she didn't wish to name any other particular place.

"I'm an herb-wife, and a good one, but I wish to be a true healer. I seek a well-known and respected healer who will take me as apprentice."

"There were none in Damascus?"

Disbelief was again rich in the trader's voice, but Hekate didn't mind. It was plain from what he said that he wasn't familiar with Damascus . . . or was testing her. She shook her head. "There were many, but I couldn't stay in Damascus."

"Doubtless you killed your clients and had to flee."

"I never practiced as an herb-wife in Damascus. I had a husband there." She sighed once more. "I can't make you believe me, but I haven't harmed any of your people, nor, I'm sure, have you heard along the road of any evil herb-wife. If you will give me charcoal in trade for my hare–you don't need to take the herbs–I will be grateful. If you won't, then let me go on my way. You have no right to keep me."

Only Hekate didn't want to go. She wanted to see that sick child and make it well; it was a nagging need in her. Fortunately she had not misjudged her man.

"Let you go?" he repeated angrily. "A woman? To travel alone? Ridiculous!" He stared at her. "Did you poison your husband?"

Hekate grinned broadly. "Would I tell you if I did? Don't be ridiculous yourself." Then she sobered and said sadly, "My husband was an old man, but good and kindly, and I was very fond of him. If you go to Damascus, ask anyone about Abu Mahound. You will hear the whole story of how his daughters forbade his wife to nurse him any longer because he did not get well." She uttered a bark of bitter laughter. "How does one get well from fourscore years of life? But I had kept him alive and happy for years, and his family lost patience–

or began to fear for their inheritance, lest he will it all to me. They desired his wealth more than his company. They said I was childless and useless–and they drove me out."

"And your husband could not call you back?"

"He was bedridden and weak. At first I was stunned, but then I grew so angry–I knew he would die without my tonics and my good cheer–that I forgot all fear and made a complaint before the king's scribe." Her lips twisted. "I suppose they actually did me a favor. What with my demands to be taken in and the complaint, the whole city knew I could not have killed him when he died."

Some note of bitterness or grief in her voice and manner convinced the trader. Hekate was amazed by her seeming sincerity; she almost convinced herself. When she stopped speaking, she drew a deep breath, as if shaken by emotion and added, "As for not being able to travel alone–I am here, alive and well, am I not? I have got this far alone. Why not farther?"

"But why are you traveling at all?"

"Because Abu Mahound's family is rich and powerful. They didn't want me in Damascus reminding all who owed him love and favors that they had driven me from the house so I could not care for him."

"His brothers would not take you?"

"They were older than he, long dead. His one nephew had been the first to say I wasn't caring properly for his uncle–he didn't invite me into his house and I wouldn't have gone anyway. For the others, my husband had only daughters, and they did not wish to share their husbands with me."

The trader looked at her, took in the silver eyes, the full lips, the fine skin, the wealth of raven hair, the rich body–which an effort could discern under the loose, shabby garments. He could understand why a woman would not wish to share her husband with the herb-wife. He shook his head.

"Well, if what you say is true, you've been ill-treated. But surely one of your husband's friends could have found a husband for you outside of Damascus."

"To speak the truth, I had enough of husbands—and their families. I had consulted many healers to be sure I was doing the best for my husband. Several of them were rich and independent—and two of those were women. Since I knew herbs already, it seemed better to follow in their footsteps."

The trader sighed noisily. "Independent! A woman! What is your name, O independent woman?"

"My name is Hekate." She grinned at him. "Will you trade some charcoal for the hare? I have another to cook for myself, but nothing with which to make a fire."

"Independent or not, I don't like it—a woman traveling alone! You said you joined some traders' caravans now and again. This road runs to Quatna. You have no place in mind so why don't you join us until we reach the city?"

"Gladly," Hekate answered promptly. Soon she would find a way to ask about the child. "I hoped you would ask me. Tell me where to leave my goods and my waterskin, and I will go fetch my bedding and the rest of my herbs."

"You accept and trust me . . . just like that?"

Hekate smiled at him. "You have had near a score of men within call since you first noticed I was not of your party. If you wished to do me harm, surely you had chances in plenty. Besides, I have a very faithful guardian waiting on my summons."

With that, Hekate let out a piercing whistle at the

same time as she said silently, *Come now, Kabeiros, and look fierce, but don't attack. Were you able to catch what the trader said to me? I tried to echo it.*

I heard most.

On the words, Kabeiros appeared in the rear exit to the camping grounds. His head was lowered, his upper lip lifted, and his ears laid back, but he stood still until Hekate gestured him forward. Then he came and licked her hand.

"Here is my guardian."

"That is a magnificent dog," the trader said, staring. "What is his name?"

"Kabeiros." Hekate's lips twitched. She guessed what the man was about to do and she was right.

The trader held out his hand and said, "Kabeiros! Here!" in an authoritative voice.

Clearly the man was accustomed to handling animals and accustomed to obedience from them. Hekate sensed just the faintest wisp of a Gift for dealing with animals. That would be most useful in his profession. Kabeiros, of course, would have smelled the magic and was, in any case, immune. He ignored both hand and command, only lifting his lips a bit farther from his great fangs.

"Well!" The trader sounded indignant, then sniffed through his beak of a nose. "Who in the world trained a great dog like that to obey a woman?"

"I was Kabeiros' choice," Hekate said. "He is my friend and my companion. I doubt he would obey anyone else, man or woman."

At that the hound looked up and nuzzled her hand, and the trader drew a sharp breath.

"He is blind!" he exclaimed.

"His eyes are strange," Hekate agreed, "but he seems to see well enough. It is Kabeiros who brought down the hares, and he has fed himself on our journey."

"Kabeiros . . ." the trader muttered, looking at the dog. "Why does that name seem familiar to me?"

"I don't know," Hekate said hurriedly, not wanting to get involved in explaining why a dog had the name of a god of mischief. "But, speaking of names, you know my name and the name of my dog. Won't you tell me what to call you, good sir?"

"I am Yasmakh the trader," he said without hesitation.

Hekate bowed slightly, acknowledging that mark of acceptance. "If you trust me to join your caravan, won't you also trust me enough to look upon this sick child? I swear I am a good herb-wife. Also, I promise to do nothing without explaining to you what I do, to do no harm to the child with or without explanation, and to tell you honestly if I can't help."

For a moment hope and anxiety twisted Yasmakh's lips and furrowed his brow. Then, as if answering an argument made many times, he said, "I had to bring her. I had no one with whom to leave her. And she enjoyed our travel so much . . . so much." He hesitated a little longer, staring into Hekate's face, then sighed. "It can't hurt her if you look at her." He bit his lip. "She . . . doesn't answer me any more."

CHAPTER 10

There was only one small tent set up, and it was to this that Yasmakh led Hekate. The hound paced beside her but sat down at the tent flap rather than entering, which was just as well since Hekate suspected that Yasmakh wouldn't want a dog inside a "dwelling." The thought was fleeting, however, her attention fixing on the pallet on which a child lay—but not quietly, although she seemed too weak to toss violently.

Clearly she had done so and was weakening. Her hair was tangled and matted and the blanket that once covered her was twisted and cast aside. She turned her head fretfully and muttered hoarsely. Hekate knelt down beside her, careful not to touch her.

"She asks for water," Hekate said.

The trader burst into tears. "But she cannot drink," he sobbed. "I've tried and tried, but the water runs out of her mouth and she cries with pain when she tries to swallow."

Hekate's eyes widened. "Mother have mercy," she

whispered, and then, louder, to the trader, "Has she been bitten by any animal, a dog or a cat or a wild creature?"

"No, that I can swear." Yasmakh shuddered. "I know that sickness. I would have killed her myself, if she had been bitten, rather than let her suffer and suffer only to die. I know there is no cure for that."

"Then I pray what ails her is not hopeless, but now I must touch her. I must look into her throat. And for that I need light. May I move her to the door?"

"I will move her," he said jealously.

He carried her, pallet and all, and laid her down athwart the tent opening. Hekate pulled aside the flap.

"Hold this," she said to Kabeiros, and he took the edge of the cloth in his mouth and kept it from falling shut. "Now you must stand behind her and open her mouth," Hekate said to Yasmakh. While he struggled to get the child's mouth open and to hold her head still, Hekate took from her pouch a small, carefully wrapped item which when unwrapped exposed a very highly polished piece of metal. Catching the light of the westering sun on its surface, she pointed it into the child's throat.

"Oh my," she said.

On each side of the throat there were usually two small lumps of flesh for which Hekate had never discovered any purpose except to make trouble. She had seen them swollen and mottled from time to time and had prescribed hot astringent gargles, which usually cleared the mottling and shrank the flesh nubbins to their normal size. In this child's throat, the lumps had swollen so that they almost touched and they were completely covered with white and yellow-green pustules.

"Can you cure her?" the father pleaded.

"I don't know," Hekate admitted, slowly rewrapping her bright bit of metal. "I have seen this illness before and I have cured it, but I've never seen so terrible an attack. And how can an unconscious child lave her throat with the liquid I must mix?" She bit her lip. "There must be a way."

Only Hekate was not really thinking of the throat gargle. She knew that was too little and too late for this child. To save her, she would have to use magic. And it was only a girl child. What if there were someone in the camp who could read or feel that she was using spells? What if these people were violently opposed to the use of magic? The Mother alone knew what would happen. Her lips parted to say she could do nothing, but she could not bring out the words.

She stared down at the pallid face with two bright red spots on the cheeks. Was her safety so precious that she would let a child die–a child? She had once been "only a girl child" herself. Was that a reason to let a child die, that it was only a girl?

Kabeiros, is there any smell of magic anywhere? she asked. *I will need to use spells to cure this child.*

Nothing I can smell or feel. Can the cure wait until we are in a place where others can have cast the spells?

No. If I do not cure her very soon, she will die.

Then cure her, Kabeiros said. *You can't let a child die because of what *might* happen.*

Hekate could feel a faint flush of heat mark her shame. Was she such a coward? She raised her head and took a deep breath.

"You know a medicine for this?" Yasmakh asked eagerly.

She swallowed a defiant impulse to mention magic. Fighting cowardice was probably the right thing to do, but not throwing caution to the winds. "Yes," she said, "but not how to use it in your daughter's case. It is not a medicine that is drunk. It must be spread over the swollen parts of the throat by . . . wait . . . I can use a feather or something of that kind to coat the throat with the medicine."

She stood up, eager to be alone so she could think out a suitable spell and how to combine the symbols so she could write them on the swollen flesh itself. A feather would serve as her pen and the throat gargle, suitably darkened, would be her ink. Then she would not need to say the spell aloud so that unless she was detected by another user of magic, Yasmakh wouldn't know she was a sorcerer.

"I will go and mix the herbs for the medicine and set them to steep," she said to the trader. "We do not have much time, for I need light to put the medicine on the diseased parts. Meanwhile, you must give the child water. No, do not expect her to swallow it," she said, cutting off Yasmakh's protest. As she spoke, she fished a little spoon out of her pouch. "Take this. Fill it and wet her lips and the inside of her mouth over and over until she stops crying for water."

Hekate hurried out of the camp with Kabeiros at her heels, aware as she turned toward her own campsite that one of Yasmakh's men—the one who had whispered in Yasmakh's ear earlier—was following her. When she got to the smaller clearing, he hesitated, then moved until he could watch her through the thin spot in the brush barrier. She was annoyed, but not surprised by the lack of trust, so she ignored his presence while she quickly rolled up the sleeping blankets and other odds and ends of cloth and clothing.

Her mind was busy with symbols and very specific

spell words. She didn't want to make the child's throat disappear instead of the pustules on the swollen flesh. And to make those disappear they had to go somewhere; it was impossible to uncreate substance, except by burning, and she could not burn them in the child's throat.

Hekate frowned slightly as she thought about the herbs she would need. Most of those were in her pouch, cleansing herbs too, but she couldn't send the pustules to a bunch of herbs; they were not like enough to where they grew. Nor could she take such diseased things into herself or inflict them on another person or living creature . . . Not on a living creature, but one newly dead? Yes. All she needed to do was command what she touched with the feather and the medicine to transfer itself to a fresh-killed animal.

I need another hare or rabbit or really anything at all larger than a mouse, she said silently to Kabeiros. *See if you can get something not worth eating because I'll have to burn it when I'm finished.*

He won't leave you alone with the child. He'll know you've done magic, Kabeiros warned.

No. I'll conceal whatever you bring in my pouch. What Yasmakh will see is me applying the medicine to the child's throat. But I will be painting the symbols for the transfer of the evil to the dead thing and the spell I will say in my mind.

Good enough, but be careful. I'd like to avoid him crying 'sorcerer' when we reach the city. There's game aplenty of small things. I shouldn't be long.

He wasn't. By the time Hekate had emptied her pouch, chosen the herbs she needed, and wrapped them in a square of clean cloth, a squall sounded not far distant. A few moments later, Kabeiros came back with a small furry creature in his mouth. At

Hekate's silent suggestion, he dropped it between the hare and the fowl. Under cover of replacing some herbs in her pouch, Hekate popped it in. That done, she tied the pouch to her belt, rolled the extra herbs and the hare and fowl into the piece of leather, and picked up her staff.

Less than half a candlemark had passed, but she cast an anxious glance at the sun, stuck her head through the brush, and shouted to the man who had been watching. "Since you are so curious, you can make yourself useful. Come in here and help me carry these bundles back to the camp."

He looked a little shamefaced at having been detected watching her, but he came and took the packages Hekate handed him. Her fearless acknowledgement of his presence seemed to make a good impression, as did the fact that she didn't mind if he touched her belongings. It was widely (if mistakenly) believed that magical objects must not be handled by common folk. Kabeiros, knowing better and free of his pack, lolled out his tongue in laughter at his companion's boldness.

She set the herbs in the special packet she had made up to steep in hot water as soon as they reached the larger camp. Yasmakh had readily supplied charcoal and a brazier; Hekate used her own little pannikin for the steeping, and managed to pour some of the liquid from it into the mouth of the small dead beast in her pouch.

Her preparations hadn't taken long, but Yasmakh was waiting anxiously by the tent, and when, without instruction, Kabeiros pulled the flap open, Hekate could see at once that, even though her mouth was now moist, the child was weaker. The little girl lay limp, clearly unconscious. Hekate let her last hope of avoiding magic slip away. The rapid decline was a final sign that she must take the chance of exposing her magical ability, or the child would die.

Yasmakh bit his lip and wept. "She didn't tell me her throat hurt on the day we left Berothah," he sobbed. "She was quiet, but I thought it was because we were leaving behind some children she had come to like. And there was nothing between there and Quatna–tiny villages that didn't even have a temple at which I could pray for her."

"Never mind that now," Hekate said sharply. "We must use the last of the light. Here, take this metal and shine the light into her mouth as I did earlier."

She set the pannikin beside her and opened the child's mouth with her left hand–there was no resistance. In her right she took a narrow feather and, with care not to block the beam of light, painted the combined magical symbols for transfer on the top of one of the mounds of putrid flesh. Under her breath she whispered the spell that directed whatever the liquid touched to move to the flesh and liquid in her pouch. As she completed the symbol, a thumbnail-sized hollow appeared in the swollen mound. Blood welled out. Hekate gasped; she had thought only the pustule would be removed, but the flesh had gone with it.

"*Stigme stasis aima*!" she breathed, activating a spell she used constantly in treating her father's slaves and servants.

The blood stopped, but Hekate held her breath, expecting a howl of protest from Yasmakh or a shout of accusation from somewhere in the camp. Yasmakh, however, didn't make a sound, and the light reflected from the bright metal only trembled a little, as it had from the beginning because of his anxiety. There was no outcry of accusation about the use of magic either.

Hekate breathed again, realizing that from

Yasmakh's angle of view, he couldn't see into the child's throat. She was pleased too by the confirmation of Kaberios' sense that there probably was no one sensitive to magic in the group.

She had no time to hesitate and began to paint the symbol on the opposite side while she wondered what would happen if she removed all the diseased flesh. She had never found any use for those nubbins, but . . . Still, if she didn't continue, the child would surely die; if she removed all the swollen and diseased flesh . . . who knew?

Until the light failed, Hekate carved away the putrid, swollen lumps of flesh. Less afraid to use magic, she checked the child's aura from time to time, but did not find much change. Also the child was breathing more easily because her air pipe was no longer almost blocked.

As Hekate sat back on her heels and began to wipe the feather on her ragged skirt, Yasmakh whispered, "Are you done? Will she live?" He continued, eyes fixed on Hekate's face, "She breathes better. Is that not a good sign?"

"I can't answer you," Hekate said honestly. "I don't know. She *is* breathing easier, but maybe that's only because the medicine has shrunk the swelling in her throat. She's still very hot with fever and she still hasn't wakened, which isn't good."

"You are very honest," he said, returning Hekate's piece of polished metal.

"I would be stupid to give you false hope, but I won't say there's no hope. I will have to repeat the treatment as soon as I have light enough to see tomorrow. Meanwhile, she should be bathed with cool water to bring down her fever and, since the swelling is down, perhaps she will be able to drink. I will give you a potion of willow bark and other herbs–I will drink some myself to prove it's not dangerous."

Yasmakh smiled at her. "There's no need."

She sighed. "Not if the child gets well, but if—all the gods forfend—I cannot save her, I don't want doubts to rise."

As she spoke, Hekate had tried to get to her feet and discovered her legs would barely support her. Fortunately Kabeiros was just outside the tent and she was able to steady herself with a hand on his shoulder. She had feared that her attempt at healing would be draining, but had been afraid to seek a vein of earth-blood to sustain her. Another magic worker, who might have been too preoccupied to notice the spells she had used, might well feel the roiling of the earth's blood. Worse yet, she could not simply sink down and sleep as she wished.

First she had to make up the potion against fever that she had promised Yasmakh; that was easy enough and she could sit while she did it. She saved what remained of the throat paint in a cup, washed the pannikin and added more water from her waterskin and herbs from the parcel rolled in the leather sheet, then set it to heat.

While her hands were busy, she considered how to be rid of the now diseased body in her pouch. She had hoped she would be able to go to the smaller camping place and simply make a fire and burn it, but she found eyes still followed wherever she went. Yasmakh might have decided to trust her, but his men did not. All she could do was seek privacy—they knew she was a woman and would not spy on her there—in the privy area.

What Hekate wanted to do was drop the diseased body into the trench and forget about it, but she feared the evil it now contained might somehow get loose and poison the whole campsite. Recalling the faint note of puzzlement—or was it disdain—in Kabeiros' mental voice when he said, "You can't let a child die because of what *might* happen," she flushed again. She could imagine what he would think of her if he knew she had considered endangering the whole campsite–this caravan and who knew how many more–just to hide the fact that she could do magic.

She had saved the child with magic and not been exposed. She must take another chance. Setting her teeth, she sought for a vein in the earth for power and rendered the body to ash with a burst of magic fire. Then she held her breath. That should have alerted anyone with even a minor Talent, but there was still no outcry. Hekate breathed a big sigh of relief and raised her skirt to use the privy for its usual purpose. Now that she need not worry about exposing herself as a sorcerer, there was no need to stir other suspicions by a second trip to relieve herself.

The conviction that Yasmakh's caravan included no one who would feel magic gave Hekate confidence enough for a good night's sleep. The fact that the child seemed somewhat better–at least less deeply unconscious–hinted that removal of the diseased flesh had done no harm. That and the child's restlessness decided her to a bolder use of the transfer spells.

Kabeiros had brought in another small animal in the first light of dawn, and Hekate went to cleanse the child's throat as soon as sunlight touched the campsite. It was not so easy. Yasmakh had to hold the little girl's head with one hand and the reflecting metal with the other, and Hekate had to exert some force to keep the child's mouth open. It was just as well that she had decided to clean away all the remaining flesh in two bold strokes because the child whimpered with the first transfer and cried out more loudly, struggling against the second. Still, it was done.

"We can only wait and hope now," Hekate said to Yasmakh. "Do you have honey?"

He nodded mutely, his eyes fixed on the child's face. "Yasmina," he murmured, "you will be better now. Papa says so and you know he is always right."

Hekate's mouth twisted wryly. Papa is always right. A chill ran down her back, but all she said was, "If you will give me a little honey, I will add it to the potion against fever so it will taste better and also soothe Yasmina's throat, which is very sore from my treatment."

"Yes. Yes, of course." He stood up, stroking the child's cheek as he rose, then, finally, raised his eyes to Hekate. They held a look, speculation shaded with fear, that she didn't like, but all he said was, "Will it hurt my daughter to travel? I have goods that will not be improved by extra days on the road."

"I don't know," Hekate admitted. "Those I treated before were in their own homes and going nowhere. All I can say is that I will walk beside the cart that carries her and if I see that her fever is rising or some other bad symptom is appearing, I'll tell you. Then you can decide what to do." Then she frowned. "But this I can say before we start. Do not put her at the end of the caravan where she will need to breath the heaviest dust."

So it was arranged that Yasmakh rode first—on a fine, high-stepping horse that told Hekate he was a man of wealth and probably of importance—followed by the small cart, which had been emptied of cargo to accommodate his daughter. Hekate walked beside it with Kabeiros. Her eyes were on the child, but she hardly saw her, only alert enough to give her the honeyed fever potion when she cried for a drink or that her throat hurt.

The compulsion to treat Yasmina had faded almost to nothing, and she took that as a sign either that the child was on the road to recovery or was beyond her help. Oddly she didn't feel strongly about either outcome. Her preference, of course, was that the child get well, but she would weep no tears and feel little pain if instead the child died. Her indifference no longer troubled her as it had at first when she feared she was becoming as heartless as her father. Now she accepted her lack of deep feeling as a sign that the children she was compelled to help would never belong to her. Only Dionysos had pulled her heartstrings—and he still did.

What made Hekate's eyes blind as she seemed to watch Yasmina was her own unreasonable and inexplicable fear of using magic. In rational hindsight, she asked herself what it could have mattered if anyone realized she was using magic to cure Yasmina. At best the spells would have been taken for ordinary healing spells and accepted—healing magic was welcome to all but a few fanatics; at worst, if she were threatened she could have used the look-by-me spell to escape. What did she fear so greatly that she had even considered sacrificing the child's life to avoid use of magic?

Fortunately, Hekate's inattention did her patient no harm. Yasmina improved throughout that first day and soon Yasmakh could not do enough for Hekate. He offered her a donkey to ride on, another to carry her bundles. She laughed and said she was no fool; the bundles were in the cart with the child and she preferred to walk alongside where she could watch her patient.

Hekate didn't mind walking and didn't wish to be troubled by a donkey's vagaries. What she wanted to do was think, but over the day and a half it took to reach Quatna, she found no answer to her cowardice, only a deep-seated reluctance to use magic. Fortunately, she didn't need it. The child was nearly recovered, only sometimes needing a draught of the willow-bark tea in the late afternoon.

To Hekate's dismay, Quatna was not an open city. The guards at the gate required Yasmakh to identify each person in his caravan and issued a badge of identification. This implied that anyone without a badge would be seized and penalized, possibly imprisoned. If it had not been for that, Hekate would have slipped away from the trader moments after they reached the first tangle of alleys.

It was not that Hekate suspected Yasmakh wished to harm her—far from it. Despite sidelong glances that hinted he knew magic, not medicine, had cured Yasmina, the trader had already offered Hekate a home in his house and the care of his precious daughter.

Without refusing outright, Hekate had spoken of her pleasure in seeing new places, finding new healing herbs, learning the medicines of new peoples. She had developed a taste for the road, she insisted. Yasmakh had not pressed his point too strongly, but he had returned to it often enough that, at the gate of the fine house to which he led the caravan, Hekate stopped. She snatched her bundles from the slowly moving cart and set them against the wall. Yasmina hopped out of the cart and stared at her.

"Aren't you coming in?" the child asked.

"No, I will say farewell here." She watched Yasmina's face but saw nothing beyond a mild regret and breathed out softly in relief. Her care for the child had not fixed Yasmina's affection on her. Now she would discharge her final responsibility. "Name to me what is in the drink you must tell your nurse to make for you if you feel hot and tired?"

Yasmina repeated the ingredients in a singsong voice. Hekate nodded. She had told Yasmakh the formula also and explained to him that Yasmina might suffer some recurrences of fever and need the potion. She had done all she could, and her lack of regret in parting from the child told her she had completed her duty. She bent to fasten one of the bundles to Kabeiros' back.

"Tell your father," she began–but it was too late, Yasmakh had come out to look for her, probably as soon as he saw the empty cart.

"Why do you not come in? Can you believe you will not be an honored guest in my house?" he asked.

Hekate smiled slowly. "You are a good man, Yasmakh, and I am sure I would be well treated and honored in your house. The question I must ask is whether I would be as free to leave it as I was to enter it."

"Why would you wish to leave? You will want for nothing, ever."

Hekate's smile broadened into a full laugh. "Except for anything to interest me. I have told you that I have grown very fond of traveling, that I am eager to see new places and learn new remedies and to find a healer who will take me as an apprentice. Is there such a healer in your city?"

"We don't have female healers in Quatna," he said, lips pinched a little in distaste. "Women are properly cared for here." He frowned. "You are a fine and beautiful woman, Hekate. I have told you I will put the care of my house and my daughter in your hands. I will even marry you without any dowry or–"

"Thank you, Yasmakh," Hekate cried, clasping his hands and then nearly laughed aloud again at his expression of consternation; clearly the thought of marrying a woman without a dowry, no matter how good and beautiful, was not completely to Yasmakh's taste. Having had her fun, she put him out of his misery by saying sadly, "But I must refuse your most generous offer."

A flash of relief, then indignation. "Refuse? Why?"

Hekate sighed. "Because I will die of boredom in your house. Besides, I don't wish to be your wife—or any man's wife. I am determined to become a healer. You know I have ability; look at Yasmina running about."

Unease marked Yasmakh's expression when Hekate reminded him of her 'abilities' and Yasmina's cure. Nonetheless, he cleared his throat and said, "Ridiculous. Why should you be barely above a servant, needing to obey anyone's call, when you could be mistress of a fine house?" He put his hand on her arm and Kabeiros growled. Yasmakh looked down. "He doesn't like me. And a city is no place for a dog of his size. You will have to be rid of him."

For one instant Hekate froze. Then she leaned closer to Yasmakh, her body rigid with threat. "I will never be rid of Kabeiros," she hissed. "I would far sooner be rid of you. And I can be!" Yasmakh let go of her arm and stepped back, staring. She straightened and smiled meaningfully. "Don't take it as a personal failing. Kabeiros doesn't like any man who thinks he has a claim on me. You have none, Yasmakh."

"Not true." Stubbornly he would not yield to a woman, even though his voice was somewhat tremulous. "You saved my daughter's life," he protested. "Now I owe a life to you. I can't allow you to travel on alone."

"I had no intention of traveling on alone," Hekate said, brows raised. "I will find another caravan and offer myself as a healer, Kabeiros as a guard and hunter. And for assurances of my skill and honesty and his ability, since I wear your badge, I intended to give your name." She met his eyes. "Will you deny me a few words of praise? Is this the thanks I get for healing Yasmina?"

"It is for your own good!" he exclaimed. "It is not safe or reasonable for a woman to desire to live alone without the support and guidance of a man."

Hekate shook her head. "I will not stay with you, even if you give me the reputation of a thief and murderess. I will simply go on alone with Kabeiros . . . and hope your lies choke you." Yasmakh stiffened and put a hand to his throat, his eyes wide. Hekate smiled again. "You don't really want me here any more, Yasmakh. You suspect all kinds of things about me, but I saved your daughter and you will never be able to say them." She nodded as he touched his throat again. "Let me go, and I will bless your name."

"Very well, very well," he agreed. "I know a good, honest caravan master who is headed toward Hamath. Will that suit you?"

"That will suit me perfectly, Yasmakh. I will wait here, by your gate, until you are ready to take me to the caravanserai and introduce me to the caravan master."

CHAPTER 11

Fifteen—or perhaps it was seventeen—caravans later Hekate walked wearily beside her pack ass in the string of animals as they moved steadily toward the river. Her glance took in the busy traffic. Colchis was a prosperous city and from her present vantage point, very beautiful.

Hekate thought that she, too, had prospered in the nearly two years since she had left Yasmakh. The pack ass had been purchased with fees she had earned and gifts from grateful patients. She could have purchased a riding ass as well as the pack animal, but she could not bring herself to ride when Kabeiros had to walk every foot of the way. And the distance from him when she was mounted, the inability to touch him, had an unsettling effect on her. From the back of an ass, she saw the man too clearly. She needed to touch the dog to remind herself of what was real, what unreal, no matter that her heart cried for it.

She put her hand on the dog's head. Now they were in Colchis. Perhaps she would find someone who knew how to untangle strands of magic trapped in a Gift—but she didn't dare think much about that tantalizing prospect until she discovered whether the Gifted were regarded with the same toleration that use of magic was.

The pack ass's head was hanging. It was tired, poor beast, and had a right to be. It was just as well that she hadn't bought a saddle ass; she couldn't have done much riding in the past three moons anyway. She shuddered slightly as she recalled that trek, in turn freezing and burning desert and nearly perpendicular mountains cut by madly rushing, unfordable rivers. No more comfortable caravanserais; no more busy markets by the city gates where she could lay out her herbs and packets of remedies.

Almost all of her profits had come from the cities—Aleppo, where she had to wait a full moon for a caravan master she could trust and Kanish and Satala where she had spent the winters. No one in the meager villages they had stopped at to find shelter since leaving Satala could pay in metal for her cures—and many needed them.

Most could barely afford the food they offered her. But in one place she had been given small rugs of unusual softness and exquisite design. Those were offered by the weaving community as a whole for a remedy she had devised for the swollen, aching finger joints engendered by their work. The salve was purely herbal, as she assured the village wisewoman who asked if the spell would need to be renewed, and she told her how to prepare it—if she could find the ingredients. But the question about magic had not been fearful, and the farther north they traveled, the more acceptable magic became.

In another place, she had been asked by the priest of the village if she had any healing spells and had exchanged one for a spell that could hold people and animals frozen in a moment of time. The priest warned her that the spell never lasted long. He thought the life-force of those it was cast upon negated the spell. Judging from how she read him and that Kabeiros could hardly smell his magic, Hekate thought the priest simply didn't have enough power to cast the spell properly. She was more concerned about the length of the spell itself than how long it would last. The invocation was so lengthy, she was sure the intended victim would have time to walk away or even to attack the spell-caster.

More interesting even than the spell was the fact that she had no reluctance at all to teach the priest her spell to stop bleeding and no reluctance–even an eagerness–to learn the new spell. When she considered casting it to see how long it would take and whether she could make it work, she again felt her body stiffen, her throat close with fear.

That was ridiculous! She had just learned the spell from the village priest. He used magic all the time–he had told her so, and the villagers clearly regarded magic as a useful tool, not something to be feared or hated. Moreover the priest had said nothing about magic being reserved for those consecrated to a god. Yet within her was a frantic warning that giving her the spell was a trap, that if she tried to use it, she would be caught and punished severely.

Once they were out of the village, Hekate had fought down her ridiculous fear and attempted to use the spell on a rabbit she spotted in a field, holding Kabeiros back from his normal instinct to chase. As she expected, the rabbit hopped off out of sight before she had finished the lengthy invocation.

Useless, she had said to Kabeiros. *Even with much practice, there is a limit to how fast words can be spoken without slurring one into another. Too bad. If it were less unwieldy, that spell could be of value. If I had stopped that rabbit, you could have walked over and taken it at your leisure.*

Don't you dare! Kabeiros had responded. *You will deprive me of half the pleasure this life affords, and atop that make me feel like a murderer. It's one thing to pit the prey's speed and skill at dodging and hiding against my ability as a hunter. It's another to kill a poor paralyzed beast. I'd have to be very weak, sick, and hungry to be willing to take an animal in that condition.*

So the useless spell had been stored away in Hekate's capacious memory. She never forgot a spell no matter how worthless it seemed or how long it had gone unused. The spells must be intact and perfect because . . .

Hekate never got beyond that because. She remembered noticing that at the time she told Kabeiros the spell was useless, remembered resolving to think about why it was necessary to remember so many spells . . . but she had never done so. At that moment Kabeiros had shot away from the caravan and around the patch of brush in which Hekate had seen the rabbit disappear. The thought had slipped away while she waited for the dog to bring back his prey and never returned until just now.

Her brow furrowed. Why now? Why was she thinking of spells and magic while she was watching the movement of boats in the river? And then she stared more fixedly. It was a perfectly calm day. No breeze stirred the leaves of the trees along the road and most of the boats in the river were being propelled by oars. One ship, black and slender with a pointed prow painted with huge, staring eyes and a high stern, was speeding up the center of the river, against the current, its large sail bowed forward as if it were filled with a strong wind. Behind the sail, in the stern of the boat, Hekate could make out a man pointing a staff at the sail. She drew in her breath, her hand stroking her own staff. Kabeiros suddenly pressed against her and butted his head into her hand.

You are looking at the ship, too, aren't you? That's strong magic . . . But Hekate, I don't smell it. The mental voice sounded uncertain, shocked. *I don't sense any magic at all!*

Neither do I, Hekate admitted, her heart pounding in her throat.

Be careful, the hound warned. *Be very careful. I thought at first that no one would fault you for using magic here. I saw people openly hawking spells along the road as we passed—*

Yes, but I thought they were worthless because I couldn't feel them.

And I agreed with you because I couldn't smell them. But it seems, instead, that their magic is invisible to us.

There was a long pause, empty of mind touch. Man and dog had both withdrawn, blind eyes turned toward the river. Hekate watched too, fascinated, as the man in the stern of the ship lowered his staff. The sail sagged, sagged more. The staff tip touched the deck. The ship's forward motion slowed. Oars were lowered into the water. The helmsman, half hidden by the man with the staff, moved his arms. The ship turned toward the dock. Wet oars flashed in the sunlight according to some pattern the helmsman or the man with the staff decreed, and the ship was maneuvered toward the docks bordering Colchis.

I wonder— Kabeiros' mind voice continued *—if our magic is invisible to them? And if they cannot sense it, will they think that what is merely magic is a Gift?*

Do you think that would be dangerous? That here, too, the Gifted are not welcome?

Hekate could feel the dog's shoulder rise and fall against her thigh. *I hope not. If being Gifted is forbidden here, we have come a long way for no purpose.*

Unless someone has a draining spell I could use against my father.

Even as she said it, Hekate knew she was not ready yet to confront Perses, even if she had a draining spell. But that didn't matter. She would remember the spell perfectly because . . .

They were at the river. Now she would need to make her farewells to the caravan master. And, indeed, she could see him making his way along the line of pack animals, counting off nine, unhooking the lead rein of the tenth, and summoning a groom who came running to take the lead.

Meanwhile the head groom was leading the nine animals onto a wooden pier built out into the river. He untied the fourth animal from the first three and his assistant came to hold them while he induced the three he led onto a broad gangway connected to a large, flat-bottomed barge. He fastened the beasts to something on the deck and went back up the gangway to lead down another three. The groom who had taken the lead of the tenth animal, now led it down toward the dock. The barge was being untied from the dock. Several men distributed themselves at the stern and began to push with long poles while two men at the prow pulled on a thick, knotted line that led across the river.

By then the caravan master had reached Hekate. "My agreement with you ends when we cross the river," he said, "but I would gladly extend it. You have been useful–and despite being a woman, no trouble. I don't know what you did to my drovers, but I can tell you they didn't even talk among themselves about having you."

"I think it is more Kabeiros than me," she said, smiling. "You know he warns off any person he feels is unwelcome to me. Since your men fear and respect you too much to consider murdering me, and since they all knew I would never rest until every person that harmed Kabeiros was dead, they left me alone. Of course, I made it plain that I was not seeking any man. And I thank you for your offer, but I must stay in Colchis for some time."

The caravan master frowned. "I hope you know what you do. This is a very strange place. The goods I find here are so rare and precious, it is worth my risk to come, but I would not stay here for long."

Hekate shrugged. "I hope to find a master who will teach me magic that I don't know. And to tell you the truth—" she grinned at him "—I cannot think of anything that would induce me to go back over the mountains and deserts we have passed. If I must leave Colchis . . . I will take passage on a ship."

The caravan master stared at her, eyes round with horror. "But that is ten times more dangerous than the deserts or the mountains," he protested, shuddering. "You dislike the wastes and the heights so you will trust yourself to a few frail boards floating on a heaving ocean?"

"Ships are not so frail, or many traders would have no goods to carry over land." Hekate laughed. "Anyway, that is moons or even years in the future. For now, I must see if I can find a master."

"Well, if you will not listen to reason, will you at least take my advice about the city?"

"Indeed I will, and with gratitude," Hekate said.

"Very well." The caravan master sighed. "You had better come on the last barge with me. When we come off the barge, we will start toward the palace on Merchants Road, but do not tie your beast to the others. You will go only a short way with us. We will pass a large market that is bordered on its north side with a broad, paved road. I will point it out to you. That is Market Road. You will turn left onto that road and follow it a fairly long way until you come to a five-way crossroad all of paved roads. Do not go straight ahead as that is the Royal Way and is reserved for visitors to the palace and for the great nobles who live around the palace. The crossroad that is *not* the Royal Way–it is not so grand as the Royal Way, but very smooth and clean–is Sorcerers Road. I would suggest to you that you turn left into Sorcerers Road and walk down until you find an inn in which you can be comfortable."

"Why not turn right? Is that also noble territory?"

"Almost." The caravan master grimaced. "To the right are the sorcerers and magicians who are richest and most closely allied to the palace. I doubt you'll find a lodging or a teacher you can afford on that part of the road. Also, you should make sure you understand what is accepted, welcomed, or forbidden before you deal with those."

"Do you know of anyone I can go to for advice about magical matters?"

He pursed his lips. "I wouldn't say I *know* any of these people or trust them either, but I've dealt with an old man called Yehoraz. I use him to make sure the goods I buy are not enhanced by magic–or if they are that the magic will last, not fade and leave me with dross. He's a sullen sort, but I can't complain that he didn't do his work. I've had no complaints about the goods I sold."

"And are you willing to tell me where to find this man?"

"Why not?" He shrugged. "Everyone likes to be recommended by his customers, and Yehoraz sells his services just as I sell my goods. He may not be willing to deal with you if he thinks you'll be a rival, but that's between you and him. So, when you come to Sorcerers Road and turn left, you walk almost down to the docks. There are many inns by the docks and they're cheap, but I wouldn't lodge there. The nobles' bodyguards come down there to protect their masters' goods and they're a rough, arrogant lot. Kabeiros is a fine dog, but he wouldn't last long against ten soldiers."

"You may be sure I'll stay away from those docks," Hekate said. "I've no reason to go there. What of other places on the Sorcerers Road? Would they be safe?"

The caravan master shrugged. "I've never lodged there, but I don't think the sorcerers would favor the nobles' guards assaulting their clients so it should be safe. The trouble is that Yehoraz lives on the street I mentioned, Porters Way, and the porters and guards take that road to the Royal Way. Yehoraz's house is about midway up that street so you'll have to use it."

"I think I could manage not to be noticed going to Yehoraz's house, but for lodging?"

After thinking a moment and making a dissatisfied moue, he said, "It wouldn't be practical for you to lodge in the Merchant's Quarter. It's not far from Sorcerers Road as the crow flies, but the palace is in between and you can't cross the palace grounds or travel on the Royal Way." He snorted gently. "You should be able to find a place on Sorcerers Road north of the Porters Way. That should bc safe."

All the while they were speaking, they had been moving closer to the pier. The barge had crossed once, returned, and taken a second load. It was midway back on its second trip, and the caravan master left Hekate to attend to the order in which the last two batches of animals would go.

While she waited for her turn to cross the river, Hekate looked about and saw that the city, or at least the commercial part of it, was spilling over onto the south bank of the river. There were mostly large docks for the barge-ferries and large, rather flimsy buildings meant to store goods that only needed a little protection from the weather. She noticed that guards lounged around the buildings, but only a few. Were there no thieves in Colchis, she wondered?

Behind and around the warehouses there were a few hovels. Maybe they were only shelter for the guards, but they might also be the lodgings of the poorest. One way to keep them out of sight. She glanced across the river. The city was *very* beautiful. She could see bands and squares of greenery, not mere gardens but large enough to be parks. And the palace . . . she couldn't make out any details from this distance, but the facades glittered reflections of the sunlight, evidence of highly polished stone or metal. Then she remembered what the caravan master had said about the nobles' guardsmen and looked again at the hovels behind the warehouses. It was also a good way for the powerless to be out of easy reach of those more powerful.

A grating sound drew her attention. The barge was being pulled close to the pier and the gangway was soon fixed into an opening in the rail that surrounded the deck. The caravan master led his animals onto the barge. Hekate with Kabeiros were the last on board. The barge was poled/pulled away from the pier, and Hekate's ass brayed pitifully as the deck moved under its feet. She went to soothe the animal and then shook her head slightly and left it to approach the caravan master.

"I have just bethought me," she said, "that if I stay

in Colchis, and take a ship when I leave, I'll have no use for the ass and it will be expensive to keep in a city. You work your string of asses hard, but you feed them well and aren't cruel. She's a good animal. Will you buy her?"

"Yes, certainly—well, depending on the price."

They haggled for a while as the barge drew closer to the opposite shore. The poles had been abandoned as the river grew too deep, and all five men now pulled at the knotted line, singing some kind of rhythmic chant. Hekate felt no magic, but she couldn't help wondering if that chant did more than keep the men pulling at the same time.

When she and the caravan master reached agreement, Hekate had lost little on her original purchase price. She thought it fair enough, a low rental fee for the months she had used the animal. Having what he thought was a good price for an animal he knew to be in top condition, the caravan master was in a mood to be generous.

"You will need the ass to get your herbs and other things to your lodging," he said and proceeded to tell her how to get from Sorcerers Road to the quarter where the merchants lodged, warning her to go the long way down Market Road and up Merchants Road rather than try to cut the distance by going on the Royal Way. Then he nodded decisively. "It's just as well that you should know where to find me. I will be in Colchis for at least a moon. If anything happens to make you change your mind about staying here—and if you come to your senses about taking a ship—I will be glad to take you back to Satala."

"I thank you," Hekate said with sincere gratitude.

She was glad, however, when the barge bumped against the pier and she was able to go back to Kabeiros and the ass without more arguments about returning to Satala. She had nothing against Satala; the fields and hills surrounding the town had been very rich in valuable herbs and there had even been a small forest where she had found a wide variety of fungi. The people had treated her well and had paid her fairly for her medicines.

Nonetheless she could tell that if she were a permanent resident she would soon be in trouble. Curious questions were asked about her reluctance to allow a matchmaker to bring men to court her. Suspicious glances were cast at Kabeiros when it became plain that he lived in the house with her rather than being relegated to the outside yard. Worst of all the town was so small that every person in it soon knew her or of her and no doubt had opinions about her.

She knew already that Colchis would be different. It must be ten times the size of Satala. As she looked up the long street called Merchants Road she saw houses with openings, not only doors but windows, facing on the street. That was very strange. In Ur-Kabos and every other town large enough to have houses rather than huts, the walls facing the streets were blank, broken only by a passage that led to the door. All windows faced an inner court, partly to keep out the direct rays of the sun and partly to ensure that no one would see the women at work . . .

Women! There were women leaning out of several of the windows and gesturing at men leading asses up the road. Ah! That kind of women. So whoring was not forbidden by the authorities of the city. The thought of authority drew her attention to the dock, and her eyes widened again. It was of stone. This was a *very* rich city . . . or some way of doing very difficult work without hundreds or thousands of men had been employed. Magic?

Dismissing that question from her mind—she

would learn the answer soon enough—Hekate watched the caravan master dealing with what was obviously an official and his scribe. She saw him gesture toward the group, and then to her dismay he beckoned to her. Reluctantly, but without any hesitation that would betray the reluctance, she went forward, telling Kabeiros to stay with the ass. She had hoped not to be singled out in any way and did not need the additional notoriety of an unusually large and handsome dog with weird eyes.

"The men will lodge with me in the Merchant's Quarter," the caravan master was saying in trade tongue as she drew near, "and they'll leave with me. This lady is a healer, who has come to study with your magic workers. Probably she'll stay in Colchis if she can find a teacher she likes."

To Hekate's intense surprise, the man only nodded at her and the scribe said, also in trade tongue, "If you stay more than three moons, you must pay the same head tax as any other resident in the city. If you buy a house, the tax collector will remind you. If you stay in lodgings, your landlord will tell you where to pay or will collect the money himself."

"I understand," Hekate said.

"Good luck in finding a teacher," the official said.

"Thank you."

Hekate bobbed her head in a sort of bow that wasn't really a bow and backed away toward Kabeiros and the ass. She was tempted to ask whether there was a list of sorcerers kept somewhere, but she didn't want to draw more attention to herself and she thought there probably wasn't or one of the efficient men would have mentioned it.

After that pleasant surprise, there were more. Having shown her Market Road and reminded her of the directions to the Merchant's Quarter, the caravan master left her with no more than a pleasant farewell. As she walked along it, Hekate noted that the market was very busy but also orderly and that men–and women–with large badges stood at the opening of each aisle to the road. No one gave her more than a single curious glance as she walked along, so Hekate stopped and in trade tongue asked one of the badged women how one obtained a space in the market. The chief warden, she was told, would arrange space for a fee. Hekate thanked her but did not ask about the fee. It was more important to find a place to stay than to arrange selling space in the market.

Lodging turned out to be easier than she had expected also. Mindful of the caravan master's warning, Hekate began to look for a place as soon as she turned onto Sorcerers Road. She was surprised again by the number of inns along the street and by the great variety of costumes she saw on the passersby. She barely stopped herself from staring rudely when a very small, slender woman with hair blacker than Hekate's own and golden skin, wearing a shimmering silk short coat and long straight pants walked by her.

As she glanced quickly at a man with truly black skin and hair like the wool of a sheep but a face of remarkable beauty, it occurred to her that if Colchis was a center for magic, people might come from far and wide. An exciting thought. Who would be more attracted to a city of sorcerers than other sorcerers? There was a chance to learn not only the "invisible" magic of Colchis but that of other lands.

Even if that didn't turn out to be the case, being surrounded by so many strange types was a most comfortable notion. She certainly wouldn't stand out. At worst she would be a stranger among strangers. Hekate again turned her attention to the inns along the street. The first had elaborate carvings around the door, an awning outside, and a carpet in the doorway. The windows on the second floor—no women hung out of those—were bordered by wooden shutters carved with trees that had fretted holes among the leaves and branches to admit air. Costly work. That inn was far too elegant for her purse, Hekate thought, and went on down the road.

Both houses and inns grew less imposing as she went southwest and she saw a few that might suit her, but the sun was still well up and she decided to look at everything before she made a choice. So she walked along until she saw something like a slow-moving maelstrom in the street which, as she drew closer, resolved itself into the meeting of Sorcerers Road and Porters Way.

Hekate drew back against the wall of a building to watch and saw that there were indeed armed men accompanying laden asses and porters and that the armed men pushed their way roughly past those already on the street, occasionally striking out at them. She grimaced and turned back, dismissing the last inn she had passed as too close to what might well become trouble.

About two hundred paces back along Sorcerers Road were two inns on opposites sides. One sat at the corner of an alleyway and the other was set behind a paved court that gave evidence animals were kept there. A fenced-off path, swept clean, led to the door Hekate entered, but she had not even got to ask the price when the landlord shouted at her to take Kabeiros outside. Animals were not welcome, nor asses in the stable, which was reserved for riding horses and mules.

I could stay outside, Kabeiros offered, sensing that Hekate had been impressed by the orderliness of the place.

So could I, Hekate snapped, walking out without a backward glance, *and so I will if I must.*

The inn on the other side of the road was marked on the door with a strange black figure, which Hekate finally decided was a black genie coming out of a bottle. The greeting she received from a portly woman seated between a tall rack of cups, mugs, and tankards was only slightly more welcoming. Soon as she entered, the woman asked if she were alone. Hekate's lips tightened, thinking a woman traveling alone wouldn't be welcome, but the woman added, "I've only the one small room left. It wouldn't be big enough for a couple, but for one person it would do."

"It must hold my dog also," Hekate said, gesturing to Kabeiros, who was pressed against her side. "He's valuable and I wouldn't like to leave him outside at night. Most days I'll be out myself, and Kabeiros with me."

The woman frowned and, when she saw Kabeiros' white eyes, sighed, believing he was Hekate's familiar. "He won't mess the place? I keep a clean house and a dog's soil *stinks*."

"Of course not!" Hekate responded indignantly, shuddering inwardly at the thought of how such talk must hurt Kabeiros.

"You'll clean it up if he does," the woman said in a threatening tone.

"I'll *eat it* if he does," Hekate snapped angrily, and then saw that Kabeiros was laughing and began to laugh too.

The woman grinned in response. "I guess it's safe," she said. "Then he's welcome. He's quiet. Better than those yapping and yowling lap things some witches cart around with them. For one night?"

Hekate realized it would be useless to deny she was a witch and said only, "Well, for the first night, but then if I liked the place and the price I would be staying longer. If the price were right, I might stay for several moons. I'm an herb-wife and I'm looking for a teacher of magic so I can call myself a full healer."

"You'd better look at the room before we begin to haggle price." The innkeeper–her remark about talking price identified her–looked toward a door in the back wall beyond the tun and shouted, "Rakefet, front."

No one came through the door immediately, but the inkeeper rose from her seat between the tun and the rack of drinking vessels. Now Hekate noticed behind and to the left was a large fireplace. Well worn but clean tables with long benches down the sides and stools at the ends filled the room that went back to where high windows let in light from the alley.

The Rakefet summoned hadn't appeared, but the innkeeper led Hekate toward a rough stair against the wall. The stairs creaked loudly but felt solid. As they went up, Hekate hid a grin. There would be little likelihood of either getting into one's chamber or out of it without the innkeeper's knowledge. Considering the woman's size and the corded muscles of her forearms, which were not padded with fat, Hekate doubted she missed any payments.

The room was at the very end of the corridor, the door facing the stair, and small was a miracle of understatement. Hekate wondered if the end of the passage had simply been walled off to provide another rentable space. A bed fitted from one wall to another on one side. A narrow window broke the wall right next to the headboard. On the other side of the window was a very small table on which stood a basin and pitcher. Under the bed was a chamberpot.

Hekate eyed the space between the table that supported the basin and pitcher and the wall. Perhaps there would be room for her herbs. Perhaps she could (very quietly) slip some pegs into wall cracks to hang other herbs. She looked at the bed. The mattress, though flat, seemed clean, with no spots of blood to imply six-legged indwellers that bit. The blanket, equally thin, also seemed clean.

Will there be room for both of us on the bed, Kabeiros?

The dog stared at the bed, but Hekate felt the eyes of the man upon her, felt a heat in the glance. She turned her head to meet that look, not down where the dog was but above her head height, but the man wasn't there.

Not necessary. The mind voice was blurred, as if dog and man were saying the same thing but with different intonations. *We have the bedrolls. We can spread those on the floor for me.*

Or for me, Hekate said. *Isn't it the woman who takes the lesser place?*

The man laughed. *Yes, but I think a dog in the bed and a woman on the floor would be too strange if the inkeeper or her servants should look in or need to wake you.* The mind voice was clear again.

"There isn't that much to see," the innkeeper said a little impatiently. "Will you take it or not?"

"I was trying to decide whether I could get all my herbs into the room," Hekate said. "I've got a loaded ass outside."

"I like animals," the woman said, grinning, "but no asses in the rooms. They aren't housebroken."

Hekate liked this woman. She laughed. "How much?"

"Three shekels of copper."

That price was so high that Hekate didn't even make a counteroffer. Disappointed in her poor judgement, she simply turned and walked out. The innkeeper followed her.

"Wait," she said. "If you only stay the one night and someone else wanted the room for a ten-day, I'd be out the whole ten-day. I wouldn't have charged you that for more than one night."

Hekate smiled. "Then I'll forgo the one-night trial. How about one shekel of copper for the whole ten-day?"

"All right, all right, I'm sorry I insulted you, but there's no need to insult the room."

"What room?" Hekate asked. "If you put a bed and a table in a closet, it's still a closet."

"Closets don't have windows," the innkeeper said firmly. "Three shekels of copper for the ten-day, but I'll throw in sheets for the bed, a towel, and even a bit of soap."

"I don't need the towel or the soap," Hekate countered. "I have my own. I'll show you the soap. Maybe you'll want to buy it for yourself. Two shekels."

"I'll look at your soap. Maybe I will buy it. Two and a half. And my name is Batshira. There's a stable around the back for the ass. It's not included in the price. You have to pay for feed–"

"You can call me Hekate. The ass is sold. She'll only be here for one night. I deliver her to the Merchant's Quarter tomorrow. Two shekels of soap for the feed."

"Done." As they went down the stair, the woman said, "I set a decent table. Most of the folk who rent rooms eat here also."

"You have the same kind of arrangement for trying the food? More for one meal than one pays for a ten-day of eating?"

The woman laughed, and the sound was echoed on a higher pitch by the girl who now sat between the rack of drinking vessels and the tun of beer. "Tried that on you, did she? No, I serve the meals and take the money. You'll pay the same as anyone else who sleeps here."

"No smart talk, Rakefet," Batshira said. "Go out and help this lady unload her ass and stable it or she'll be too late to eat altogether."

Two pair of hands for the unloading made a difference, but Hekate wished she had told Kabeiros not to help when she saw how Rakefet stared at him as he seized several bundles in his jaw and carried them up the stairs.

Don't be too clever, Hekate warned him, but it seemed his cleverness was not what attracted Rakefet's attention.

"How beautiful he is," she sighed to Hekate. "If only it were a bitch and I could have a puppy. We need a dog like him in the inn–we had two, but when . . ." She stopped abruptly and picked up two armfuls of the herb packages. "Oh, how nice they smell," she said, and went in and up the stairs.

Hekate looked after her thoughtfully. Possibly it wasn't because Batshira and Rakefet thought Kabeiros was a familiar that they looked at him so intently. When Kabeiros returned she said, *I wonder what happened to the two dogs Rakefet mentioned? I wonder if that's why Batshira didn't object when I said I'd keep you inside with me? I wonder if perhaps we aren't far enough from Porters Way. Could some of those armsmen have decided to make merry at the inns and the dogs tried to stop them?*

A good reason for keeping me in at night, Kabeiros agreed. *I'd have a better chance against them where I could get under tables.* He took another batch of small sacks and went in.

Although the idea made Hekate uncomfortable, there was no incursion of guards up Sorcerers Road that night. In fact it became very quiet after sunset. The dinner was good, plain, and not seasoned so highly that Hekate felt as if her throat and stomach would burst into flame. Although she pointed out the table where the long-term residents sat and said they were pleasant people, Batshira didn't urge Hekate to join them. She just nodded when Hekate said she was tired and would prefer to meet them one by one at breakfast time or later. Batshira shrugged. It wasn't required that they all sit together, she remarked.

Hekate thanked her and went up to her room as soon as she finished her meal. Kabeiros had eaten exactly the same food for which Hekate had paid a guest's price even though Rakefet offered to feed him free on scraps in the kitchen.

"I can't take the chance that it's tidbit-passion that keeps him with me," she said, hoping to divert Rakefet from the notion that Kabeiros was a familiar. "We go along together as friends and companions, not mistress and slave. He has to remember that."

She wasn't sure she had convinced Rakefet, but she found she didn't care much. Being a familiar was about equally more safe and more dangerous. No one would try to steal a familiar; on the other hand a fanatic might try to kill one. Still, Batshira and Rakefet seemed more interested than frightened and what Batshira had said implied that they were accustomed to witches' familiars.

In any case, they were safe once the door to their room was closed–at least from too great curiosity. Kabeiros sneezed and Hekate followed him a moment later. The odor of the herbs confined in that small space was overpowering. Hekate rushed–all of two steps–to open the window. Both had sneezed again, but in moments opening the window displayed an advantage of the tiny room Hekate hadn't thought of. Although the window was small, it let in enough air to cool the whole space very comfortably. And the scent of herbs diminished quickly until it was merely refreshing.

Sheets had appeared while they were eating. Hekate tucked them over the mattress, aware that they were rather harsh and stiff with recent washing, aware too of the way her arms ached and a great desire to just drop across the bed and close her eyes. She was more exhausted than she had realized, having been supported by excitement. She had to force herself to unroll the bedrolls for Kabeiros and to undress. Then, groaning with weariness she tumbled into bed.

CHAPTER 12

Hekate woke with Kabeiros prodding her with his wet nose. *We have to be more careful,* he said. *The sun rises on the other side of the building and the alley is almost dark until near noon. I think you've missed breaking your fast. I only woke because I heard Rakefet making the bed next door. She wasn't pleased about something the guest had done.*

Hekate stretched and yawned. *I can set a time ward if it's necessary, but I'm just as glad we slept late. We can break our fast in the market, which will give us a chance to roam around in it. The only other thing I have to do is to bring the ass to the caravan master. That will fill what's left of the morning. Somehow I don't feel that sorcerers are early risers, so the afternoon will be the best time to call on Yehoraz. If my guess is wrong, no doubt one of his servants will tell us what time to come tomorrow morning.*

Her guess, however, was accurate enough. Yehoraz was seeing clients when Hekate arrived with Kabeiros. She was pleased to see others in the waiting room of the small house and she examined the people with interest, if surreptitiously. From their modest clothing and quiet manner, she assumed they were merchants and craftsmen and women who needed the kind of commercial sorcery that the caravan master used. From their number, it seemed that Yehoraz was honest and reliable. From the fact that no one stared at Kabeiros, she guessed that Yehoraz had dealings with other workers of magic.

If so and he were willing to make some arrangement with her, it would be a good ending to an excellent day. She had had a profitable morning, richer by five shekels of silver as agreed for the price of the ass. In addition she had secured a place in the market where she could sell her salves and potions.

Contemplating how well everything had gone since she arrived in Colchis made Hekate slightly uneasy, but the feeling was not justified by her meeting with Yehoraz. He was old, but still straight of body and healthy looking, and his scowl relaxed just a trifle when she told him he had been recommended to her by the caravan master.

"To what purpose?" he asked. "I see by your dog that you know magic already."

"Not your kind," Hekate replied honestly, "but magic is not my reason for seeking you out today. I am an herb-wife, a good one. I have rented a place in the market–"

"I know nothing about herbs," Yehoraz interrupted, starting to rise from his chair.

"Nor did I think you did, or I would not have come here. I don't expect assistance from those I might come to rival. What I desire from you is to learn the language of Colchis. Trade tongue will not do for explaining the use and the purpose of some of my salves and potions."

"Ah, you wish me to teach you the language quickly by magic."

"Exactly. Can you do it? Will you do it? And how much will it cost me?"

Yehoraz's scowl relaxed completely. He almost smiled. "The three essential questions and with no extra words. Unfortunately, I cannot be as succinct. I can do it, but it is a long and complex spell and requires that I invade your mind. And the price and whether you are willing to pay comes before whether I am willing. The price is a mina of silver—"

"Sixty shekels!" Hekate exclaimed. "That's high."

Lips twisted, Yehoraz said, "I didn't set that price. It's set by the merchants and crafts guilds and it's set to prevent those like you from flooding into the city and taking away the work and the livelihood of those born in Colchis. I would make a greater profit if I could do the spell for many for a reasonable price instead of asking a ridiculous price and getting one or two clients a year."

Hekate nodded. "And if you don't keep to their price, no member of the guilds will come to you for spells. I see." She frowned. "But who does pay such a price?"

"Ambassadors to the court of Colchis. Occasionally a merchant or trader who is involved in a legal case. Others are content to learn the language slowly and less perfectly, which is what I advise you to do."

He waved at the door, and it opened. Hekate could not detect the smallest feel of magic. Kabeiros sniffed and then lifted his head to look at her. Suddenly an idea came to Hekate; before she could think or the fear of using magic could restrain her, she created a mage light—a large one, bright enough to light up the rather dim room. Yehoraz gasped.

"How did you do that? What is it?"

"Are you unacquainted with mage lights?"

"Magic torches I know, but a light that has nothing to which to cling?" He gasped again as Hekate elevated the light and took away her hand. "It will stay where you place it? For how long?"

"That depends on the power with which you invest it," Hekate replied. "If you can connect it to some source of power or contrive some other way to feed it, yes. It will stay wherever you will it to stay, or follow you about, and stay bright as long as it has power."

"But . . . but I felt no power when you lit it," Yehoraz whispered.

"And I felt none when you opened the door."

On the words, Yehoraz gestured again and the door closed. "I hope no one heard us," he said.

"Why? This is the house of a sorcerer. Surely the casting of spells is a common thing?"

"Common enough, but the mage light isn't common here, it's unknown. And magic that can't be detected . . ." His eyes were large, avid.

Hekate shook her head. "I wish I could use that for barter, but I haven't the faintest idea why you don't sense my magic or I yours." Hekate wished she did know. When she left Colchis it would be good to be able to do a kind of magic no one could sense. She didn't mention that to Yehoraz, though, only said, "That's too deep a mystery for me, I fear. Let's start with simpler things. I will teach you the spell for the mage light. If you can use your own power to cast it and it works with your magic, we will have a better basis to talk."

"Not now," Yehoraz said uneasily. "This is my time for clients and visitors. Tell me where your house is, and I will come to you."

"I have no house. I am in the Inn of the Black

Genie and I'm not sure the innkeeper would be pleased if we were casting spells in her parlor."

"No, that wouldn't do. We'll have to use my workroom. Unless I . . . No, the workroom will be best. Can you return here after dark?"

"I'm not too eager to be abroad after dark."

"You have no warding spells?"

Hekate found she couldn't admit she didn't like to use magic. Yehoraz might well not believe her, since she had just done so. "If no one can feel the wards, would they protect me?" she asked. "One man or two I don't fear. Kabeiros could drive them away, but if a troop of armsmen is looking for pleasure . . ."

"I'll send a servant for you." A calculating look lit his eyes. "Can you put a mage light into his hand or set it over his head?"

Hekate giggled. "So anyone in the street will see that your servant has something new and wonderful? Yes, I can do it, but that will take a shekel off the mina I will owe you if you give me the language of Colchis."

To her surprise, the lines of habitual discontent on Yehoraz's face relaxed and he laughed heartily. "I will need to be careful," he said, "or I will end up owing you metal for bespelling you into knowing our language."

Hekate laughed too as she left, but the way home was not as uneventful as the walk to Yehoraz's house. Almost at the meeting of Porters Way with Sorcerers Road, one of the guards passing with a small train of pack asses reached out to seize Hekate where she stood flattened against a building to be well out of the way. She twisted away, before his hand could close and Kabeiros came in front of her snarling. The guard reached for his sword, but another man pulled him away to keep up with the pack asses, telling him as they walked not to be a fool; killing a dog that size was no small piece of work and would probably involve all the men. The woman would resist him even more if he killed her dog and scream her head off. He would be unable to take her with him, and he would be reported if he left the train. Worst of all, the pack train would be opened by the confusion to attack by thieves.

They were gone up the road before the reasons to leave her alone ran out, but Hekate resolved no matter how uneasy it made her feel that she would use the look-by-me spell as soon as there was no one to see her cast it. Which made her wonder suddenly why she had agreed to return to Yehoraz's house? Why did he want her at night when she would be alone with him and his servants, when there were no other clients to hear if she made a disturbance?

She didn't know whether the spell would cover Kabeiros, but she put her hand on his shoulder and, swallowing her fear and reluctance, found a deep doorway and cast the spell. She could feel a vein in the earth flicker in response to her draw; she could feel her magic as it took hold; and she could tell when they passed two porters with one guard and a bit farther along another train of pack asses, that the spell was working. She left it in effect as she walked up Sorcerers Road, only dismissing it as they stepped under the lintel of the Black Genie.

Over her evening meal, which she again took in a private corner, Hekate puzzled not so much over the important and incomprehensible absence of the "sense" of power in the magic done by Colchis' sorcerers but over Yehoraz's peculiar reactions. It was not unreasonable that he should be pleased when she told him a past client had recommended him, and his eagerness to learn a showy and harmless spell like that for the mage light and how to perform magic with undetectable power were both completely normal behavior. But why couldn't she teach him the spell then and there? It wasn't difficult. And why had he laughed and joked when she demanded a price for her spell in contradiction to his previously dour manner? She had thought he would be angry. It was strange but she liked him . . .

What did you think of Yehoraz? she asked Kabeiros.

I liked him. A good man. A sad, lonely man.

Lonely? He has clients enough and servants.

But no friends. I suspect the clients are afraid of him and too subservient. I guess because of what the caravan master said about the sorcerers to the northeast of the Royal Way, that they either scorn Yehoraz for taking common folk as his clients or that he was . . . ah . . . expelled from their group for something of which they disapproved.

You don't think he has any nefarious purpose in asking me to come back at night?

He was uneasy about working on the mage-light spell in his own house . . . You remember, he wanted to work in your house. There was a pause while the dog licked his nose contemplatively. *I wonder if he was thought to be too . . . daring . . . in the spells he tried.*

But toward me. It was most peculiar the way he laughed when he should have been angry over my demanding a shekel of silver for the spell.

The dog lolled out his tongue. *Spells don't take on me. If you look strange or act strange, there's going to be a very bloody, very frightened sorcerer until you are back to normal. But I don't think he means harm. I think you put him at ease by showing you were his equal, at least in some things, and still being willing to share. With a court so close, I would guess the sorcerers are very jealous of each other, that they try to steal from one another and are punished for violating any strict protocol–*

"Are you talking to the dog?" Rakefet asked in an undertone, setting down a second beer, which Hekate had not ordered. "Batshira says you aren't to do any spells in the house. Like you or not, that's forbidden."

"No spells," Hekate assured her, smiling, although she didn't deny she was talking to Kabeiros. "I went to see if Yehoraz would teach me Colchis speech, but he asked such a price that I doubt I can afford his spell."

"That's the merchant and craft guilds," Rakefet said with a grimace. "They don't want a lot of foreigners with strange ways–and maybe better products–able to talk and teach. As long as a foreigner can't talk right, he's marked for what he is. Innkeepers'd like the spell more common. It'd mean more visitors, but . . ." She shrugged. "Will you be late coming back? Someone will have to let you in."

"I don't know," Hekate admitted, "but I should be back before the drinking is finished. You won't have to wait up for me."

Rakefet's innocent confirmation of the reason for Yehoraz's price added to Kabeiros' good opinion of the man and soothed Hekate's doubts. By the time she finished her dinner, Yehoraz's servant was waiting. As soon as she came out, Hekate made a large, bright mage light and set it over the servant's head. He kept looking up at it nervously, and Hekate assured him, swallowing a grin, that it would not fall on him and burn him. She moved it once, to dart threateningly at a group of armsmen coming down the street toward them. The men backed off, wide-eyed, and the mage light obediently returned to hang over the servant's head.

When they came to the house, the servant said, "Please, my master will wish to see this."

Hekate obligingly left the light following the servant. Yehoraz came down from his consulting room and gaped at the light, moving wherever the servant went.

"She can make it move anywhere," the servant said, sounding a trifle breathless. "She made it jump at a bunch of guards, who were making rude remarks. They shut their mouths and stood aside."

"Will you teach me that too?" Yehoraz asked.

"It comes with the spell," Hekate replied.

As she spoke she realized that the spells that attached the mage light to a place or person and for movement didn't really come with the mage-light spell. They were merely used together so often, that they had been sort of curled up together; the separate symbols now blended into one in the mind and the words also blended . . . An excitement began deep in Hekate's gut and spread up to her chest, making her heart pound so that she had to forcibly control her breathing. She fixed the idea in her mind and to cover her excitement, said to Yehoraz, "The spell comes in three parts, but I don't consider one complete without the others, so I will teach you all three."

"For one shekel of silver?"

Hekate couldn't help laughing, "Yes, although I admit that if I had thought of it being three parts before I said I would give it to you for one shekel, I might have asked three."

He smiled at her slowly and his face changed, the hard lines softening and the bright, cold eyes seeming to become a warmer brown. "I will credit you with three shekels gladly . . . if I can learn the spell and make it work." He stared at the mage light and shook his head. "Nothing. I sense nothing at all. I see it is magic. I know it is magic. But I can't feel magic at all, and that's one of my Talents." He gestured for her to follow him. "Come. I'm most eager to try this spell."

As they followed him up to his consulting room and out through a well-concealed door at the back, Hekate said, *Kabeiros?*

He knew what the question meant. *I smell the spell,* the dog replied. "Earth-blood and heat and your special scent.* He was silent while they went down two flights of stairs, the landing between them holding a locked door that Hekate suspected led to a back alley. *They use some other source of power, not the blood of the earth,* he remarked as Yehoraz unlocked a door at the bottom of the second flight.

*I never thought of that," Hekate said. *Oh, Kabeiros, if we can learn what it is . . . I will explain later, but see if you can get any idea of what Yehoraz draws upon when he casts the language spell.*

The door opened. Hekate braced herself to repress the revulsion she had always felt in her father's workroom, but no such sensation assailed her. There was no stench of evil, no contorted forms frozen in stasis to recall their suffering. Shelves held jars of magical substances–Hekate recognized hens' teeth, the shavings of a unicorn's horn, a vial that must be dragon's blood–and there were two skeletons, male and female, one of which animated and came forward.

"Service, master?"

"No, Naor," Yehoraz said. "I will not need you or Nili tonight." He turned to Hekate. "Will we need artifacts for the spell? I think I have–"

"Only a sheet of parchment so I can show you the symbols and write the commands."

He watched her avidly, his eyes widening and his head nodding with familiarity. "I know most of those," he said, "but never put together in that way, and there are terms I have never heard. Will you say them?"

"Of course."

It was so strange to fix her eyes on the symbols for the mage light separate from the mark that would place it where she desired it to be and the two marks that would permit it to move as she willed. The revelation she had had became clearer and a new notion seized her so hard that she almost tripped over the words, saying them one at a time, slowly. In slow response a misty spot formed, brightened, and drew together on her hand. Yehoraz drew in his breath. Hekate held out the light to him, pushed it off her hand onto his. It sat there, glowing. She muttered, "*Thialuo psuz.*" The light went out.

Yehoraz breathed heavily, staring into his hand. His brow was shiny with sweat.

He stinks of fear, Kabeiros said.

Hekate kept her face still, but she laughed in her mind. *I was suspicious of him. I never thought that he might be equally suspicious of me. What if that spell . . . ah . . . did some harm, bound him in some way. But he must know now it is harmless, not even hot in one's hand.*

Not yet, Kabeiros said. *It might be something that seems innocent until he casts it himself. I wonder if he will gather the courage to try?*

Almost before Kabeiros finished his thought, Yehoraz, still sweating, leaned over the table, fixed his gaze on the first symbol and pronounced the spell words. Since he had not extended his hand, the mist of light gathered slowly over the parchment and gradually formed a mage light. Yehoraz stared at it, pushed his hand under it, extended it toward Hekate, who took it into her hand willingly. Yehoraz began to smile, although he was still sweating.

They then went through the other two parts of the spell in the same way. When Yehoraz had a mage light that would hang suspended over Hekate or Kabeiros, without either offering any protest, and move about the room, he breathed a huge sigh of relief.

"Well," he said, finally wiping the sweat from his face, "we have both honored the first part of our bargain." He hesitated, looking at Hekate intently. "You are a strange woman, to part with such a spell so cheaply."

Hekate grinned. "Because among my people it's a cheap spell. Even hedge witches can make a mage light. Oh, if they aren't strong, the light is faint and weak and moves very slowly, but to me the spell is nothing. I have many, many others. Teach me the language of Colchis, and we can more readily discuss what you would like to have as your pay, although I can pay part in true silver. I sold my ass, and I have some earnings from my work as an herb-wife."

"You don't suspect me of evil? What if I cast a spell that makes you my slave or puts you into a trance so I can make you teach me everything you know?"

"You will be dead," Hekate said, smiling sweetly. "I imagine that will release me from whatever you tried to do to me. Kabeiros will watch. He is . . . a little more than a dog. If you try to fasten a hook into my soul, he'll kill you. He can do it before your servants can get here to save you."

"But the servants will kill him!"

"I doubt it," Hekate said, still smiling. "Kabeiros is very hard to kill and I will be recovering quickly once you are dead and your will is gone. And if Kabeiros is hurt–" she hesitated, smiled again "–your servants will be very, very sorry for a very long time."

Yehoraz shook his head. He looked younger now that his lips were no longer drawn thin and down and his eyes were wider open. He looked worried, too.

"It was stupid to say that. I never intended you any harm, mistress, but I was surprised by your seeming trust and wished to warn you. I had not thought of Kabeiros. Most familiars are not so large and strong."

"Kabeiros is not a familiar, not enslaved. You need not hope he will be glad to be released from my will. He *is* free and he has chosen to travel with me and be my protector."

Yehoraz was beginning to sweat again. "This is not an easy spell. Will your dog understand if the spell hurts you that it is necessary?"

"I hope so," Hekate said drily, "because it would do neither of us any good if the spell broke in the middle. I'll tell him the spell will hurt–" she did so.

"Tell him . . ." Yehoraz looked from Hekate to the hound. The blank white eyes met his gaze steadily. He looked away. "As you say. As you say. Well, you should sit down in this chair–" he gestured to the side where a large chair padded with leather cushions stood.

Hekate sat down. Kabeiros walked around until he could see her face clearly and also sat down. Yehoraz took a beaker and some flasks and jars from the shelves. He brought these over to Hekate and showed them to her. At her nod, he poured a drop of this and a bit of that into the empty beaker and mixed it all carefully together. When he was done, he chanted sharply for a few minutes, took the rod with which he had been mixing and marked Hekate's lips, ears, throat, and forehead repeatedly, until the small beaker was empty.

Hekate took a chance and opened her senses as

wide as she ever had. Nothing. Nothing at all . . . or was there the faintest tickle, no, not a tickle, a prickle, like the sensation one felt in an arm or a leg upon which one had slept, but fainter, much, much fainter . . . if it was there at all. Hekate deepened her search, and it was gone.

Now Yehoraz put the rod and the beaker away and began to chant again. Hekate forgot her search for power. Her head began to ache, and *ache,* and ACHE. As the chanting went on, the sensation went far beyond an ache; long, thin skewers were piercing her head. She gripped the arms of the chair, her knuckles whitening. She bit her lips, barely able to keep herself from screaming, but she had experienced this kind of learning before and Kabeiros was standing, growling softly.

She waved at him to sit down again, being unable to use mind talk to reassure him. The chant rose in volume. Yehoraz gestured. Hekate gasped. He gestured again. Her eyes rolled up. She heard Kabeiros snarl and managed to gasp, "No. This must be." Yehoraz came close and touched her lips, her ears, her forehead, her throat, then clapped his hands together. The most piercing pain of all accompanied the sound, dragging a wail from her, and then the agony began to ebb. Hekate blinked and breathed out. Kabeiros sat down beside her again.

Yehoraz wiped sweat from his face. "For a moment there, I thought your dog had lost patience and that I was a dead man."

"He doesn't like to see me suffer, and I think he was a little annoyed because you didn't use a sleep spell. Of course, I wouldn't have . . ." Her voice trailed off and she began to laugh as she realized she had been speaking the language of Colchis in an instinctive response to Yehoraz's remark in that tongue. She rose from the chair, held out her hand. "I'm delighted, even if my head feels as if it will split open any moment."

Yehoraz grinned. "Sorry about that. No one has ever been able to soften the reaction. Have I fulfilled my promise to teach you the language of Colchis?"

"Indeed you have."

"Then you owe me fifty-seven shekels of silver—or several new spells on which we can agree."

"That was the bargain and I hold by it. I will even barter the equivalent of fifty-nine shekels—since that was what I said at first . . . but of your mercy, not tonight. I will come back any time you say . . ."

"Oh, of course." The old man laughed but raised a brow. "You are stronger than anyone I know if you can even think about magic after that spell."

Hekate was not comfortable with that remark or Yehoraz's expression. She sighed. "I can think about it. Whether I could perform it is another thing entirely. Shall I come tomorrow at the same time?"

"If you are recovered and willing, I will be waiting eagerly."

Porters Way and Sorcerers Road were both empty when Hekate and Kabeiros walked home. As they turned from one into the other, they could hear a confused noise farther down toward the docks. As quietly as possible they hurried up Sorcerers Road—Hekate had not tried to cast the look-by-me spell in her present state—and reached the Black Genie without trouble. The inn still had customers in the main room, but Hekate went directly to the stair.

"Got it?" Rakefet called in Cholchis.

Hekate closed her eyes and winced.

"Up to bed with you," Batshira said. "Rakefet will bring your breakfast and let Kabeiros out in the morning if your head still hurts."

Mumbled thanks were accepted with a wave of the

hand, but what Hekate wanted far more than food or rest was to be alone with Kabeiros, who during the whole walk to the inn had been emanating a suppressed excitement. It was that, far more than her headache, that drove her to her room.

What is it? she asked, wincing and putting a hand to her head as overused pathways in her brain responded with a sharp pang to use of mind speech.

Lightning, Kabeiros said. *When Yehoraz cast that spell, I smelled lightning.*

Lightning? Hekate repeated. *I didn't know lightning had a smell. But there was no lightning . . . except in my head.*

Kabeiros whined in frustration. *I'm not sure it *is* a smell, exactly, but when those flashes in the sky come really close–and there's no rain–there is . . . I don't know . . . something in the air. But of course there was no lightning. We were inside in a deep cellar. I think it was the power he was using that I smelled. I don't know how to explain it better, but it was a too-dry smell that should have made my fur stand on end, sharp, prickling–*

Prickling! Hekate exclaimed, and grabbed for her head again.

The gesture was automatic; she was hardly aware of the pain that caused her to make it. She remembered sensing a prickling in the air when Yehoraz began his chanting. Slowly she lay down on the bed, her brow creased. When a soft scratch on the door heralded Rakefet with food, Hekate left the frown in place and closed her eyes. To her relief the girl did not speak, only put the pitcher and basin on the floor and the tray of food on the little table. When she left the room, Hekate sighed softly.

He draws his power from the air? she thought to Kabeiros. *How can that be? The air is . . . too thin, too spread out . . . except when there is lightning.*

We have a hint and I think we have it right. Kabeiros sounded excited. *He didn't use the blood of the earth even when he cast your spell for the mage light. He used his own power–and the spell worked! You will teach him other spells and we will watch him closely when he repeats them. I will smell higher, as if a scent is running in the wind. You should feel 'higher.' Try to ignore the sense of the earth's blood. That's so strong to you that it's shutting out all other sensings.*

CHAPTER 13

It wasn't easy to shut out the sense of the earth's blood, and Hekate was rather frightened of trying. She feared that if she closed off the sense, she wouldn't be able to find the veins of the Mother again. That, at least, turned out to be a vain fear. When the desire to use the "invisible magic" became stronger than her fear, she did try. It was like being deafened, shut in a black room, suspended midair so she lost even the sense of touch. Terror dried her mouth and almost stopped her breathing, but the full sense of the Mother's touch resumed the moment she opened herself.

The experiment having been made, the terror of being shut off from all warmth and power became less and she dared try in Yehoraz's presence. At first the sense of deprivation was too strong for any fainter power to make an impression. However, over the moons that followed while she taught Yehoraz spells, until he said the full price for the language of Colchis was paid, and then bartered spells with him, Hekate began to feel the source from which he drew his strength.

It was, indeed, "higher." Some energy existed far above the clouds where there was a rushing about of she knew not what but it could be tapped. Patient trials made the source clearer; repeated effort showed her the source was not as diffuse as she had believed. There were running streams and eddies and even whirlpools of power that she could draw upon. Then one day when there was a violent thunderstorm, Hekate drew so much power she almost "burned" and had to send what she had received down into the earth. There the power ran at once into one of the veins of the earth. It was all one power, Hekate realized, just drawn in different ways.

That removed the last of her fears about using that power. She had been a trifle concerned that the Mother would be angry, would think her ungrateful and greedy to be seeking more power than she already had. But it was one power, all the Mother's power . . . only Kabeiros assured her that when she drew from the air he could no longer smell her magic, only the faint, acrid sense of lightning.

Although she had come to like and trust Yehoraz, Hekate never used the power of lightning in his presence and continued to assure him she could not feel his magic any more than he could feel hers. This was not completely a lie; all she ever felt was that very, very faint prickling, but now she *saw* the power those of Colchis used, saw the power as swirls and flows of color in the air around her and as sparkles and stabs of light when the power was used.

Had Yehoraz *needed* to use the power of earthblood, Hekate would have tried to teach him how to reach it because she felt she owed him a considerable debt. The need to teach him to make each spell anew so he could use it with his own power had taught *her* how to take apart spells she had used from childhood and for which she had lost the true structure. From that, she learned how to fold together other, greater spells.

The freezing spell, for one, she could now invoke with two gestures and three short words. Now Hekate combined that with a technique her mother had taught her in secret when she was a child, to invest a spell in an inanimate object—an amulet, a precious stone, even a ceramic cup or saucer. Then the spell could be invoked from its container with a single common word, a key. She had delivered healing spells that way when she wanted to hide that she was using magic.

In gratitude, she gave Yehoraz the freezing spell; she invested it in a very pretty piece of clear quartz that looked as if it contained snowflakes. All Yehoraz had to do was to touch the crystal and say the three invoking words. For an unTalented person, that would have been the end of the spell, for the power with which Hekate had invested it would be drained. However Yehoraz was a sorcerer; having frozen and released one of his servants, he attempted to recharge the crystal by feeding it lightning power. To Hekate's delight, the spell worked perfectly a second time. Yehoraz stared at the crystal and then began to weep.

"Dear Mother," Hekate cried, "what have I done wrong? How have I hurt you? You are my friend. I would not harm you for the world!"

"No harm. No harm." The old man patted her shoulder. "But you are ten years too late." He was silent, caressing the stone. Then he said in a rush, "If you had come with this ten years ago, I would still be living in a lavish house two doors down from the palace gate. I angered Medea, for I would not do what she desired, and before I could explain why, she had blasted me. I almost died, and when I recovered, my great spells would not work."

"I am very sorry," Hekate said, lips thinning. This Medea seemed to be another Perses.

"No. No. Those were tears of gratitude. I'm not sorry at all. I was just thinking how merciful are the gods. I would have used this spell if I had it, and perhaps far worse would have befallen me. Because she blasted me, I came here and did small magics for small people. And I became *free*. For the first time since I came from my school, I wasn't afraid. Living near and serving the court was spiritual death. I became hard and cruel. I found myself looking at every other sorcerer who should be my friend, as if I expected to be robbed or killed. No! I would not go back, but the spell will be useful . . . very useful."

"Nonetheless what Medea did was very wrong. Perhaps she needs to be taught a lesson."

"No!" Yehoraz touched Hekate gently. "You may be as strong as she, but you haven't the ruthlessness. You can both do terrible things, but she *would* without a thought, and you would stop to think . . . and be destroyed. Besides, she is the king's daughter and has mundane powers as well as sorcerous ones. Let her be. She didn't mean it, but she made me a happy man. I have more than enough to eat and drink. I have, thanks to you, spells that will make my clients devoted forever. But it would be an infinite asset if I, too, could invest amulets with spells."

Hekate had not intended to part with that secret, but Yehoraz swore that the art would go no further. "I have a woman whose husband beats her. If I could give her an amulet that would make his arms and legs numb every time he began to hit her . . ."

Hekate's silver eyes narrowed; Yehoraz knew she had a weakness. "Very well, I'll show you, but it isn't easy. You can't simply transfer the spells. You must go back to the beginning and do each part of the spell separately."

It wasn't true. Hekate was able to transfer her spells to the inanimate container in their finished form by means of a transport spell she had devised, but she didn't want to make it easy to invest an innocent-seeming object with an evil spell. Not that she suspected Yehoraz of doing that; he was a good man . . . but not a very strong one. She was afraid he would be unable to resist showing off his ability or might be pressured into teaching a less scrupulous sorcerer the skill.

The difficulty Yehoraz had in transferring a spell to an object brought a new advantage to Hekate because he knew that spells fade, no matter how carefully nurtured. Thus, he implemented his work with a very tiny binding spell that sealed the power inside the spell and, incidentally, concealed it. The binding spell was new to Hekate. Yehoraz taught it to her, laughing with delight over having something to give her, aside from his company and his advice.

Needless to say, the ability to create amulets and invest innocent-looking things with magic did wonders for Hekate's business. She had been doing well as an herb-wife because her salves and potions were good in themselves. Now they were doubly effective—a little spell here and there helped immeasurably and being invisible passed any scrutiny by a practicing sorcerer or a priest. Add to that amulets that could easily be disguised as jewelry, say to aid a merchant in testing the quality of goods or the truth-telling of those with whom he dealt, she was growing quite rich.

However, her personal problem remained. Although she used magic constantly now, she was still subject to her fear and distaste for casting spells, and that constant miasma of unease frequently made her miserable. She knew the fear was ridiculous; in Colchis magic was a way of life, so much so that there were laws governing its use and standard fines and punishments for misuse. Reason, however, had no effect on Hekate's anxiety and she grew more dissatisfied than ever with the inner compulsion to avoid magic.

She admitted that on the road to Colchis the reluctance had proved useful. She and Kabeiros between them had found other solutions for problems for which she would ordinarily have thoughtlessly used magic. That restraint had kept her from being noted as a witch and having that reputation passed from caravan to caravan.

Still, in a city in which magic was practiced freely, to need to think about and force herself to cast a spell might become far more dangerous than being known as a spell-caster. Another puzzle was that she felt no anxiety about building new spells or learning new ways to make them quicker and more effective. Also, she loved magic and loved to work with it. In fact, learning and teaching Yehoraz what she knew actually relieved her fear and made her happy.

That thought brought her back to that forever unfinished "because." She could teach and learn spells, which must be kept perfectly in memory because . . . Unconsciously she turned her head to look south, which happened to be at a blank wall. She stared at it unseeingly, a slow-growing horror twisting her lips, her hands clenching on what they held, her throat and mouth drying with fear.

Her mind tried to slip away from that horror, to wonder about a spot on the wall, to think about the bags and bundles of herbs piled against it, but this time there was no interruption to let her mind squirm free. Kabeiros was asleep. The inn was almost silent. Because . . . She gripped the word and the rest of the phrase came to her. Because . . . Because she was supposed to bring the new spells home to Perses.

Whether she made a sound of distress or he sensed her fear, Kabeiros leapt to his feet and a moment later Hekate found a weight of dog against her shoulder and a large, wet tongue lapping at her face. She hugged Kabeiros hard and buried her face against his smooth fur.

You remember that I told you I had this ridiculous fear of using magic except to teach or learn spells?

I remember.

I have just fought my way through the deception covering that fear. I am sure now it must be some compulsion set on me by my father. I know, too, why I was happy to create new spells and teach them to others. Tears filled her eyes and she wiped her cheeks on Kabeiros' soft neck. *I was always supposed to learn every new spell I could and bring it home to him.* She swallowed hard. *I don't remember ever teaching him a spell. I suppose he somehow lifted them from my mind . . . *

She was shivering and nauseous. Kabeiros licked the tears from her face. She held him tight. "I wish you were a man," she whispered.

I wish so too. The mental voice was somehow blurred. *The man wishes he were a man.* There was a wry mental chuckle. *The dog doesn't care.*

Kabeiros, I haven't forgotten. I've asked every sorcerer, every witch I've met, about anyone who's tried to 'cure' shape-shifting. Yehoraz has asked, too, but we must be careful. Shape-shifters are no better liked here in Colchis than elsewhere, even if magic is accepted. And there could be danger for you. Yehoraz is a dear, sweet man and wise in some ways, but he's no tower of strength and he knows you're more than a dog. I think Rakefet and Batshira . . . no, probably they think you're just a familiar. But no one will even admit shape-shifting exists.

The dog sighed heavily. *Admit, no, but mostly their eyes shifted and always to the same direction.*

The palace.

Yes.

Hekate sighed. *I suppose I'll have to go and introduce myself to Aietes and Medea.*

Not yet, Kabeiros said, resting his head against her. *I'm not that desperate yet.*

However, Hekate was not to have the choice about when to meet Aietes and Medea. Less than a ten-day later, Rakefet came into the market, rather breathless and looking uneasily over her shoulder. Hekate cut short a pleasant conversation she was having with a satisfied client, and as soon as the client was gone, Rakefet plucked at her sleeve urging her into a quiet spot away from other waiting clients. Kabeiros remained, guarding Hekate's wares.

"Batshira sent me," Rakefet whispered. "There was a message for you from the palace. Tomorrow morning you are to present yourself to the king. A guard will come to escort you. If . . . if you wish to disappear before then . . ." Her eyes were large with fear.

"Thank you, Rakefet," Hekate said, blinking with shock. "You and Batshira are very kind–and very brave. But if I were to disappear, you would be in great trouble because the king would know you warned me."

"No, no. We were *supposed* to tell you when you came back to the inn. Mother only thought if you knew a few hours earlier . . ."

Having absorbed the shock, Hekate shook her

head. "It's still very good of you both, but I don't think there's anything to fear—at least, not yet. If the king intended me harm, why warn me a day in advance? That's silly. He could have sent a guard at any time to arrest me right here. I'm known well enough in the market."

"But if you are taken . . ." Rakefet whispered. "It would be too late."

"True, but if I flee, must I not be guilty of something? And I'm not." She shrugged. "I'll think about it. If I don't return to the inn, you may have whatever I leave there."

Calmer, Rakefet said, "Well, it's true he could have sent the guard here. And guards come for merchants, to get them through the gates. It was just . . . Mother and I *like* you, Hekate. We know—" she looked toward Kabeiros and lowered her voice even further "—you're greater than most of the sorcerers up past the Royal Way. We don't talk, but . . ."

"There's been gossip about me?"

The girl nodded. Hekate sighed and patted Rakefet's shoulder. "It's all right. I'll manage."

Frowning, Hekate returned to the waiting clients and attended to their wants, which fortunately were simple, thinking furiously all the time. Kabeiros must have caught some of those thoughts—as they grew closer over the years of companionship, he sometimes did receive a sort of spillover from her mind—so he wasn't surprised when she was free and told him of Rakefet's message. He had been thinking about the problem, too.

I hope you're right, he said. *I agree that it would seem stupid for the king to give you warning, but it may also be that he's just confident no one can escape him.*

But I'm sure I've done nothing forbidden, Hekate protested.

A king's will can make the most innocent act forbidden. Still, I think as you do that the threat isn't immediate. Such a message most likely means he's curious. Perhaps Yehoraz couldn't resist speaking of the 'invisible magic' or the amulets that could be triggered with a single word. The king might want those secrets. What will you do?

Give him the 'secret' of the amulets at once and act wide-eyed with surprise that it's something he didn't know. As to the 'invisible magic,' I'll tell him that the magic of Colchis is equally invisible to me and that I'll gladly cast spells or do whatever he asks to give him the answer, but that I don't know it myself. I must trust in my shields; if he gets through them, we'll both be in deep trouble.

The dog sighed again. *True enough. I think your plan is best, but I also think it best that I don't accompany you into the king's presence. You can transmit what's said to me, if it's safe to do so. If you come out again, I'll be waiting patiently by the door. If you don't, you can tell me where they have taken you and I'll come and get you out.*

Good enough, Hekate agreed calmly, although she wasn't sure she would call for Kabeiros' help.

It would depend on the kind of guards the king used. If they were stupid common men, Kabeiros likely could manage to release her by taking out the guards one at a time. If they were well-trained and responded as a group, they would surely kill him. But if she didn't call him in an attempt to save his life, she might well doom him to a more horrible death, a slow death of the soul as the dog lost its humanity.

One thing, however, she came to see before her day's work ended—that it was useless to try to escape. There was no way she could get far enough from Colchis to elude the king's grasp if he wished to seize her. Unless . . . if she took a ship? Then she remembered the long black vessel that moved upriver without oars, with full sails when no breeze blew. She couldn't think of a ship that would be swifter than the king's vessels. No, the best she could do was to build the strongest wards possible and hope it was curiosity that drove Aietes to summon her, not anger.

She was as prepared as one can possibly be for the totally unknown when she took her staff in hand and went to wait in the street for Aietes' guard. Although Batshira had not asked her to meet the guard outside, her voice was gruff with emotion when she thanked Hekate for her consideration.

"A week's free lodging," she said.

Hekate widened her eyes. "Are you *that* sure I won't be returning?" she asked.

"That was a low blow," Batshira said, laughing.

Hekate laughed too, but she didn't feel at all like laughing when she saw the guard coming down the street through a wide aisle the people left around him . . . it. The thing was plainly not human, although it stood upright on two legs, had two arms, and was clothed and armed like a man. Hekate could not see the head under the full helmet it wore, but the face was gray-skinned and naked; there were nostrils but no nose; and the eyes—the eyes were not flesh at all, but bright, many-faceted stones.

Taking a deep breath, Hekate stepped into the street. "I am Hekate," she said. "I believe you have come for me."

The creature stopped and regarded her. "Lady Hekate?" Its voice was flat, with a metallic ring as if it spoke through the wire strings of an instrument.

Hekate nodded. "I am the Lady Hekate."

The thing bowed a little, turned, and led the way back up the street. It moved lithely. A well-trained human athlete could not have been more graceful. Kabeiros rose from the shadows at the side of the building. They had talked about how to act and had decided not to call attention to Kabeiros. He would simply follow discreetly.

The guard was silent and they walked up Sorcerers Road to the Royal Way. He crossed that road, continuing along Sorcerers Road, which first showed large, fine houses set back behind metal gates and then seemed to become almost a rural lane broken only by tree-bordered paths. Along one of those, straighter than the others, Hekate caught a glimpse of a house as large as the palace of the ruler of Ur-Kabos. The homes of the great sorcerers, she thought. Yehoraz must have lived in a house like that before Medea blasted him—before he could explain why he had not been able rather than would not obey her. Hekate pressed her staff deeper into the earth and drew more power into her shields.

The guard's pace slowed as they approached a gate in a stone wall, which was some five man-heights tall, built of polished stone so smooth, so well fitting, that climbing it was clearly impossible. A guard stood at the gate, a perfect duplicate of the guard that had accompanied her. Neither spoke, but the gate guard lowered his spear and pulled the gate aside. Hekate, who was watching on the "higher" plane of magic, saw a bright flash of light pass between them.

Kabeiros had closed the distance between himself and Hekate and her guard when the palace wall came into view. Now he stood beside Hekate, between her and her guard; the gate guard either did not notice the dog or had been instructed to allow him entrance because he made no protest when Kabeiros followed Hekate into the inner precincts.

This was a wide area paved in polished black stone that seemed to go around the whole palace. Hekate looked up . . . and up . . . and up, and to the right and the left, which was possible because the guard was walking slowly to avoid bumping into any of the large number of busy people who moved about the area. Many were servants engaged in obvious tasks like sweeping or hauling goods in small handcarts. Many others were well dressed, some with scrolls, others having baskets or covered rolls or well-made carrying bags, all moving this way or that with deliberate purpose.

Of greater importance to Hekate was that no one looked particularly frightened; among the well-dressed people with business in the palace there were a few frowns, but those seemed more thoughtful than worried. And no one glanced even twice at her or her guard. The creatures seemingly were commonly used as escorts and messengers.

Her particular escort wove his way with remarkable dexterity to a wide portico of white marble. Hekate glanced right and left, a long way right and left. She blinked. The portico also seemed to go all the way around the huge building. An effort kept her from shaking her head. The palace at Byblos, far grander than that at Ur-Kabos, would not, she suspected, have served as an out-kitchen to this place.

The guard mounted the white marble steps and crossed the portico. Directly ahead were immense double doors which, open, could probably admit three or four war chariots. A guard stood before them, but when, again, that flash of light passed between the two strange creatures, although the door guard nodded, he did not open the vast double doors. He gestured to a dark recess in which a human-sized door stood already open.

Kabeiros, having followed without eliciting any notice, entered the dark recess, went through the door and stopped, still within a sort of very short corridor. Hekate's guard took no more notice of this than he had of anything else the dog had done.

As she went forward without the hound, Hekate felt bereft. Then she saw directly ahead, across a wide corridor paved in black slabs, another pair of bronze double doors. These doors, like the small one beside which Kabeiros sat, were open and beyond them was a great hall paved and pillared in a cream-colored, green-veined marble.

The guard marched ahead into a wide avenue between the pillars. Hekate followed and saw a chamber so vast that the farther end was obscured. Brass torches were fixed to each pillar and also to the side walls, each at least five man-lengths distant. What were obviously mage lights burned on each torch. The power expended was shocking. For one moment Hekate opened her shields enough to use mage sight and could see the power pouring through the room. Even so, the light was dim, which was why, she realized, she could not clearly see the far end of the chamber.

She was startled and tightened her wards immediately when the guard hesitated long enough to exchange a flash of light with another of the creatures, which Hekate had not seen approach. The second guard pointed to an aisle—one of several, Hekate now saw—left free to approach a dais through a moderately large audience of silent people. The guard led; she followed. As she passed them, she saw irritation on their faces, not fear; the kind of irritation one feels when a customer or client is served ahead of you out of turn.

Expression? But the room had been too dim . . . Hekate looked about, realizing that the area around the central—or perhaps it was more accurate to say an off-center—dais was bright as day. Instinctively she looked up and gasped. A huge metal framework, high-arched to resist its own weight, covered the entire central section of the room over the dais. Inside each section of the framework was a substance clear as water, but hard enough not to sag. Hekate would have said they were slices of crystal, but whoever heard of crystal sliced as thin as parchment? She longed to look at it with mage sight, but she was afraid to drop her wards, even for a moment, this close to the dais.

As she and her guard grew closer, the sound of voices drew her attention. She could not see the speaker, who was on the same level as she, on the floor before the dais, but she could see those on it more clearly every moment.

On the dais was a throne chair in which sat a big man, doubtless King Aietes. His hair was brown and curly as was his beard, which was full but neatly trimmed at about four fingerwidths' length. His lips were full, curved upward a trifle at the corners, which gave him a look of good nature, and, to Hekate's relief, his eyes did not belie that; they were a dark brown and gazed directly at the person speaking and their expression was mildly amused as he replied.

To the left of the chair stood a tall, well-built young man. His hair was fair, his eyes blue, and he was smiling down at a boy of about ten, whom he held by the hand. He had a look of Kabeiros about him; he, too, had underlying sadness in his expression, even as he smiled.

To the right of the chair was a woman, no, a girl. Although her lush body cried woman, there was something about her—her carriage, the way she held her head, the smoothness of her skin—that betrayed her youth. Young or old, she was outstandingly beautiful, her pale-skinned face was broad at the temples and softly heart-shaped with high cheekbones that made the most of enormous, almond-shaped eyes, tilted up at the outer edges under winged eyebrows, which almost touched a waterfall of blue-black hair.

Those eyes. Hekate looked down at the floor. A witch's eyes, not silver like Hekate's own but almost colorless, marked only by the black pupil and a black ring around the nearly invisible iris. Hekate didn't dare open her shields, but now that the shock of the girl's beauty had diminished a little, Hekate was almost overwhelmed by her aura; it was so intense she could feel it beat against her, like the warmth of the sun. This must be Medea—the Medea who had blasted Yehoraz.

Afraid the wild mixture of curiosity, fear, and resentment would somehow leak through and betray her, Hekate turned her attention to the king and the new petitioner who had come forward. The man was well-fed—perhaps a bit too well-fed—rubicund of countenance and wearing an expression of anxiety that didn't sit too well on him.

"Sire, I beseech you to consider us. You are safe behind your walls and your guards, but you have so well governed, that your city is the most prosperous in the world. That very prosperity has driven us to populate the south bank of the river and there we are almost naked to any raider who sails up the river and desires to attack us. If we are so easily robbed, the prosperity of Colchis will be damaged. Who will want to bring their goods to a place where those goods can be easily lost?"

"I am not unaware of the problem," Aietes responded, "and I have given it some thought. There are three principal ways to solve it. First, the merchants could all band together and hire enough guards to fight off any assaults from reivers. Second, I could enlarge my navy considerably and have the river mouth always under observation and patrol so my ships could attack any pirates. Third, I could close off the river with illusion so that no thief could find it."

"But then the merchants could not find it either," the petitioner protested.

"Oh well, each merchant with Colchis as his destination would take aboard a mage who would have a key to the illusion." King Aietes smiled.

"And who would pay the mages?"

"The merchants, of course."

"Then I think an increase in the navy—"

"Which would necessitate a substantial increase in tariffs, docking fees, and perhaps other taxes. Warships do not build themselves, and the mages who ride them and assure that they will be where they are needed when they are needed also must be paid."

"Sire, Sire," the merchant cried. "I cannot make such a decision for all my peers without a word to them. And yet it has taken me near a year to obtain this audience. Must I go back and tell them I have no news, that we must wait another year?"

"Master Merchant." The mellow voice was that of the blond man to the king's left. "Nothing worth having is free. You have yourself praised the good governance of King Aietes. You are not the only one who has petitions for him, which is why each must wait his turn. Now think of his generosity in not simply applying to the problem of raiders the remedy that would cause him the least inconvenience and assessing you for the cost. Any solution will take time and have a price. Warships are not built in a day, nor is an illusion that disguises the whole coast generated without long preparation. Even if you take your protection into your own hands, you will find that you cannot assemble a good and reliable fighting force overnight. I advise you to take King Aietes' generosity to heart."

"Of course." The Master Merchant bowed. "I understand. I am grateful."

"Good. Then go back to your living quarter and discuss these expedients with your fellow merchants. When you have come to a conclusion as to what would best suit you all, come to me. I will bring your answer to the king so that you do not need to wait for a formal appointment, and I will bring his answer to you."

"Meddling again, Phrixos?" The girl smiled as she spoke, which almost made the words into praise.

Almost, but not quite. Hekate knew without any doubt that Medea did not like Phrixos, not at all! Her eyes flicked to Aietes' face and to Phrixos'; only Phrixos seemed unaware of the bitterness under the honey—thick, smooth, and sweet—of Medea's voice. Hekate's eyes came back to that beautiful face and widened. One blemish existed in the perfect beauty. Medea's lips were perfectly bowed, very red, full and soft, but the smile exposed her teeth, which were just a little too small for her mouth and, in addition, as sharply pointed as if each had been filed.

King Aietes laughed but looked hard at Medea. "He meddles to my great benefit," he said firmly. "Phrixos, I will leave the whole in your hands, for the merchant has spoken of a real and growing danger. As the fame of Colchis spreads, greedy eyes turn to us. There was that raid on the lower docks by Porters Way and Lord Nodeleya and Lady Tshuva lost a whole shipload of goods, not to mention the buildings that were burnt and the people killed. That was only one ship. What if ten had come?" He turned to the merchant. "Master Merchant, I will give Phrixos the power to carry out whatever decision he makes for the protection of the city."

The man called Phrixos bowed his head to the king and said, "Yes, lord," then turned to look at the Master Merchant. "Come to my house after the Court is over, and we will make arrangements for your easy access to me," he said, smiling.

The merchant seemed well pleased with that arrangement and stepped back into the crowd. Another man pressed forward, but the king's guard forestalled him.

"Here is the Lady Hekate," it said.

The eyes of everyone on the dais turned to her. Hekate clutched her staff tighter. Phrixos smiled. Aietes looked faintly puzzled. And Medea cried out, high and angry, "By the names of all the gods, she isn't there!"

CHAPTER 14

"A simulacrum? An empty shell?" Aietes exclaimed, half rising from his throne chair.

"No, I am not!" Hekate cried. "I am me. I am real. I am no simulacrum!" With the words, she created a mage light and left it suspended just above the hand holding her staff. "No simulacrum could cast a spell!"

Aietes sank back into his seat. "I have never heard of a simulacrum that could cast a spell. Usually they can barely speak and walk." His eyes sought his daughter's.

"Usually?" Medea hissed. "What is usual about this circumstance? About what we have heard of her? Why could a simulacrum not be created carrying one or even several spells? I say we must destroy—"

"Gently. Gently," Aietes remonstrated, waving back the guards who were closing in on Hekate. "I don't wish to damage either the person or if it is a construct, the construct. Such a creation is worth study. And it is not inimical to us, Medea. If it is a simulacrum and if, as you claim, it carries one spell, why not a spell of destruction? The mage light can do no harm even if it is floating free. And I would like to know how she did that!"

"It could snap forward and touch you before you could avoid it. How do you know what it can do if it touches you?" Medea snapped.

"Shall I dissolve it?" Hekate asked. "Would that come under what a simulacrum could do? What can I do to prove I am real? I don't wish to be cut to show I bleed red blood."

While she was speaking, Phrixos had released the hand of the little boy, stepped off the dais, and cupped his hand around the mage light. "It is harmless to me," he remarked, and raised his hand so that it fell on Hekate's shoulder. "She is warm and of flesh."

"I don't care!" Medea shrieked. "She isn't there! I see her with my eyes, but I can't feel her. I can't sense her. She has no soul! No matter how perfect, she's a simulacrum!"

"No," Aietes said quietly. "Calm yourself, Medea. I think Phrixos is right—"

"Phrixos is always right!" Medea spat.

"About the woman," Aietes continued. "I agree that I don't feel her as I feel others, but I can't sense the spell that holds the mage light either."

"What?"

Medea's huge eyes turned to the mage light that held steady over Hekate's hand on the knob of her staff. She stared at it. It shone placidly. She muttered under her breath. It didn't move or flicker. She gestured, spoke aloud in a language unfamiliar to Hekate. From the corner of her eyes, which she kept fixed on Medea, Hekate could see the swirls of lightning power around the mage light, but they didn't affect the earth-blood power Hekate had used to create it. The mage light remained unaffected. Medea looked at Hekate.

"Who are you? What are you?" she asked, eyes narrowed.

"I am called Hekate." The answer acknowledged that she had a true name kept unknown. "I am an herb-wife—or, I was an herb-wife until I came to Colchis and found those who would teach me healing spells. I am now a healer."

"What other spells do you know? I don't wish to have someone carried here from a sickbed so you can show your healing skills."

Hekate shrugged. "I know a few illusions, such as may entertain at a celebration."

She saw a thread of light dart from Medea toward her and pulled a touch more power into her shields but without shifting her eyes or allowing any change in her expression. The thread of light touched her wards and dissipated into a blurred mist. Hekate frowned thoughtfully at Medea.

"I am very good at personal illusions," she said, pointed a finger at her head, drew it down her body to her feet, muttered a few meaningless words, and shifted to the crone.

It was perhaps a dangerous chance to take, but she was tired of arguing about whether she was real or not and even Medea would acknowledge that a simulacrum could not change its appearance. She had proof enough that neither Aietes nor Medea, who was, Hekate suspected, the more powerful of the two although less experienced, could feel her. That would make it impossible for them to sense that the crone was not an illusion but a true form of Hekate so her shift should not betray her.

The guards had sprung forward as she began to mutter and gesture, one throwing himself in front of her so that she could not cast a spell at those on the dais, the second reaching for her. When she changed form, however, both hesitated, and in that time Aietes bade them let her alone.

"So," he said, "you are no simulacrum. An illusion atop an illusion—that is too much. Now you need to tell us how you can do magic no one can sense and why we cannot touch you as we can touch everyone else."

"I wish I could," Hekate said most mendaciously but with seeming sincerity, "but I don't know myself because *I* can't sense *your* magic. I'm sure you and the Lady Medea have been trying to scry my soul, but I feel nothing."

Aietes raised his hand to rub his lips. As he did, a bolt of light flew from his fingertips. Hekate ignored it, keeping her eyes on the king's and not flinching or blinking when the bolt shattered on her shields.

"Yet when you learn a spell, it will work for you?"

Hekate's lips parted to speak, but she was interrupted by Medea, who said, "Dismiss that disgusting illusion! If we must talk with you and be nauseated by what you say, at least spare our other sensibilities."

"Yes, my lady."

Hekate repeated her meaningless "spell" and shifted back to the woman, straightening away from the staff on which she had been leaning her bent body. She was aware of Medea's keen scrutiny and of the flash of anger that betrayed Medea had not sensed the dismissal of the "illusion." As she looked toward the king to answer the question he had asked, Phrixos bent close to speak in Aietes' ear. Hekate waited. The king sighed, then nodded and beckoned to the guard who had accompanied Hekate from the inn—at least she thought it was the same one; they were to her eyes identical.

"Take Lady Hekate to the first waiting chamber," Aietes said. The guard came forward. The king held up a hand and said to Hekate, "I can see that I must speak to you at length, but this is a time of petition for my people and I must not scant them. You will have to wait."

"Yes, my lord," Hekate said.

She bowed to Aietes and again to Medea, watching each carefully as she transmitted to Kabeiros the information that she was going to have to wait, for how long she knew not. To her relief, neither showed the smallest sign that they were aware of what she was doing. She had not previously aimed a clear communication at the hound, for fear they would sense it although she had "echoed" their remarks and her replies, hoping Kabeiros would be able to catch something. Now she shifted her attention to the guard and "sent" that she would be in the first waiting room . . . wherever that was.

The guard showed no response, but as Hekate moved toward him, Medea said, "Wait!" and the guard, who had been turning, stopped. So did Hekate. "Where is the black dog?" Medea asked. "We were told that she was always accompanied by a large black dog with white eyes. Does he hold her soul?"

"No, of course not," Hekate said immediately, allowing a touch of anger to show in her voice. "Even if you can't sense it, my soul is just where it should be, within my own body." She bowed to the king. "King Aietes, I didn't intend to hide Kabeiros. I just didn't think it fitting to bring a dog into your palace. Kabeiros is waiting for me by the outer door."

Aietes shook his head at Medea. "That the soul can be lodged elsewhere is a tale, Medea. Even the gods can't move their souls around." Then he looked at Hekate again. "Nonetheless, I would like to see this dog myself."

"I will fetch him," Hekate said.

"You can't summon your familiar?"

"Kabeiros isn't my familiar. He doesn't store or focus my power . . . such as it is."

Although Kabeiros was resistant to her magic, Hekate wasn't sure he would be equally resistant to that of Aietes and Medea. Her spells didn't "take" on him, so she had no way to shield him and didn't want Aietes and Medea trying to take him apart to find what wasn't there.

"I have heard he is a very strange-looking dog." Aietes' doubts were clear in his voice.

"That's true, my lord. His eyes are all white. He was left on a midden near my house—because he was believed blind, I suppose. Perhaps I am too tender-hearted, but I couldn't leave that puppy to die of hunger and thirst. I told myself a dog doesn't use his sight as much as his smell and hearing. I brought him home, and it worked to my advantage. It was as if he knew; he has always been devoted to me and when my husband's family put me out . . ."

"For what?" Medea's question was sharp, suspicious.

Hekate shrugged. "For being childless—as if it were my fault when my husband was past fourscore years."

"And you were not powerful enough to hold your own against them?" Medea's suspicions had not been allayed.

"Powerful?" Hekate shook her head. "I knew nothing then but herbs, and in that city—"

"Enough!" Aietes cut her off and gestured sharply at Medea, whose lips tightened; however, she stepped back. Then Aietes spoke to the guard. "Take Lady Hekate first to the door to fetch her dog. Then bring her and the dog to the first waiting room. Stay with her until I come."

Hekate went at once, but as she and the guard made their way out of the bright center of the chamber and through the dimmer, almost forest-like aisle, she remembered that the guard had obeyed Medea when she said, "Wait." If there were a contest of wills between Aietes and Medea, who would win? Aietes right now, Hekate thought, but not forever; perhaps not even for long.

Father against daughter. Hekate felt chilled and reminded herself firmly that Aietes was no Perses and Medea was the last person in the world to need her help. Then she wondered whether she should warn Aietes. Warn the father against the daughter? Hekate restrained a shudder and decided if he didn't understand the danger a warning would do no good because he wouldn't be perceptive enough or strong enough to resist Medea anyway.

When they went through the audience-chamber doors into the corridor, Hekate called aloud, "Kabeiros, come," so the guard should hear her give the hound a verbal order. But it wasn't the dog she saw at first. The shadowy man almost leapt to his feet as the solid hound rose more slowly from his haunches.

What happened? Kabeiros' face was twisted with anxiety. *I almost tried to follow you twice. I smelled the magic of your wards—a burning smell—as if they had been damaged. Are you all right?*

Hekate felt startled and frightened. The touches on her shields had seemed insignificant; then the damage Kabeiros sensed had been undetectable to her. She passed her tongue nervously over her suddenly dry lips.

*Both Aietes and Medea tried my shields, but I

felt no weakening. We may be in worse danger than I thought if–*

No. I must have smelled the testing. The wards are as usual now, just smelling of your kind of magic.

Was that true, or had Kabeiros only offered reassurance so that fear shouldn't weaken her? She was distracted from that concern as the shadow of the man reached her, ahead of the dog. He put out a hand, as if to draw her to him, and Hekate leaned toward him, wanting desperately to be enfolded in a supporting embrace . . . but she only felt the dog lick her hand. Tears stung her eyes, and she had to force her eyes away from the man and make herself pat the dog's head. It seemed to her that before she had looked away, the shadow eyes were bright with shadow tears.

The guard, who had waited until the dog reached Hekate's side, pivoted to the left and walked along the wide corridor which, as Hekate had thought, went all the way around the building. They didn't go so far, however. At what Hekate estimated must be an area that was behind the dais in the great audience chamber, the guard stopped, turned left again to face the inner wall, and opened a door.

The room was not large, but it was plainly not a prison cell either. Although Hekate held the dog close, curiosity dulled the pain of wanting the man. Facing the door at which they entered was a beautiful mosaic of a garden. About midway a gate wrought of some dark metal was pictured. Through the gate the mosaic showed a paved walk that disappeared into the distance.

Against the wall on the right was a narrow table that held a pitcher and several glasses on an oval platter. Above it were three mosaic portraits, very well done, particularly the eyes, which had a lustre that was nearly living. Hekate could see no sign of active power around those eyes, but the lustre might have been lent by old usage. By the other wall there was a divan flanked by two comfortable chairs. A low table stood before the divan.

"Sit," the guard said, and went to stand with its back to the door.

Although Hekate and Kabeiros had plenty of time to review everything that had been said, done, and felt while she was in the audience chamber, their wait was not as long as Hekate feared it might be. Before the slight nagging sensation in her belly resolved into real hunger, Kabeiros, who had been sitting by her knee facing the back wall, stiffened and rose to his feet. Hekate turned to look and also rose to her feet.

Along the path pictured in the mosaic came two figures that quickly approached the wrought metal gate. As the man put his hand out to touch the gate latch, Hekate saw he was Aietes, the woman Medea. Neither Phrixos nor the child was with them. And then they were in the room, standing with their backs to the gate as if they had actually passed through it.

Both looked at Kabeiros, who looked back, perking his ears and wagging his tail very slightly in an ingratiating manner. He and Hekate had decided that meek compliance was their best hope until all hope was gone. Then, if necessary, they would both attack and try to escape. But that didn't seem an immediate threat.

"You never answered my question," Aietes said, coming forward. He seated himself in one of the chairs and Medea went to the other—neatly flanking Hekate and Kabeiros. "When you learn a spell, that spell will work for you?"

"Yes, my lord. And I have taught the spell of the

free-floating mage light to other sorcerers. When they cast the spell, it works just as it should . . . but I can't sense it any more."

The king waved at Hekate to be seated, and she resumed her place on the divan with Kabeiros at her knee again. But now he had his back to her so he could watch Aietes and Medea.

"You've taught that spell to others?" Medea repeated. "Why would you give away so valuable a spell?"

"I didn't give it away, my lady. I bartered it for learning the language of Colchis and for other small spells—a binding spell I didn't know and several finding spells, which are very useful in my business. And the floating mage-light spell is not valuable among the people from whom I came. It is a simple spell, taught as soon as a child is known to be Talented by making fire."

"Teach me," Aietes ordered.

Hekate nodded and smiled. "Gladly, but I need something with which to write the symbols so you can fix them in your mind, my lord. And if you want me to write the words, I will need a sheet of parchment."

"Write," Aietes repeated without expression. "You are a well-educated herb woman."

Hekate felt the hound by her side stiffen as if he sensed a threat, but she answered calmly, "My husband was a man of substance, but he was old. He did not trust his family—with good reason as it turned out—so he had me taught to read and write. That way, he could continue to conduct his business without the interference of his dishonest nephew or his daughters' greedy husbands."

Aietes nodded, but his eyes still assessed her. The expression was skillful, she realized, as she swallowed a strong temptation to make further explanations that might well reveal more than she wished. She attempted to look eager and hopeful, but when she glanced down at Kabeiros she realized that the shadow of the man Kabeiros was gone. That nearly startled her into a reaction, but Aietes had turned his head to look at the guard; Hekate swallowed hard and drew more power into her shields.

The guard, however, remained motionless by the door. Nonetheless, a few moments later, the door opened and another guard carried in a small wooden lap desk. A gesture from Aietes sent the second guard to Hekate, who took the desk.

She opened it at once, found a capped inkwell, a split reed for writing, and sheets of—of all surprising things—Egyptian papyrus. Knowing she had seemed startled, she fingered the writing material as if she didn't recognize it. She wasted no time on inquiring, however, but quickly drew her symbol for light and the glyphs for *epikaloumi eustropsos*. Below these she drew the single upcurving line with attached triangles for wings that signified the ability to float and the glyphs for *didomi elapsrotes*, and finally the shattered, double-headed arrow for motion and the glyphs denoting *exesti exelthein*.

She then invoked the mage light, demonstrating how the three commands were almost piled one atop the other. "But there is no reason why you cannot do each separately, that is, create the light on a support and then apply to it the other two commands. It only takes a little more power to combine the spells from the beginning, however, and then you can do what you like with the light. Of course, you must keep each symbol clearly in mind or draw it with a gesture when you say the commands."

Suspicion had given way to interest in Aietes's expression and he held out a hand for the sheet of papyrus, which Hekate handed to him. After studying it for a moment he set it on the low table.

"My spell for the mage light is different than yours," he said. "It's longer and more complicated to tell the truth. However, that spell is familiar to me. Could I use that and then apply these other two?"

"I have no idea," Hekate replied, eyes bright with speculation. "I've never tried to mix the spells I was taught here in Colchis with old ones I learned as a child and those I learned along the road. It–" she gestured, frowning "–they were mostly for different purposes. And healing spells . . . One must be specially careful with healing spells. I would *never* mix those. I don't *think* mixing would cause a backlash, but I don't know. Perhaps you should summon a palace sorcerer to try instead of risking yourself, my lord?"

He looked at her. "You are remarkably generous with inviting others to share your spells." Then he smiled. "The spells seem simple enough. Would the backlash from them be strong?"

"Not if they are just ill done. As I said, these are the first spells taught to children and no one wishes a child to come to real harm. I think the backlash is little more than a stinging slap. But that is just for not doing the spell right. A mixture with other magic . . . That might be another matter altogether and much more violent. I just don't know."

The king grinned like a mischievous boy. "And make a big bang? I used to do that often as a boy. I think I'll try again."

Hekate felt the hound pressed against her thigh stir slightly and her attention moved from the spells themselves to Aietes. She could see now that there was what appeared to be a faint glow under his skin, and she realized that he–and likely Medea too–had warded themselves before they came to the room to speak to her. Most cleverly warded, too, and likely covered with a binding spell because she hadn't seen any swirl of lightning power around them.

When the king started to gesture and whisper, Hekate politely turned her eyes aside so as not to seem to spy on the spell he was creating. It was safe enough not to watch; Kabeiros was watching and her shields were at full strength. A casual glance at Medea was also swiftly withdrawn; Hekate fixed her eyes on her own hands in her lap. The princess, who had feigned utter indifference to the spells Hekate was inscribing, now had her eyes fixed on the parchment on which they were written while her father was occupied.

Even with her eyes lowered, Hekate saw a flash of light and drew breath to command the stasis of any spell; she had no intention of being accused of deliberately harming the king if the spells did backlash violently and had little hope that Medea would stand witness that she had warned Aietes. However, her caution wasn't necessary. The brilliant light held steady–unlike an explosion of power–and when she looked up, Aietes was smiling broadly. Midway in the room a very brilliant mage light hung and as Hekate looked at it, it moved upward to rest at the ceiling.

"The two magics work together very well," Aietes said to Hekate. "And now that I have cast them, I can sense your spells as clearly as my own. Well, Medea?"

The princess shrugged. "I sense them also. But not that." She pointed to Hekate's mage light, much fainter than that of Aietes', which floated where Hekate had left it. Her head snapped around to Hekate. "Why?"

"I don't know," Hekate wailed in a really fine simulation of fear and frustration. "Do you think I haven't tried to discover why your magic is invisible to me and mine to you? If I knew, I would tell you gladly. You are far too powerful for me to try to hide such a secret, and what harm would it do me if you knew? I might indeed try to hide it from fellow sorcerers, but the king and the princess of Colchis could never be rivals for such as I. Moreover, you would be pleased with me if I told you. Do you think I don't know how much good that could do me?"

In fact, Hekate thought it might not do her any good at all. She wondered if the precious pair might kill her to be sure they were the only ones who retained the secret of the different sources of power for magic.

Aietes shook his head, his eyes on Medea. "Since I can't read her at all, I can't truth-read her, but what she says makes good sense." Then he looked at Hekate. "Would you be willing to allow several of our court mages to examine you?"

"Yes, of course," Hekate agreed without hesitation.

What she had heard from Yehoraz indicated that the king and more particularly the princess were stronger than any of the sorcerers who served the court. Her one concern was that several working together could breach her shields if the "burning" Kabeiros had sensed was damage to them rather than the smell of the lightning power dissipating itself against them. Still it was far safer to agree readily than to arouse greater suspicion by refusing.

Aietes stood. Hekate rose also and said, "Please, my lord . . ."

"Yes?"

"I'm getting very hungry," Hekate said in a small voice, "and my clients will wonder what has become of me. Some may hear I was summoned to the court. If I don't soon return, they will believe I am somehow tainted with your displeasure and won't use me any more. Please, my lord, may I go about my business now? I will hold myself ready to come again any time you wish to send for me."

"Medea?" Aietes looked at his daughter.

Medea's exquisite face was expressionless. "I agree with you, Father, but I have a question or two I wish to ask Hekate–" she smiled suddenly, exposing all of the sharp pointed teeth; Hekate barely retained a shudder "–to do with the dog, not magic. Then I will let her go."

Hekate rather expected Aietes to sit down again, but instead of acting curious about Medea's continued interest in Kabeiros, an expression of unease flicked over his face and was swiftly wiped away. When he spoke, he almost seemed not to have heard her.

"Very well," he said. "For me there's little more to learn from her in the matter of spells. Illusions I can make. Spells to entertain are useless to me as are those for finding. Binding . . . I think I know every binding spell there is. Let her go. We know where to find her and I will make sure she cannot leave Colchis until I am completely satisfied about the magic she uses."

"Good." Medea nodded agreement.

Hekate pretended to turn to the princess, but she was watching Aietes in her wide peripheral vision. She expected him to approach the mosaic and wanted to know whether he had translocated himself–which Kabeiros had once told her was possible to the great mages of Olympus–or if he had translocated Medea and she him. However Aietes didn't satisfy her curiosity. He walked to the door to the corridor rather than the gate in the mosaic. The guard moved aside and he exited the room in a most mundane manner.

Now Hekate gave her full attention to Medea, but the princess did absolutely nothing. She sat quite still, staring straight ahead–a gaze that took in neither Hekate nor Kabeiros. Actually, she seemed to be listening. Hekate sat still and silent, daring to do no more than once lick her dry lips, hoping the princess was not as inimical and dangerous as she feared.

Suddenly Medea turned her head to the guard and said one sharp word. Hekate gasped as the bright faceted stones that were the creature's eyes dimmed. Her gaze flew to Medea, and she saw to her intense surprise that the princess was pallid, her breath coming quickly. After a few moments when nothing more happened–the guard still stood with its back to the door although its eyes were dead–Medea slowly looked away. She still did not speak to Hekate, but took on the listening expression again. This time it did not last long. After one more glance over her shoulder to make sure the guard still stood, she spoke, not to Hekate, but to the dog.

"Come out of that shape!" she ordered sharply. "I wish to see the man form."

Kabeiros whined and Hekate burst into tears. Medea's lips thinned to near invisibility.

"I don't know what protections you use, but in this I mean you no harm. Dismiss them. I need to know if I can sense the dog's change. Come! Be a man!"

She knew. It was too late for lying. "He can't!" Hekate cried.

"I don't believe you!" Medea spat–and there coiled before them a huge serpent.

It was *very* beautiful. The pointed face was scaled in silver, the lidless eyes unusually large. Beginning between them was a wide V of brilliantly green scales bordered in dark red. Those spread out over the narrow portion that separated the head from the immense body and the green was patterned with varying shapes in black-bordered silver with accents of the dark red. The snake moved. The patterns also moved, binding the eyes. At first Hekate couldn't look away, but a blow struck her thigh and a man's cry of agony tore through her mind. She looked down to see Kabeiros convulsing on the floor.

There was no time for spell-casting, not even for the word or two she would need; worse, there was no spell she knew that was adequate punishment for Medea's cruelty. Without thinking, Hekate grabbed her staff from where it leaned against the divan and struck the serpent with it, sending through it a blast of power. The serpent screamed, and Medea lay back in the chair, her skin bright red, as if she had been burned. Kabeiros lay still.

Hekate grasped the staff between both hands so the sharp steel point was aimed directly at Medea's throat. The princess's eyes widened, bulged with fear; her mouth opened on a desperate unvoiced plea. Hekate, face twisted with a terrible rage, raised the staff to strike.

CHAPTER 15

No! Don't kill her!

The hound's voice was faint and blurred, but hearing it aborted the downward thrust that would have plunged the steel point of the staff through Medea's throat. It also drew Hekate's eyes to the black body on the floor. The hound was moving, his feet scrabbling for a grip on the polished stones. In that moment of inattention, Hekate lost her advantage. When she turned back to Medea, flashes of light were streaming at her from the princess, who had managed to push her chair back out of Hekate's reach.

If you harm her, we'll never escape, Kabeiros said, his mental voice clearer.

The daggers and streams of light shattered into bright sparkles that diffused into nothing. Hekate saw that with her inner eye; her outer ones were fixed on Medea, who was plainly shocked by the failure of her attack spells. Pretending she had never noticed Medea's attempt, Hekate parted her lips in an expression of fear and pleading, and let the staff droop in her hands, as if she had not the strength or will to carry through her threat and was terrified by what she had done. Meanwhile she noticed that the red had faded from Medea's skin. Likely she had been lightly burned when the serpent's shields were destroyed by the lash of Hekate's power.

Actually Hekate was glad Medea's shields had been strong enough to resist that blast. Neither was she tempted to send any destructive spell against her now that her shields were burnt away. However, it was no scruple against murder that made Hekate lower the staff; Medea would be no loss to the world. What kept her passive was her knowledge that Kabeiros spoke the horrible truth. If she killed Medea, escape from Colchis would be well-nigh impossible.

Whatever Aietes' doubts about his daughter, if she were killed, those doubts would be forgotten and he would muster the whole strength of Colchis to take revenge. Neither could Hekate hope simply to disguise herself and travel separately from Kabeiros. Aietes knew she could wear an "illusion." It would not be beyond the king's power to prevent any and all persons from leaving Colchis until he laid his hands upon the one who had murdered his daughter.

Unfortunately leaving Medea alive was almost as bad a choice. Now that the princess had exposed herself to them as a shape-changer, she might well intend they both die to keep her secret. Not that it was much of a secret. Judging from the reactions of anyone who dealt with magic when she asked about shape-shifting, most of the magic workers already knew.

Undecided between the evil of a living, malevolent enemy and a corpse that would be a catastrophe, Hekate put out a placating hand to Medea. She had no time to speak, however, and it seemed as if her plea had come too late. The princess had already turned her head to the guard, who still stood against the door with dead eyes.

Hekate took a breath to utter the freezing spell, praying that Medea's shields were gone or weak enough to let the spell take hold; it would at least give her and Kabeiros time to think. But Medea didn't speak the words that would bring light to the guard's stone eyes. Instead she turned back to Hekate, taking in her seemingly desperate grip on her staff and the pleading hand outstretched. She glanced briefly at Kabeiros, who lifted his lip to show his tearing fangs and tried to steady his still-shaking body. And then Medea laughed shortly, her expression one of utter contempt.

"Fear for your lives, do you?" she asked, sneering. "Well, you have cause enough. You had not courage enough to strike, and you have lost your chance forever."

That Medea spoke instead of acting was a good sign and the look of contempt gave a reason to hope. "I didn't," Hekate cried. "It was an accident–"

"A spell that damages my shields was an accident?"

"That was no spell, my lady," Hekate said, trying to sound desperate. "I couldn't cast a spell that fast. Nor do I know any spell strong enough to damage your wards. It was only the power I had stored in my staff. I beg your pardon, I do, but when I saw you torturing poor Kabeiros for something he can't help, I lost my control over the staff and the power poured out."

"I wasn't torturing the dog," Medea snapped. "I was trying to find out–" And then the first words Hekate had spoken came back to her. "Not a spell?" Medea's eyes narrowed, but after a moment's thought, she nodded slowly and her eyes shifted to the staff. "So you store power in the staff."

"Yes, but it isn't mine. It's Kabeiros' staff." Although Hekate gave no sign of it, she noticed the interest that flashed across Medea's face. She continued eagerly, "I just carry it for him in the hope that some day we will discover a cure for his affliction. Really, truly, he cannot change back to a man."

Medea nodded again, briskly this time. "Perhaps that's the only true thing you've said since you came into the palace," she said, but for once she looked young and brightly interested. "What should be a clean node of power is all tangled up with a draining spell that constantly draws away the power to shift. If I had such a spell—" She stopped abruptly, her lips thinning. "You deserve to die for trying to protect a shape-shifter as well as for striking me," she remarked. "You know that. I could call that guard awake with a single word, faster than you could bespell me. My father's guards are impervious to magic and this one could call as many more as he needed to subdue you."

Hekate dropped her head, as if she could not meet Medea's gaze and made her outstretched hand tremble. Kabeiros allowed his ears to droop and dropped his tail between his legs. But actually Hekate felt a strong sense of relief from the hound and her own fear was receding. If Medea had intended to kill them, she would have wakened the guard and given the orders at once. Feeding the princess's feeling of contempt was more useful now than threat. Medea wanted something and she would believe she could get it more easily from cowed opponents than from aggressive ones.

"Please, my lady," Hekate whined. She felt like gagging at the sound of her voice, but if it won her freedom it was a small price to pay. "It was a mistake, an accident. No one deserves to die for an accident. Surely there is some way I can make up to you for my affront. And . . . and my lady, if you kill me and my dog after the king said we could go and that he still wanted to investigate my magic, won't he wonder why we were destroyed?"

"My father trusts me," Medea snapped, but doubt flickered behind her eyes.

Hekate made no reply to that, simply pleading again to be released for mercy's sake and swearing that she had seen and heard nothing unusual. Medea stared at her and then laughed again.

"Say I became a serpent," she said. "No one would believe you if you told such a fantastic story."

Hekate smiled tentatively, tremulously, as if hope were wakening in her. "No one will even believe I was at the palace, except the very few who saw the palace guard come for me, and they will not speak of it for fear."

Medea stared at her, looked speculatively at Kabeiros, then shrugged. "You will not be free to leave the city. You understand that?"

"Indeed, my lady. Why should I wish to leave? I have a good business here–" Hekate hesitated and tried to look calculating "–and if I come and go to the palace, I'm sure my business will improve. No, indeed, I won't leave the city, and I'll come here gladly any time you send for me."

The contempt had returned, more markedly, to Medea's expression. Plainly she considered Hekate very stupid as well as lacking in courage. However she didn't speak to Hekate, merely turned her head and snapped one word at the guard. Slowly the light returned to his eyes, but Medea was already looking at Hekate when full brilliance was restored.

"So you have nothing more to tell me about the dog?"

"No, my lady," Hekate said, as if no time had passed between King Aietes leaving the room and the guard being . . . Hekate's mind hesitated over the proper word and then chose shut down, as if he were a water wheel or some other mechanical contrivance. But she had continued saying, "I don't know how or why he sees although he looks blind, and I don't know of any magical quality he has, except being unusually clever. Sometimes I swear he understands everything I say."

Medea did not look particularly grateful for Hekate's support of her pretense, and Hekate cursed herself for being distracted by thinking about the guard and allowing herself to seem too clever. She needed Medea to believe she was stupid. However, the princess only turned to the guard and told him to see Hekate out of the palace. Hekate bowed, the dog wagged his tail very slightly and ran to the door as if eager to be gone. Hekate took her staff in hand and sidled out between the divan and the low table, leaving the papyrus with the spells lying there.

She had gone only a few steps toward the guard, who had already opened the door, when Medea said, "Wait. I think I will bid you leave that staff with me."

Hekate stopped and stared with her mouth slightly open, but mentally she cried, *Kabeiros?*

Leave it. Leave it, he replied. *If I am ever a man again, I can make another.*

"It is useless now until I gather more power for it," Hekate said, walking back toward Medea.

"Nonetheless, I will take it. I think I would prefer that you did not have a great store of power, which you might wield as a weapon again. Leave the staff with me."

"Yes, my lady," Hekate said meekly, and handed it over.

She was afraid, until they were actually passed

through the outer gate of the palace, that taking the staff had been an attempt by Medea to strip her of a weapon so she and Kabeiros could be more easily killed or taken prisoner or have an accident on the way out. However, nothing untoward happened and she and Kabeiros safely reached the inn, where she assured Batshira and Rakefet that the king had only been curious about her magic, but that he had been too busy to investigate fully and she would have to return. Then she set out for the market.

I thought after she asked for the staff, that we wouldn't get out of there alive, she said to Kabeiros as they walked. *Why do you think she wanted it?*

Probably to use just as you did. She knew that your spells could work with their magic. She knew that the staff was not yours originally. Thus she concluded that she could store her own magic in it and release it as you did without using a spell. I think it will work. The staff was never sealed to me. Perhaps that will pacify her for a bit, but we had better begin to plan a way to escape from here.

Not yet. There was suppressed excitement in Hekate's mental voice. *Didn't you hear what she gave away! I know now what is interfering with your ability to shift. The draining spell that sorcerer was using is caught in the shifting power. As I guessed, he was trying to kill you and was prevented somehow.*

Then why could I be a man in the caves of the dead?

Some magic dies in the caves. Mine didn't and yours didn't. We both could find the earth's blood and feed from it, but the otherplanar creatures could not pass and my father's magic— Hekate's mental voice stopped as if she had drawn a sharp physical breath. *Sweet Mother, Kabeiros, could we both have the same enemy? Could the sorcerer who attacked you be . . . my father?*

It would be convenient, Kabeiros said dryly, *but not very important now. How long do you think it will be before Medea attacks us? How can we be gone from here before then?*

You are sure she will attack?

As I am the sun will rise. Her spells would not hurt you; your power did hurt her. Can she let you live?

Hekate sighed. *You're right, of course, but I think she won't act yet. She has the staff to play with and she thinks I'm stupid and cowardly. I also think there's something more she wants from me. Besides that, she's not ready to challenge Aietes yet and he said he wanted me to be examined by his mages. I hope she'll wait until he's satisfied. Anyway, there's no way we can escape yet. We're being scryed. If we make a move, Aietes' creatures will be down on us.*

The dog was silent for a long time, then when they reached Hekate's place in the market and she was about to unlock the box that came with each space, he said, *I think I have in mind the word Medea used to stop the guard, but you will have to say it aloud so that I can hear it. Can the scryer hear what we say?*

Some can, some can't. I would guess Aietes' or Medea's scryers can. But I'm about to open my box. I think I'll extend my shields out to cover the whole workplace. That will seem natural enough.

On the words a thin silver hemisphere sprang up around them. Kabeiros put into her mind the word *mrznutise*. Hekate said it. Kabeiros shook his head, repeated with the emphasis slightly different. Meanwhile, Hekate had unlocked her box, spread the mat on which she sat, dropped the cushions one at each end. She repeated the word. Kabeiros shook his head, said, *Your voice must be harsher, like metal on metal.* She tried again as she lifted out a smaller locked box full of amulets and placed it by her cushion.

No more now, she told Kabeiros as she called the shield back into her body. *I can't keep my shield up too long or it will be suspicious.*

They would have had little chance to try anything more even if the scryer had not watched so constantly because Hekate had hardly settled on her mat when the first client arrived. After that she had a constant stream of clients, most of whom wanted to know why she had been called to the palace, what it was like, to whom she had spoken there . . . so many questions that she apologetically cut each person short, pointing out that others were waiting.

Among those waiting were servants from three sorcerers who lived in the great houses on Sorcerers Road past the Royal Way. Hekate had never met these people nor had they previously shown the smallest interest in her. Yet today, within hours after her return from the palace, each had sent a servant to purchase an amulet. She guessed that all of them either had informants in the palace who had reported on her interview with the royals or that they were acting under Aietes' orders.

Hekate blandly offered the box and allowed the sorcerers' servants to chose among the contents. All the amulets she had ready prepared, she told each servant, were charged with a "feel-good" spell that calmed anxiety. If they wanted other healing spells, Hekate said, they must describe the illness or allow her to visit the patient and she would prepare the amulet overnight. She wrapped each amulet in a scrap of cloth and handed it over.

After the second servant departed, she beckoned to one of the small boys who ran errands in the market. She handed him a similarly wrapped amulet, briefly touching his hand. The boy blinked once and set out without any verbal instruction, just as had the other sorcerers' servants, but that boy would deliver an uncharged amulet to Yehoraz and was bespelled to tell him that she had attracted the attention of the palace and that there was a scryer watching her. The boy would also say that she had not mentioned Yehoraz's name, and that she would not come to his house again. If he needed her for something, he should come to the market like any other client, which would not single him out in any way.

With that burden gone from her mind, Hekate answered one or two questions for each client, using superlatives of praise, over the guards, over the palace itself, over the wisdom of Aietes, the cleverness of Phrixos, and the beauty of Medea, all the time wondering how so many people had so quickly discovered that she had been summoned. When gathering dusk finally freed her from needing to think about her clients' needs, she realized the news had not really spread so quickly. The guard had come the night before; there had been time enough, if even one client had heard of it, for that one to spread the news to another until nearly all knew.

Now she was quick about folding her mat, piling the pillows atop the folded mat and, lifting her much-depleted chest of amulets, spreading her shield again. As she unlocked the box, and tossed everything inside, she made another two attempts to reproduce the word Kabeiros had heard.

The scryer was still watching when Hekate went to bed, and was there in the morning. Hekate had not bothered to wake in the night to check whether she was watched all night. It was logical she should be. If she were going to bolt, she would do so at night, so the scryer would watch all the more intently through the dark. But Hekate had no intention of running away, despite the danger.

Medea had already given her one valuable piece of information and might have more to impart. Of course, the princess didn't have a draining spell—she had spoken enviously of the one tangled in Kabeiros' shifting power—but now Hekate was far more interested in restoring Kabeiros' ability to shift than in the spell to drain her father. And it might be possible that in separating the draining spell she might learn it, so finding one answer would provide the other.

Hekate was reasonably sure that Medea had been trying to tease free the draining spell—or, more likely, tear it free, considering the agony inflicted on Kabeiros. If she could discover how the princess thought she could do that, Hekate reasoned that she could find a gentler way to accomplish the same purpose. Unfortunately, Hekate admitted she had not the faintest idea of how to pry information out of Medea. She could only wait and hope.

However, there was no message from the palace that morning. In fact a ten-day passed without further interference—except for the unbroken attention of the scryer and the arrival, at intervals, of five sorcerers' servants—two of the original three wanted more amulets and three were new. Fortunately the flow of ordinary clients had decreased to normal and Hekate could close and open her stall to obtain a midday meal, which permitted two more shielded moments to practice the word Kabeiros had heard.

She could say it by the end of the ten-day, although neither she nor Kabeiros was certain his memory of the word was perfect . . . or had remained perfect over the time they had been working with it. Moreover, Hekate knew that if the princess had held a symbol in her mind when she spoke, neither she nor Kabeiros could guess at what that symbol was.

In that time, she had also accomplished something that she knew would work; she had devised a ward with a bright mirror finish. Now if Medea tried to bespell her, instead of merely dissipating against Hekate's shields, that spell would reflect back on its caster.

Hekate hoped the spell Medea cast would not be devised to kill. However, she suspected that even if that was Medea's intention the reflection, distorted by the necessarily curved surface of the mirror ward, would not be very effective. Only effective enough, Hekate thought, to give Medea a good shock.

Only Medea didn't send for her. The only way Hekate knew she was still of interest to the palace was that she could feel the scryer constantly. Fortunately there was no way for a scryer to tell one spell from another; too much went on in the mind of the maker. The scryer could report that Hekate was devising spells, but not much more than that. Ignoring the minor irritation, Hekate went on with her life.

Following her usual custom, she didn't open her stall on the tenth day. She did her own shopping, mostly buying trinkets she could use for amulets. Then she returned to the inn and invested the trinkets with "feel-good" and finding spells. In a last attempt to protect Yehoraz, she did them in her chamber, as if that were where she always worked, hoping that Batshira would not sense her spell-casting and remind her that she was forbidden to do magic in the inn.

Another ten-day passed and with it came the end of the cool, bright days that marked autumn. The sky grew gray with dense cloud, only the faintest bright spot marking where the sun moved. A nasty wind blew; Kabeiros and Hekate both shivered on the exposed mat; about midmorning it began to rain. Hekate closed her stall and went back to the inn. On the third such day when she returned to the Black Genie, she complained bitterly to Batshira, who laughed at her.

"Colchis is a city of magic, yes, but even Aietes and his daughter cannot change the weather. Winter has come. There will be two, perhaps three, moons of this weather–and no, you can't use the inn for business."

"Where can I go?"

That was the right question. Batshira grinned widely. For a finder's fee, she bound herself to discover a chamber or apartment that Hekate could use to see clients or work spells. That was accomplished in so short a time, that Hekate wondered wryly whether knowing of the available space had sparked Batshira's firm refusal to allow Hekate to use the inn. However, she remembered that Batshira had been willing to risk warning her when the first summons to the palace had come and paid over the finder's fee without complaint.

She was glad she had done so and had stationed a "cryer" at her stall in the market to direct clients to her new place of business, for an inhuman guard arrived half a ten-day after she had settled into her new quarters. This time it waited until her last client had departed and led her to the palace as dusk was turning into full night. And the first thing King Aietes said when she was brought into his presence was that he was pleased she appeared to be planning to settle in Colchis.

"I would gladly do so if I were welcome," she answered a trifle absently as she looked around.

The guard had guided her not to the audience

chamber or the small waiting room, but to a handsome apartment fitted at one end with cushioned chairs and a divan for conversation and at the other end with a polished table and chairs for dining. This was not the king's own apartment, Hekate guessed, but a place he used for meeting with ambassadors and other important dignitaries. She was a little flattered but more interested in the table as she had been summoned before she had a chance to eat her evening meal.

The hope presented by the table was not in vain. Soon after the king acknowledged that even his best sorcerers could not detect her spells in the amulets but that they assuredly worked, he gestured her toward the table and a meal was carried in. Hekate ate heartily and was permitted to put a plate of cold sliced beef on the floor for Kabeiros.

The king was surprisingly interested in the feel-good spell itself. Some who came before him, he said, were so terrified or so angry that they could not tell a coherent tale. A spell like hers, which would not last more than a few candlemarks or a day, would do the petitioner no harm and ease his own work. If he were speaking the truth–and Hekate had no reason to think otherwise; she had seen him attending to petitioners herself–the spell would be used for a good purpose. Not that she could have refused to give it to him, even if she suspected the worst, but this way, when they were finished with the sweetmeats that ended the meal, Hekate taught it to him with true pleasure, which showed.

It was another very simple spell, one of the first her mother had taught her when she realized her own powers were bring drained away. Hekate had used it constantly within her father's household, where without it all the servants would have been in a constant state of panic.

When Aietes had the spell, he cast it on a human servant brought into his presence by a guard. The man's relaxation together with his alertness and clear understanding of where he was was sufficient evidence that the spell had been effective. Having dismissed guard and servant, Aietes looked at Hekate almost apologetically.

"That is a good spell and I am glad to have it, but I am no wiser now about what makes your magic beyond my senses or why you, yourself, are like a painting or a statue–visible to the eye but empty within." He shook his head. "Well, I hoped to spare you, but several sorcerers are waiting to examine you."

Hekate smiled at him sweetly. "So long as they tell me what they discover, I am very willing." She stood up and tightened her shields around her. "I am ready." Then she smiled. "Thank you, my lord, for feeding me first."

As she spoke the words she felt a pang of fear. Could that most excellent meal have contained some drug that would weaken her resistance to probing? She asked Kabeiros as they walked, but he had no answer for her except that in the portion fed to him he neither sensed nor smelled any unusual drug. And in the event, the meal was either innocent or whatever was administered was not effective because the sorcerers singly and together discovered nothing. She was as impenetrable to them as she had been to the king.

That was not the last of it, of course. She was recalled to the palace within the ten-day, earlier in the day this time, to be examined by three women, as if the gender of the sorcerer might have some influence. After that, although the scryer still watched, two ten-days passed without a summons and Hekate thought Aietes might be satisfied. She wondered how long she would have to wait for Medea to make her move, but it was to the king she was escorted in the middle of the third ten-day. This time he handed her one of the amulets which had held a triggered spell.

Most amulets were invoked immediately by the client's touch and the spell worked until it was exhausted, usually for several days growing steadily weaker. Those with a triggered spell were invoked by a word or an action, released a strong spell, and were immediately empty. Hekate explained and Aietes stared at her for a moment in silence. There was no threat in his expression.

"I thought I knew magic," he said, "but what you do is remarkable. Quite remarkable. Amulets are common enough, of course, but to trigger a spell hidden in a thing . . . that is new to me."

Hekate shook her head. "Just different, my lord, not remarkable. It is a healer's trick, and would not be necessary to you. If a person is very ill and needs a spell that will bring sleep or ease pain, either the healer must go to that person or have the person brought to her even if his condition is well known and the spell could be delivered in an amulet. But if the healer herself did not deliver the amulet, which would make the thing useless because the healer could deliver the spell itself, the greatest good of the amulet, which is when it is first invoked, would be lost on a messenger who doesn't need the spell. Thus the need for a triggered spell. Then the amulet could be delivered inactive and the patient could trigger the spell with a single word."

"Teach me," Aietes said.

Hekate sighed. What a king could do with such a device to hold spells made her uneasy. "This isn't as simple as the other spells."

The king smiled. "Somehow I didn't think it was,

but we don't have to finish the work today. You can come again as often as needed."

"My business, my lord," Hekate murmured.

"Come after dusk." He smiled again. "I will provide an evening meal, and we can talk about magic."

So they did. Six days out of ten a guard came for Hekate and took her to the palace and brought her home again. The winter passed and the skies were often clear, the wind mild. Hekate moved back to her mat in the marketplace three days out of every ten for she had noticed that the poorer clients did not come to the apartment on Sorcerers Road. Aietes asked about the move and she told him the truth.

"I would charge them the same, but perhaps they were afraid my price would rise, or they were overawed by the house. Why should they do without? And I like the market. I gossip with the other stallholders. They have very interesting things to say."

The king looked at her for a time without speaking, but a ten-day later she noticed that he no longer bothered to shield himself against her. From time to time, Hekate would be washed by an impulse to drop her own, but caution prevailed. Then one night when the moon was full, Hekate was flooded with a violent temptation to dismiss her own wards. Why should she not? Aietes trusted her, why should she not trust him? He had other protections, but—

Then Kabeiros, who was lying on the floor apart from her rather than sitting pressed against her thigh, said, *Your magic will still be invisible, but your mind and soul will be naked to Aietes' gaze. Do you want that?*

CHAPTER 16

The mental voice was thick and dull, like a man just roused from sleep—roused unwillingly because the instinct to protect her both for the dog and for the man was stronger than torpor, came before life itself. Suddenly Hekate's throat closed with fear—not because she had almost given herself into Aietes' hands to do with what he pleased, but because she had not heard Kabeiros' voice for so long—for ten-days? moons?

With a terrible pang of remorse, Hekate realized that she had spoken very little to Kabeiros over the whole winter. Between her business every day and the king's summons nearly every evening, she was too tired to do much more than tumble into bed and fall asleep when she reached her apartment. Although she enjoyed her evenings with Aietes, she needed to be wary and the hours spent with him were always a strain. Still, he was a fascinating man, although not as strong a sorcerer as she had first believed.

She discovered very soon that *his* magic had not

produced the wonders of Colchis, although he was a master of illusions and of binding spells of which he had taught her many. Bit by bit after he had ceased to shield himself against her, Hekate learned what Aietes could and couldn't do.

Not that she had tried to probe him; he would have known that at once, she was sure, and never trusted her again. Hekate could not decide whether he was deliberately giving her the information as a sign of his trust or whether he didn't realize just how much she was learning about him, because what she now knew came through the wonderful tales he told, mostly about his great-great-grandfather, who had been a foster-brother to the god Hephaestos.

In an infantile attempt to stop a quarrel between his mother, Hera, and his father, Zeus, Hephaestos had been picked up by the leg and flung away so violently he had been crippled. His terrified nurse had fled with him to Hermes, who had "leapt" with them to the farthest place he knew, Colchis. There the king had taken the nurse and her three-year-old charge into his protection.

When he had grown into his powers, Hephaestos had built the palace of Colchis and given other artifacts to Aietes' ancestor out of love and gratitude, although those emotions were not so common among the gods. Among those artifacts were the dragon's teeth–Hekate had been startled by receiving an image of a fang longer than her hand–which if planted under certain conditions, grew into the stone-eyed servitors, who were Aietes' guards.

None of that was of any importance now. Hekate put a hand to her head and choked on her remorse. Her pride and vanity, her insatiable curiosity, were a curse. Like a babe with a new bauble, she had cast aside the solid worth of a familiar friend for the gaudy tinsel of novelty. Because she was no longer hungry for conversation with a trusted equal as she had been when they were traveling or when they had first come to Colchis, she might lose Kabeiros.

Aietes was speaking, but Hekate had both hands pressed to her temples. *Kabeiros,* her mind whispered, *Kabeiros, forgive me.* But there was no response.

She looked down at Kabeiros and it was only the dog lying there on the floor. The image of the man she used to see was gone. Had it ever returned after Medea had attacked him? Had she failed him so long ago as that? Hekate stared wide-eyed but unseeing at Aietes.

"What's wrong?" he was asking anxiously. "Hekate, what's wrong?"

"Forgive me, my lord," she muttered. "Suddenly my head hurts unbearably. Will you permit me to go home?"

Aietes looked startled, but he said immediately, "Of course, my dear. Shall I summon a litter for you?"

Hekate tried to swallow her grief and misery. There was now rage in Aietes' eyes and ice behind the gentle voice in which he spoke to her. But she could not be concerned with Aietes any more. Kabeiros was more important.

"Thank you, no," she whispered, dropping her hands from her head and closing her eyes for a moment. "I think the walk in the cool air will do me good."

As she spoke, a guard opened the door. She rose and then had to bid Kabeiros to come, which further frightened her. How long had she needed to give him orders as if he were, indeed, a dog? When the man had been present with the dog, he had always listened to her conversations and been on his feet and ready to leave as soon as she moved. She put her hand on his head, whispering silently, *Kabeiros, Kabeiros, forgive me.* But there was no response.

Once out of the palace, she hurried down Sorcerers Road as fast as she could. Not a hundred paces from the gate, the sense of being watched struck her with almost physical force. Hekate shivered and walked faster, one hand locked on the loose skin at Kabeiros' neck. The watcher, who had glanced at her only infrequently over the past moon, had returned with greater than usual intensity. Perhaps Aietes had been made suspicious by her sudden retreat; perhaps the pace she was setting was too fast for someone who had claimed an aching head. Hekate didn't care although her mind instinctively provided the excuse that she had been hurrying home to her herbs and simples to obtain relief.

In her apartment, aware of the scryer's even more pressing attention, she shook some powder into a cup, added water, and drank it down. Then she sank onto the carpet where Kabeiros lay and laid her head upon his shoulder.

Kabeiros, she cried as strongly as she could make her mind voice sound, *come back to me. Come back. Where are you?*

What is left of me is here.

Oh, forgive me. Forgive me. Hekate embraced the dog and began to sob aloud.

The dog barely stirred.

Please, Kabeiros. Please. I've been so tired at night. I didn't realize how I was neglecting you. Why didn't you scold me? Why didn't you remind me that I'd promised to talk to you all the time so that you wouldn't forget you were a man?

It didn't seem important. The mental voice was still dull, although somewhat clearer. *While you needed me, while you had to hide your magic in the caravans and even here at first, I was a man for you. But now you have found another man, more interesting than foolish Kabeiros, likely more powerful too. What will you do with me when you marry Aietes?*

Hekate was so shocked that her sobs checked. After a moment of stunned silence, she echoed, *Marry Aietes? Sweet, merciful Mother, where did you ever get such an idea?* She sat up straight. *I will never marry Aietes!*

Won't you? The dog finally looked at her. *He intends to marry you. It has been in his mind, more and more strongly, since he dropped his shields.*

Why didn't you warn me?

Warn you? How could you not know? I assumed you were pleased. If I could read the intention in him, how come you couldn't?

Hekate stared into Kabieros' white eyes and slowly shook her head. *I have no idea. Perhaps he could have buried the idea so deep that I didn't notice . . . but then, how would you have read him so clearly? I don't know how . . . wait . . . let me think. Sometimes I would feel confused when Aietes and I were talking, as if his words were blurred. Several times I was tempted, although not so strongly as tonight, to open my wards to better understand.* Her lips thinned. *Do you think he's been playing with me all this time in the hope that I would drop my shields so he could discover the secret of my 'invisible' magic?*

Possibly, but then why should he bury his thoughts about marriage from you? The dog also sat up and his "voice" was clearer, quicker. *Surely showing you that intention should have been an inducement to openness.*

Not if he guessed how I would feel about marriage to him!

*How *do* you feel about it?*

Hekate shuddered and leaned forward to clutch Kabeiros to her. *The only man I will ever marry—if that man should be willing to take me—is you, Kabeiros. I have surety enough, over the years we have been together, that we are alike in mind and spirit, that there is nothing with which I would not trust you, mind, body, or soul. There is no other man—most certainly not Aietes—about whom I could say that.* There was a long pause, and then Hekate said, wonderingly, *I love you, Kabeiros. I . . . I didn't know it until now, but I love you.*

Suddenly the man was beside her, squatting in and around the dog, one immaterial arm around her shoulders, one hand stroking her cheek and hair. The dog panted gently and turned his head to lick her cheek.

But I am not a man. The anguish in the mental voice drew tears from Hekate's eyes.

You will be! You will be! I will never give up, never! I have been bewitched, flattered that a powerful mage-king should talk with me, should tell me his secrets and tales of the gods. Forgive me. It won't happen again. I am come to my senses.

My forgiveness is easily won, but will that of Aietes be? Dog and man shook his head, but the mental tone was all human, ascerbic. *I hope it's not too late. How does one tell a king that his attentions, which have been encouraged for some three moons, have become unwelcome?*

The dry mental tone, completely undoglike, delighted Hekate, who released him and straightened up. *I don't know,* she admitted. *We'll have to think of something.*

We! Kabeiros exclaimed. *You got us into this . . . * The mental voice began to drift.

Kabeiros! Hekate bellowed.

The dog jumped. *What? Why are you shouting into my head?*

I thought you were drifting away from me.

Oh, no. I just had a thought. It's very strange you didn't sense Aietes' intention of marrying you, and what you said about sometimes finding him hard to understand made me wonder if his desire to have you for his wife might have been hidden by an outside force.

Outside?

The dog lolled out his tongue in silent laughter. *Do you think Medea would be very happy to have a mother-by-law?*

Hekate's eyes opened wide and a slow smile curved her lips. "She would have a litter of kittens!" Hekate was so enchanted with the idea that she spoke aloud, then recalled the scryer and added silently, *Yes, Medea. Now that you've called her to my mind, I wonder how I could have forgotten her all this while. Do you think my shields were not so impenetrable as I believed and Aietes spelled me to forget his daughter? If you're right and he wanted to marry me . . . well, what woman would want a daughter-by-marriage like Medea?*

I think your shields are sound. I think it was the way Aietes spoke to you, took you into his confidence—or seemed to—that made it seem he had only himself to please. It was a kind of suggestive idea that takes unobtrusive root.

Do you think they could have been working together, Aietes winning my confidence and Medea waiting to seize my mind when I dropped my shields?

The dog was silent, his mind withdrawn into thought, the skin above his eyes wrinkling in his concentration. Then he heaved a great sigh.

*I am also at fault. Because I was alone, I allowed

myself to sink into the dog who felt less. I've been lax in my duty to protect you—*

"No!" Hekate cried aloud, and put her arms around him.

Yes. I haven't been paying attention to the smell of power around us. It's very faint and I have to strain to pick it up . . . and I was in no mood for straining. That doesn't matter now.

Hekate hugged the dog to her. *We're together again.*

The dog reared back a little, and Hekate released him. *Still, I can't believe they worked together,* he said. *I don't think Aietes would trust Medea to get into your mind. And why should he? If you dropped your shields, he would seize your mind himself. Besides, if they were working together, Medea wouldn't have blocked Aietes' thoughts about marriage . . . unless those were no part of the plan?*

That's possible, but I still think you're right. I can't imagine Medea taking at all kindly even to the pretense that her father might marry again, particularly to a very strong sorcerer.

So we are agreed that if Medea interfered, Aietes was unaware of it. Now how can we use her to convince Aietes he doesn't want you to wife?

Hekate grinned. *By telling her the absolute truth: that I only realized today that Aietes thought of me as more than a friend and that, although I respect and admire the king, I have no desire at all to be queen. We need to think about this some more, but I might also tell her I wish to leave Colchis because I have despaired of untangling the draining spell from your shifting power or of finding anyone in Colchis who can help me do it. Oh, wait . . . another idea occurs to me. Why don't I ask her to tell me how she intended to do that as a bribe to leave Colchis forever?*

Never mind about asking how she intended to get the draining spell out of my power node. I know that. What she planned was to burn away the shifting power–

Hekate uttered a wordless cry and clutched the dog to her once more. *But that would kill you!*

The dog leaned away from her to loll out his tongue in laughter again. *Did you think that would trouble Medea overmuch?*

Serpent bitch!

Now, now. Let's not malign my species or that of the serpent, which is a clean beast, even if venemous.

Then the dog's mind went blank. Hekate tightened her grip on him. *Never mind her, Kabeiros. I will spread my shield so that it covers you also.*

No, Kabeiros said, *you can't afford to thin the wards so much. I'm not afraid of her. I was just suddenly reminded of how she shifted to the serpent form. Why did she do that, Hekate? Why did she expose herself to us?*

Because she wanted to see you shift so that she could learn how it works? I have no idea what I do to shift, do you?

*No, and what you say is possible, even probable. I agree that she wanted to see me change, but still there was no need for *her* to change form. She could have just told us she knew I was a shape-shifter and ordered me to change. No. She needed to be in the serpent form.* He paused then went on slowly, *Yes . . . yes. It is because she has powers in that form that she does not have in the human body.* His mental tone quickened. *Think, Hekate. As a dog I can smell magic. I cannot sense it as a man, except for being able to see the flow of earth-blood.*

You have it! Hekate hugged him, then released him and bit her lip. *But can she cast spells in serpent form? You told me you couldn't do spell-casting as a dog.*

Kabeiros ducked his head in the equivalent of a shrug. *I don't know. I think not, but you can cast spells in any of your shapes–*

Those I use are all human. I couldn't cast spells when I once took the body of a cat. That was one reason I never tried to perfect any animal form.

You mean I could shift to a form other than the dog?

Hekate nibbled on her lower lip. *I don't know. So little is known about shape-shifting. No one–as far as I know–has ever dared to study it because it is so hated.* Her silver eyes glowed with interest. *Now that is something you and I must do–you can study me and I you–when we have found a safe haven. Think what we could accomplish if we could win control of shifting–*

The dog had looked away and Hekate caught her breath, knowing his pain. She hugged him tight again. *You will be freed. I am bound to it and bound again. We will leave Colchis and seek our answer in Olympus.*

That's a very good thought. Hold tight to it. I, too, think it a good time to leave Colchis and seek Olympus. But how do we leave Colchis with Aietes not willing to let you go?

Medea must find an escape for us, but I am not quite sure how we can use her shape-shifting to . . . And I have thought of another problem. How can I get to see Medea to tell her what we need to tell her?

They came to no conclusion, although they discussed the matter on and off until they went to bed. In between they talked about what Hekate needed to take with her when they left Colchis and how to convince Medea to help them escape. That was a somewhat more fruitful discussion. The necessary herbs and amulets were laid aside in several packs, the one most essential made up so that either Hekate or Kabeiros could seize it and carry it, the other two to be taken if possible. They did not talk much about confronting Medea; both knew that if the devices Hekate had designed did not work exactly as she hoped, they might both die.

In the event, getting to see Medea was not a problem at all. Ignoring the heavy presence of the watcher, Hekate set out for the market the next morning. She had barely settled herself on her mat, when a rather strange figure cut in front of the two clients waiting and loomed over her. Hekate looked up and saw a tall man, cloaked in black—although the weather was mild—wearing a most peculiar beard. The hair above his lip had been allowed to grow down around his mouth on each side and was braided into long strands. Another braided strand grew from the center of his chin. His eyes were black and very narrow, set above wide, flat cheekbones, and his skin was a dull ochre yellow.

Without a word, he pointed a finger at her. Light that only Hekate could see streamed from that finger and dissipated against her shields. Annoyed, she hastily added the mirror shield to the others.

"Yes?" she asked coldly, but as if she hadn't noticed the attempt to bespell her.

Kabeiros was not as polite; he rose to his feet, snarling. The sorcerer hastily directed two more blasts of light—first one at Kabeiros, which thinned to a shining veil as it touched him and then slipped off into the ground as water slips off an oiled surface, the other at Hekate, which hit her mirror ward and bounced back. She had one moment to see his unbelieving and horrified expression before his own spell hit him. Then he stood staring stupidly at her, eyes glazed, waiting for her commands.

"Tell me what it is you want me to do," Hekate said, guessing at the kind of spell the sorcerer had cast and asking what she hoped would produce the most unrevealing answer.

She was aware of her clients and the merchants and clients in the stalls to either side of hers. They wouldn't have seen or sensed the magic exchange, of course, but quick glances showed her that they were somewhat awed and frightened. This sorcerer was known, and feared, among the common folk of Colchis.

"You must come to my house," the man in the black cloak replied, his voice flat and without expression.

"Very well," Hekate responded calmly.

She leaned around him and told her waiting clients that an emergency had arisen, then rose from her mat and packed everything into the box that came with the stall. There was nothing there she could not leave behind. It was a shame the potions and lotions must be abandoned . . . No, she would leave the key and the spell with Batshira to be given to Yehoraz. It would be her farewell gift to him.

As she worked, she asked Kabeiros if he was all right, whether the spell had hurt him? He replied he hadn't even been aware that a spell had been cast at him. *The dog,* he remarked, as they set off in the wake of the black-cloaked sorcerer, *has always been impervious to magic and that seems to be as true of the high power as of the earth power.*

But Medea hurt you. Now that they were to confront the princess again, Hekate was worried about Kabeiros.

That wasn't a spell, he replied calmly, trotting along beside her. *I'm sure that was something only the serpent can do. As long as she is in human form, I have no need to fear her. And if she changes, this time I think she'll aim her will at you.*

And meet the mirror. I wonder what a distorted form of her own will will do to her?

There was amusement in Hekate's mind, and the dog snorted gently as they crossed the Royal Way and walked along the upper reaches of Sorcerers Road. The black-cloaked man turned into a gate leading to one of the most secluded of the houses. Something in his stride warned Kabeiros who told Hekate to beware, that the reflected spell had worn off. Hekate shrugged. She had made no attempt to use the spell to question the man because of the watcher and she doubted he was likely to try any more spells against her.

I wonder, Hekate mused, *whether it was a very short-term spell because Medea is here already and he didn't want her to know he had bespelled me or whether the mirror's distortion weakened it.*

In either case, beware! Kabeiros warned.

You may be sure— Hekate didn't complete the assurance she was about to give Kabeiros because at that point they passed some kind of barrier—Hekate saw it as a very faintly glowing line of mist—and the watcher was gone.

Almost at the same moment she became aware of that, Kabeiros said, *The smell of lightning is gone. I think magic isn't supposed to work here—but I still smell your shields. The ward is against the high magic, I think.*

The absence of power gave the black-cloaked sorcerer's garden a peculiarly dead feeling. Hekate watched his back speculatively. If this was his work, he was a powerful mage, far more powerful than those whom Aietes had ordered to examine her. So he hid his power from the king . . . from Medea too?

Not possible if she was here to meet them; she would be aware of the ward against power. It was a shield of a magnitude Hekate had never come across before and she was tempted to ask how such a ward could be constructed and powered. Only she was not supposed to be aware of it.

They entered the house—that too was dead feeling—and Hekate suffered a definite twinge of envy. Kabeiros, sensing her curiosity, growled a soft warning. A great deal, possibly even their lives, depended on Medea underestimating them. To expose that they were aware of the high magic might be fatal. Hekate sighed and nodded.

The corridor was lit by square openings in its roof. A faint breeze wafted down from them, so they weren't covered with that impossibly thin crystal that roofed Aietes' audience chamber. No obvious doors broke the walls of the corridor, which was paneled in dark wood. The panels alternated between those carved with delicate, fantastic scenes of gardens, high-humped bridges, peculiar houses with upcurved roof beams, and tiny people in strange clothing and those carved with angular symbols in which Hekate could find no familiarity at all.

The sorcerer went about two thirds of the way down the corridor and touched one of the symbols. If he murmured a word, Hekate did not catch it; she hoped Kabeiros might have heard, his ears being keener. A door swung open to reveal a small landing and a flight of stairs. Midway down the stairs was another landing on which the sorcerer stopped and murmured a word. The door, this one not concealed in any way, opened. He stepped aside and waved for Hekate and Kabeiros to enter. The door closed behind them, and something in the way it shut made Hekate think it would not be easy to open again.

Medea was sitting on a high-backed, intricately carved chair of black wood set on a dais. On each side of the chair stood one of the stone-eyed guards. Hekate felt at once that this room was not dead—although she couldn't feel the watcher. Still, magic would work here . . . magic had been worked here . . . much magic.

Hekate bent her lips into a smile and started forward, saying, "Lady Medea, thank you for summoning me. I didn't know how to reach you—"

The princess turned toward one of the guards and said, "*U pozorisnom komadu.* Kill her."

The guard stepped forward, drawing his sword. "You are making a mistake, my lady," Hekate cried, but there was no more time for explanation. "*Mrznutise!*" Hekate shrieked, and unbidden, the image of the dragon's tooth came into her mind. The result left her open-mouthed with shock.

Both creatures collapsed to the ground, swords and armor ringing hollowly as they struck the stone floor. Hekate stared wide-eyed as weapon and armor as well as the guards' bodies fell to dust and disappeared, leaving on the floor two curved and shining teeth, a handspan long.

Medea screamed, then began to moan, "Fool! Fool! You don't know what you've done! How could my father have been so besotted that he taught you that command?"

And the serpent was there, coiled in the high-backed chair, bending its beautifully marked neck to reach the side of the chair where the mouth gripped Kabeiros' staff and lifted it so the metal tip pointed at Hekate.

"No! Don't! Please!" Hekate cried as she stepped in front of Kabeiros and drew into her mirror shield every bit of the unused earth-blood, which virtually pooled on the stone floor.

Even so, the blast of power that struck Hekate sent her staggering backward, which drove her against Kabeiros. Unbalanced, she fell heavily, but fortunately the dog's quick reaction permitted him to move when Hekate bumped him and position himself so his body cushioned her head. That saved her from knocking herself unconscious, which could have been utter disaster; unconsciousness would have dissolved her shields and left her naked to Medea's wrath. Hekate was still shuddering with relief as she levered herself upright, but then she realized she had been in little danger.

The room seemed full of sparkles of light as released power scattered. Wherever wisps of Hekate's hair were not confined, they stood away from her head, writhing. Kabeiros' fur was also all standing on end and little crackles came from it when he moved. The serpent was gone. Medea was limp and sagging, supported by the arm of the great chair, her head hanging, her eyes glazed. Hekate breathed a sigh of relief when she saw that the princess was still breathing.

Should I put a compulsion on her? Hekate asked Kabeiros. *Her shields are down.*

No! Kabeiros exclaimed. *It would be too dangerous to trust the spell–it might fade or fail suddenly–so you would have to convince her anyway, which would be harder because she would sense the spell and the hatred she would feel . . . It would expose your real power also. No, we're better off trying to convince her without any magical aids.*

She hates us anyway. But there was little energy in Hekate's argument; she wasn't fond of coercion spells and she dropped the idea as Medea began to stir.

"I begged you not to loose that blast at me," Hekate sighed, as soon as sense came back into

Medea's eyes and she straightened in her chair. "If you had let me speak, my lady, I would have warned you. Spells cast at me sometimes just die and sometimes bounce back . . ."

Hekate spoke as if she hadn't seen the serpent, didn't know that what had been directed at her had not been a spell but a blast of raw power, hadn't recognized the staff in which the power had been stored. Medea stared at her, open-mouthed, for once looking as young and vulnerable as an ordinary frightened girl of her age.

"Who are you? What are you?" Medea breathed.

"I told you when you first asked. I am an herb-wife who has learned magic—more magic than I ever expected to learn and more than I need or want. How I do that magic and how I am protected from magic, I can't tell you. Neither can your father, who has been testing and prying for moons and has discovered nothing."

There was a pause and then Medea asked, "Are you a goddess?"

"If I am, I don't know it," Hekate replied, but her brow was suddenly creased in a thoughtful frown, and she allowed her voice to hold a note of doubt. "I believe," she added slowly, "that I was born in the ordinary way and I know I had a father and mother, who were not gods."

As she spoke the words, her lips thinned. Was it possible that Perses was a rogue "god," driven from Olympus because of his evil propensities? Not that what she had heard of the Olympians made them good and pure. The tales that Kabeiros had told in the caves and on the journey to Colchis made them out to be very human—proud, petty, greedy, selfish, and lustful, but also occasionally good-hearted and generous. None was truly evil.

She pushed that thought away. Even to think of

Perses weakened her and she needed all her strength . . . Yes, strength. It came suddenly to Hekate that appearing weak was no longer any protection from Medea. It was time to abandon that ploy. Possibly the opposite would work. Certainly a Medea wide-eyed and trembling, asking if Hekate were a goddess was less dangerous than the Medea who thought she could squash Hekate like a bug.

Let the princess fear she was a goddess. There were tales enough of gods who had lost themselves and didn't recognize their own powers. Let Medea think she was an immortal and further attempts to harm her would be useless.

Let her think me a goddess? she asked Kabeiros.

Try. Mother knows acting a simpleton didn't help.

She had no time for a further exchange with Kabeiros, because Medea was saying, "If you *are* a goddess, you knew Ming Hao was my messenger and you knew I wished you ill. Why did you come? Are you planning to punish me or teach me?"

"No, I am not," Hekate said, allowing a touch of contempt to color her voice. "For all your malice, you have done me no harm, and I need you to find me a ship out of Colchis."

"A ship?" Medea's eyes widened, then narrowed. "For what does a goddess need a ship?"

"I never said I was a goddess . . . you said that. I said, and it's true, that I don't know. I can do things I never expected, but some of those things happen without my will or intention. You think I threw back your spell at you, and I suppose I did, but I don't know how. Since I have come to Colchis, my powers have increased hugely but they are nearly new to me. At present I have no way to escape Colchis.

In fact, I didn't know the sorcerer was bringing your summons, but I hoped it was so."

"You *wished* to see me?"

"Yes. I told you I need you to get me a ship. I think you're the only one powerful enough to do that against the king's order and save me."

"Save you? I just ordered you killed. How can you believe I would want to save you."

"Because you *can't* kill me, can you?" Hekate smiled.

For a moment Medea looked as if she might try again, but she only said, "Not by magic, it seems, and since you already can control the dragon's tooth guards–" she choked over the words, but continued "–and will soon be queen of Colchis, too–"

"But I don't want to be queen of Colchis!" Hekate interrupted.

Medea stared at her, then said, "Liar."

Hekate shook her head firmly. "I'm not lying. That's why I need to leave Colchis against the king's will. I only learned yesterday that Aietes wants to marry me." A flicker of satisfaction showed in Medea's face, and Hekate's suspicion was confirmed; it had been Medea who had fogged her mind from time to time. "So it was you who hid his intention from me. You fool! Do you *want* me as a mother-by-marriage, Medea? If I'd known Aietes' intention, you would have been rid of me much sooner–and I wouldn't have learned as much as I did from your father."

"You liar! You would have learned more, using his lust to lead him to indiscretion. How, how did you induce him to teach you the command that would return a servitor to his original form?"

"He never told me anything about the guards." Hekate smiled pityingly. "You were the one who taught me that word. Don't you remember? The time you almost killed Kabeiros because you chose not to believe he couldn't change? I saw you turn off the guard so you could play your games in private, and I heard the word, and I remembered." Hekate paused then went on, threateningly, "I remembered *everything* about that meeting. Now, I want out of Colchis." Her silver eyes grew darker, met Medea's colorless gaze.

"You heard and remembered . . . I thought you were nothing, an herb-wife with a silly trick . . ."

"Then I *was* nothing. I have learned a great deal. Have sense. Arrange for a ship to take me away before I learn more."

"You only want me to find you passage on a ship so you can tell my father I was trying to be rid of you. You want to make ill-will between us."

"No." Hekate shook her head almost sadly. "King Aietes is a wonderful man, handsome, intelligent, and a powerful sorcerer, but—" she put her hand on Kabeiros's head and held Medea's gaze with her own; Medea knew that Kabeiros was a man as well as a dog "—I have a man already. I want no other and, in particular, I don't want to be bound to the duties of a queen. I need to be free to pursue my own destiny."

She gave a little emphasis to the last word, to remind Medea what that destiny probably was. The princess looked down at her hands, now folded sweetly in her lap and slowly shook her head. She seemed pensive, slightly sad.

"My father won't let you go. He is really set on having you totally within his power so he can use your invisible magic. You know, I suppose, that coupling creates a special binding. I am very much afraid that if you wish to be free, you will have to . . . ah . . . render him powerless. Then, of course, I could—"

"No, Medea," Hekate interrupted coldly. "I will do King Aietes no harm. I am very fond of him. I consider him a friend and it grieves me greatly that I must leave and without even a kind farewell. However, I am thrice bound to other duties. Don't try again to make me harm your father."

"I never said you should harm him!" Medea burst out. "*You* are trying to injure me in his opinion. You've already done me great harm. Last night you told him I was tampering with your mind–"

"I told him nothing, but you did meddle in serpent form, didn't you? And look where it has got us, you silly child!"

If Medea heard her, she gave no sign of it. Eyes fixed, she shrieked, "He came raging into my chamber and threatened to destroy my powers. He told me he intended to marry you so he would have you, whom he could trust, and not need me any more to assist him."

"All the more reason to be rid of me, you fool," Hekate said to Medea and then to Kabeiros, *Why is she fighting what she should devoutly desire?*

I would guess because she cannot bear that anyone who bested her should escape without punishment.

Hekate's eyes narrowed. *You know, Kabeiros, the world would be a better place without this one.*

Let her be. It is for the Mother to judge her, which She will do in Her own time.

Mentally, Hekate sighed but continued to speak to Medea in what she hoped was a reasonable tone. "Medea, if I don't leave Colchis, you will have to . . . one way or another. Soon there won't be room in this city for both of us. Remember, you said yourself that coupling creates a special bond. Are you sure that you want me for a mother-by-marriage?

Are you sure who would win the contest of wills in a coupling beween your father and me?"

Medea actually paled. "Very well. Very well. But it cannot be today."

She wants time to arrange for your assassination, Kabeiros said.

I guessed, Hekate replied mentally with utmost calm, and then said aloud, "You know it must be today. After what passed between you and your father last night, he will insist on settling matters between us at once . . . so he will know how to deal with you. I need to be well away from Colchis before the time that I usually go to your father in the evening. And I tell you plainly, if I am still here, I will agree to marry him and tell him everything. Now, will you help me escape from Colchis this very day?"

"And how would I explain that to my father?"

"Why explain anything? Why should you know anything about my leaving?" Hekate smiled. "In any case, you would have a much harder time explaining my death. After last night, do you think Aietes will believe you innocent?"

Medea stared at her, lips thinned to an ugly line, but then they softened and she began to look more thoughtful than angry. "You will never be able to return to Colchis," she said.

Hekate nodded. "I know, and I am sorry for it. I like the city and the people and I am truly fond of Aietes. But I have other, more driving needs. I will not return."

"You must not be seen going down to the dock, the one at the foot of Sorcerers Road. You must allow me to bespell you to invisibility. And you must leave the dog here. Everyone knows the dog."

Laughing, Hekate shook her head. "Send a message to the market or to the Black Genie with the name of the ship and when it sails and leave all else to me. And do not think I will be unaware that you will instruct the captain to be rid of me. When he tries, I will teach him a lesson that will make him your enemy forever."

Medea shrugged. "You will not listen to me, so I will not be responsible for what befalls you. There is no need for a messenger, which might betray me to my father. The *Sea Foam* will start down the river at dawn. Tell the captain, if you wish, that it is by my order that you leave Colchis."

CHAPTER 17

Wearing the look-by-me spell, Hekate came aboard the *Sea Foam* in the late afternoon, during a busy period of loading. There were guards to prevent thieving, clerks to write down what was brought aboard, examiners to see that what was listed on the bill of lading was actually in the packages, as well as the slaves who carried the goods. In the crowded conditions, the danger of touching someone was greater; however, there were so many people and things to distract the eye from her, that even if she did bump someone she only needed to step aside and she would never be noticed.

Weaving this way and that, she made her way below the decked-over area and found a place that seemed fully loaded. There she crammed her bundles into the spaces left by the curve of a number of barrels and squeezed herself behind bales of what she thought was cloth. Having sat down to wait until the loading was complete, she had time to think. The ease of her escape thus far was surprising.

Had Medea accepted her arguments? Certainly she seemed relieved when Hekate agreed that she would never return to Colchis. Perhaps Medea had decided it was better to be rid of a hated rival than to garner an empty satisfaction in Hekate's death, which would make more trouble for her. Perhaps . . . Still, when Hekate had left Ming Hao's house, the watcher had not touched her again. Had Medea blocked the scrying? Was it necessary? The watcher could have been Medea's, not Aietes', all along.

Not that Hekate had done anything either Medea or Aietes would have found suspicious. She saw a few clients at the market, then she had gone to the Black Genie to eat dinner. There she had followed Batshira into the kitchen, a thing she had done many times before. This time, however, she cast a no-see-no-hear spell and told the innkeeper she was leaving Colchis. She gave her the key to her rooms and another moon's rent. Over that time, little by little, Hekate said, Batshira should give to Yehoraz the herbs and amulets from the rooms and take the other contents for herself.

That done, she went back to her apartment, gathered up her three bundles, and cast the look-by-me spell. Kabeiros had not followed her from the inn; he had gone off on his own toward the market. From there, he had told her, he would take a long and winding path, not infrequently stopping to consort with other dogs in the city, down to the dock area, where he would find *Sea Foam* and conceal himself near the ship until she called for him.

Too easy, Hekate wondered? Not if Medea was helping her to leave. Hekate had no doubt that Medea knew ways to blind or divert a watcher and, she suspected, was capable of fixing Aietes' attention, too. Had she approached her father with tearful apologies, with promises of amendment of her ways?

Had she even needed to? Aietes was fond of Medea. Wouldn't he regret being so harsh to her? Hekate smiled. Likely enough it was Aietes who came to Medea with apologies. If so, that was the best luck that could befall her, Hekate thought. Aietes would not send for her that evening if he were trying to placate Medea, so he wouldn't know she had fled until the next day at least.

Hekate sighed. She could hope for such good fortune, but there was no way to know anything for certain. She must watch and wait. Taking a polished circle of metal from her special bundle, Hekate scryed the upper deck at intervals, keeping her observation short so no minimally Talented person would "feel" the watching. As evening approached, the loading reached a peak of activity, then began to diminish.

By dark, the clerks, examiners, and porters were gone and the captain and two officers went ashore. Bread, cheese, and wine were distributed to the crew who ate quickly, then rolled themselves in blankets and bedded down on the deck along the hull. Only one guard remained to watch the landing plank until the captain should return, when Hekate assumed the plank would be pulled in.

Having waited until there was no more murmuring or movement from the blanket-covered crew, Hekate extracted herself from behind the bales, walked softly and carefully to just behind the guard, and threw one of her amulets, making sure it rolled noisily into concealment behind some casks. The guard's head turned to the sound. Hekate called silently to Kabeiros, who came out of the shadows beside one of the dockside buildings.

The guard cast a look about the street to make

sure no one was close enough to reach the ship and board it while his attention was distracted. Then he went to check on the noise behind the casks. He found the amulet, lifted it, and froze. Kabeiros dashed across the dock, leapt up the plank, and ran across the deck to slip into the dark underdeck where Hekate joined him.

They were safely behind the bales, black Kabeiros invisible in the black shadow, Hekate shielded by the look-by-me spell, before the guard moved. He was unaware that he had lost some moments, and turned alertly to scan the dock again. It was empty. The guard returned to his post, looking curiously at the amulet and wondering from where it had come. It was possible that one of the crew had lost it and it had caught on a rope and simply fallen off. Nonetheless, the man tucked it carefully in his belt, resolved to tell the captain what had happened. Colchis was a strange place.

A very dull two days followed for Hekate while the ship, which had left port after suffering only a cursory check for forbidden goods or pasengers, sailed down the river and turned southward along the coast and then almost due west. Hekate didn't mind at all. She had brought aboard sufficient food and water for several days, knowing that it might be possible for Aietes' ships to overtake them within that time. Afterward, she was reasonably sure they would be out of reach, unless the captain actually stopped and waited–and she knew how to deal with that.

She needed no occupation either because as soon as she had shifted the bales to make a fairly comfortable nest for herself and Kabeiros, she was overtaken by an irresistible urge to sleep. In her few wakeful periods, that puzzled her, until she remembered that she had slept away almost the whole of the first week in the caves of the dead. She needed to allow herself to unravel, she decided after thinking about it. She had slept in the caves of the dead to recover from the tensions and anxieties of living with Perses; now she slept to rest after the strain of so much healing magic and wariness in the presence of Aietes.

As with all ships, except under unusual circumstances, *Sea Foam* beached each evening. The crew went ashore to hunt and cook and to sleep far more comfortably than they could on the deck. When it was dark, Kabeiros also went ashore to hunt and to empty his bladder and bowels, which he did again at dawn. Hekate was also able to take care of her needs, using a bailing vessel that she then washed out in the ocean.

The result was so satisfactory that Hekate was seriously thinking about remaining in hiding for the whole trip, pilfering food and water or sharing Kabeiros' quarry, which she could cook by magic.

On the third day, she was much less sleepy and mentioned this notion to Kabeiros who cocked his head at her and asked, *Don't you think it strange that the captain didn't search for you or send a message to the palace to say you hadn't come aboard?*

Likely he told Medea or sent a message to her when he went ashore. Also, I suppose Medea told him I would come secretly, and you know how ship captains are. The tides are more important than the orders of a land-bound lord, even one such as Medea. Doubtless he will be at sea for some time, moons or even years, and he assumes her orders would be forgotten. If he's an honest man, he can always repay the passage money when he returns—if she paid him anything, which I doubt.

Or repay the blood money if you aren't dead?

That dry comment brought a thoughtful expression to Hekate's face. After a moment she said, *Now that I think about it, it is strange that he didn't set a search for me. If I were a ship captain, I wouldn't like to have an unknown person aboard, specially a person with the character Medea must have given me.*

And I saw from where I was hidden that the captain took two officers with him. Would he bring witnesses to a meeting with Medea? Would she permit it?

Not if she didn't want anyone to know she was involved in my departure—even less if she were going to bid the captain toss me overboard or be rid of me in some other way.

Is it possible, Kabeiros asked, *that he never saw Medea? Never received any orders from her at all?*

Hekate stroked Kabeiros' silky fur and sighed. *It is not only possible but probable. Why should Medea bother to make arrangements with the captain. Not for my welfare. She could have known about the ship and sailing time because she was getting or sending something by the *Sea Foam*. She knew I wouldn't come aboard openly for fear of Aietes' spies, so I wouldn't have to confront the captain while ashore where I could be put off.*

Yes. Kabeiros nodded like a man; Hekate saw his head move in the dim light that seeped under the deck from the open area in which the rowing benches stood. *And Medea would guess you would conceal yourself for as long as you could in case Aietes pursued the ship.*

Suddenly Hekate stiffened. *Kabeiros, I think she's done something to the ship. I think she intended to sink this ship with all aboard. That way she would be sure of being rid of me and no one else would be alive to be questioned.*

How like Medea! Kabeiros remarked. "Now what do we do?*

I think we have no choice but to go to the captain.

I agree, but how are you going to tell him about the danger to his ship without being blamed for it?

Hekate laughed softly. *I'll tell him as little of the truth as possible and any lies that are necessary to get him to thoroughly inspect his ship.*

Mentally, Kabeiros chuckled. *You are a wonderful liar. How did you learn the art so well?*

Any amusement was missing from Hekate's mental aura when she said, *By living with Perses.*

Kabeiros growled softly, then after a moment asked, *Do I stay here or go with you?*

*Come with me. I don't *think* the captain will order me thrown overboard without question, but if we are wrong and he did speak to Medea, you might need to protect me until I can cast a spell. And I will go as the crone. An old woman is less threatening . . . and less likely to interest the crew if they are long away from women.*

Kabeiros got to his feet and Hekate stood as soon as she had space to rise. Then, old and bent, but still wearing the look-by-me spell, she came out into the open belly of the ship, stepped on an unoccupied rowers' bench, and from there onto the broad plank that ran from prow to stern between the decked-over areas. Kabeiros leapt up after her, drawing exclamations of surprise and a few gasps. The crew watched the huge, black dog with open mouths and round eyes, which grew even rounder as Hekate drew near the captain and dismissed the spell that kept her from being noticed.

"Who in Plutos are you?" the captain roared, stepping back a pace. "How did you get aboard my ship?"

"I am called Hekate, and I came aboard your ship in the same way I walked from under the deck to here, bespelled so no one would see me. I am sorry that you are so surpised. I thought my passage with you had been arranged."

"Arranged? By who?"

"The Lady Medea, who cast upon me the spell that kept me hidden–"

"Medea?" The captain's voice rose to a roar again. "So that was why she wanted to speak to me? I didn't go. That woman is poison."

"You didn't go?" Hekate echoed. "When was this?"

"When I made port, three . . . no, four days ago. Why didn't she tell you I hadn't agreed to take you?"

Hekate frowned. "I'm afraid it was because she was annoyed with us both," she said, but she was thinking that Medea already had a grudge against this ship and its captain.

"Why should she be annoyed with me?" the captain protested. "I've traded in Colchis for years without trouble and often carried cargo for King Aietes."

That was how Medea knew the *Sea Foam* was in port and when it would leave, Hekate thought, but she shrugged and said, "You didn't obey her summons. That would be enough."

"And you?" the captain asked, but he sounded less angry, almost sympathetic.

Hekate sighed. "I crossed her pet sorcerer, Ming Hao. She sent for me in the market and told me to leave Colchis that very day. I hadn't even time to tell my clients. She named this ship and the time it would sail."

"From what I've heard about her, I'm surprised you're alive. But she had no cause to take a spite at me," the captain added indignantly. "I didn't refuse to obey her. I sent an excuse. I even asked for a new time to come to her."

"After you planned to sail?" Hekate laughed. "You didn't fool her, though. She knew when you planned to leave port because she told me the *Sea Foam* would sail exactly when it did sail. Captain, I think within moments after you sent your excuses, Medea set some enchantment on your ship."

"An enchantment on my ship?" The man's voice scaled up to a near screech. "Because of you?"

"No, oh no! I had nothing to do with that. Your doom was decided before she spoke to me. I think she bid me take this ship so that I would drown with you and your crew."

"Drown? You're mad! Even Medea can't reach me in the middle of the ocean."

"No, she can't," Hekate said quickly before he began to think that she might be Medea's agent and she might be guilty of the damage, whatever it was. "But she could easily have set a spell on some cargo you loaded or something some slave brought aboard–"

The captain was staring at her, eyes wide. "On an amulet?" he asked, starting to breathe quickly. "An amulet seemed to fall from the sky onto the ship. One of my crew who was acting as watchman brought it to me. It seemed harmless. It didn't do anything when he touched it or later when I touched it."

"An amulet could easily carry Medea's spell," Hekate said gravely, blessing the Mother that she had used what was clearly a magical artifact instead of a pebble or twig to carry the spell that froze the guard. "And I know the Lady Medea can make objects move through the air. I saw her do it with a globe of light. So the amulet could have been sent and dropped on your deck."

"But it didn't *do* anything."

"Are you sure, Captain? Won't you please look over your ship very carefully and make sure there is nothing wrong with it? If that amulet brought some kind of curse, it would fix itself to the ship at once so when your man touched it the magic was already gone from it and it was harmless. It is harmless now, I assure you. But the curse itself, that might act only slowly, like rotting the wood of your ship or . . . or . . . oh, I don't know anything about ships, but won't you please look to see the ship is sound?"

"You're a witch yourself!"

"Not really. I can only do small healing spells. I'm a healer. That's how I fell afoul of Ming Hao. I healed a client he had cursed. Perhaps if a curse was set on your ship, I could remove it or stop it from working."

The captain's lips thinned. "How do I know you didn't bring the curse aboard yourself?"

"Are you mad?" Hekate gasped. "If your ship sinks, I and my dog, Kabeiros, will drown with the rest of you. I cannot fly through the air nor swim well enough to save myself. You may be sure that I did nothing to harm your ship and that I will do all in my power to save it."

That argument had the force of reason. The captain, because he had traded in Colchis for many years, had met and dealt with many sorcerers. He had seen them move small objects but never themselves or anything large or weighty. Logic also said that there would be little reason for a sorcerer to pay him to bring goods or carry them if he could move them at no cost himself. If she would drown, she wouldn't harm the ship. He nodded brusquely at Hekate and ordered a half dozen of the crew to do an inspection of the ship.

At first nothing seemed wrong. The men walked along the hull, checking the caulking and prodding the boards to test their soundness, and no sign of weakness appeared. Even at the level of the rowers' benches, the men could find no sign of damage, although two hesitated over the lashings that held the planks of the hull together near the prow where the waves often splashed. However, as soon as a man descended below the waterline and pulled aside a rack of amphorae of oil, he set up a frightened shout.

Thc captain ran down, looked, exclaimed in horror and bellowed for Hekate to come at once. She stared where she saw his eyes fixed, but didn't understand what was turning him gray under his weather-beaten brown.

"Stop them!" he cried. "Stop them!"

"Stop who? What?" Hekate asked. "I don't know what's wrong."

"The roots. The roots that are used to lash together the planking of the hull. They're *growing*. They're twice the thickness they should be. Look. Look. Another thumbnail's width and they will force apart the planking and let in the sea."

Hekate didn't understand, but she touched the dark brown ropelike thing the captain's trembling finger indicated and muttered the spell she used to draw moisture from swollen tissue. Water began to drain out of the lashing and trickle down the hull. The brown rope shrank to a thinner, darker rope, and Hekate could see that the two boards it encircled were pulled more tightly against each other.

"Is that what–" Hekate began.

The captain was not paying attention. He was looking wildly up and down along the hull. "They are all growing," he breathed, his eyes starting with terror. "The hull will be pulled apart before the end of the day."

He jumped to the central walkway and screamed for the lookout to find a beach on which they could land. From there he ran to the deck near the prow from where he shouted for his steersman to sail closer to the shore and for two sailors who were staring open-mouthed to shift the sail to hold the wind. He bellowed curses against sorcerers and magic in between ordering the rest of the sailors to take to the oars to move them more swiftly.

Kabeiros, who had remained on deck when Hekate went down, slunk aside into the shadow and began to make his way as inconspicuously as possible to join her. He found her working her way around the hull, touching each lashing that seemed to be swollen and uttering the spell that leached out moisture.

Thank the Mother for allowing me to use the high magic as well as the low, Hekate said to him, when he stood beside her, to defend her if the sailors turned on her. *But even with drawing power from the air, I will never be able to keep all the lashings drained. They are drinking water from the sea, which is limitless.*

If you can keep anything from bursting for even a few candlemarks, we'll probably be safe. The captain is looking for a place to beach the ship.

Hekate breathed a long sigh of relief. *If I don't have to keep working at draining these roots, I'll try to tease out the spell Medea used. Then I'll be able to stop it or change it.*

You'd better explain that to the captain as soon as he comes down here again because he'll be able to see that you can't control the damage with what you're doing.

Hekate made an exasperated sound. *How do I

explain negating the whole spell when I want him to believe I am only a healer?*

You don't have to explain removing the spell. Everyone knows that most spells wear off after a few days. As soon as you find a way to counterspell the hull, you can tell the captain that the spell just wore itself out. There's nothing sorcerous about that.

Hekate was about to answer, when the captain's voice came down from above. "Witch! Damn you! Get up here!"

"No!" Hekate shouted back. "I've dried about a third of the lashings. I don't want to drown any more than you do. Let me finish my work."

Sputtering with rage, the captain leapt down from the deck to the median plank and then to the bottom. One hand was rising, possibly to strike at Hekate, but he was met by Kabeiros. The huge dog's snarling threat made him pause, and in that moment, Hekate drew his attention to what she had done.

"How?" he gasped. "How are you doing that?"

"It is a small spell that I use to ease dropsy," Hekate said, as she moved from one lashing to another. "It is no cure. I know no cure for the disease, but this spell draws out the water that gathers in a person with that sickness and for a few days relieves the pain."

"But that is a person," the captain muttered. "This is a dead part of a plant . . ."

Hekate shrugged. "It was the first thing that came to my mind, so I tried it. It it hadn't worked, I would have tried something else."

"You've saved us, then?"

"Not really." Hekate touched another lashing, muttered the spell. "Look at the first one I did. Already it's not as hard and dry as this that I've just bespelled. Likely it will take another three days to get as thick as this next lashing, but the curse is still working and I can't cast spells night and day."

"You mean even if we get to shore and save our lives, my ship is lost to me?" His voice trembled.

"Oh, no. A curse, even Medea's, seldom lasts more than a few days without being renewed. If you beach the boat so that only a few lashings are in the water, I can keep those dry until the curse wears off. Then the ship will be as good as new . . . at least, the lashings will be good as new. If some other damage has been done by their swelling, I wouldn't know that."

"Caulking," the captain muttered. He stared at Hekate's back, eyes narrowed, then said, "But this will delay me several days, mayhap even a ten-day. Not only will those waiting for cargo be dissatisfied and perhaps withhold payment, but all that time I will be feeding you and that monstrous dog. And he showed his teeth at me. A threat like that would be death for a man in my crew. I won't have a dangerous dog aboard my ship–"

"Captain," Hekate said, taking her hand from the lashing she was about to bespell and turning to face him; she looked older, more bent, her voice rough with fatigue, "my dog and I have a special bond. If he should be harmed, I would not wish to live and there would be no purpose to my expending my strength to dry your lashings. You will have us both, or I will go overboard with Kabeiros. Look!" She pointed behind the captain to a bare trickle of water coming between two planks. "Will you wager your life on finding a place to beach before the water comes in all over?"

He stared at the trickle of water, then at Kabeiros, who stood quietly beside Hekate. "What land?" he roared up at the lookout.

"Cliffs and forest," the lookout called back.

"It was probably you who brought this curse on us," he snarled resentfully.

"I doubt it, but it's possible." The crone leaned against the hull, cackled, and pointed; two more trickles crawled down the ship's side.

"The dog can stay," the captain gasped.

Hekate turned her back on him and touched another lashing. Water dribbled from it down the hull, through the open planking of the lowest deck and into the bilge. After a while, the captain called for two sailors to bail out the extra water that was accumulating. Hekate moved along the hull, touching and whispering. Kabeiros moved with her; soon she needed to brace a hand on his back for support.

Later the captain was called by the lookout and went up on deck to consider a cove where the ship might be pulled from the water. It was very rocky, however, and he bade his men sail on and keep looking. Had Hekate not been more than two thirds around the hull, it would have been a hard choice between the chance of striking a rock and the chance of the lashings swelling too far.

When he came down again, Hekate was sitting on a low keg, her head down on Kabeiros' shoulder. "What are you doing?" he yelled. "While you're cuddling that beast, the water is coming in."

She didn't answer at once. She had never been so depleted of power, blind and achingly empty. After a moment she whispered, "I have done what I can. I don't want to drown, but I can do no more. I must rest and eat."

"Eat? Eat? Passengers who pay fare eat."

Again Hekate had to gather strength before she could reply. "I understood Medea was to pay."

"I never saw Medea," the captain snarled.

"Very well," Hekate said. "When I have eaten and

drunk and have strength enough, I will try to dry the rest of the lashings because I don't want to drown–unless you feel staying afloat is not worth the price of one meal. If so, I will just rest here until we sink. As to the dog, you need not worry about feeding him. He's hunted for himself every night and will continue to do so. If you make shore, and you feel you don't need my services, I will leave–and you can deal with whatever other little toys Medea has left aboard on your own."

The sailors who had been bailing had stopped and were listening to the conversation. One of them took a half-full pail, raised it to the median plank, and climbed up after it. A few minutes later, a big man about the captain's age let himself down to the lower deck. He carried a leather mug in one hand and a cloth-wrapped package in the other.

"What are you doing here, steersman?" the captain asked.

"Making sure your greed don't sink this ship," the steersman answered without expression.

Ignoring the captain's order to get back to his steering oar, the steersman shoved another keg within Hekate's reach. On that he placed the mug and opened the cloth, in which was wrapped a wedge of cheese, a handful of olives, and a round of hard bread. She tried to take the mug, but her hands would not grip it, and the steersman lifted it, supported her head, and let her drink. When she had swallowed about half the sweet wine, she pulled away and he put down the mug. She reached for the cheese, bit, chewed, took an olive. At first she had to eat slowly and the steersman looked around at the hull.

It was apparent what Hekate had done, for where she had not drained out the lashings, they were swollen enough by now to interfere with the proper mating of the planks. The water coming in was already more than a trickle, but not yet so much that the men bailing could not hold their own. If the boards opened more, they might not be able to keep up; worse, the distortion the swollen lashings caused might damage the whole hull.

"Lady," the steersman said, "I can see you are exhausted and have done much already, but all your work will be for nothing if you cannot finish. The bad will destroy the good."

"I know," Hekate whispered, but continued to eat.

"I can hold you up," the steersman said. "Will that help?"

"In a moment," she said.

The captain had been silent, staring at the leaking hull. When Hekate had finished the olives and cheese and was dipping the bread into the remains of the wine to soften it, he said, "Send another man down to support the old witch, if you don't think she's shamming. You are needed at the steering oar. A beach may be found at any time."

Without even turning his head, the steersman watched Hekate. As soon as she had finished the bread and emptied the mug, he lifted her to her feet, and when she sagged against him, carried her to the ship's side. The captain watched with an expression that boded the steersman no good, but he said no more and climbed up to the median plank and then to the deck.

Hekate didn't notice. She was concentrating on drawing off just a touch of the steersman's strength, not enough to do more than make him feel a little tired. He had no Talent, it was life-force itself that she was taking, not to increase her power but to give her physical strength. That, together with the food and wine, made her able to begin again. Almost it was not enough to finish, and for the last few lashings she had to draw from Kabeiros, who sank to his belly on the wet floor.

She dried the last lashing with darkness closing in on her. Later she became dimly aware of shouts and the sound of feet pounding above her. She thought she should get up and go on deck if the ship were sinking, but hadn't the strength. And Kabeiros lay limp beside her. She couldn't go without him. Maybe some of the barrels would float, she thought. Surely the cold of the water coming in would wake her.

What woke her, however, was the captain's voice. "Well! Well! I'm glad to see you made yourself so comfortable. Even paying passengers are not allowed to use the cargo for their own comfort. You'll have to pay extra for that!"

Hekate sat up slowly and looked around. Kabeiros sat beside her warily eyeing the captain. She was very hungry again, but mostly restored. Someone had laid her down at the edge of the underdeck, and it was true that bales of cloth had been moved to make her a bed. She remembered her last thought, but clearly the excitement she had heard had not been the ship sinking. A glance at the hull showed it to be dry as far as she could see, and the sailors who had been bailing were gone. The ship was not rocking as it did while at sea. They had found a beach in time, it seemed.

"I can't pay at all," she said clearly, hoping her voice would carry. "I have very little metal, only a few copper pieces." That was a flat lie; Hekate had brought a great deal of gold and silver—all she had earned while at Colchis. However, she was sure if she admitted to being able to pay, the captain would try to have her throat slit to steal the money. "What I brought was my herbs and simples, some potions and powders. I will be able to treat most sicknesses and wounds, and I will gladly do that for you and the crew to pay for my passage."

"Nonsense. You must have some trade metal. How could you start on a long journey without the means to pay for food and lodging?"

"I had little choice," Hekate replied dryly. "Don't you remember that Medea summoned me from my work in the market and bid me go? She gave me no time to go to my lodging for what I had saved. I had barely time enough to gather up the supplies I had at my stall."

"Well, no one here will give you anything. Doubtless it's your fault our ship was cursed. You'll get nothing from me or my men. Take your filthy dog and go. Whatever you brought aboard is forfeit for the evil you've brought on us."

Slowly, Hekate rose. "I'll go, but I will take what is mine with me." She nodded at Kabeiros, who had come from the dark part of the underdeck dragging her three bundles by their ties. "I nearly died to save your ship. That's enough service to pay for three days aboard her."

"You'll starve on the road," the captain sneered.

"Oh, no," Hekate answered calmly, lifting one pack to her shoulder and taking the other two in hand. "Kabeiros will hunt and I will gather while we're in the wilderness. When we find a house or a village, I'll be welcome. There are few places in which a healer is not eagerly greeted."

"You'll starve, and I'll be glad of it, old witch, for you'll do no healing. I'll take what you have in those packs." The captain drew a knife.

Hekate dropped one pack to the ground and laughed aloud as the captain drew it to him and undid the bindings. Out of the pack crawled a serpent, which struck at the captain's reaching hand and then at his bare feet. He screamed and leapt up to the median plank, but somehow the serpent was there with him and he ran for the upper deck. Hekate redid the bindings on the bundle, listening to his screams diminish as he went down the ladder from the deck to the beach.

She had to stand on a cask to reach the median plank and lifted herself to the deck with some difficulty. The form of the crone did not lend itself to gymnastics. As she walked toward the ladder, she could hear the captain still screaming about the serpent and the shouts of the crew as they tried to keep him from running off into the forest that edged the beach.

Thanking the Mother for their preoccupation, Hekate climbed down the ladder. Kabeiros, unbalanced by the bundle fastened to his harness, slipped and slid behind her, feet scrabbling for a hold on the narrow treads. Unburdened and with a man's intelligence, he had learned how to climb the ladder without difficulty, but he had no way to grip the treads and the pack pulled him backward. Twice he would have fallen if Hekate had not been there to brace his body. She was bruised and gasping when they were at last on solid ground.

"There is no serpent!" the steersman was shouting, and then he saw Hekate and advanced on her threateningly. "What did you do to him, witch?" he bellowed.

"Nothing," Hekate said, shaking her head. "I did nothing. He came aboard and demanded trade metal. I told him the truth, that I had only the few copper pieces I had with me in the market because Medea had not given me time to go to my lodging and gather my possessions. I said there was only herbs and suchlike in my packs. Then he ordered me off the ship to make my own way and said he would keep my packs. He seized one and opened it, then screamed there was a serpent and ran away."

"You said you were a healer. Did you have a serpent in the pack?"

Hekate laughed. "Do you see a serpent?" She dropped the bundles to the ground and said, "Open them and look."

"You open them."

Obligingly, Hekate opened the packs. One held bundles of herbs, folded stalks and stems–which a madman might see as a serpent–and a box full of black seeds, nut hulls, and dried somethings which gave off a noxious smell. The second had more herbs in which were nestled small stoppered and sealed flasks and pots. The third contained a worn gown, two shifts, thin and gray with washing, a much-mended shawl wrapped around a box of cheap trinkets.

"What are those?" the steersman asked suspiciously.

"Toys for the children. If they drink down the potion they need for healing, they can have a toy."

The crew, which had been casting uneasy looks at her in between restraining the captain, now advanced on him right through the empty space to which he pointed, screaming, "Snake. Snake." They took away his knife, wrestled him to the ground, and bound him.

Gesturing to Hekate to do up her bundles again, the steersman advanced on the captain. "Where is the snake?" he asked.

"There. There. There," the captain screeched. "Near my feet. It is striking at my feet."

"Has it bitten you yet?" the steersman asked.

"No, or I would be dead."

"Isn't it strange that it should strike but never bite

when you cannot move away? There is no serpent, Captain. No one sees it except you."

"It came out of her bundle, I tell you. See. See. It still weaves back and forth. It will kill me."

"It hasn't so far and we have opened all her bundles. There are no snakes in them, nothing but what she said was there, herbs and suchlike. What were you looking for?"

"Gold," the captain gasped, twitching his feet from side to side. "I know she has gold. An old woman like that doesn't go on a long journey without metal to supply her needs. A young one could sell her body, but who would even buy a drink to have so ancient a crone? But she wouldn't pay, not even for her fare, not even when I told her she must go alone into the wilderness."

"Go? But she's not finished with the ship!" the steersman exclaimed. "The roots by the prow that are in the water are still swelling. She must dry them."

"The curse will wear off. She admitted that herself."

"But will the roots go back to being dry after the curse wears off?"

"The serpent is there on your feet! Man, it will bite you. Jump away. Run."

The captain's eyes followed something that crawled back and forth over the steersman's feet, but no one else could see it and the steersman clearly couldn't feel it. Those crew members who could see the captain's face whispered among themselves and to the crewmen who were watching Hekate.

All of them were sure she had caused the captain's condition, but none—not even the steersman—was willing to confront her. Worse might befall them than the harmless vision bedevilling the captain. What if they began to see other crew members as monsters and attacked each other? And what of the ship? What if the curse did not wear off?

Hekate had quietly repacked her bundles and lifted one to each shoulder, the third to Kabeiros' back. She never looked at the captain or any other member of the crew, but started to walk slowly toward the forest bordering the beach. The steersman ran after her.

"Mother," he said, his voice pleading, "it seems that the captain's greed has addled his brain. You can't go off into the wild all alone. Stay with us."

"I think the danger of being alone in the wild is less than the danger that your mad captain will order me thrown overboard when a new fit seizes him."

"But the ship is not healed. Will the lashings return to normal when the curse wears off?"

"I have no idea," Hekate admitted. "I didn't set the curse on the ship. I don't even know how such a thing is done. I'm an herb-wife and I know some small healing spells and that's all."

"Mother, if the lashings do not heal by themselves, we will be castaways on this beach. Please stay, at least until the next port, which is not far. I will make sure no harm comes to you, that you go ashore with everything you brought aboard, and that you are fed–and the dog too."

Hekate put down her bundles. Kabeiros sat down beside her, panting. The steersman offered further inducements, further guarantees of her safety. Eventually she shrugged and looked at the semicircle of men watching and listening.

"The rest of the crew must agree also," she said. "With the captain's approval, you could be overwhelmed by the others and your promises made worthless."

There was no problem about the crew agreeing.

They were all nodding as she spoke. Each man then came separately, and allowed her to touch him in binding, swearing on his gods, and, more important, on the mercy of the sea that Hekate and Kabeiros would be kept safe, fed, cherished, no matter what the captain ordered. But then they gathered and begged her to remove the curse that was driving their captain mad.

Hekate shook her head. "Whatever you all believe, I didn't curse the man and I can't remove the curse, just as I can heal the lashings but I cannot remove the curse from them. I have nothing to do with curses."

"Then what ails the captain?" the steersman asked.

"I don't know. Perhaps he knew he was wrong to try to rob me after I had worked so hard to keep us all alive. Then when he saw the herb stalks in my bundle, he thought it was a snake. But madness is beyond my skill to cure. The best I can do is offer a potion to make the captain sleep. Perhaps when he wakes, the serpent will be gone."

At first the captain would not agree and screamed that the serpent would bite him while he slept and, when the crew insisted there was no serpent, that Hekate had bewitched him so she could poison him. Hekate offered to drink some of the potion herself and after she did, the steersman forced it down the captain's throat and had him carried aboard. Of course, the serpent was not gone, when the captain woke–Hekate saw to that.

With the captain out of the way, her relations with the crew improved over the five days it took her to unravel Medea's spell. She healed small sores, removed deep driven splinters, soothed uneasy guts. Making the crew less fearful of her was important because she didn't want hysteria to sweep over them at sea and end with her overboard. And, despite her apparent reluctance, Hekate was as eager to stay with the ship as the crew were to keep her.

She didn't fear the wilderness, but her packs were heavy, each having a substantial sum in gold and silver hidden by illusion in it. No matter that the chunks and twists of metal looked like nut hulls, seeds, stinking black dried dung, or pots of salve, the weight of the metal was there, and Hekate didn't want to carry it. The spell Medea had put on the ship intrigued her, too. Surely the princess of Colchis had not discovered how to revive the dead?

The answer was not so earth-shaking. In fact, it was so simple she almost overlooked it—a basic piece of sympathetic magic. Medea had someone bring her some of the root fiber used for lashing together the planks of a ship and cast a spell for drinking in water on it. Then most likely she had sent one of her tame sorcerers aboard the *Sea Foam*, perhaps disguised as one of the crew, with the enchanted root in hand. He would only need to go around touching all the roots in the hull, transferring the magic from the seed root to those on the ship.

More intriguing to Hekate was the renewal spell Medea had woven into the simple water-drinking spell. The vindictive princess had, in fact, made sure the "curse" would never have worn off. The renewal spell drew power from high or low magic and fed itself and fed any spell to which it was connected.

It took Hekate most of the five days she insisted the *Sea Foam* remain on the beach—ostensibly to let the curse wear off—to tease the two spells apart, but the renewal spell was well worth having. Hekate had known a way to make an illusion spell that drew from the earth-blood to feed itself, but that spell needed to be on the earth and could not be moved. Now she had a way to make any spell she devised "immortal."

PART THREE:

THE UNBINDING

CHAPTER 18

It took Hekate years to reach Olympus, but she had been in no hurry. Traveling again, she discovered she had developed a strong taste for new places, new people, and new ideas. Having learned from Yehoraz the spell for drawing a language from a person's mind, she never needed to be marked as a stranger, although usually it suited her best to use trade tongue. There were advantages as well as disadvantages to being an outlander. And most often, despite the discomfort, she used the form of the crone.

She had learned caution, and traveling by ship required no physical effort. The form of the old woman with her cloth-wrapped bundles was no threat to anyone and no temptation to men or to thieves. And, oddly, Kabeiros seemed happiest and most affectionate when she was the crone.

Occasionally, if she didn't like the selection of ships in a small port, she would join a caravan. She selected those that included other travelers, especially women. Then the crone would arrange a place for her newly widowed granddaughter or greatniece-by-marriage or some other relative by marriage, begging the caravan master to care for the lone creature, and the woman Hekate would do the more strenuous traveling.

She always left the impression that she had a large and loving family. When she sailed, the woman bought space for her grandmother aboard a ship that regularly took passengers and had a good reputation for arrival of the travelers. This most beloved old lady wished to go home to some more-western land (Hekate picked a new one each time) to see a younger, favorite son, but her older son expected her to return and awaited that event eagerly.

Neither in caravan nor ship did she have another experience like that on the ship that had taken her from Colchis. She thought of that ship from time to time and regretted that she had resisted the temptation to add Medea's self-sustaining loop to the illusion that kept the serpent as the captain's constant companion. He knew by the time they made the port where Hekate left them that the snake was not real and that it wouldn't bite him, and he could function . . . but not well.

He deserved the punishment, but Kabeiros said it was enough, for he shied away from her like a frightened horse and spoke to her, when it was absolutely necessary, most respectfully. The crew, too, Kabeiros said, didn't deserve to be ruined by the loss of the ship and the cargo, and any emergency at sea or trading venture could turn to disaster if the captain were distracted. So she hadn't made the spell permanent.

Despite his own griefs, Kabeiros was sweet-natured. He did not carry the scars on his soul that Perses had left on hers. Hekate always yielded to his kinder judgement when the matter was not of their safety, and she never expected to see the *Sea Foam* again. She had laughed to herself as she packed her bundles. By now none of the crew blamed her for the captain's "lunacy," but they would watch him closely in the future and might curb his greed to prevent a second attack of guilty madness. So Hekate just said her farewells and walked away, knowing that the spell would fade as time passed.

The old crone had disappeared in the narrow, dirty streets of Trapesus. A day after *Sea Foam* had left port, a tall, strong young woman, carefully veiled, had enquired about passage westward for her grandmother, who wanted to go home to Greece. Only a few on the docks had ever heard of Greece, and no ship was headed there. The moving rocks, the Symplegades, cut off the narrow passage of the Bosphorus from the Propontis, but perhaps at Sinope, a larger port, someone would have more information.

She was satisfied. She hadn't expected to find a ship that went to Greece, but she had the name of a port to the west. The next day, the crone inquired about ships and fares to Sinope. Her master was dead and she wanted to join her daughter in that city. She looked poor and was offered deck space at a reasonable price, so she bought a place for herself and her master's dog, whom no one else would keep.

It took the rest of the summer and into the autumn to travel from Trapesus to Sinope, but the ship made port and laid over at Hermanssus, Cerasus, Cytorus, Themiscrya, and Carusa on the way. The crone and the hound enjoyed themselves. At each town where the ship stopped to load and unload cargo, the crone visited the market and set up a stall if it were permitted.

If itinerant merchants were forbidden the market,

she was allowed a small mat on the dock near the ship. She offered for sale foreign lotions and potions, amulets for protection, for good luck, for faithful love (but never to induce love), and gathered in handfuls of copper and now and then a piece of silver. Some of the metal she bartered for herbs, spices, and exotic roots and for new amulets to replace her supply; the remainder she shared with the captain and won his goodwill.

She spent the winter in Sinope, fortunately a city that was indifferent to foreigners. If you paid the fees, you could buy, sell, even practice magic . . . but Hekate admitted to no magic. The amulets, she claimed, had been purchased in "the east" as they were, charged with good fortune or other blessings. She was an herb woman, no more.

She almost spent more than the winter in Sinope. The ships going westward were few and far between. The land to the west was more barren. Only Cytorus and Heraclea were towns large enough to make trade worthwhile. Caravans were even less frequent. Only the wild tribes traveled that barren interior. The moons of early spring passed; high summer was close before a ship traveling west docked.

Wave Leaper, however, was worth waiting for. The woman Hekate was told that the ship was going all the way to the Bosphorus, the passage guarded by the Symplegades. Ser Ottah, the captain, whom Hekate immediately recognized as an Egyptian although she did not say so, informed her that he could not be certain of the actual date. They might not make port in Cyaneae until the next spring, and from there her grandmother would have to travel overland to Byzantium.

He hoped, he told Hekate, to arrive at Cyaneae, a town just north of the Symplegades where they made a blue dye of surpassing beauty and tenacity, before winter, but he could not give a bond for that. It was later in the season than he usually arrived at Sinope. If the weather turned foul too soon, he would stay in whatever port he could find, as he would not risk his ship in the winter storms.

The woman Hekate pursed her lips. She understood the problem. If *Wave Leaper* wintered over where the crone had no friends or relatives, she would have to pay to live–find goods or metal to provide her with rent and food. Hekate said that her grandmother was a famous healer and could support herself wherever trade was allowed to foreigners. Then she shrugged.

"I will give you metal or trade goods enough to support her over the winter, and you may give her the metal or goods wherever you overwinter or take care of her needs. If more is owed you, she can trade in herbs or in service. As I said, she is an unequalled healer."

If Captain Ottah looked a little surprised at such trustfulness, Hekate was indifferent. Attached to the gold and silver pieces the crone delivered to him before *Wave Leaper* sailed was a compulsion to treat with honesty, generosity, and kindness the person who gave him the metal–and Medea's renewal spell was wound into the compulsion. Hekate could have renewed the spell herself by touching Ottah now and again during the voyage, but she preferred not to need to think about it. Until the end of his life, Captain Ottah would be kind, generous, and honest to Hekate.

As the voyage progressed, Hekate came to believe that the compulsion spell was unnecessary. Captain Ottah was a delight: an excellent seaman, a fair master, a good host with a lively sense of humor and a wonderful knowledge about places and people. When Hekate confessed that the tale of a younger son in Byzantium was false, that she was traveling just because she was old and wanted to see what she could of the world before she died, he laughed immoderately. When he could speak, he remarked that he who had spent all his life traveling looked forward to settling in one place. It was only reasonable, he said, that she, who had lived always in one place, should want to travel.

To her delight, he suggested that she visit Greece, although he warned her strictly against using any magic at all there, even simple healing spells. He smiled at her when he said it, showing that he knew she had used more than pounded leaves and draughts of willow bark steepings to cure the foot of a seaman who had driven a splinter deep where it had festered.

"If they don't kill you outright," he said, "they bind you and leave you as a sacrifice to the king of the dead."

Hekate sighed. "They only treated the Gifted that way in Sinope," she said. "Magic was not loved, but usually it was tolerated–if no one had a grudge against the magic maker."

That set him off and he told tales of his youthful years in Greece, when he had accompanied his father on trading missions, tales of how they dressed and what they ate, small things but those that made a deep impression on him because it was his first voyage out of Egyptian territory.

"And I never went home again," he said with a sigh.

"But if you passed the Symplegades coming from the Mare Aegaeum to the Pontus Euxinus, why not the other way?"

He laughed heartily. "I wasn't captain then, just a seaman. I was a third son with no hopes of my father's business, so I struck out on my own. And the ship I sailed on didn't pass through the Bosphorus. At Byzantium I left the ship and went overland to Cyaneae–which is how I started to trade on my own. There are caravans that travel that route several times a ten-day."

However, Hekate was not to need that knowledge very soon. There were contrary winds and sickness struck the whole crew at Cytorus where they were forced to remain for a full moon. It took all Hekate's skill to save Ser Ottah. Kabeiros grew very silent again while she cared for the captain, but although she did not neglect the dog, her mind and attention were plainly elsewhere.

Wave Leaper barely made Heraclea. A nasty storm tore away their sail and the crew had to row to reach that port. Hekate had taken the place of the cook and had bailed to free more men for the oars. And when they came to port, the captain said he would go no farther, that the crew was free to seek another ship or he would do what he could to reduce the cost of lodging for those who wished to overwinter at Heraclea and finish the voyage with him.

Hekate was satisfied to do that; she was in no hurry. But she was surprised when Ottah did not give her the metal she had entrusted to him at the start of the voyage and let her fend for herself like the crew. Instead he found her a more comfortable lodging than she would have chosen for herself and even hired a little maid to care for her. When she protested that her funds would not cover such expenses, he laughed and said she had earned her comfort and that he did not wish to forgo the pleasure he had in her company.

Truthfully she was glad to have someone with whom to talk and jest. Kabeiros had been not only unusually silent but sullen since she settled into her new quarters. She grew very sorry that she had gone aboard the *Wave Leaper* in the form of the crone instead of wearing the woman's body.

"If I had thought about it," she said one night after Ottah had left to walk back to his own lodging in a pouring rain, "I could have gone as the woman since I intended to bespell him anyway."

And he could have stayed the night in your bed rather than going home to his own? Kabeiros said. *And what would I have done? Gone to sleep in the alley?*

"What would you care?" Hekate snapped. "You are forever telling me that the dog isn't interested in humans. And you needn't be so self-pitying. There are two chambers to this apartment. There would be nothing to stop you from sleeping on the divan or the rug in here."

Whereupon the dog got up and went to the door. *Let me out,* he said.

Hekate ran to him. "No, don't go out, Kabeiros. You'll get all wet. It's raining very hard."

Open the door, he repeated. *I need to remind myself that I am a dog.*

He was not back by the time Hekate was ready for bed. She wasn't sure whether she was more frightened or resentful. She had not neglected him. Indeed, she had included him in most of her conversations with the captain, specially when Ottah told tales of the sea or of cities he had visited. In the periods when it was normal for her to be a silent listener, it was easy to make mental asides to Kabeiros and to enjoy his sometimes caustic remarks.

Other times she had been a bit irritated by Kabeiros' comments, which tended to point out what he felt must be exaggerations on Ottah's part–and she had said so. But she had never left him out of her thoughts or ignored his remarks. Lying in bed, listening for Kabeiros' scratch or short bark at the door, Hekate had asked herself what this attitude meant. When (she wouldn't let herself think 'if') Kabeiros had control of his shifting again and could live in the world as a man, if they were to live together, would he want all her attention? Would he object to her having friends of her own? Would he grow sullen and angry every time she enjoyed another man's company?

She fell asleep at last without ever hearing a sign from Kabeiros. He didn't return until she was up and dressed and eating the breakfast the little maid set on the table. The girl had looked about for the big black dog and asked where he was, and Hekate had snapped at her that he was about his dog's business, which was none of her affair. She had felt guilty but too ill-humored to apologize.

The child was very fond of Kabeiros. She had been terrified of the huge dog when Ottah first brought her to serve Hekate, and Kabeiros had put himself out to win her trust, wagging his tail and pressing his head against her hand very gently so that she could pat him. Her first lesson about the household in which she was to serve was that she didn't need to fear the black dog and she had come to love the creature. Now she always made sure his bowl was full of water and asked if she should prepare food for him.

It was the maid who opened the door when he scratched and he stopped halfway in to lick her cheek, which made her giggle. If he glanced at Hekate, it was too quickly for her to see and she said, "Where the devil have you been?"

The little maid laughed as she always did when Hekate spoke aloud to Kabeiros, but this time Kabeiros did not reply under cover of the maid's amusement. He leapt up on the divan, turned once around, and went to sleep. The maid made no comment on that. Her second lesson had been that the black dog was *never* reprimanded. He went where he liked, lay where he liked, and if he chose to rise up on his hind legs, put his forepaws on the table, and snatch a tidbit from Hekate's plate, even that was not criticized.

Hekate was so annoyed that she pushed aside the remains of her breakfast, took her cloak, and left the apartment, slamming the door behind her. Outside she went down a few steps and then hesitated, listening for Kabeiros to tell her to wait or, if he still was not speaking to her, for a scratch at the door or a bark to indicate that he intended to accompany her, but no peace token was extended.

Fuming, she went down the rest of the stairs and headed for the market. She had intended to rent a stall as soon as she knew the *Wave Leaper* would remain in port in Heraclea but somehow she hadn't done it. Instead she had accepted with pleasure Captain Ottah's invitation to go about with him as he negotiated for new cargo, sharing meals with him and talking of the advantages of trading for oneself or carrying goods for others.

She found the talk and expeditions of such interest that they reconciled her to wearing the body of the crone. No one looked askance at her keeping company with the captain as they would have done had she been a handsome young woman. The bailiffs and shipping factors all called her Mother and addressed their most persuasive arguments to her, assuming she must be old and wise in trade for the captain to bring her with him. She and Ottah laughed heartily together over the mistake, but sometimes it was useful when different aspects of a cargo were presented to her and to him.

Her mind was so busy with past pleasures that she passed unseeing along the stalls, starting when a hand caught her arm and a market warden called out to her. He remembered her from an earlier examination of rental possibilities because he had had a terrible cough when she spoke to him, for which she had given him a remedy. That act of kindness was now repaid; there was a stall open—the holder had fallen sick and abandoned it—that would suit her perfectly.

She was indeed satisfied with what was shown to her—a small but weathertight shed in which she could store her goods and even see to a client if the weather were inclement, and an outside apron of dirt packed so hard that even the rain of the previous night had done no more than slick the surface. Hekate contracted for the space at once, fishing in her thin purse for a few coppers to hold her right until she could return later in the day with the rental and fee.

She felt surprisingly pleased with the transaction, and hardly regretted that it would curtail her time with Ottah. It was only when she was on her way back to her rooms, thinking how pleased Kabeiros would be, that she realized she had rushed out to rent market space to pacify the hound. Her desire to pacify him when it was he that had made the quarrel by being totally unreasonable, annoyed her so much that she didn't tell him what she had done. And he annoyed her still more when she came in; he didn't speak but lay on the divan, only the dog showing, nothing of the shadow man.

Even angrier than before, Hekate changed to her best gown—not that any gown could do much for the crone, bent and hollow-chested as she was—and went out to dinner with Ottah and the crew. She was sorry the moment she stepped out of the house. Heraclea was not a particularly dangerous city, but dockside was not perfectly safe either, and she was accustomed to having the protection of the black dog.

No harm befell her, however, and Ottah saw her home. She told him about renting a stall and when he offered any support she needed, thinking she sought clients because she needed living expenses, she assured him it was more to keep up her practice in healing than any need. He was regretful that she would not be available as a companion, but admitted he had little more to do. His cargo was sold and, by his reckoning, his hold would be full for the spring voyage.

When they reached the house, Ottah looked down and then up at her in surprise and asked about Kabeiros. He had not noticed until then that the dog was not with her, simply assuming he was. Hekate made some excuse, she didn't remember what, because she was busy fighting a terrible temptation to shift to the woman and to go home with Ottah, leaving Kabeiros to wait and worry.

Almost, almost she yielded. Only the thought of the long explanations, of the admission that she was a real sorcerer and knew a lot more than healing spells, of the real chance that Ottah, Egyptian or not, would withdraw from her in horror when he learned she was Gifted, a shape-shifter, held her back. So she said her usual good-night and went up the stair. The heavy key that hung at her belt opened the door, but she didn't even glance toward the divan. She went through to her bedchamber and went to bed.

The next morning, to her infinite surprise, not only was Kabeiros sitting in his usual place, but the shadow man was present . . . and he was hardly a shadow.

Kabeiros! she exclaimed, silently because the little maid was scurrying about with dishes and platters. *You are almost real. You look as if I could touch you.*

Not real enough, unfortunately, he said, with a smile that twisted the lips of the shadow but lacked mirth. *I was thinking last night that my trouble might be within myself, a result of lack of trying to be a man.*

I can't believe that! You must have tried to shift.

She was eating as she spoke, holding out a tidbit to the dog as she often did. The little maid noticed nothing strange.

Did I? Kabeiros asked doubtfully. *Shifting had always been so easy. Like breathing. I thought 'dog' or 'man' and I was dog or man. I didn't think how. I just was. And when I tried to shift and I couldn't . . . I do remember the terror that seized me. I remember trying again and again and being more afraid each time I failed. But I *don't* remember asking why I couldn't shift or looking within myself to see what was wrong. My friends tried to help, but they didn't really know any more than I did and I soon fled and became more and more the dog, until I came by accident to the caves of the dead . . . and became a man.*

I don't know. Hekate's eyes lit with enthusiasm. *There's no sense blaming yourself after all this time. Who knows what really took place? But we can work on it. Perhaps if I lend you power–not that you need power but more might do the trick–you will be able to change. We can do that between clients. Few will come these first days, until my reputation has a chance to spread. We will have time.*

Clients? And are you sure the market will be a good place to work? What if I do change to a man right there where everyone can see?

I have a shed and it has a door. I can pretend to be working with my herbs, preparing potions.

You have a shed? His mind echoed the words as it had previously echoed "clients."

Hekate blushed a trifle. "Oh, I forgot to tell you. When I went out yesterday I went to the market and I rented a stall. There are two or three moons more before the weather clears enough for sailing and I have done no healing for a long time. I need to practice my skills because, as you have told me and Ottah, too, no spells are allowed in Greece. I bet they will have witch-smellers about, too. I need to cure without witchcraft.*

She had practice in plenty in the moons until the *Wave Leaper* sailed, except for the first few days. These she devoted to Kabeiros while she pretended to mix herbs and compound salves. First she tried to pour power into the hound, but he was as resistant to outside transference of power as he was to spells. Foiled of the most direct route, she tried to teach Kabeiros to draw power from the blood of the earth. He could smell it and she was marginally more successful in this attempt. If he walked the blood-lines, he could draw some power through his naked paws. It was enough to allow him to sustain the less shadowy appearance of the man, but did not come near feeding enough to the draining spell to make the man real. Last of all, Hekate tried to enter the dog, find the organ that ruled his ability to shift and pick the draining spell from it, thread by thread if need be. That, too, failed. She could no more penetrate the hound than could a spell.

After that failure, the dog was silent and only a dog. Hekate pleaded with him not to give up hope, blaming her own lack of skill and knowledge for the failure, but her voice trembled with fear. She knew she was lacking neither in skill nor in knowledge. When she had arrived in Colchis, perhaps, but she had grown enormously in the years she had spent there. She had freed herself from Perses' compulsion not to use magic; she had learned to use high magic as well as low; she could create spells, weave them together, take them apart, bind them, make them immortal. Yet she could not penetrate the dog's shields.

For a ten-day she might as well have been pleading and reasoning with a true hound. Then she remembered that she *didn't* know everything. The dog was *not* impervious to all magic. With hope in her own voice and face, Hekate reminded Kabeiros that Medea in serpent form, *had* reached past the dog's defenses, whatever they were. The princess had used her Gift for that. True, her spells as a human sorcerer were as ineffective as Hekate's own, but the serpent's Gift had reached inside the hound, found his power and the draining spell that spoiled it . . . and had nearly killed him.

Hold on. Hold on, Hekate begged. *As soon as spring comes we will be on our way to Olympus. The gods are greatly Gifted. Think. If Hephaestos could build the palace at Colchis when he was little more than a child, his Gift as an artificer is near incredible–and he was only one of the minor gods. Surely among the great ones, one will have a Gift that will free you.*

Perhaps, Kabeiros replied, but his voice was dull.

Hekate would have been in utter despair, except that she was soon too busy healing, and Kabeiros was roused from fading into a dog's uncaring by the need to watch her clients, to listen to what they said to each other and report that to Hekate. She was not a teller of fortunes and didn't care about the clients' private lives but, strangely enough, they would often tell a fellow sufferer of symptoms they would not describe to their healer.

Hekate's success was not totally owing to skill and good fortune. Some of it began with a new favor from Ottah, who sent members of his crew and others to her. Seeing her stall crowded, local people began to come out of curiosity and soon out of need. It was not surprising, then, as the year turned toward spring, and she told her clients she must depart, that there were pleas and protests. She calmed those by leaving recipes for certain potions and salves with several healers she had learned were skilled and honest.

To one woman, whose eyes told Hekate more than the woman knew herself, Hekate came on the evening before *Wave Leaper* sailed and brought a half-dozen healing spells for deep troubles that salves and potions would not touch. She told the woman how to practice the spells and how to test them.

Hekate would have been horrified to learn that when she was gone, the woman set up a shrine at the crossroads in the market and worshiped Hekate. When others laughed, she insisted that a goddess had visited Heraclea. They laughed less when her healing spells, taught her—she never failed to say—by Hekate, worked wonders. The woman spread the spells among her sisters and daughters so that more worshipers were drawn to the shrine. They came as dusk faded to darkness because that was when Hekate had come to her first disciple. As in legend, the goddess had moved on, but the worship persisted and spread.

Hekate knew nothing of that. Her heart and mind reached only toward Olympus. Perhaps her desire was strong enough to magic the weather. The long voyage to the Bosphorus was swift and sure. A following wind, not so strong as to whip up huge waves but strong enough to drive the ship forward at a good pace, never failed. It died just enough every evening to allow them to beach *Wave Leaper* without difficulty, and blew again the next day. It even shifted to southerly when they needed to stand out to sea to avoid the Symplegades and turned westerly again when they needed to come back to shore.

At Cyaneae Ottah tried to convince Hekate to continue on with him. If she merely wanted to see new people and new things, he said, she would certainly do so if she came along on his voyage, for which he would demand no fare. *Wave Leaper* would be taking the northern route along the coast of Thrace and the land of the Getae to Olbia and then south. She had never seen those lands, had she?

She refused him gently, laughing and saying he might not have seen the last of her, she might yet return to the shores of the Pontus Euxinus. First, however, she had to go to Greece. And when he protested that would be dangerous for such as she, she shrugged and told him her goal was one place where magic must be welcome–Olympus.

"No, no," he begged. "You are old, but you are very strong and won't die soon. I know what you desire. Because you are a witch, you think you can win immortality in Olympus, but it's a vain hope. You'll never find the place, and even if you do, the gods don't so easily give up their secrets. And they are known to punish the audacious."

She shook her head. "I've no such foolish dreams," she said. "It's for Kabeiros that I go." She shrugged and put her arm around the unresponsive hound. "He wasn't always a dog. He is bespelled . . ." Even to Ottah and in the last hours before separation, she wouldn't admit Kabeiros was a shapeshifter.

"I knew he was more than a dog. I knew." Ottah sighed. "No one is bound to a dog as you're bound to Kabeiros."

"Nor have I been completely honest with you about more than my lack of a younger son in Byzantium. I have no sons at all, and didn't come from Sinope but from Colchis."

"Colchis! I have heard tales . . ."

"Too many are true. If you don't have to make port there, don't. But even in Colchis, and it was a city of sorcerers, there was no one who could set Kabeiros free. There are only the gods of Olympus left."

She said it softly, looking anxiously over her shoulder at Kabeiros, who had walked away to lie down on some folded blankets. His eyes were closed and there was no sign of the shadow man. He was not totally withdrawn into the dog. He came alert quickly when there was doubt or danger, but he hardly spoke–no more little caustic comments or seemingly sober remarks really designed to make her laugh when she shouldn't. More than her heart ached. She kept seeing the man, almost real, and her body ached for him, too.

Ottah saw the inflexible determination in her. He wondered if the dog had been a brother or a husband or, even though she had denied children, a son. He told her first what his route would be and where, if she decided to return, she could leave messages for him or meet him. Then, sighing, he went with her to the caravanserai and helped her make arrangements to start her journey west.

CHAPTER 19

Winter was closing in on Greece by the time Hekate and Kabeiros reached their goal. Kabeiros the man surfaced again as they set foot on his homeland, and as she gathered her bundles, he began to warn her about how to behave. Fortunately they came ashore at Heraclea, on the border between Thessaly and Pieria. When they had heard the name of the final port, both agreed at once to sail on that ship; it was a good omen Hekate felt for the same safety and ease of travel they had had since leaving Heraclea in Bythnia.

Added benefits appeared once they docked. Heraclea was a large enough port to have shops that supplied anything a traveler could want, but small enough not to be either a sink of iniquity or a major focus of the king's authority. It did have a local lord, but his port officer knew he would not be interested in an old woman, who carefully husbanded her few pieces of copper. If the officer had followed her, he would have seen her bartering for a heavy woolen blanket rather than a fur-lined cloak and thick-soled, tall, leather huntsman's boots.

The large, strong dog might have been of more interest to a lord who enjoyed the hunt, except that it slunk along behind the old woman with its tail between its legs. A single glance showed the official it had no disposition to fight and didn't even chase rats. At first it didn't occur to the lord's officer to wonder how the poor old woman fed a dog of that size. He might have accused her of stealing when the thought did come, but they were gone from the town by that time and he had heard no complaints about them.

A number of the merchants from whom Hekate bartered goods were horrified at the thought of an old woman setting off to travel in the winter. She pacified them by naming the nearest inland village–Kabeiros had discovered the name for her and the names of some people who lived there. The place was only a day's walk distant, even for an old woman, and she said she had family there waiting for her. Then she and Kabeiros left at night, Hekate having artfully arranged some of her worn summer clothing over the heap of straw on which she would have slept. Last, she stole a small, sturdy mule, leaving more than its worth in twists of silver.

The village Hekate had named was south of Heraclea, in Magnesia. She and Kabeiros set off northwest into a land that was essentially wilderness, except for a few isolated farms. Away from other humans, Hekate changed form to the woman, sighed with relief, and strode forth at a pace the crone could never match. She had no fears of the wilderness. In it she was free to use magic to ward away wild beasts, to keep her warm and protected from the weather, to cook her food, even to lighten the load on the little mule, which was mostly two trusses of hay and grain for its food.

What was more she didn't fear to expend the power to accomplish even the most trivial things. The blood of the earth under her feet ran more like a wide river than a little stream–and it ran from the northwest, from the mountain the local people called Olympus.

It was plain from the land that no one went that way. There were game trails here and there but no sign of any hunter, and the only obstacles Hekate found were two rivers she had to cross. In the winter with waters mostly frozen into ice in the mountains, they were easy enough to ford and magic dried clothing and fur so none were chilled.

In the late afternoon of the second day of travel, Hekate looked ahead into another narrow, arid, empty valley that came to an abrupt end in a sheer cliff.

It is here, Kabeiros said, and sneezed.

Hekate grinned. The illusion was large, but not quite as good as those of Aietes, and, in any case, illusion was useless against anyone who could sense magic. It flowed thick and rich, so rich that it felt hot rather than comfortingly warm, from whatever was behind the illusion.

She cast a protection over her little mule and drew extra wards around her in case there was a sting behind the gossamer web that deceived the eyes. Those were wise precautions because she felt a more violent magic run off her shield and saw it flow over and off Kabeiros. For a moment that had all her attention, in case his natural protection wasn't perfect and he should be hurt. The shadow man, who had been walking beside her disappeared, but Hekate didn't know whether that was the effect of the defense of Olympus or a withdrawal because his invulnerability was not a hopeful sign to Kabeiros.

As she tried to think what to say, the dog showed Kabeiros had not withdrawn too far. He turned his head and said, *Look.* And she did, and saw that the valley was much, much larger than that depicted in the illusion. In fact, she could not see the end of it at all; it must stretch many miles.

From where she stood, a wide dirt road passed through what were clearly tilled fields, although now they were lying fallow. Dividing the fields far along the road were wooded patches, and beyond the fields to north and south the land rose, at first gently into hilly pasturage and then, at a good distance but where she could still see clearly, more suddenly into high cliffs.

There was no sign of habitation, but the road was marked with and smelled of manure. Draft animals of some kind came along the road often enough, even in winter, for their soil to remain evident. As she thought "winter," Hekate noticed that the air was much warmer, not summerlike but no colder than late autumn. But it had been full winter, threatening snow, on the other side of the shield/illusion. Kabeiros sneezed again.

Magic on magic, he said. *I've never smelled it so strong.*

"Well, there's no sense standing here," Hekate said. "I don't see any signs of a welcoming committee, even a hostile one. Maybe they've got the local people so cowed that even if they manage to pass the spell at the entrance, whatever it is, when they see they have actually penetrated the valley of the gods, they retreat to safer ground."

We'll know soon enough, Kabeiros agreed, starting forward, *but for now I think I will keep the man hidden. The mages of Colchis couldn't see my man form, but they couldn't see any of the low magic. Perhaps they can here, and I would prefer to keep secret the fact that I can think like a man.* He hesitated and added bitterly, *Even if that's all I can do like a man.*

It will not be so long now, Hekate soothed. *A few weeks, perhaps, to find my balance and discover what I can offer these mages to try to cure you.*

They walked along briskly for some time, once passing a very ordinary-looking peasant leading an ox that drew a small two-wheeled cart laden with hay. The peasant looked at Hekate with her dog and her mule, but he said nothing and Hekate let him pass because she didn't know what questions she wanted to ask.

Soon after that encounter, the tilled fields gave way to a kind of tamed wilderness. There were tall trees rising out of grassy or mossy ground with here and there neat patches of berry-bearing brambles and bushes that she suspected also bore berries or, perhaps, nuts. It was like a park. They were coming close to the city, she thought, the kind of city that didn't want to be too close to the peasants that fed it. Hekate shrugged as she walked. She would have to answer questions at the gate, she assumed, but she would know better what answers to give when she had seen the city.

They came at last to a wall . . . but there was no city, only the wall, long overgrown. Hekate stopped and stared, and in her mind Kabeiros began to laugh crazily.

Dead and gone, his mind was in chaos. *Long dead and gone.* The crazy laughter echoed again. *While I lived like a dead man in the caves of the dead, the 'gods' all died.*

Don't be silly, Hekate snapped. *That illusion

at the head of the valley wasn't set before these vines grew.*

How do you know? You have illusions that you say will last until the earth moves. Why not these, who called themselves gods?

"Because," Hekate said dryly, aloud, having got over her shock, "the wall goes in the wrong direction. Have you ever seen a city wall that did not *cross* the road? Yes, sometimes a track will go around, but not the main road."

In fact, a little farther along they found a gate from which the vines had been cleared, invitingly open.

"It's a temple," Hekate said, looking at the carvings on the gate posts, "and someone still comes here." She stood listening, then asked, "Do you hear any sign of life?"

No. Kabeiros' panic had been conquered. *But there's a fountain still running or a spring of some kind.*

After a moment of silence, Hekate said, "I . . . I must go in. I am being . . . drawn, no, called, within."

Hekate! he warned, but it was too late.

She had already passed through the gates and Kabeiros hurried to catch up as she walked along a narrow path. Once it had been much wider; once processions had passed along it, but now brush and creepers were encroaching along the sides. Only the center was clear, but that had been swept free of fallen leaves and blown earth, showing that the path had been laid of white marble.

Without hesitation Hekate passed under a broad stone lintel and into the temple itself. It was a small, round building. Once the stones might have gleamed pure white, now they were stained and streaked where rain had penetrated the failing roof. Hekate barely noticed. At the center of the temple on a low plinth there was an image. Only by the most careful examination—or an act of faith—could she see a shape: a head, sloping shoulders, long shadows that might mark arms, a sweep of stone into a broader base that could be the skirt of a gown. Her gaze went back to the head, to the long, oval face, an indentation across it that might have been eyes, a slight bulge or perhaps only a lightening of color that marked a high-bridged nose, and below that other shadows that could limn a mouth.

"Mother?" Hekate breathed.

She walked around the image and her breath caught. From whatever position she took, she saw the same face. The long eyes under the high brow followed her; what could have been the nose changed shape slightly; but the mouth . . . when she had reached her first position again, she could swear it was smiling.

"She smiled at me!" Hekate said to Kabeiros. "Thank you, Mother! I will go in hope because You approve."

Kabeiros looked up at her. She sounded like a little girl, and she waved gaily to the image as they left the temple.

"If we stay here," Hekate said, turning into the road again, "I will see what I can do about fixing that roof. Not that the Mother will care. Her strength doesn't come from Her worshipers, like the strength of a blood-mage from the bodies of his victims. She is the same whether any worship Her or not. The shrine to which my mother took me had no temple at all, only a wooden image that looked a lot like this one, although this is stone. Our Lady stood right out in the open in a forest glade."

I don't think worship of the Mother is popular here, Kabeiros said, his mental tone neutral.

"Oh, no." Hekate laughed. "I suppose they

worship themselves, or each other. You needn't warn me. I won't start to preach. The Mother can look out for Herself. As far and as long as I know Her, She only gives, never takes. She needs nothing from us." Hekate laughed again. "As to what She gives, one needs to be careful in asking; you might get *exactly* that, which wasn't what you wanted at all."

They progressed in silence for somewhat less than a quarter candlemark when Kabeiros hesitated, poked his nose down at the ground, and then sniffed under a tall stand of tasseled grass.

Wait, he called. *There's something behind here.*

Hekate returned and peered over the tall grass. "Could be," she agreed. "There are old trees on each side of this grass stuff and it forms a gentle curve, as if it were once a walk. Shall we go back and look? I have a feeling that we won't find any inns in Olympus. If any part of what was once here is still standing, it might be a good place to sleep."

She left the mule tethered behind some brush, and they pushed their way through the growth, careful near the road not to damage the grass too much. Just out of sight around a hedge, which had not completely grown together, there was a house. Hekate and Kabeiros stood and stared at it.

It wasn't white and shining as the temple must once have been. It was of huge gray blocks of granite, seemingly crude but each set so close and finely on the others that no mortar was necessary. Nothing lightened the somber facade, only the granite itself sparkled where the sun touched it and reflected from minute grains of quartz. Two doors of gleaming black wood with matching handpulls of brass stood closed in the center of the building. On either side were three tall windows, tightly shuttered. A tall facade hid all but one central peak of the roof which seemed to be of slate and perhaps had a window or a door.

That it was an impressive, almost an overwhelming, house was not what held Hekate and Kabeiros gaping. It was all perfect. Amidst the riot of overgrown grounds, the house was clear of vine or weed, even of moss grown on the roof.

Stasis? Hekate asked Kabeiros.

Mother knows, he replied. *This whole place stinks so of magic that it's hard to pick out one spell.*

Should I try to break it?

Kabeiros hesitated, then said, *Not now. To break a spell so strong and so old might wake some kind of alarm and would surely be considered an aggressive act. Let's find the city first. Who knows, perhaps we can ask permission to use this house . . . if you like it.*

I think I do, Hekate said. *I like how close it is to the Mother's temple, and it doesn't look like decorated pastry. I like the somber look of it. Well, we'll see.*

So they went on. Almost opposite the hidden house, a small lane led south. The grass on either side of it was cropped smooth and Hekate thought she caught a glimpse of a low, white house farther in. She didn't take that lane, however; it looked too much like the purely residential streets in Ur-Kabos and, like them, probably led nowhere but to more private houses.

Beyond that there was another overgrown lane to their right; then the main road seemed to fork left. Since the fork seemed wider and better traveled than the road that ran straight on, Hekate and Kabeiros bore to the left and very soon came to a wider and perfectly paved road that went south. Hekate looked at the new road in some dismay. It was, like the path to the temple, of closely fitted blocks of white marble. A few dusty footprints marred the surface, but not a single oval of a hoof, not a heap of manure, nor a straight track of a wheel.

I don't think our mule will be welcome here, Hekate said.

*I'm not sure *I* will be welcome here.* Kabeiros sounded dismayed.

That problem we can deal with when we meet it, Hekate said. *You aren't likely to leave a pile of dung anywhere. The mule is. I'll take it back to our house . . . *

The words "our house" echoed in her mind and she laughed, but Kabeiros had no doubt about which house she meant and they hurriedly retraced their steps. They hobbled the mule behind the hedge, where Kabeiros had found a broken fountain from which some water still flowed.

After a moment in which she had glanced around the deserted grounds, Hekate said, *I think I'll change my clothes. There isn't any sense in walking into the city wearing stained and dusty travel clothes. That will just cry aloud that we are strangers.*

The dog backed away from her as if she had threatened him.

"What's the matter? Do you think it would be more dangerous to—"

No. No. The words were blurred and mumbled as if Kabeiros was having difficulty speaking at all. *I . . . I need to look at the warding from all sides. Do what you like about clothing.*

He was gone before the last few words came to her mind, running with his tail low, as if some dreadful danger was on his heels. Hekate stood staring after him. She had no particular inclination to look around or send out a testing probe. Kabeiros would never run from danger, specially not from danger to her. If he ran from her it was she who posed the danger to him. But how? Why? And why when she said she would change her clothing?

While she mused, she got the pack that held her clothing and extracted a light green tunic and a dark and sober gown, decently trimmed with twining vines in silver and light green. Then she removed what she was wearing, including the tall huntsman's boots. Naked, she washed her face, arms, and legs and used some rough sacking to dry herself.

It occurred to her, while she was rubbing the last drops of water from her legs, that Kabeiros had been more and more distant since they left Heraclea–not less human; he had been alert to every chance and every danger and quick to offer advice, but less close. He no longer walked near enough for her to rest her hand on him as he always had when she wore the form of the crone. He lay on the far side of the fire when they slept instead of lying pressed against her . . . and it was winter; the warmth would have been welcome.

Could Kabeiros love only the crone because it was she with whom he had spent those months in the caves of the dead? That was ridiculous, she told herself as she drew on the undertunic and then the gown, found a clean place to sit, and laced on sandals. The crone and the woman were the same person–even the maiden was the same person. But he had been in man form when she was with him as the crone. Could that have made a difference?

She sighed, unable to understand and unwilling just now to spend more time puzzling over the problem. A mental call brought Kabeiros loping around the edge of the house. Hekate then extracted from the bundle a strong leather wallet and put into it some silver and gold.

After going a small distance along the wide street

that had caused them to get rid of the mule, they discovered it was not as devoid of life as the roads they had traveled thus far. Several men and women, plainly but decently dressed, passed them. Two entered a westbound street, also marble paved and wide. Hekate thought of following them, but they were walking slowly, talking, not as if they had errands or other business to do. Several other people came by ones and twos from narrower, but also well-paved side streets.

Hekate breathed several sighs of relief when no more than a single curious glance was cast at them from anyone. A dog, it seemed, was not a very unusual sight and her clothing would pass. They went by two more side streets on the left and one on the right. Then, at last, their road met another, not only equally wide and equally well-paved, but lined with elegant columns.

Beyond that crossroad, there seemed to be only one more side lane. After that, the road ran through the same kind of tamed wilderness or parkland they had passed before reaching the deserted temple. To the right, however, the street with columns showed more life, and Kabeiros reported he heard the sound of many voices and smelled many people.

They turned into that street, passed an open grassy area, and then walked into a modestly busy market. Hekate stood with her hand on Kabeiros' head and stared around.

"Is that a new dog for Lady Artemis?" a woman's voice asked.

Hekate's hand closed possessively on the ruff of fur on Kabeiros' neck.

Say you want Lady Artemis to look at the dog, Kabeiros urged her sharply.

Hekate was not willing to go as far as that. "I'm not sure," she said to the woman.

The woman who had spoken was very tall, her brown hair pulled back into a bun at the nape, and a heavy felted cloak thrust aside so that Hekate could see she wore a simple white garment pinned together on her left shoulder with a brooch and belted at her waist with silver links. The garment left her right shoulder bare. Her expression was severe but not unpleasant.

"He is a beautiful dog," she said, and then, with a touch of sympathy in her voice, "I can see that you love him. Well, you need not fear to leave him with Lady Artemis. He will be very well cared for."

"But what if I bring him to her and then realize I cannot bear to be parted from him? Will she be angry with me?"

"Likely not," the woman said.

However, Hekate thought she didn't sound very sure and Kabeiros chuckled in the back of her mind.

From what I've heard about these 'gods,' they don't take kindly to being denied their desires.

Then perhaps we shouldn't use this pretext.

I think we must. This is a quick and easy introduction to one of the great mages, and she is twin sister to Apollo—one of the greatest. Besides, if Lady Artemis is as familar with dogs and as powerful as the daughter of Zeus should be, she won't take me for a dog for long. You can explain our need to her . . . but I think you should be well warded, in case she takes offense at your pretense.

Actually, it wasn't the pretense that Hekate had a dog to sell that annoyed Artemis; it was because Hekate had brought a male who wasn't part of Artemis' family into Artemis' presence without invitation that they were nearly skewered with arrows. But not immediately. At first all had gone well. They had had no trouble following the woman's directions and finding Artemis' house, as all they had to do was continue to the end of the market, turn right on the lane there, and enter the first paved path to the left. There was a gate with a finely wrought bell, which Hekate rang.

The servant who came down the wide portico steps to answer was an older woman, gray-haired and with thin-drawn lips. She glanced at Hekate, began to shake her head, then looked down at Kabeiros, smiled, and opened the gate. As they entered, a cacaphony of howls and barks could be heard coming from somewhere behind the house.

"You have a dog to sell," the servant said–not a question but a statement, as if this was a common occurrence.

"Only to show Lady Artemis," Hekate said, ignoring Kabeiros' urging that she agree. She found she could not even pretend such an idea.

"You can wait in there."

The servant pointed to a chamber that opened through a wide arch from the entry hall. Obediently Hekate walked in, drew breath, and stopped dead. Straight ahead a tiny stream ran, falling out of the back wall of the place, which seemed to be of rough stone with plants growing from crevices. Across the stream, a doe and two fawns bent to drink. Behind them, a little distance away, a stag with magnificent antlers stood with raised head.

From a dense thicket of bushes, which masked the wall to Hekate's right, eyes gleamed. After a moment's study, she made out rough brown fur and a hulking shape . . . a bear. Nearer, just at the edge of the thicket, a fox crouched. On the far left was a grove of young birches, which stretched to shadowy distance, among which were more deer; that, however, was only a painting.

It isn't real, Kabeiros said, his nose twitching.

Perhaps not, but it is magnificent workmanship. I wonder who made it?

You can ask. It's a harmless enough question.

Before Hekate could answer, footsteps sounded in the entryway and a tall, broad-shouldered but very beautiful woman came through the arch. Her hair was a golden-brown, elaborately dressed in braids and curls but caught up on top and close to the sides of her head so it would not get in the way. Her eyes were almost the color of her hair, large and almond-shaped with thick, straight lashes. The nose was perfect, straight, with delicate nostrils. If there was any fault, it was in the mouth, which was well-formed but held too tightly.

She wore a gown of thick, gleaming, white fabric. Silk, Hekate thought, like the cloth that came to Colchis from far to the east. The gown was pinned on the left shoulder to leave the right arm bare, like that of the woman who gave them directions in the market, but the skirt was kilted up well above the knees for ease in running. On her feet were tall huntsman's boots, much like those Hekate had discarded. A quiver of arrows hung from the golden belt at her waist, and a short, dangerous looking horn bow drooped from one hand.

She looked first at Kabeiros, a quick glance, then at Hekate, to whom she said, "What do you want for him?"

"I . . ."

"Oh, out with it! Whom do you want killed and why?"

"Killed!" Hekate echoed, eyes wide with shock. "I don't want anyone killed. What a horrible thought. Are you the executioner of the gods?"

Artemis stared at her, then suddenly laughed. "I suppose I am, in a way. All of us can kill, but I'm the one who's asked to do it." The smile that remained after the laugh ended was very bitter. Then she shrugged. "I don't mind killing, and the death I deal is always quick and painless." She smiled again. "Some of them don't like that."

Hekate shook her head. "I beg your pardon, Lady Artemis, we seem to be here, Kabeiros and I, under false pretenses. I don't want anyone killed, and I haven't the right to sell Kabeiros."

"Kabeiros, is it?" Artemis now gave her full attention to the hound. In a moment, her eyes widened. "That is no dog!" she exclaimed. "It is a man. In my house!"

The bow lifted, an arrow, extracted from the quiver so quickly it seemed almost magical, was notched and aimed at Kabeiros, the bow drawn.

"*Teleia stigme*!" Hekate spat, and pointed.

Artemis froze into position.

What now? Kabeiros asked, rising to his feet. *Does this mean that shape-shifting is forbidden in Olympus?*

I wouldn't jump to that conclusion, Hekate said, walking over to Artemis. She touched the fingers bent around the bow and arrow and murmured, "*Entautha monos thialuo teleia stigme*," and removed the bow and arrow from Artemis' hands. *I would say this is one nasty lady who just doesn't like men.*

But she can't go around killing every man on sight, Kabeiros protested.

No, no. I suspect it's only males that invade her territory that she kills. This is her house, after all. What's more important is that she saw at once what you were.

*Are you sure *that* isn't why she tried to kill me?*

Sure? No, I'm not. If that's true, we must leave—

For where? The hound stared up at her. The face showed little expression, but an angry despair emanated from his posture, the raised hackles, the lifted lip. *This was our last hope.*

No. Hekate's mind voice was flat and ashamed. *We can go back to the caves of the dead. When you are a man, you are open to my magic. I didn't want to go back.* Her mind withdrew and she looked into the imaging of a forest scene. "I am afraid of Perses," she said aloud.

**I* don't want to go back to the caves of the dead,* Kabeiros said. *Perhaps it's true she hates men. If not, perhaps she is one who hates shape-shifting and not all feel as she does. What can we do to pacify her? Shall I go away? No, then she might exercise all her spite on you . . .*

How? I don't think she's accustomed to casting spells. It was her bow she reached for to inflict punishment. And she had no shields against my magic. That last might be an accident. It's possible Olympians don't bother with shields in their own homes, but I think they really don't use magic much.

Kabeiros came closer and smelled the arrow. His nose wrinkled. *The arrowheads are bespelled illusions.*

Bespelled how? What kind of illusion?

He sniffed again. *I don't know. It's not like a made spell. It's like . . . like something scented with a person's body.*

An essence of her Gift made into a spell? Could it be that these people don't know how to create spells? If so, I could barter for almost anything. What do you think she would trade for that freezing spell?

Provided you could get her to listen instead of trying to kill you, almost anything she has.

Hekate sighed, then slowly dropped to her knees. She put the bow and arrows close beside her where

Artemis could not easily grab them, then released the spell.

Artemis immediately made the gesture of loosing the arrow from her bow and simultaneously shouted, "Opis!"

"Please, Lady Artemis, forgive me," Hekate had time to say before another woman, garbed much like Artemis and with the same broad shoulders, burst through the arch, bow in hand. Hekate froze her and turned back to Artemis, who was staring with wide eyes and open mouth. "Please listen, Lady Artemis," Hekate pleaded. "I mean no harm. I didn't know it was forbidden to bring a man into your house, but even if I did know I would have had to bring Kabeiros. You see, that's why we sought you out, for your knowledge of dogs. The problem is that Kabeiros cannot be a man. He is bound to the form of the dog."

"What did you do to my woman?" Artemis cried, ignoring what Hekate had said. "How did you get my bow?"

"I took your bow from your hands while you were frozen as is your woman now. The spell does no harm. It is purely a defense. I beg you to forgive me for using it against you, but I couldn't let you kill Kabeiros. He is bound to the form of a dog, I tell you. No man has violated your house."

"Bound to the form of a dog?" Artemis' glance flicked from her frozen woman to Kabeiros and back to Opis. "Loose my woman," she said.

"I have no desire to be shot," Hekate pointed out. "The arrow will fly before you can bid her not to shoot . . . if you bid her not to shoot. I'm afraid I must take her bow, as I took yours. Kabeiros, come sit on Lady Artemis' bow."

"Don't touch the arrowheads. They are death," Artemis warned Kabeiros, then bit her lip and shook her head. "I forgot he's a man. I meant to save the dog."

Kabeiros lolled out his tongue and sat down on the bow without touching the arrows at all. Hekate was pleased with his response. He was immune to magical spells—at least, she had not yet found one that affected him—but magic that was actually part of a Gift might be different.

With Kabeiros watching Artemis, Hekate approached Opis and removed her bow as she had with Artemis. The "goddess" watched her with bright eyes, clearly fascinated.

"You said words," she said, and then her eyes widened. "Are you a Titan?"

"*Thialuo*," Hekate said, releasing Opis, and then to Artemis, "A Titan? What's that?"

Opis had also completed the gesture of releasing her arrow and then stared open-mouthed at her empty hands. "It's all right," Artemis said to her with unexpected wry humor, "My 'guest' is collecting bows."

"She wants too much for the dog, does she?" Opis snarled, flexing her hands. "Shall I take him?"

"It isn't a dog," Artemis said. "I don't want him." She contemplated Hekate for a moment, then added, "You can go, Opis." And, as she saw the worried doubt in her woman's eyes, smiled. "She wants me to turn her dog into a man. She won't try to harm me."

She followed the woman to the archway, whispering in her ear, then came back and seated herself on a padded bench that pretended to be a fallen log. She gestured Hekate to another, which faced the painted wall. Hekate took the bows with her and set them on the bench together with the quivers. The arrowheads in Opis' quiver were ordinary bronze. Hekate thought about breaking the death-illusions of the arrowheads and then decided not to annoy or frighten Artemis with any further display of her ability.

"You asked what a Titan was," Artemis said. "They were an ancient enemy of my people, vanquished and cast out of Olympus in the time of Kronos, Zeus' father. They did magic as you do, with words and gestures . . . created spells."

"I am certainly no Titan if they lived in the time of Zeus' father. That was long before I was born."

"Oh, there are still some Titans about, just not here in Olympus. Not very long ago, several attacked the outlying farms." She sneered. "Imagine attacking the helpless native slaves. I killed one of them right at the edge of the city." She hesitated, stared at Hekate calculatingly, and added, "His spells took much longer to cast than yours. He began one, but my arrow was quicker. The fool wasn't afraid of me. He said, 'Little girl, go away,' and then that his name was Gration and he was about to reclaim the treasure from his grandfather's house. I wonder if there is a treasure there?"

Hekate raised her brows. "Has no one looked?"

"There's no way to get in. Oh, I suppose Zeus could blast the house . . . but perhaps his lightning would only destroy the house and not break the spell that binds it."

"Is that the house near the shrine of the Mother?"

Artemis' face stiffened. "Whose mother?"

"An old shrine, abandoned," Hekate said, unwilling to start any argument. "After we passed it, we came to an overgrown path. The house was behind a hedge."

"And you entered it?"

"No, of course not. I don't go into houses uninvited, even those clearly long abandoned. I didn't know to whom it belonged and it wasn't my right to enter, but I admired it. It's a handsome house."

"Very plain." Artemis wrinkled her nose. "Can you break the spell on it?"

Hekate shrugged. "I might be able to. I don't know. I didn't examine the spell. That wouldn't have been right."

"It's *my* right," Artemis said. "I killed Gration. His property is now mine."

"If you give your permission, I would certainly be willing to examine the spell and see if I could undo it. If I can remove the wards, would you permit me to stay in the house after you had taken from it anything you wanted?"

"Why should you want to stay in the house?"

"I thought there might not be any inns in Olympus and Kabeiros and I might be here for ten-days or even moons. We would need a place to live while we looked for a solution to Kabeiros' problem. He wishes to be able to be a man sometimes."

"He's better off as a dog."

"Perhaps, but it's his body and he has a right to use it as he likes. We have come a long way to Olympus to discover if any of the gods can cure his affliction. You saw at once that he wasn't a dog. If you could cure him, Lady Artemis, I . . . I would give you anything, anything I have."

"The freezing spell?" Artemis asked eagerly. "How could you give me a spell?"

"Just as you can create from your Gift the illusion of an arrowhead that carries death, so I can form my spell in such a way that you can take it within yourself. When you wish to use it, you need only think of drawing it forth and say the key words to invoke it."

"So I will have used it once, and then it will be gone. That's a small price to pay even for the use of Gration's house, not to mention anything else."

"Well, I did intend to pay you a rental, but I can bind to the freezing spell another that will root it to your power. Then, when you use it, it will simply put forth another bud of itself. However, I warn you that it will draw from your power, and if you use it often, that might weaken you."

"I will take the renewing spell instead of rental. If you have another spell that I think useful, perhaps I will sell the house to you."

"Cure Kabeiros, Lady Artemis, and I will build spells to your order, any spell you desire!"

There was a silence, after which Artemis shook her head.

"Can't you forget he's a man and just think of him as a sick dog? I would–"

Don't annoy her, Hekate, Kabeiros' mental voice was sharp and urgent. "It's not that she won't. It's that she can't. I can smell her fear and her confusion. And she can't admit she can't because she's supposed to be a goddess who can do anything.*

"Forgive me, Lady Artemis," Hekate said, bowing her head. "You have your oaths and your bindings, of which I know nothing. Perhaps they forbid you to act in Kabeiros' case. I must bow to that. If, however, I can undo the spell on Gration's house and then transfer to you the freezing spell, would you be willing to introduce me to others who might be willing to help poor Kabeiros?"

"If and if." Artemis' voice was sharp, but Hekate thought she was more defensive than angry. "There is some proving to be done before we consider rewards."

"That is fair, Lady," Hekate replied calmly, but thought once she had undone the wards, she could slap them right back on, if Artemis planned to cheat her. "But it will take me some time to examine the spell and find a way–if I can find a way–to undo it. I don't think you would wish to stand and watch me while I work. Nor would you wish to leave me completely on my own at Gration's house. Perhaps it would suit you to send a servant, or more than one, with me to watch me. Then if I manage to unlock the wards, one servant could run to fetch you while the others made sure I didn't enter the house and take anything you might want."

"You are a most sensible woman," Artemis said. "When will you be ready to begin?"

"When I have eaten and rested, Lady Artemis. Kabeiros and I have walked a long way today."

Artemis' eyes narrowed for a moment. "You can eat and rest here," she said, and then called again for Opis and told her to see to Hekate's refreshment. "And when she is ready, Opis, accompany her to Gration's house and see if she can break the spell that seals us out."

CHAPTER 20

The shield protecting Gration's house was a good one, but no better than Hekate could do on her own. It held one phrase that was of value because that phrase allowed the spell-caster to define the area to be shielded. However, Hekate thought Gration's spell could only be used in Olympus itself because it drew a huge amount of power. That didn't matter where the blood of the earth welled in neverending fountains and flowed into veritable lakes of power. Elsewhere such a spell could dry up its source of power very quickly.

While she worked on Gration's spell, Hekate remained the guest of Artemis, Opis accompanying her to Gration's house and then back to Artemis'. She and Kabeiros were lodged in a comfortable room at the back of a long corridor that ran along the side of the woodland reception chamber. Hekate wasn't sure whether the hospitality was extended because Artemis suspected she would get into Gration's house alone and steal or because Artemis feared she would find another "god" who could cure

Kabeiros and give that "god" her freezing spell. She asked no questions. She was safe and comfortable and well fed, as was Kabeiros.

Artemis' behavior implied to Hekate that the Olympians did not trust one another nor anyone else. This would have made Hekate vastly uneasy, except that Artemis' house was open and unguarded. Plainly, while she suspected she might be cheated, Artemis didn't fear any attempt would be made to hurt her. Whether that forebearance would be extended to those who were not native Olympians, Hekate couldn't guess.

On the evening of the second day, Hekate removed the shield around Gration's house. She called to Opis, and together they crossed the line where the overgrowth had stopped. Then she called Opis back and reinvoked the spell (actually it was somewhat altered for the better). Opis bellowed in protest but it was too late, and Hekate said blandly she would leave the house unguarded only in Artemis' presence. Her face was expressionless, but Kabeiros' tongue was lolling out with laughter. Hekate intended to show herself just as wary as the "goddess."

The sun was near setting when Artemis, bringing half a dozen maidservants, came to the house. Hekate dismissed the stasis with a single word and gesture, intending to impress Artemis even more without alarming her. Whether or not she was successful remained in doubt. The "goddess" only rushed into the house, calling for torches to be lit, and began a hunt for the Titan's strong room. For all Hekate knew, she may have hunted far into the night; Hekate found a comfortable bed and went to sleep.

By morning, Artemis was resigned to the fact that there was no treasure in the sense of a huge repository of metal and gems. Hekate helpfully sent

Kabeiros to sniff for hidden rooms or areas disguised by illusion, but he didn't find any. Artemis was annoyed, but not surprised and said she thought Gration was a boastful liar. She busied herself with collecting all the jewelry in the house and all the bejeweled and golden artifacts. At noon the maids served a meal.

Having eaten, Artemis went back to scouring the place, all the while assuring Hekate that these were just toys to remind her of her victory—more hard won than she had first implied—over Gration, that her worshipers supplied her with jewels and gold in plenty. Hekate thought that Gration was not the only boastful liar, but she said nothing of that, only promising to tell Artemis if she found a treasure room.

She doubted Artemis believed her but sat down in the antechamber with Opis while Artemis searched. With the glittering gauds gone, she liked the room even better. It was simply a very large chamber, furnished with comfortable groups of chairs, divans, and tables, all in soft earth tones, lightened here and there with a dull gold or a flick of sun yellow. The walls were not disguised forest glades or manicured gardens; they were smooth, polished stone colored like pale sand, and they were hung with remarkable pictures.

A quick survey showed Hekate the beginning—a desperate battle scene, dominated by two figures, one of which was opening the earth to swallow the army of the other. The next picture showed the defeated fleeing (among whom, because of highlighting, Hekate was sure were Titans). A whole series of scenes followed the defeated on an incredible journey in which passes through mountains had been opened by a massive figure who seemed to be drawing heat from the rock, which was then pulverized by the hammer blows of the Titans. Then a valley was depicted; it was rocky and barren, but under the scrub brush and tangled hummocks of grass, the artist had depicted a red glitter that was surely meant to be earth-blood—the valley of Olympus as first seen.

Next to last was a picture of a city being built. The houses were of hewn granite rather than polished white or patterned marble, but Hekate was sure it was Olympus from the Titans' point of view. The last painting was not finished. It showed two crowds of men confronting each other. On one side was the man who had sucked the heat from the rocks; on the other was a man even bigger, dark-haired, dark-eyed with an expression of acute distress and one hand extended in a plea or a welcome to the first tall person. Behind the men were women, some standing proudly alone and others clinging together in twos and threes.

It was near evening again when Artemis came back, several bundles improvised out of cloaks being carried by her women servants. She looked around, commented on what a dull room it was, and then said that Hekate could have the house furnished as it was if she wanted the furniture, which was terribly old-fashioned, for the freezing spell.

Hekate had given the matter thought and was ready. She held her hands before her breast and in them grew a silvery sphere. This she held up to Artemis' face and said, "Drink."

The "goddess" stared at her, mouth thin with tension.

"Do not fear. Remember, I depend upon you to bring me into favorable notice of the other gods. I assure you, this is only the freezing spell you desired, bonded to the renewing spell so that as long as you have power or can draw power, the spell will not fail. You can use it as often as you like, but I warn you again, that if you use it too often you will grow empty and weak. That's nothing to do with the spell. That's only dependent on your own power."

It wasn't the whole truth, for Hekate had also bound to the renewing spell a very gentle compulsion to like her. The compulsion would not prevent Artemis from being angry with her nor induce any strong fondness, just encourage a mild friendliness. Aside from that the spell was harmless.

A moment of tense silence passed, then Artemis bent forward and put her lips to the ball of silvery light. It disappeared quickly.

"Now bring the spell to your mind, point your finger at whomever you want to freeze, and say, '*Teleia stigme.*' " Hekate grinned as she saw Artemis' hand rise. "Not at me. The spell won't work on me or on Kabeiros."

Artemis swung around and pointed at a maidservant. "*Teleia stigme,*" she said, and began to laugh with delight as the girl froze. Then she blinked and whirled to confront Hekate. "What have you done?" she shrieked. "You've seduced me into freezing one of my maidens! Release her. Release her at once!"

"Lady Artemis, be calm. You can release her yourself. I'm not the king of tricksters that would teach you a spell you couldn't reverse. Now, simply point at your maiden again, see her in your mind going about her normal business, and say, '*Thialuo.*' "

Release accomplished, the girl who had been frozen finished the step she had been about to take and then stared around at her companions, who were crying out with relief and delight and rushing forward to embrace her. Artemis grinned, looking suddenly like a young girl herself. Then a speculative gleam lit her eye.

"Is it permanent?" she asked Hekate.

"No. No spell is permanent."

That wasn't the truth, because the renewal spell, attached in a different way, would make any spell permanent; Hekate wasn't about to tell Artemis or any "god" that. If Artemis was any indication, these powerful yet totally untaught and quite uncontrolled Gifted individuals should be trusted with as little as possible. Perses had taught Hekate how dangerous spells could be in the hands of a monster without conscience.

"Oh." Artemis sounded rather disappointed, the gleam in her eyes dimming. "How long would a spell last? I mean, if I hadn't released Britomaris, how long would she have remained frozen?"

"I can't tell you that." Hekate laughed at the expression on Artemis' face. "I don't mean it's a secret I don't want to reveal, I mean I don't know. Different spells wear off at different times. It depends on how much power is needed to keep the spell active and how much power you are able to invest in the spell when you cast it. Spells can be renewed by touching the bespelled person or thing and adding power—"

Artemis shook her head. "I don't know what you're talking about."

"I don't know how to explain it better." Hekate sighed. "I was taught from a child. How do you make the arrowheads?"

"I . . . I wish for arrowheads, and then they are in my hand."

She wasn't telling what she actually did, but Hekate didn't blame her. She herself was divulging as little as possible.

"I hope it will work the same way," she said. "When you cast the spell, wish as you do for arrowheads, but wish harder or only lightly. Then see how long each freezing spell lasts. You needn't be concerned for whoever is frozen. The spell does no harm—unless it were to last for several days because you have so much power. A person needs to eat and drink and void. The freezing lets them wait longer, but not too long."

"Is there a way to freeze the body but not the mind?"

Hekate shuddered at the thought of being aware and unable to speak or move. "I don't know. I never tried."

"Think on it," Artemis said, smiling slowly. "If you can give me a spell like that, the house is yours."

"And in the meantime?" Hecate asked, quite prepared to be told to go.

Artemis laughed. "Stay, if you like, as long as you like. I saw your face when I asked about freezing the body and not the mind. I *would* use it as a punishment, but not unreasonably. When you realize I'm not a monster and are willing to trust me, I'm sure you will be able to create the spell I want."

"I will think about it," Hekate said.

She would need to discover how long a spell cast by Artemis would last. If it were not too long, being frozen for some hours or a day would be better than being slain. Still, she would do no more for Artemis until she fulfilled her part of the bargain over the freezing spell.

She said firmly, "And now for Kabeiros' trouble. Will you make me and his problem known to the other gods and goddesses and ask if any are willing to help me?"

"If you do not give any of them the freezing spell."

Hekate hesitated, then nodded. "That's fair. I'll not give the freezing spell to any other . . . well, I have it, but I won't use it unless it means my life or Kabeiros'."

"If you have time, I would rather you called on me and I will come and protect you."

"Call on you . . . how?"

Artemis grinned. "Oh, there's something you don't know? Can you speak mind to mind?"

"With Kabeiros."

"Can you scry?"

"If I must. I don't like to spy on people."

"Well, Calling is like scrying, but with voice only, no vision. When I've got home, you can Call me and see if I hear you."

"That's very kind, Lady Artemis, but I would be afraid to Call at an inconvenient moment. At your own best time, if you would Call me, I will answer if I hear. But about meeting the other gods–"

"You are fixed on letting a man have this power?"

"It's a Gift he was born with, and his right. He's taking nothing from me nor from anyone else."

Artemis made a moue of distaste. "Very well, that was our agreement. You've fulfilled your part. Tomorrow I'll take you to my mother, Leto. There's no one in Olympus she doesn't know, and her greatest delight is to help people."

Hekate signified her satisfaction with that arrangement and Artemis departed with her maidservants. When the house was quiet, she and Kabeiros explored it thoroughly. They even found a substantial stable off to one side, and Hekate laughed heartily as she established their one small mule in a huge stall, clearly meant for a horse able to carry a heavy man. After she had spread oats and barley in a manger, piled hay in a crib, and carried water from a stream diverted to supply the stable, she said to Kabeiros. "Either we must be rid of the mule or get a groom."

It's a big house, Kabeiros pointed out. *We need more than a groom. We need servants to cook and clean and go to the market.*

And how do I pay them? she asked, shouldering two packs and draping the third over Kabeiros' back; he held it steady with his teeth fixed on a strap.

Probably not at all. I'm sure that all the 'gods' are served by slaves. You'll buy those you need with spells from whatever 'god' has too many. I'm more concerned with paying for food and drink–

Hekate winced.

What's wrong? Kabeiros asked anxiously.

Drink. Dionysos. When you said 'drink,' I felt a drawing toward Dionysos. I wonder why? He's too young–

Not now. We've been away from Ka'anan a long time. If your binding to Dionysos is drawing you, we must go at once.

No, not yet.

Hekate put her hand on Kabeiros' shoulder, but he trotted forward so suddenly, it slid away. She looked down at her hand, and her eyes misted with tears. It was almost as if he hated her in this form. He would talk to her, but he wouldn't let her touch him. Blinking back the tears that obscured her vision, she found the back door and opened it. They entered a huge kitchen, spotlessly clean, with shining pots all ready to be lifted from their hooks and used.

What do you mean, not yet? Kabeiros' voice was loud and sharp in her mind, impatient, as if he had asked the question before.

*First we must see what the 'gods' can do for you. I'm not sure I even felt a draw to Dionysos, just . . . for a moment an uneasiness . . . *

In the name of the nameless Mother, are you mad? It took us how many years to get here? It isn't as if we are within an hour's walk of Ka'anan. Who knows what will have happened or how painful your binding will be by the time we return?

She stared at him, then shook her head. *You told me these 'gods' had a way to leap from one place to another. Perhaps I can buy a spell for us that will take us to Ka'anan in the blink of an eye. They don't know magic, but they have these Gifts. At least we can wait for tomorrow and see what Lady Leto says.* She hesitated, then looked away and added, aloud but very low, "I know you cannot bear to be with me much longer. I'm sorry, Kabeiros. I don't know what I've done. Perhaps when you can change your shape again and are not bound to me, when you are free to go if you wish–"

The dog lifted his head and fixed his white eyes on her. *Are you mad?* he asked again. And then, *Oh, you fool!*

He dropped the pack that had been balanced on his back and ran out the door. Hekate looked after him, but he had already disappeared into the shadows of oncoming night. After a few moments she lifted the pack that carried their food to a huge table of polished marble in the center of the room and began to unpack their supplies. Miserable as she was, the sight of the few pieces of dried meat, the small bags of barley and millet, the carefully wrapped wedges of cheese, and low pile of flat, hard, journeybread huddled together on that enormous table made her laugh.

There were stools under the table and she pulled one out, sat down, and, because she couldn't bear to let herself think about Kabeiros, she looked around. On the wall that held the door through which she had entered were three large hearths; each had some complicated erection of metal rods and chains. Hekate smiled again at the thought of hanging her little pot on any of the massive hooks attached to the chains or of roasting her one-rabbit supper on a spit plainly meant to hold several sheep or deer or even a couple of oxen.

One side wall had a single door, the other two, and the wall opposite the outer door, had one. Hekate looked toward her supplies, realized she couldn't see them, and called a mage light into being. Then she shook her head; she hadn't eaten since noon but she wasn't hungry. Her eyes turned toward the open back door. Impatient with herself, she rose and turned her back on the temptation to run out and call Kabeiros. Instead she walked to the door to her right.

Behind it the mage light illuminated a long passage with doors along the way. She opened two, which were identical bedchambers, small and austere but not grim. Each had a window, a narrow bed, a plain but sturdy chest, and a three-legged stool. Near the door, the corridor formed an L with another. Sending the mage light down that, Hekate saw several larger, more ornate doors, which she assumed closed off the bedchambers of Gration and his family.

She went back to the kitchen and opened the first door on the left wall. There was a tiny antechamber that had doors at right angles to each other. The nearer one, on the inner wall, opened into a dry storage chamber; the chamber behind the other door was at the outer corner of the house and had a clear stream running through it, providing a place to keep milk and cheese and even to cool wine or beer.

The farther door opened into a narrow serving pantry that led to a huge dining room. Hekate did not bother to send the mage light far into the room. A glimpse of the immense table surrounded by tall-backed chairs made her back out. They were a convivial people, the Titans. Tears came to her eyes again and she forced them back. She would never have any use for seating for so many guests.

The wall opposite the hearths had a single door that opened into the back of the reception chamber. Serving tables flanked it, providing space for the servants to place food and drink for visitors. Hekate sighed and closed the door, returning again to the kitchen where she picked up the bundle that held her clothing. This she took to the bedchamber nearest the reception room in which she had slept the previous night. Kabeiros would look for her there first . . . if he came back at all.

Eventually she went back to the kitchen and ate. The back door stood open, but the black dog did not appear in it. She wept a little, finding it very difficult to swallow. He might come back–probably he would because he had nowhere else to go and no other hope of regaining the man's form–but when he recovered his full powers, he would leave her. The tears fell a little faster. It had been so good, so warm, not to be alone. She wiped away the tears angrily, moved her supplies to the storeroom, which was warded against pests both insect and vermin.

Hekate left the door of her bedchamber open as well as the back door, but she was very tired and despite her misery she fell asleep. She had no idea that Kabeiros had returned until she went into the kitchen and saw two dead rabbits on the table. She would not let herself search for him, partly because she was too afraid she wouldn't find him. She began to gut and skin the rabbits, hoping the odor would tell him she was awake and bring him to her, but even after she cleaned up, he didn't come. She made some tea and choked down some journeybread to break her fast, wondering what she should do next if Kabeiros had left her, until Artemis' voice rang in her head.

Come to my house, and I will take you to Leto.

She couldn't tell Artemis that she didn't know where Kabeiros was, so she said, *I'll come as fast as I can, but remember Gration's house is at some distance.*

You can't leap to the marketplace?

I can't leap at all, except on my two feet.

Hekate was aware of an odd pause, which somehow reminded her of a physical sigh. Then, *Perhaps I should take you to Hermes first. He can sell you a leaping spell that will take you to the marketplace from wherever you are in Olympus. This time I will come to Gration's house, since Hermes is closer to you than to me.*

Should I meet you there? That would be halfway for each of us.

Have you done something to Gration's house that you don't want me to see? Artemis asked suspiciously.

No, my lady. I was only— she hesitated, her eye having caught a shadow moving by the door; her heart leapt, beating double time as joy flushed her cheeks *—trying to save you some effort. You are welcome here at any time.*

A sense of satisfaction, even a mild pleasure at the warmth of Hekate's welcome, came across although Artemis said no more. And then Hekate was aware that the communication was ended. She looked down at Kabeiros, who was sitting, facing her from beyond the table. He showed no sign of remorse for the pain he had caused her. Hekate gave him a sour look.

I'll thank you in the future to tell me that you're going hunting. And what took you so long? I had to go to bed with the back door open. Anyone could have walked in.

Here? Nonsense. And I had to go out past the tilled lands to find game. That's what took me so long. I heard Artemis. Do you know where to go?

For a wonder, I do. Artemis pointed out a number of the 'god's' dwellings and I remembered.

Hermes' house was larger than Gration's, all of the ubiquitous white marble. The servant who opened the door to her was plump and bright-eyed. He was polite, but Hekate kept her eyes on him. There was something about him that promised mischief. He did nothing; however, that might have been because Hermes was waiting at the entrance to the reception room and could see them.

Although his coloring was similar to that of Artemis, Hermes could not have been more different. He, like Artemis, had golden-brown hair and a handsome nose with clean-cut nostrils. His eyes were also large and almond-shaped of the same light brown, but with enough green to let them be called hazel. The major difference was in the mouth. Artemis had hers too firmly under control, the lips tucked back so hard that the lovely curve was spoiled. Hermes' mouth was made for laughter.

He was laughing when Hekate was shown into his reception chamber. This might have been a small square in a prosperous city. An elaborate fountain played in the center of an area of marvelous tiles. At a safe distance from water droplets but close enough for the sound of falling water to be soothing were several small tables with chairs around them. Behind was the facade of an elegant drinking house, and the surrounding walls showed stalls full of merchandise with alleys and streets stretching away into the distance.

"So you are Lady Hekate the fearsome spell-caster," he said. "I don't believe I've ever seen Artemis so awestruck. An altogether rewarding experience."

"Yes, I'm Hekate, and this is Kabeiros. I thought Lady Artemis would meet us here."

Hermes chuckled. "She said she had other business, and I couldn't tell whether she was afraid of you or didn't want to see me make a better bargain than she did. I understand you traded her a single spell for Gration's house. That does seem a rich reward for one spell."

"Only for the right to live in Gration's house; I don't own it. And Lady Artemis will never need to barter for another spell for that purpose. She can use the spell as often as she has power enough."

"I see. She didn't mention that. So what spell did Artemis find so valuable that she would want to use it over and over?"

Hekate smiled. "You will have to ask her that, Lord Hermes."

"Well, will you trade that spell to me for a leaping spell?"

"Not that one. That's my agreement with Lady Artemis. I will not offer the spell I bartered to her for the use of Gration's house to any other person in Olympus. Nor will I myself use the spell in Olympus, except in a great extremity of need. But I have spells enough." She grinned. "How would you like to walk unseen through the city streets you seem to love so much?"

"You have a spell of invisibility?" The jocularity was gone from Hermes' voice; he sounded a little breathless.

"Invisibility is greatly overrated and, because of the amount of power needed to keep the spell active, often useless. I have a simple spell that hardly draws power, which I call the look-by-me spell."

On the words, she murmured the key and took two steps sideways. Kabeiros remained where he was. Hermes gasped.

"Where are you?" he cried, then laughed in amazement. "If that's not true invisibility, I don't know what is."

Hekate walked quietly to the place she had been standing beside Kabeiros. Hermes' glance skittered this way and that avoiding her. She whispered, "*Eimi oraton.*" Hermes gasped again as his gaze became able to fix on her.

"You *were* invisible," he said.

"No. I merely made you–and everyone else, although no one else was here–unwilling to look at me. I can put the spell on you and you can test it–"

"I am sure Artemis tested the spell you gave her, so I won't bother. What do you want for it?"

He was very eager. Hekate smiled. "For that spell, because it is small and nothing, I would like the ability to leap from wherever I am to Gration's house."

"I can give you a home point at Gration's house, but whether you would be able to leap there from 'wherever' you were I don't know. That, too, is a matter of power. If you have enough, you go; if you don't have enough, you will be drained to no purpose."

"Ah, I understand. The power is related to the distance. For example, if I wanted to go from the market to Gration's house, that would take little power. To get to the house from outside Olympus would take much more power."

Hekate didn't mention that she thought there was enough power in Olympus to carry her to the moon.

Hermes seemed no more aware of the flood of earth-blood, so rich she could see it right through the paved floor of his house, than Artemis had been, and she had no intention of telling him or any of the others about it. They were powerful enough. She wondered briefly from where the Olympians' power came. Did they absorb it unaware from the earth?

"Exactly," Hermes said.

Hekate brought her attention back to the immediate situation. "Now," she said, "what we have been talking about is a one-time use of a spell, to you the look-by-me and to me one leap from anywhere I have power enough to Gration's house. Before we go ahead, I must tell you that I have a spell of renewal that I can attach to the look-by-me so that you can use it, as Lady Artemis can use her spell, whenever and as often as you desire and have power."

Hermes' beautiful eyes narrowed and Hekate was amazed at how shrewd they now looked. "And you would add the same renewability to my spell so you could use it over and over." He smiled. "But you could have done that without telling me."

Hekate's lips thinned with distaste. "No. In trading, I am honest. When I sell a spell, you get exactly what I describe, nor do I take more than I bargained for in payment."

Hermes looked down, and to Hekate's surprise a faint color rose in his cheeks. Then he asked rather defiantly, "Would it be possible for me to attach that renewal spell to spells I received from other people?"

"You would first have to separate it from the look-by-me spell." Hekate grinned at him. "If you think you can do that, then it should be possible to bud it and attach it to any other spell. However, I work with magic, with spells that are created not with an extract or a distillation of a Gift. I would be glad to teach you–"

"How many years would that take?" Hermes laughed. "Could I buy the renewal spell separately?"

"Certainly, but I would not agree to keep that spell for you alone." Then Hekate laughed also. "Let me discover first whether my renewal spell will bond with the essence you provide me for leaping. If it will, then we can talk about whether you would be able to do the bonding yourself for any spell you received."

She gave him the look-by-me spell and taught him the key words to invoke it and to dispell it. Then he called for servants to bring refreshments to her while he tried out his new toy and disappeared. She ate and drank, fed Kabeiros. Hermes reappeared suddenly before her, laughing with delight, his hazel eyes sparkling with pleasure and mischief.

"I must see Gration's house, see the place where you want my spell to bring you," he said, then looked at her sidelong. "But I must warn you that I am a thief. If you show me your house, I could leap there wearing my look-by-me spell, and steal–"

"If you can steal anything from Gration's house, I will stand by and cheer you on. There is nothing left in it except the heavy furniture. Artemis went through and removed whatever she and her maid-servants could carry. And I have nothing, except some worn travel clothing."

"Ah, but you won't be poor for long. For the spells you sell, the other Olympians will shower you with gold and jewels and every kind of adornment for your person and your house."

"I had rather they showered me with food and drink. And speaking of food and drink, do you have any extra servants?"

He shook his head. "My people are all family to me and are trained in ways that would not be suitable for your household. You might ask Aphrodite if any of her children are ready to go into service with another household, or Hestia will know. And your spell has given me so much pleasure already and will provide so much in the future, that I'll give you two for one, a spell for the market as well as one for Gration's house."

The essence that Hermes drew from himself appeared very much like any of Hekate's spells, formed into a silvery ball between the young "god's" lips. Mischief gleamed in his eyes as he leaned forward to put his mouth to Hekate's, but she didn't respond, stepping back, all her senses fixed on the spell—only it wasn't a spell. To her, a spell was made of strands and knots, the strands twisted and curled around each other, the knots catch-points that fixed the shape. Patient teasing could find a loose end and then open the mass so that Hekate could sense each individual word that made up a strand and see the symbols that formed the knots.

Hermes' ball of light was just that, a ball of light. All Hekate could sense within it was a twisting swirl of energy. Ignoring the young "god's" mischievous invitation, she reached toward him and pinched the spell from between his lips. To her relief, it held together. She cast the renewal spell and bade it spread itself over what she held; obediently one silvery ball spread flat and slid over the other, but Hekate sensed that the moment she relaxed her will they would slip apart. She reabsorbed the renewal spell and cast the binding spell. That did cling to Hermes' ball of light, and then she added the renewal spell outermost.

Now the whole spell felt solid and Hekate drew it within her, fixing it in the outermost layer of her crowded repository. She had a feeling that, if it worked at all, it was a spell she would use frequently. When she looked outward again, Hermes was staring at her, wide-eyed.

"I should not have laughed so much at Artemis," he murmured. "I never believed you could change my spell. How did you do that?"

Hekate smiled at him and said, "If you want to learn, I'll teach you–for a price. Now, how do I invoke the spell?"

"You say '*Dei me exelthein agora*' and . . . No!" He grabbed for her arm as she repeated the words, crying, "Wait!" but it was too late. He was caught up in what felt like a blast of lightning and dropped, rocking off balance with the force of arrival, in front of his favorite drinking house. He breathed out, a whoosh of relief and exasperation. "Well," he said, as Hekate looked around in a dazed sort of way at the people calmly giving their orders and drinking what the servers brought to them, "you certainly have enough power."

"I never lack for power," Hekate said absently, and asked, "How is it that no one is surprised to see two people appear out of nothing?"

Hermes laughed. "I often come here. They are accustomed."

"Oh." Hekate grinned and looked down to where Kabeiros usually sat to see if he were equally amused. He wasn't there! Her eyes went wide and wild and she grabbed for Hermes, her nails digging into his arm in her anxiety. "Where is Kabeiros?" she cried. "Is he lost otherwhere?"

"He's back in the house," Hermes said, frowning and prying at her fingers. "Unless you gave him the spell and he didn't know where we were going."

Hekate was white with shock. "Sorry," she murmured, smoothing Hermes' arm where spots of red showed how deeply her nails had dug into the flesh. Then she sighed. "How stupid of me. I can't give Kabeiros the spell–I can't give him *any* spell. He's totally resistant to magic."

"Well, then, leave him at home or put him in a kennel if he's destructive."

"Put him in a kennel!" Hekate echoed in horror. "He is a man!"

As she spoke she realized that, unlike Artemis, Hermes hadn't sensed that Kabeiros was more than a dog. So not all the Gifted had that ability. Likely that meant Hermes would not be able to help cure Kabeiros' condition; on the other hand, by his indifference to her statement she understood that shapeshifting must be a common enough thing in Olympus.

"Hmmm." Hermes had been following his own thoughts about bringing Kabeiros along. He shrugged. "Just grip him firmly by the neck and he should be transported with you. He's heavy, but you brought me along without any difficulty. And you don't have to use *that* much power to leap a short distance. I'll take you back now." He took her hand. "Watch what I do. Then we can all go to Gration's house so you can pick out where you want to arrive."

An instant later, at Hermes' house, they could hear Kabeiros' frantic barking. Hekate ran from the hall into the reception room, hoping Kabeiros hadn't savaged any of the servants in his frustration over being unable to find out where Hekate had gone. He hadn't yet, merely menacing them with exposed fangs, trying to frighten them into telling him what had happened. She called to him to stop, and he whirled around, so angry he didn't speak. In fact, like a dog, he snapped at her. Then he backed off, snarling.

"I'm sorry," she said. "I thought there'd be more to it than just the words."

Kabeiros still didn't speak, just turned again and sat with his back to her. Hekate had wanted to throw her arms around him and apologize for leaving him unable to communicate and frightening him, but his snarl reminded her of *his* fit of temper the previous night and the horrible time she had spent wondering to where he had disappeared and whether he would come back at all.

"Didn't like it, did you?" she snapped at his unresponsive back. "Well, I didn't like it when you took off last night without a word to me. When you turn civil, so will I!"

Hermes raised his brows and glanced from one to the other with a knowing smile; then, however, he frowned and asked, "Why didn't he just shift back to a man and *ask* my servants where you and I had gone instead of barking at them and threatening to bite them?"

"Because he can't," Hekate said, sighing heavily. "He's trapped in the form of the dog. That's really why we've come to Olympus. My magic won't touch him, but a strongly Gifted woman was able to reach the spell. It's—" she hesitated, afraid to mention that the spell causing the disruption of Kabeiros' power was a draining spell, and went on "—it's tangled up in his organ of power so he can't use the power and the power feeds the spell so it won't die . . ."

"I'm very sorry," Hermes said to Kabeiros, who had turned to look at him. "I didn't know." And then to Hekate, "So why didn't this Gifted woman remove the spell?"

"Because it would have been easier to kill Kabeiros than to take the time to disentangle the spell from his power. I could stop her from killing us, but I had no way to control her."

"You have nice friends."

"Medea was no friend."

Hermes took in her expression, shuddered slightly, and held up his hands in a gesture of surrender. "I have to be in Egypt this afternoon," he said. "Let's get over to Gration's house so I can give you the second spell."

The now-bland voice and expression confirmed that he would ask no more questions about Medea or the spell holding Kabeiros to the dog form—at least, Hekate thought, he would ask *her* no more questions. His inquisitive nature wouldn't allow the subject to die.

As they walked, Hekate asked how to find Leto, saying she hoped that Artemis would have remembered to tell her mother that Hekate needed introductions to other Olympians. Hermes grinned and said he thought she would, adding he thought Artemis believed Hekate would turn her into a statue if she didn't. Hekate was too clever to respond to that provocative statement, and asked about Leto again.

"Oh, sorry. You leap to the market and go up the right-hand path toward Zeus' palace. There is a cross path leading to the palace doors, which will be open—Zeus' doors are always open, but I don't think you want to draw his attention yet. The lord of all gods isn't too enthusiastic about his subjects learning magic. He's aware of our Gifts nearly from birth and thinks he can control them, but created magic is too unpredictable. Likely that's why Kronos drove out the Titans." He cocked his head on the side. "Are you a Titan, Hekate?"

"Artemis asked me the same question," she said. "I don't believe so. In the land I came from, use of magic is far more common than being Gifted—in fact, being Gifted, as Kabeiros was, is a quick way to die. However, I know my mother was no Titan. She was a woman native to Ka'anan. I know nothing about my father."

"You don't know him?"

Hekate shuddered visibly. "I know him all too well, but he never spoke of his past. Are Titans forbidden to come to Olympus?"

"No, not at all." Hermes laughed. "Maybe in Kronos' time, but not now. Zeus' mother Rhea was a Titan, and Leto is a Titan, the daughter of Koios, who was their leader." He sighed. "I was told that Kronos mutilated Koios horribly, and kept him prisoner for a long time. Finally when he saw that his own people were disgusted, he sent Koios into the Underworld, but that was all long before I was born."

Hekate recalled the paintings on her antechamber walls. If she was interpreting them aright, the "gods" and the Titans had been allies, had been defeated together, and had found Olympus together. She also recalled Koios' outstretched hand, as if he was pleading with or welcoming a friend.

"But the gods and the Titans came together from . . . from wherever and found Olympus together. What was the war about? Why did Kronos want to be rid of them?"

"I don't know. I told you all that was long before I was born, but if you want my opinion it was because the Titans' magic was growing stronger and stronger. The Gifts of Kronos and his party had always been more powerful than the magic of the Titans, and Kronos dominated the entire group. When the Titans found this valley, however, they insisted on staying here. Kronos wanted to settle among the natives so he and his people would have their choice of slaves. Instead, they captured a large group of natives and brought them back to Olympus.

Then they found that the Titans' magic was increasing in strength. If you really want to know, though, ask Eros. He actually came with Kronos."

They had reached Gration's house by then, and Hekate took Hermes to the reception room. He laughed when he saw the pictures and said he had been thinking Hekate omniscient as well as a master sorceress, but now he knew where she had her information about the start of the Titans and Olympians.

Then he wasted no more time, but drew forth a new spell, which she treated as she had the first.

"For this one you must say, '*Dei me exelthein katoikia*,' and it will take you here."

"What does *katoikia* mean?" Hekate asked.

"Home," Hermes responded.

Hekate sighed and then smiled. "I have never had a home before." She looked around the handsome room. "It would be wonderful."

"You will have to arrange matters with Zeus if you mean to stay here permanently." He shrugged. "I would offer to help, but Zeus is annoyed with me . . . as usual." He sighed. "I really do have to be in Egypt this afternoon."

And he was gone.

CHAPTER 21

Hekate discovered that from the market she could not only reach Leto's home but also that of almost every other Olympian. Most of the dwellings of the greater "gods" were clustered around Zeus' palace. Not really surprising because nearly all of them were tied to him in some way, some were his children, others his siblings. Leto had been his mistress, and Artemis and Apollo were his children by her.

Leto had no Talent at all—so she said. Hekate didn't believe it; she was reasonably sure that Leto had suppressed whatever abilities she had for so long that they were all but smothered. However, like Hermes, she had not been able to see the man/dog dichotomy in Kabeiros.

Only about a third of the gods could sense it, and who could and who could not was totally unpredictable. Hebe, a pretty, plump creature with seemingly no wits, who had come on an errand to Leto and met them by accident, had burst into tears as soon as she came into the room with Kabeiros. She had run to kneel beside him, weeping profusely over the trap in which he was caught, but when Hekate had asked if she would be willing to try to free Kabeiros, she had refused almost hysterically. It was magic, she had cried; she would have nothing to do with magic.

That was disappointing in one way but very hopeful in another. If worse came to worst, Hekate thought she could bend Hebe to her will. Not yet, not ever if she could avoid it, for what she would have to do might change Hebe forever. But it was helpful in another way. Leto, who had been very doubting of Hekate's tale, was now convinced and agreed to make arrangements with other Olympians to examine Kabeiros.

Some whom they sought out with high hopes felt nothing. Paieon, whose Gift was healing, and who could sense the smallest irregularity in the health of the body, was amazed when Hekate told him of Kabeiros' problem. He had not felt the man in the dog and, although he tried, after he learned the truth, he could not find the entangling spell nor even Kabeiros' organ of power. Asklepios, also a healer, worked with magic, and Kabeiros was as opaque to him as he was to Hekate.

Aphrodite instantly knew Kabeiros was a man—she could even talk to him, which few others could do, and playfully made Hekate burn with jealousy—but she could not sense the spell disrupting his organ of power. Eros could. Eros was so beautiful that he took away Hekate's breath . . . until she looked into his eyes. They were the eyes of a reanimated corpse. Hekate could think of no way to bend Eros to her will; what could you offer a dead man? with what could you threaten him? She wondered how Aprhodite could bear to live with a walking, talking dead man.

But hope was kept alive. Hestia could sense the spell. Indeed, she almost fainted when she sought it out. Leto had asked Hestia to visit Hekate to judge how many servants she would need and to suggest where to obtain them. Hekate decided to use the visit for a double purpose, since she had no desire to draw Zeus' notice and Hestia lived in Zeus' palace and kept house for him and Hera. So far either Zeus was willing to ignore her or he hadn't yet become aware of her–which was likely enough, Hermes told her, if the king of the gods was pursuing another native maiden. It seemed safer to ask Hestia's help in Gration's house, which Hekate did.

"It's a draining spell," Hestia whispered, turning pale. Hekate rushed to support her to a chair. "Zeus used such a spell on our father Kronos. It was terrible. Terrible." Tears came to her kind blue eyes and ran down her cheeks.

"Zeus used a *draining* spell," Hekate whispered. "Does he still use it?"

"No, no." Horror darkened her blue eyes. "Only that one time. The sorcerer from whom he took it . . . died. And no one knew of your renewing spell, so after Zeus used it, the spell was gone." Hestia shuddered hard and said more firmly, "And it's good that it's gone. I shouldn't have told you about it. We've all agreed that such a terrible spell must never be used again, must never be mentioned."

"It *is* terrible," Hekate agreed, holding the distraught woman's hand. "And poor Kabeiros is trapped in the form of a dog. He cannot speak or . . . or do anything a man does."

Love me, Hekate thought. If he were free of the *need* to stay with me, surely I could make him love me. We are good companions. We laugh at the same kind of foolishness. We both love to travel. I desire him. . . .

"Will you help him?" Hekate pleaded, and the dog came forward and rested his head on Hestia's knee.

Hestia turned even whiter. "I cannot," she whispered. "Oh, don't ask it of me. I haven't the power. If I touched the spell, it would drain me dry. I would die. Oh, I'm so sorry for poor Kabeiros, so sorry, but I'm afraid . . ."

Hekate soothed her; Kabeiros licked her hand. But when she was gone, Hekate said to Kabeiros, *We can't push her now, but she might be able to do it.*

No. Kabeiros lay down on the floor, head on his paws. *No. She's a good woman. I won't have you torment her for my sake, and I certainly won't take the chance that drawing the spell out of me will kill her. She doesn't have much power—*

*Oh, power! There's enough power here in Olympus to fly to the moon, or pull it down to earth. I could feed her power. The trouble isn't power, it's her fear. Unfortunately in magic fear can do what nothing else can do. Until I can convince her that the draining spell can't hurt her, it *might* kill her.*

Let her be! Kabeiros exclaimed.

For now, Hekate agreed, *but there's hope, Kabeiros, there's hope.*

There was enough hope to sustain them both through the spring burgeoning into summer, through the summer and the long autumn, through another winter. It wasn't that there were so very many Olympians, but they had their own lives and their own affairs. Nor could Hekate and Kabeiros spend *all* their time hunting a cure for him. They had to live.

Weeks were spent finding servants and months in training them to behavior that satisfied Hekate. And they all had to eat and drink. Hekate bartered spells for supplies, for hay and grain for the mule, for beer and wine, for bread and meat. Kabeiros went hunting with Artemis—they both enjoyed that; she was willing to accept him as long as he acted like a dog—and he brought home game. They settled into life in Olympus.

No one could predict who would react to Kabeiros' entrapment. Hephaestos saw the spell and the power organ the most clearly. He told Hekate that the spell was not, as she had thought, mingled with Kabeiros' power but, like her binding spell, clung to the organ and sent tendrils down into it. But when Hekate offered any spell in her collection, any ten spells, any hundred—offered herself—if Hephaestos would only remove the spell from Kabeiros, he shook his head.

"I'm not unwilling, I'm unable." He limped away from her and sat heavily in a beautiful leather chair. "I can't think of a way to loosen that dreadful thing except by pulling the tendrils out one by one . . . but before I could loosen many, they would grow back, seeking to eat Kabeiros' power."

"You're a master artificer," Hekate pleaded. "I know how great you are. I saw the palace in Colchis. It is a wonder beyond wonders. Don't let this stupid spell defeat you. Think of a way to seize it and lift it away from Kabeiros all at once."

Hephaestos blinked at her. "An artificer. I never thought of dealing with a spell as an artificer . . . But a sphere? How to pull something off a sphere all at once without tearing the sphere apart?" He nodded. "I can't promise, but I will certainly think on it."

Hekate and Kabeiros flicked back to Gration's house filled with satisfaction, talking about whether there was any way Hekate could help Hephaestos. Over the next winter they worked on the problem with occasional amused assistance from Hermes, who was always willing to fetch esoteric magical supplies from distant lands. Hekate constructed spell balls and covered them with the binding spell, which Hephaestos tried to lift away from the spell beneath. He had not yet been successful, but he wasn't discouraged. With each failure he found himself more fascinated by the problem and with new ideas for solving it.

Thus Hekate was less enthusiastic than she might have been a few days before the vernal equinox when Leto sent a message to say that Apollo had agreed to see them. He had been very reluctant to admit them to his presence, for which Leto had apologized profusely, assuring them that he wasn't usually so difficult, at least not as difficult as Artemis . . . and then she had blushed and said that wasn't what she meant at all.

She was all excited when Hekate and Kabeiros arrived, flushed with pleasure because Apollo had come and told her to invite them, all on his own without any urging. And if they would come with her . . . She gestured them toward the door of a small side chamber but didn't enter herself.

Hekate immediately raised her shields and reinforced them. She was prejudiced against Apollo because Hermes didn't like him and she adored Hermes—when she wasn't fighting an urge to murder him. As for Apollo, she was surprised when she saw him, not because of his beauty—all Olympians seemed to be beautiful—but because Apollo was the first Olympian she had met who actually looked like a god.

His features were much like those of Artemis but coldly composed. His hair was a bright gold and his eyes a piercing gray and he stood perfectly still when she entered the room, his bow in one hand, his lyre in the other, examining her gravely. A very short, dazzlingly white tunic was pinned on his left shoulder with a brooch in the likeness of a rayed sun. It covered him to midthigh, leaving his long legs, strong arms, and right shoulder bare.

"You have been troubling my beloved mother," he said softly, face and voice devoid of any expression beyond dignity. "Others have died for less." His lips thinned. "Unfortunately, I haven't the right to destroy you."

Beside Hekate, Kabeiros voiced a full-throated growl and crouched to leap. Hekate laid a restraining hand on his shoulder. She said nothing, silver gaze fixed on Apollo.

"Man-dog," he said, "I'm sorry. I see your twisted power and the thing that eats away at it. Evil magic destroying the good and natural . . . but I am constrained from helping you as I am constrained against interfering with the witch Hekate."

Constrained from helping. Hekate's heart leapt. Surely that meant he could help if the constraint was removed . . . or a stronger constraint was applied? But with this Olympian, Hekate's courage failed her. Her mouth went dry at the thought of trying to force Apollo to her will.

To find time, she said, "I *am* a witch, but why should you wish to interfere with me? I am careful to do no harm."

"Your existence is harm," he said, distastefully. "A necessary evil. You will bring change to Olympus, perhaps a necessary change, but one I hate."

Hekate blinked. "The use of magic," she said.

Apollo nodded. "Witch. Wielder of magic. But you will leave Olympus soon."

"No," Hekate protested. "We must find a cure for Kabeiros . . ."

She let her voice fade, recalling Apollo's implication that he, too, saw the draining spell and power source and that he was "constrained" not to separate one from the other. She glanced at Apollo and away. She had dismissed the idea of bribing or intimidating him, but he had also said he hated the use of magic in Olympus. What if she offered to leave Olympus, never to return . . . She was surprised at the pain, at the lump that rose in her throat when she thought of leaving Gration's house, of leaving her soft-footed, soft-voiced servants, who smiled whenever they came across her or Kabeiros, of leaving Hermes, Hephaestos, Aphrodite, and even dead-eyed Eros. But she would do it if Apollo would return to Kabeiros the use of his power.

"No," Apollo said, as if he had read her thought. "There is another way."

Whereupon he walked right by them, ignoring Kabeiros' bared teeth and resounding growls, and went out. In the corridor, he kissed his mother—and disappeared.

Once that might have impressed Hekate. Now it eased her pounding heart to know that Apollo was "human" enough to need to trade with Hermes. She wondered what he offered Hermes in exchange, entertaining for a moment some thoroughly lewd ideas, but Leto appeared in the doorway and diverted her thoughts.

Hekate thanked Leto profusely, but Apollo's mother shrugged. "He said he couldn't help you, but I thought it would be better if you heard that bad news from him. I hope he wasn't . . . rude. He doesn't like to admit that he isn't all-powerful and it makes him a little . . ."

"No, he wasn't rude," Hekate said, smiling and wondering what word Leto would have chosen if she hadn't leapt into the breach. "Thank you again, Leto, for your great kindness and for all the help you've given us."

On the words, she gripped Kabeiros' nape and

leapt back to Gration's house where, as they landed, Kabeiros said, *Arrogant bastard.*

That made Hekate laugh aloud. *Now, now, Kabeiros,* she said mentally while giggling physically. *You know that's quite literally true. Apollo is a bastard. But since the blame for it would fall on Leto, who's really been very kind, I hope you won't use that particular epithet any more.*

If you like. But Kabeiros' mental voice was vague, as if he was thinking of something else, and then he said, *But which is true—that he could draw off the draining spell but won't, or that he didn't want to admit he couldn't?*

Before Hekate could answer, the elderly native man that Hekate had bought from Athena for a bargain price because he had lost his youthful good looks poked his head around the edge of the archway. He served as Hekate's porter and greeter, and he knew every one and just how to treat every person who came to her house.

"You are back, my lord and my lady." Philo understood Kabeiros was not merely a dog and always addressed him as a man and his master. "Good. I was beginning to worry. There's a messenger from Zeus waiting."

"Zeus!" Color rose in Hekate's cheeks, but she shook her head at her servant's suddenly anxious question and told him to fetch the messenger.

To Kabeiros she said, *Apollo *told* us we would leave Olympus. Perhaps he's a better seer than Hermes was willing to admit and he Saw . . . But we can't leave now! You know that if we don't keep after Hephaestos, he'll start another project. I swear if Zeus tells us we must go, I'll freeze him solid, bind the renewing spell to the freezing spell, and bury him under his own palace. And I'll add that spell that Artemis wants so he knows every minute . . . *

Hekate! Kabeiros' mental voice laughed, even though Hekate could feel his anxiety. *Don't borrow a measure of barley.*

Now Hekate had to laugh. That was an old, old tale about a man who was sent by his wife to a neighbor's house to borrow a measure of barley. On his way, he began to think of a polite way to ask for the barley, from which his mind expanded the conversation to the neighbor's wonder at his needing to borrow barley and his own resentment that the neighbor should question him about his husbandry, going though a long passage of "and then he said," "and then I said," ending in his neighbor refusing to lend the barley. At that point, the man reached his neighbor's door, and when the man opened it, shouted at him for refusing to give him one rotten measure of barley and struck him in the face. Kabeiros, of course, was warning her not to work up a rage at Zeus before the Olympian did anything to offend her.

Thus she was polite to Zeus' messenger, a very pretty boy called Ganymede, and when he said Zeus wanted her to come to the palace, she and Kabeiros followed him on foot through the streets–since the child didn't seem to have a leaping spell. Coming up the walk from the market, she was almost blinded by the glitter of the sun on the polished white stone. She knew the place was as magnificent within as without; there were things more wonderful than in the palace at Colchis. However, Hekate was too anxious to appreciate them, and the moment Zeus walked into the small, private chamber to which she had been led she forgot everything beyond the sudden aching need that filled her.

"Dionysos!" she cried, the binding cutting her heart.

In all but the too-large eyes and an expression that

Dionysos had never worn when he looked at her, it was the face of the boy she had nurtured she saw. Zeus stopped just inside the doorway, eyeing her warily. Blue flickers showed at the tips of the fingers of the hand he had half raised.

"Who or what is Dionysos?" he asked.

Hekate caught her breath. The binding had place and purpose. Dionysos must come here.

"Dionysos is your son," she replied. "Semele was his mother." Her voice grew cold. "Remember Semele? You covered her with a shower of gold. Unfortunately that didn't save her. She was sacrificed to the king of the dead."

"Poor Hades," Zeus remarked blandly. "He doesn't deserve Semele. Even I didn't deserve her. What of the gold?"

"I have no idea, but I saved your son."

Zeus shrugged. "I have many sons."

Hekate stared at him; Kabeiros growled. Suddenly Hekate felt a roiling in the sea of earth-blood beneath the palace floor and sensed around Zeus the faint pulsing that denoted a shield. So Zeus, at least, knew magic as well as being Gifted, sensed her fury . . . and was afraid.

"Not sons like Dionysos," she said. "He bred true. He is pure Olympian, greatly Gifted."

"You mean he plays magic tricks like yours?"

Hekate smiled slowly, unpleasantly, at the attempt to prick her into showing her magic was no set of cheap tricks. But he knew that already, or he wouldn't have erected shields against her. Her sense of his suppressed fear made her calm.

"Magic? No. Dionysos has no need of magic. He has Gifts enough without. For one, he is a seer of uncommon strength and can See both immediately and far into the future. And I have never known his Seeing to be wrong."

While she answered him, she prodded at the shield and found it weak and with lapses she could put a shaft through. For just a moment she was tempted, and then recalled the measure of barley. Zeus had done no more than open the door and look sour. She would be better off if she could pacify him. Besides, the sour expression had faded from his face.

"A seer! Truly?" Zeus' expression now betrayed a lively interest.

"Truly," Hekate assured him.

She didn't bother to tell him that interpretation of Dionysos' predictions, particularly those for the far future, was sometimes very difficult. More than two thirds of the time she had guessed wrong and only understood what he had been trying to tell her after the event had taken place. Nor did she tell Zeus that Dionysos could drive others into frenzies of hate, panic, and terror.

That Dionysos was a seer had interested Zeus enough so she only added, "He is very young. I had to leave him in the care of his aunt and had no chance to test all of his abilities. The other Gift I know best, I don't understand. It has to do with a fruit used to make wine, not dates but a small round fruit that grows in bunches–"

"Grapes," Zeus said, but he wasn't terribly interested in that ability.

"I need to bring Dionysos here," Hekate said. "He Saw that he would come to Olympus after he had established this fruit, this grape, in Ka'anan and other lands."

Zeus frowned and shook his head slowly. "I would like to see my son, since you say he is well Gifted, but it would be dangerous to bring him here. My wife, Hera, is not very welcoming to my children born of other mothers."

"No?" Hekate laughed aloud. "Then be sure to warn Dionysos that Hera is your beloved wife and you don't wish harm to come to her."

"Harm to come to *her*?" Zeus echoed, stared at Hekate hard for a moment, and then asked, "So if Dionysos is as powerful as you say, why didn't he make his way to Olympus as have my other true sons?"

"I told you he was too young and, besides, he had Seen the time when he must come to you. You Olympians do not count years, since they matter little, but Dionysos is–" she hesitated and looked down at Kabeiros, who said, *Less than twenty years, but not by much. I've lost count myself.*

"Who is that speaking?" Zeus asked sharply, and his shields tightened, although Hekate thought she could still get though them.

It was interesting that he "heard" Kabeiros but could not determine from where the "voice" came. How fortunate that he had betrayed the ability before she and Kabeiros engaged in some less-than-diplomatic comments. Hekate took warning never to judge any Olympian's Gifts before she was able to test them in some way. She allowed herself to look surprised.

"That voice is Kabeiros'," she said. "He wears the guise of a dog because a spell has got tangled in his organ of power and prevents him from shifting to a man. I understand that you are a master shape-shifter–a bull, a swan . . ."

Zeus cleared his throat. "Ah, yes, the black dog with white eyes," he said, but then he brought his brows together in a black scowl. "You tell the same tale to everyone, and Artemis, Hephaestos, and others–even little Hebe–confirm that the tale is true. Nonetheless, I find it hard to believe. I think you had other purposes in coming to Olympus. You're a Titan, aren't you?"

"Lord Zeus," she said, now completely sincere and hoping he could sense it, "I swear I don't know. When Lady Artemis asked, I said 'no' in good faith, but I didn't even know what a Titan was at that time. I thought they were some kind of giants. When Hermes asked, I was more doubtful. I told him the truth, that my mother was not. She was of a well-known family in Ka'anan."

"And your father?"

Hekate looked away and put a hand on Kabeiros for support. "I know nothing of my father's antecedents," she said in a low voice. "To tell the truth, he is a truly mighty sorcerer and I am afraid of him. He accepts no restraints; he indulges in blood magic and calls and binds otherplanar creatures to his will."

"That was exactly what Kronos said of the Titans of Olympus. He said their power knew no bounds, that in only a little time their magic would overwhelm the Gifts of the Olympians. I didn't believe him. My mother Rhea had no dangerous magical powers. She had a few small spells, which she used to hide us from his wrath. And Leto has no magic at all. But you . . . you are a different thing entirely. I can easily imagine you spreading magic through Olympus and setting one of my turbulent children against another until this peaceful valley is a shambles of blood and death."

"I never would!" Hekate exclaimed. "Lord Zeus, with your permission and approval, I deeply desire to make Olympus my home. I have come to love some of the Olympians and I have a house I love and I am oath-bound to bring Dionysos here. As to the spells, you know I have been careful. I have given to your people in trade only that which fits with their Gifts."

Zeus's lips parted to voice a denial, but he closed his mouth and thought. "So you haven't," he said, sounding suprised. "And why is that?"

Hekate smiled, with gentle amusement this time. "For the same reason that you objected to my teaching them magic at all. It had come to my attention that most Olympians, even some of those I love best, are . . . to say the least, willful and accustomed to having their way. To give them a whole new way to enforce their will . . ." She shuddered.

"That sounds very sensible," Zeus said, "but you could not have known and loved Olympians when you first made your way to our valley—and I would like to know how you pierced the illusion and escaped the punishment spell."

"I have no wish to offend, but the illusion was child's play to me. I can offer you a far better illusion, bonded to the blood of the earth so it will never need renewal. As to the punishment spell: it could not pierce my shields and Kabeiros is immune to magic." She sighed. "If he were not, I could have freed him of the evil spell that binds him."

Zeus continued to frown, but more thoughtfully than angrily. "What you say is tempting and reasonable, but I still think you had another purpose in coming to Olympus."

"I had several," Hekate admitted. "I had to come to a place where shape-shifters are not anathema. I wanted to live in a city that accepted magic. And I had to leave Colchis in a hurry because I offended Princess Medea. Moreover, I am beginning to think that fate had a hand in my coming. I had almost forgotten Dionysos, but it was like a bolt through my heart when I saw you." She smiled at him again. "If you wanted to be rid of your beard, you wouldn't need a mirror if Dionysos was in the room, so much alike you two are."

Zeus immediately looked interested. "So he resembles me in feature?"

"Exactly, except that his eyes are larger and a little staring. You are the handsomer for that, but still, hair, forehead, nose, mouth, chin, the shape of the face . . ." She hesitated, frowning. "Now I remember, too, what he said before Seeing he must come here. I felt terrible when I knew I had to leave him, and I asked if he wished to come with me to a place of refuge, and he said, 'I can't go there now. I must meet you there some other time.'"

"He Saw that? How long ago?"

Hekate looked down at Kabeiros. "How long?"

Five years. Perhaps six.

"Six years foreseeing," Zeus said with satisfaction. "That's a sensible kind of interval. One could do something and hope for some success." Zeus nodded. "Dionysos may come. I will test him, and if he is truly my son and strong enough, he may stay–if he can protect himself from Hera. But that brings us back to the original problem. What can you do about the magic spells that you've sold Olympians?"

In the excitement of realizing where Dionysos belonged, and gaining Zeus' permission for him to come to Olympus, Hekate had temporarily forgotten Zeus' objection to magic, or, rather, to anyone except himself using it.

She said, "I can do nothing about the spells I've already bartered for goods. I'm sorry if it was forbidden. No one who traded with me admitted it was forbidden."

"It's not precisely forbidden, although I explained why I'm not very happy about the use of magic."

"And I agreed with you. My lord, I told you I wish very much to make Olympus my home. I'm happy here and there is the possibility that one of your people will find a cure for Kabeiros' condition. Can we come to a compromise?"

"What kind of compromise?"

"You have agreed to receive Dionysos. I will go to fetch him from Ka'anan. That will take almost a year, I think. For the privilege of being allowed to live in Olympus, I will give you a new illusion to cover the valley."

"And a new deterrent spell? Ours didn't seem to deter you."

Hekate reviewed her spells and shook her head. "Mine would kill. I'm sure yours will be sufficient. And I promise that during the year I am traveling, I will seek for a better spell of deterrence or, perhaps, create one. Also, during the year I am gone, you will have time enough to study those Olympians to whom I have sold magic and see what effect the spells they now own have had upon them. If there is some type of spell you think particularly dangerous, I would even agree not to sell that."

"But when you return, you will continue to sell spells although you know I don't like it. Why?

"Why?" Hekate repeated, looking amazed. "Because I need slaves to keep my house, I need food and drink to feed them and to feed Kabeiros and me, I need hay and grain to feed my mule. What else have I to trade?"

The expression that Hekate had noted Dionysos never wore when looking at her returned to Zeus' face. "You are a very beautiful woman," he said. "You could have come to me and I would have seen that you were supplied with your needs."

He stepped forward and put out a hand to lift Hekate's chin and she shifted to the crone.

"Beautiful?" She cackled with laughter as Zeus pulled his hand back and stepped away. "When my body is lusted after by a man, this is what happens to me."

"Surely you can control it," Zeus snapped.

Kabeiros growled and took a step forward, his hackles rising, his teeth bared. Zeus waved a hand at him and began to speak a spell. Hekate pointed and said, "*Mha thon Dia*!" Zeus stopped speaking, his mouth open but wordless. His eyes bulged until he was completely the image of Dionysos.

"Stop, Kabeiros!" Hekate said sharply. Then, to Zeus, "Forgive me. I couldn't let you try to bespell Kabeiros. I believe he is immune to magic, but you are very powerful. I have done you no harm. If you agree not to attack us, I will remove the impediment to your spell-casting."

"I am shielded," Zeus gasped, eyes still staring. "How did you get through my shields?"

"Your shields are not very strong," she said quietly. "And there are . . . spaces through which my magic can pass."

There was another silence during which their gazes clashed. Then, diplomatically, Hekate looked down.

After a moment, Zeus turned and went to sit in a high-backed chair against the wall. Hekate stood quietly with her head bowed. Finally Zeus asked, "Could you have killed me?"

For perhaps ten heartbeats Hekate considered the consequences of both yea and nay. Then she said, "Yes."

"So, why didn't you?"

Involuntarily Hekate's arms went around herself, and she huddled in, making herself small in rejection. Terrible memories flashed by, memories of horrors she had seen and heard, of Dionysos' vision of her father making blood sacrifice.

"No," she breathed. "I do not kill with or for

magic. Never. There are other ways if killing is needed, a bow, a knife, Kabeiros' teeth." She swallowed hard and stood tall. "Besides, I am *not* an idiot. Your people love you, Lord Zeus. Oh, I know they argue and complain, but every one acknowledges you as king in Olympus and is satisfied with your rule. One by one I might withstand, but if harm came to you they would all band together, and I would never survive." She pointed at Zeus again and said, "*Metatheto mha thon Dia.*" Zeus drew a long breath. "I know the spell again."

Hekate nodded. "I've done you no harm," she said. "You are as you were before."

He stared at the crone, shuddered slightly, and said, "Rid yourself of that disgusting form. I will not force you. I have seduced many women and with some I used deception, but I have never forced one." And when Hekate stood before him as the woman again, he asked, "Where are your shrines, your worshipers?"

"I have neither shrine nor worshipers–as far as I know," Hekate said. "I'm no goddess, nor near to being divine." Now it was her turn to shudder. "I can think of nothing more horrible than being responsible for doing something about the prayers and pleas of people wholly unknown to me."

Zeus laughed. "You don't *have* to listen, you know."

"I'm not an Olympian," she said tartly, and then as the full meaning of the words struck her, tears came to her eyes. She sighed. "No, I'm not an Olympian," and she bent and hugged Kabeiros to her. "I will go," she whispered.

"No. I'll not banish you, but I need some assurance . . . Whom do you worship?"

A very slight hesitation showed that Hekate knew what she was about to say would not be welcome.

Then she shrugged. "I worship the Mother," she said defiantly.

Zeus winced very slightly. "You would," he muttered, but then his expression cleared and his lips pursed thoughtfully. "You truly believe, don't you?"

She made the sign of completion. "I do."

"Then you will swear, by the Mother, that you will never knowingly harm me personally or bring harm to Olympus."

Hekate thought that over and then said, "I can swear I will never knowingly bring harm to Olympus, but I cannot swear not to harm you. I can swear never to direct at you a spell that will disable you or kill you, but you might be harmed by a passive defense I erected."

"What kind of *passive* defense could harm me?"

"I have used a mirror shield as a defense. If you cast lightning at me and it bounced off my mirror and struck you, you would be harmed. Certainly a spell Princess Medea cast at me gave her a severe shock when it bounced back."

Zeus sat quiet, watching her. Hekate guessed he no longer regarded her as a personal threat, that he accepted as true her claim that she would only defend herself, not attack. Now, she thought, he was weighing the risk of having her remain in Olympus against the uses he might make of her skills in the future.

"Let me hear how you would word the oath," he said at last.

"By the Mother, I swear I will never knowingly bring harm to Olympus or its inhabitants, and in particular I will never knowingly work a spell that will disable, injure, or kill the Lord Zeus nor affect his power, although I do not swear to eschew passive defense against him if he attacks me or

Kabeiros."

Another thoughtful silence, then Zeus nodded sharply. "Done," he said. "Now swear."

Hekate brought to mind the ruined temple and the stone that stood on the altar there. When it was clear in her mind, the strange eyes that were not eyes fixed on her, she repeated the oath. For a single instant the well of power within her was utterly empty; the floor beneath her feet was only polished white marble, the faint red glow of the earth's blood of which she had been constantly aware was gone; her sense of Kabeiros as a man, as anything beyond a dog was gone; only her physical senses remained. Terror stopped her breath, but before she could cry out or fall unconscious, struck down by horror, everything was back to normal.

"I understand," she whispered, trembling, not speaking to Zeus. "I understand, Mother. I will not again take Your name in vain to confirm a silly swearing."

Oddly, Zeus must have felt something too. He had a hand raised to his cheek, as if he had been sharply slapped. His face was white and his lower lip caught between his teeth. He stood up from his chair, but kept one hand on it for support, and he gestured at Hekate.

"That's all," he said. "You are free of Olympus, to come and go as you please. Now go!"

CHAPTER 22

Hermes wasn't able to take Hekate and Kabeiros anyplace in Ka'anan. He had never been there and could not find a home port. However, he was able to leap them to the docks of a port city of Egypt. Ships left regularly from there for Byblos and Hekate was able to secure passage on one that carried two other women as well as several traders. She bought the passage in the form of the crone but came aboard later as the blonde, barely nubile, blue-eyed girl.

The girl was a form Hekate's father had never seen, and he had never known her to be accompanied by a black dog either. Nonetheless they didn't linger in Byblos, staying only long enough to gather supplies and take a night's rest before they set out for the mountains.

Kabeiros had been totally withdrawn all through the voyage and had not even offered advice about the supplies Hekate bought, accepting the pack she strapped over his shoulders without a word. Hekate did not prod him, racked alternately by guilt for abandoning the quest for a cure for his condition and resentment over his blaming her for leaving Olympus without a greater struggle. At first she had tried to explain to him the growing need she felt to bring Dionysos to Olympus and also her feeling that it was best to be out of the way so Zeus could rationalize accepting her without further irritation. Now she was mentally as silent as he.

The second night, Kabeiros disappeared from the campsite before Hekate had selected the precise area into which to settle, unceremoniously pulling loose the bindings and dumping his pack. Hekate stood looking after him, but only for a moment. Then she set up her camp, prepared her meal, and wondered what she would do if he didn't return. Here in Ka'anan Kabeiros didn't need to communicate to anyone. He could find the caves of the dead and be a man without any of the useless help she offered.

She need not have concerned herself about being abandoned. Dusk was just turning into dark when Kabeiros came back, dragging the body of one of the local small deer.

He dropped it by the fire and said, *I must go to the caves of the dead. I cannot be a dog any longer. This should be meat enough to last you to wherever you wish to go; there's no need for you to come with me. I know the way.*

An icy hollow formed between Hekate's breast bone and her belly. Kabeiros wanted to be rid of her completely. She sat for a moment, looking into the fire, and trying to find sufficient pride to say "go." But pride was a cold, lonely thing and Hekate had been bitterly lonely for most of her life. Being with Kabeiros was never lonely, even when he was angry and wouldn't open his mind to her. He was *there.*

"Don't be ridiculous," Hekate said, struggling not to pant with terror. "I must go to the caves of the dead with you or without you. It's true that no spy will report seeing Hekate, Perses' daughter, in Byblos and I'll try to go around as far from Ur-Kabos as I can, but both the valley of the Nymphae and Dionysos' aunt's house are well within the distance Perses can scry. If I am in this area more than a day or two, he will sense my aura. The only place I can be safe, if it takes Dionysos more than a few hours to reach me, is the caves of the dead."

The hound made no immediate reply, and Hekate drew her knife and began to butcher his kill. She laid the head and the entrails on a mat of small branches of brush, cut off the lower legs and added those, then divided what remained of the carcass into four smaller pieces and cast a spell of stasis on the meat so she could carry it without spoilage. Kabeiros watched her from across the fire for a while, and then lay down, his head on his paws turned away from her.

It was all Hekate could do when every task was finished not to lie down beside him and weep into his soft, thick fur. She wondered how fate could be so cruel as to make one partner of an oath-bound pair love deeply while the other was tormented by the closeness and only longed to be free. In her misery and because she found Kabeiros' gorging on the brains, intestines, and other organs revolting, she never noticed that the dog had not eaten.

They remained by the fire, silent, until dull misery numbed Hekate and she lay down on her bedroll and slept, waking in the morning with tears on her cheeks, although she had no memory of her dreams. She gathered up her supplies, rolled the bedroll, strapped on Kabeiros' pack, and set out north and east into the mountains.

While aboard ship, she had asked Kabeiros what he thought they should do. Receiving no reply, she abandoned any attempt to draw him into a discussion. By the time they came ashore, she had decided to go first to the valley of the Nymphae to discover whether they had any way of communicating with Dionysos. She could Call him, but when she thought of doing so, her heart clenched within her. What if Perses should hear and recognize her Call?

Hekate told herself she was a fool. She had never known a Call to be intercepted. There was no reason her father should be listening—if that was even possible. As far as she knew, he wasn't aware of Dionysos' existence or of her connection to Dionysos. She had always visited him as a side trip to gathering herbs and had been careful never to carry a watcher with her. Her reasoning was all useless; Hekate found her body was slick with cold sweat.

She berated herself for her fear. It was ridiculous to fear Perses when she had outfaced Medea and the Olympian gods. Surely he was not a stronger mage than Aietes or Medea and the Olympian Gifts were more dangerous than spells, which took time to cast. Even as she tried to reassure herself, her breath came shorter and harder and her steps quickened. Suddenly a cold nose was thrust into her hand.

The caves of the dead are safe, Kabeiros said. *And there's no smell of magic anywhere.*

She kept her mind closed because she feared that if she opened it to answer him all that would come across would be a babble of senseless terror, but she clutched the loose skin on Kabeiros' neck gratefully and pulled him closer so she could keep one arm around him. He endured it for a time, but since no one can live in a peak of terror for very long, Hekate's panic soon subsided and Kabeiros slid away.

They stopped at noon to rest and eat and again at dusk, but Hekate did not unpack more than the food for the meal and didn't unroll the blankets. Both felt they were near their goal and needed to reach it. They passed well to the north of Ur-Kabos, then angled eastward, Hekate creating a small mage light to help them find the path in the dark. Then the moon rose. At first it was little help, merely silvering the treetops, but then the path opened into a clearing.

Grass, like the treetops was silvered by moonlight, as to the right and left were the trunks of trees. Between the trees was dark, here and there dappled with a faint light as branches moved in the breeze and let the moon shine through. Across the clearing, however, was utter blackness, and spilling out of that blackness a long tongue of raw earth, which also looked black in the draining light of the moon.

Both were tired, but that blackness held an irresistible attraction for each. They surged forward, Hekate, driven by her fears, a step or two ahead, the mage light hanging faithfully above her. Reaching her haven, she flung off her pack and turned, arms wide, toward Kabeiros. He, remembering he would shift shape, had hesitated outside the cave mouth just long enough to pull open the strap holding his pack before he took the last step. He was still close enough behind Hekate that she found herself collapsing under the oncoming weight of a naked man unable to balance himself on two legs when he had spent so many years walking on four.

Instinctively Hekate clutched at anything she could grab, which was not very helpful since it was Kabeiros' body and that was falling with her. Fortunately, he had already put out his hands to catch himself, so Hekate only struck the ground with her own weight and a little of his. Still it was enough to knock the wind out of her, and she lay, gasping for breath, enough stunned to continue to hold tight to Kabeiros.

The midsummer day on which they had started the last part of their journey had been mild and, although the night was much cooler than the day, they had been walking fast, so Hekate had never felt chilled. She had been wearing only a thin, Egyptian linen undertunic, and a light wool overtunic under her cloak, which was thrust back over her shoulders. The cloak, bunched behind her, had softened her fall, but both tunics had been twisted and raised, leaving her mostly naked.

"Let me go," Kabeiros groaned. "For the Mother's sake, let me go."

"Let you go?" Hekate repeated in a tone of delighted surprise. It had become apparent to her while she was catching her breath, that the bare male flesh pressed against her was in a state of high arousal. Hekate giggled. "Not for the Mother's sake. She approves heartily of the coupling of man with maid."

"You idiot! Not this man with this maid."

Hekate's arms trembled, but she couldn't release her precious burden. Was it possible that the Mother had touched Kabeiros and forbidden him to love her? Without forbidding her?

"The Mother?" she asked doubtfully. "When did She forbid us? I've been at Her shrine many times, and you were with me. I never felt any coldness. How could She touch you so strongly that you felt unwelcome and I didn't know? Why didn't you tell me, Kabeiros?"

"Stop asking questions and let me go."

A suspicion began to tickle Hekate. "Are you claiming the Mother's disapproval for some reason of your own?"

"You fool! How can you desire a dog?"

Hekate giggled again. "You aren't a dog now," she whispered, and wriggled her hips.

Kabeiros gasped. "Stop. Let me explain."

"Later," she breathed into his ear. "As we are now, you will make no sense and I will hear no sense, no matter what you need to say. One coupling doesn't make a life bonding nor break one. Let us content each other now. Later we'll talk."

They did no talking, however, until long past the next morning. After the explosive release of their passion atop the long day's march, Hekate and Kabeiros slept as they were, still joined, until the pressure of Kabeiros' weight began to crush Hekate. She stirred under her burden, seeking relief, and woke Kabeiros. Half asleep, he half understood the problem and turned with her so that she now lay atop him.

Now, however, her cloak fell over his face. In trying to push it aside so he could breathe, the pin came loose and he pushed off the cloak entirely. Willingly misunderstanding, Hekate lifted herself just enough to pull off both over and undertunic. Kabeiros made an indistinct sound of protest, but it was too late. The wall of restraint he had raised had been breached already and Hekate's squirming stirred him in another way. Breathing hard, he seized her hips and began to move them. It took no time at all for Hekate to realize what was going on and begin to cooperate fully. Their second mating was less violent, but no less satisfying.

Some time later even Kabeiros' tougher body began to feel bruised. He tried to escape Hekate's embrace without waking her but did not succeed. She was frightened at first, thinking he intended to leave her, and gripped him fiercely, but he assured her he only wanted to get the blankets to make them a little more comfortable. By the time those were pulled free of the packs and spread on the floor, both were awake enough to feel renewed desire and also guilt for the almost impersonal hunger with which they had mated.

Neither knew what to say. Hekate was terrified that if she confessed love to the man, Kabeiros would flee her entirely. She could tell from his heightened color and averted glance that he was embarrassed, but she was afraid to ask why. Tentatively, she took his hand and, when he didn't pull away, drew him down beside her. After only the most token resistance he sat . . . close enough so their thighs touched. Hekate stroked his face and pressed her lips to his shoulder. He pushed aside her wealth of blonde curls and kissed her nape. Her hand slid down his body, stroked his thigh; his found her breast. Not long after, they were coupled again.

They woke easily, almost simultaneously, near noon, and, still wordless but with gentle and sustained caresses, they made love once more. It was a lovemaking that knew no need for haste or greedy grasping. In silence it acknowledged that this was not the last time, that love would come again. Replete but not exhausted, they rested, content to be silent and together, until Kabeiros, gazing idly over Hekate's head, stiffened somewhat in surprise.

"Look," he said, "the trees have nearly no shadows. The sun must be almost overhead."

Hekate yawned and stretched, accidentally pushing away the cape that had covered them, which exposed Kabeiros' chest. She smiled to herself and tickled his nipple. He caught his breath, pulled away, and sat up, pulling the cloak around him. This, of course, left Hekate exposed. Reaching out hastily, Kabeiros found her undertunic and handed it to her.

She blinked at it, as if she wasn't sure what to do with it.

"Put it on," Kabeiros said. "You'll be all over gooseflesh in another moment. And I'd better see if I can find a tunic or some cloth among the offerings." He started to rise and then sank back, knees shaking as if his legs wouldn't support him.

"Not for my sake," Hekate said, and drew a finger down the side of his leg, which had been exposed by his movement.

"No, for mine," he retorted. "You seem to be planning to be rid of your binding to me by killing me in a most unusual and untraceable way."

Hekate stared, shocked, until she saw the glint in his amber-colored eyes and remembered that this was the man who had provided a much needed fountain as an image of a dog urinating on a post. Even as she realized he was joking, she found herself torn between relief and exasperation. She knew he hadn't intended to couple with her, that his need had overpowered him when they first fell together to the floor.

What she didn't know was why he had fought so hard to resist. He had said he wanted to explain, but now he was avoiding explanation. Did he just not care for her and think it unfair to "take advantage"? Had that last "sweet" loving acknowledged a kind of defeat, a willingness to stay with her since he had mated with her? Was his escape from the cruelty of telling her he could not love her this need to jest? If so, she would help him. It was better to laugh than to cry.

"Oh, no," she said. "How could you think I wanted to be rid of you? I'm a devoted worshiper of the Mother in Her guise of fertility goddess and you are the perfect phallus."

His lips parted, then shut tightly. Hekate

swallowed. Then he bent his lips into a smile, tried to rise again, and fell back with a groan.

"You won't have use of me long at this rate," he said. "You'll have to find someone who can turn himself into stone. I know it's said that dogs can bind together for hours, but it doesn't seem to carry over into the man form."

"Ohhh . . ." Hekate let the sound linger. "You do well enough."

He uttered an indignant snort and made a third attempt to rise, succeeding this time by straddling his legs and bending his knees. Hekate giggled but realized that it wasn't only a lingering weakness from four couplings but a problem with balancing. She jumped up in time to steady him and they made it across the trough. There a wave of despair and terror seized Hekate and she wavered on her feet, until Kabeiros dismissed the spell.

The offerings were piled carelessly in heaps just beyond where the worshipers could see, as if whoever had collected them could hardly bear to remain. It struck Hekate odd that a dead spirit should react to Kabeiros' spell, but Kabeiros had spotted a man's tunic among the goods and tottered forward to pull it on. He made one attempt to fold the blanket and almost fell over, so Hekate took it from him, but he walked more steadily to a second pile of goods where he saw a handsome rug. He did fall over when he bent to pick it up, but he righted himself.

Meanwhile Hekate had found a cushion and another rug. They carried those back into what had been Kabeiros' living quarters, where Hekate was again made breathless by the beauty of the stone formations and the way quartz and semiprecious stones reflected the mage lights Kabeiros waved awake. A glance around showed that nothing had been disturbed. They might have left only a few moments or hours before rather than having been away for years.

After a little while to appreciate the wonders she had almost forgotten, Hekate went and got the packs and distributed the food they had carried into the proper chambers. Then she hurried to use the privy cave, almost bumping into Kabeiros who was coming out. He was decently clothed in a white undertunic and the embroidered overtunic he had picked out of the offerings, but his feet were bare.

"You need sandals," she said.

"Yes," he agreed, but he looked uncomfortable. "I know it's foolish," he added, "but I feel as if I'm stealing. I never minded taking what I needed while I was here. I felt that I had earned it by casting the spell when it was necessary and keeping the offerings in good order."

Hekate smiled at him. "Let's steal some wine and break our fast. Then I'll go out to the valley of the Nymphae and you can spend the rest of the day putting the offerings in order. It's two or three candlemarks' walk to their valley, and probably I won't stay long with them so I should be back before dark. Go get us some wine while I broil some of the deer you brought in."

When they were seated at Kabeiros' stone table, eating slices of the meat broiled on slabs of rock heated by earth-blood power and some grain roasted in a little oil, she said, "Is there a chamber that could be fitted out for Dionysos to sleep in?"

"Dionysos," Kabeiros repeated, stiffening slightly. "Will you bring him back with you? I thought you didn't know where he was."

"I don't," Hekate replied, "but I just realized that, being a seer, and a strong one, he may have had a Vision of my coming. If so, he might have decided to meet me at the valley of the Nymphae. I . . ." She hesitated, and then went on regretfully, "I guess I would have to bring him back. Now that he's no longer a child, the Nymphae won't let him stay."

Kabeiros shrugged but something about the blankness of his expression and the tension in his body told Hekate that he would not really welcome Dionysos' company. She wondered if his reason could be the same as hers, but shut the thought out lest it take too hard a hold on her and lead to more hurt.

"Please, Kabeiros," she said, "find a place, not too near us, and make it ready. I don't want to hurt him, but I don't want him in our bedchamber either."

He looked away when she said our bedchamber, and Hekate reached across the table and touched his face, then ran her hand caressingly down his shoulder and arm. When she turned her hand to draw a finger back up his arm, he pulled away.

"Let me alone! Have you no mercy?" he asked bitterly. "If Dionysos is already waiting for you, we will not be using the bedchamber for long. We will leave here . . . and I will be a dog again, but my man's mind will remember . . . and desire . . ." He stopped speaking and swallowed.

"Then I have given you pleasure?" Hekate murmured. "I could not be sure."

He started to get up and Hekate closed her hand around his arm. "I must bring Dionysos to Olympus, and I must speak to Hermes. For that small time it will do you no harm to remember our love play. It will whet your appetite–"

"Small time?" Kabeiros wrenched his arm free, got up from the stone stool, and turned his back to her. "No one will *ever* find an answer to my curse. I will be a dog–"

"There *will* be an answer," Hekate interrupted sharply. "I have bound myself to it! But I didn't mean to wait for that. Kabeiros, what is to prevent us from coming back here any time we want, as often as we want?"

"To travel for months to spend a few days and–"

"No, no. Don't be silly. We can leap from here to Olympus–"

Kabeiros sighed and reseated himself. "It's too far, Hekate. I know you are strong, but to carry me and Dionysos is too much."

"Hmmm." She took a bite of the meat and chewed it. "I had forgotten that Dionysos won't have the leaping spell. Anyway, you're probably right that it's too far for one leap. There's power here, but not enough, I fear. We'll have to return to Olympus by ship, but that's not all bad. I can find homeplaces in several convenient ports."

"But if Hermes hasn't seen them, how can he fix his essence–or whatever it is–to those places?"

Hekate looked a little shamefaced. "Well . . . I don't really need Hermes any more. I've been playing with the leaping essence, or whatever it is, and I . . . I can bud it just like a magic spell."

Kabeiros shook his head. "Some day you're going to play with something that will burst like a firepot in your head and leave you with burnt brains."

She frowned. "No, usually there's a warning kind of feeling to a bad spell, but the point is that the leaping thing isn't mine to play with. That's what I have to talk to Hermes about. I suppose I must pay him for each leap even though I don't get the spell from him."

"You certainly must talk to him, but likely Hermes won't care. He's so enchanted with the look-by-me spell–"

Hekate made a sour face. "I should never have given it to that busybody. He knew too much before.

Now he knows everything. If Zeus casts me out of Olympus, it will be because Hermes has unearthed one secret too many."

Kabeiros laughed. "It's just as well that we've been away so long. Maybe he'll forget where Hermes got the spell." He was silent for a while and then, looking more at ease than he had since she had a man's face to read, said, "If we can jump back and forth . . . Yes."

He said no more, but finished his meal with good appetite speculating easily about what food was likely to come in as an offering, whether the dog should go hunting, or whether they would be gone before they needed more meat. When the meal was over, Hekate left for the valley of the Nymphae. Kabeiros said an abstracted good-bye, but he was shaking his head while he examined the disorganized piles of offerings. Clearly his mind was on how best to arrange them for removal by the servants of the king of the dead.

The body of the girl was even lighter and stronger than the body of the woman. Hekate covered the distance from the caves to the outskirts of Ur-Kabos more quickly than she expected. As she hurried around the north end of the city, she was sorely tempted to enter it and see whether it had changed. Soon after she suppressed that dangerous notion she was racked by the even more dangerous desire to send out a probe and find out what her father was doing.

The urge was so strong that her pace slowed until she was standing still, facing the city wall, which was invisible behind the trees. She had actually begun to walk toward the city, her mind fixed on using high magic for the probe so it would be invisible to Perses when her toe struck an upstanding root with enough force to break the thought and make her cry out. She bent to rub the sore toe, but stopped with her heart pounding in her throat.

Was she mad? Perses *should* be blind and deaf to high magic, but who knew from where he came and what abilities he kept hidden? She had been afraid he would sense her aura, and now she had considered sending out a probe? Oh, no, that couldn't have been her own thought . . . She turned from Ur-Kabos and began eastward again as fast as she could without drawing undue attention.

Her father had set a trap spell for her! So frightened that she could hardly breathe, Hekate ran faster, but the fear and the rapid pace soon brought her to a halt. She stood gasping, leaning against a tree, expecting every moment to feel the weight of her father's watcher settling on her. But it didn't, and after a time she gathered her wits and began to tell herself that it would have been ridiculous for Perses to set such a spell and expend the energy to keep it going for so many years.

That calmed her and she set off toward the valley of the Nymphae again. As she went, she thought about that desire to probe for her father. It seemed stranger and stranger the more she thought about it. She didn't care where Perses was or what he did. As she calmed, she grinned, wondering if so much association with Hermes had made his intense curiosity contagious. But that was more ridiculous than Perses setting a trap spell . . . No, that wasn't so ridiculous. Perses had many and bitter enemies. It wasn't ridiculous at all for him to set a trap spell—not for her but for anyone who had any knowledge of him at all.

Her toe still ached, and Hekate smiled down at it. Good fortune alone had saved her from exposing herself. Well, that was a lesson. She wouldn't travel near Ur-Kabos again unless Kabeiros was with her. He would have smelled that spell and warned her. The dog form was certainly useful; if only he could change back and forth when he wished. Hekate sighed and turned further north, working her way through the cedars and cypresses to where ash and oak began. The ground was rising steadily and in a short time there were only ash and oak trees, thinning as the ridge became more barren.

Eventually she found the cleft that was like the center of an upper lip. She breathed a sigh of relief, glanced about to make sure there were no shepherds in sight, and walked off the top of the ridge, which seemed to drop hundreds of stadia into a bare, rock-strewn ravine. That was pure illusion, and Hekate smiled with relief because her work was still protecting the valley. She paused on the other side to examine the spell she had set so many years before. She knew a better way now, one that didn't draw so much power, but there was power in plenty in the earth here, and she left things as they were.

She went down the lushly grassed hill, crossed the stream, and entered the grove in which the house of the Nymphae grew. As she came into the tiny clearing before the vines that curtained the Nymphae's door, the three emerged with a tall, blond young man behind them.

"Hekate–" the three voices said together.

"Hekate?" the young man repeated doubtfully.

Hekate laughed and shifted form to the woman.

"You did not need to do that," one of the Nymphae said.

"We knew you at once," a second agreed.

"But Dionysos did not," the third pointed out.

"I didn't know you could do that!" Dionysos exclaimed, and looked so young and innocently amused that Hekate held out her hand to him.

He stepped around the Nymphae and took it. He was taller even than Kabeiros; Hekate's head came barely to his shoulder. As a youth, he had been transparently pale. His skin was still white, but it had a healthy glow, and around his head, holding back shoulder-length golden hair, was a many-stemmed wreath. They walked to the turf-covered bank where they had talked when Dionysos was a child—nothing changed in the valley of the Nymphae—and sat down.

"Are you celebrating something?" Hekate asked, looking at the wreath, and then, "Did you See my coming and leave your aunt's house in the middle of a party?"

A shadow passed over Dionysos' face. "I am not often invited to parties in my aunt's home. I am not living with her any longer."

"Was she unkind to you?" Hekate asked anxiously. "I didn't know. Why didn't my binding tighten? Was I too far for you to Call me?"

"No one can be unkind to me." For a moment Dionysos' face could have been graven from marble and his eyes were hard and bright as sapphires. Then his brow creased with concern. "And knowing what you had fled from here, I wouldn't Call." He frowned. "I can deal with men, but that . . . that thing." He shuddered.

"The guhrt?" Hekate patted Dionysos' hand, offering comfort. "It's gone—back to its own plane, I hope. Kabeiros and I got rid of it."

"Kabeiros?"

"You knew I went to the caves of the dead?" Dionysos nodded and Hekate continued, "There I encountered a man named Kabeiros who protected the caves with a spell and collected the offerings for the servants of the king of the dead to take to the underworld."

"Are you sure he didn't collect them for himself?"

Hekate laughed. "Quite sure. He left the caves to come with me and protect me on my journeys, and he took nothing with him."

Dionysos started to get up. "If you have a companion, you won't want me."

Hekate caught at him. "Won't want you? What can you mean? Kabeiros is my lover, that's true, but you are my friend, Dionysos. Now you are a man grown, you are even more my friend. No one can have too many friends, and I have too few."

He settled back and his face was that of a boy again, cheerful and expectant. "You've been away a long time. Have you been to many strange places?"

"Indeed I have, and I'll tell you all the tales . . ."

She looked up. The Nymphae were standing close by, actually between their house and the turf-covered bank where she and Dionysos sat, almost as if they were herding Hekate and Dionysos away from their most private place.

"You've hidden our valley," the breezelike voice of one of the Nymphae said.

"And that magic has held good, as you promised," the second sighed.

"And it will continue to hold as long as the earth lies quiet," Hekate assured them. "I examined it on my way in and the spell is good, the linkage to the power of the earth firm."

"Yesss," the word was slightly sibilant through the third Nymph's sharp teeth. "And care of Dionysos was the price we paid for that shelter."

"So we took him in, when he returned," the second said.

"But he is a man grown now, not a child. We can care for him no longer," the first said.

"I thank you," Hekate said, "for all you've done, and I understand."

Unfortunately it was clear from his expression that Dionysos didn't understand and was bitterly hurt. He muttered that even the Nymphae didn't want him. Hekate felt a well of sadness from him and also more dangerous emotions stirring beneath. She stood up and took Dionysos' hand, pulling him up with her.

"It's time for me to go to the caves of the dead, isn't it?" he said. There was a tremor in his voice. "I knew long ago that I would have to go there."

Hekate laughed. "Yes, but you are no sacrifice. You will leave the caves, just as I left them, whenever you wish. For Kabeiros and me—and for you, too—the caves of the dead are only a temporary resting place. And I'll show you a wonderful magic trick to getting there."

To be more secure, she put her arm around him, hugged him tight, and said, "*Dei me exelthein ta loisthia spelaion*," while her mind made a clear picture of the mouth of the caves of the dead. She heard an exclamation from Dionysos, oddly truncated and, equally oddly, completed as they touched ground in the dark cave mouth.

"How did you *do* that?" the young man gasped.

Hekate grinned at him. "I didn't do it at all. It's not a spell I made. It's . . . I don't know what—an essence? a distillation?—of the Gift of a young Olympian called Hermes. He can somehow form a piece of his Gift into a bit of power that acts just like a spell."

"Did you steal it from him?"

The question made Hekate laugh aloud. "Not from Hermes. He is the master thief, and anyway, Dionysos, you should know that I don't steal. I bartered with him spell for spell."

"Would he barter with me?" Dionysos asked eagerly. "A spell like that could spread my worship all over whatever part of the earth can support the vine of the grape."

"Spread your worship?" Hekate echoed.

"Oh, yes," he said with a charming mixture of pride and amazement. "I am the god of wine, and many temples have been raised to me. This is such a wine as you never drank, not sweet and thick and cloying like date wine. The wine of the grape is a fine quencher of thirst, sweet or almost astringent. It is much less likely to make you sick—although if you drink enough even of grape wine you will be sick. And it is a great opener of hearts—"

"Are you sure that is such a good idea?"

Hekate turned, let go of Dionysos, and leapt lightly across the blood trough to kiss Kabeiros gently on the mouth. Aloud she said, "Dionysos, this is my dear companion, Kabeiros," and before Kabeiros could look surprised at the display of intimacy, she said mind to mind, *I have told Dionysos you are my lover. I wanted to remind him of that. He must have had some bad experiences with his aunt because he feels no one wants him. Make him welcome, please, Kabeiros.*

Dionysos had not heard the mental exchange and frowned slightly at Kabeiros, not like a jealous man but in response to what Kabeiros had said. "Why not?" he asked.

"Because open hearts often lead to drawn knives," Kabeiros replied, smiling. "A thin veneer of lies is often the perfect grease for a smooth relationship."

Dionysos grinned. "You may be right. It's true enough that a beaker or two too many can cause a slip into some wild behavior."

"But what is this about temples?" Hekate asked, coming back across the blood trough with Kabeiros, who held out his hand to Dionysos.

The younger man smiled and took the hand, but

his eyes were on Hekate, and he said, "You knew of my Seeing about planting vines?"

"Yes."

Dionysos touched the wreath of intertwined stems around his head. "These are the vines. They live as long as they touch me, and they never grow fewer, no matter how many I plant in the earth. It has come to me how to nurture them, how to ferment the fruit, and I taught these skills. Moreover, where I pass the grapes are sweet and perfect and ferment into a drink like no other. Those who followed my teaching have grown rich and have raised temples and leave offerings to tempt me back into their vineyards where my touch, or even my thought, can produce a wine like ambrosia. If I could only leap in an instant from one vineyard to another, I would be . . ." His voice drifted away and he cocked his head at Hekate. "Ambrosia, the drink of the gods! Surely only a god could leap as you did—"

"But you know I'm not a god," Hekate said, laughing.

"Then this Hermes, who bartered spell for spell with you, would he barter his spell or essence or whatever for something I had?"

"I'm sure he would, as soon as you are in Olympus. And if you had nothing to barter at first, I believe Hermes would lend you a spell until you could pay him." Hekate now put her arm around Dionysos again and said, "I've found your father, and Zeus is the leader of the Olympians. Olympus is a city full of people who have great Gifts, so no Gift is an anathema. I've told Zeus about you, Dionysos, and you are invited to come and live in Olympus.

"And you?"

"I will live there too. Zeus—" she chuckled softly

"—will be a lot happier with you than he is with me. In Olympus, Gifts are what is accepted. My magic and spells are suspect."

CHAPTER 23

Hekate was surely no seer, for no prediction could have been further from the truth than her statement that Zeus would be much happier with Dionysos than he was with her. Not that Zeus didn't welcome his son kindly. At first he was pleased to see him and very willing to acknowledge him as son. Later, when he took the full measure of Dionysos' Gifts, he bitterly regretted what he had done, but by then he had learned to his horror that he was as powerless against Dionysos as any common native.

In the beginning Zeus wanted this son close to test him and also protect him from Hera, although he soon realized that Dionysos needed protection from no one. Before he learned better, Zeus asked Dionysos to stay in his palace, insisted on it, although Dionysos told him he was welcome in Hekate's home until his vines had replaced the harsh and sour grapes that were native. Still he was glad of Zeus' invitation and soon accepted it because Hekate was seldom at home. Besides, it was easier for him to approach the other Olympians from the palace.

His memory of the leaping spell firmly in mind, Hermes was the first, and Dionysos and that young mischief maker found an instant rapport. Having sampled a few draughts of Dionysos' wine, which he had carried with him by ship from Ka'anan and then transported on the backs of two asses, Hermes became an instant devotee. He was delighted to give Dionysos his spell, on the understanding he would be repaid when Dionysos came into his full worship. In addition, Hermes volunteered to take Dionysos to places where he could leap, like Egypt, and offered to accompany Dionysos for the fun of it when he found new places to visit.

Conversions of winemakers were easy. Two beautiful men, taller and stronger and much fairer than the natives, appearing out of thin air went a long way to making a man's mind pliable. Then a taste of the wine Dionysos carried completed the job. Dionysos was certain that when those who planted his vines and followed his way of pressing and fermenting the grapes grew rich, he would be worshiped in Greece as he was among the people of the Fertile Crescent. Hermes believed him. Although he pretended mild contempt, Zeus believed him too, which might have been the root of the trouble between them.

Hekate was hardly aware of any problem. Aside from reiterating that Gration's house was open to Dionysos at any time, she didn't interfere with the new Olympian's life. She had a new focus for her attention. She had learned part of a spell absolutely forbidden in Olympus and all her mind was fixed on keeping the secret and on completing the spell.

When it was far too late, Hekate wondered whether it was Dionysos' calm assumption that he would join the pantheon of Olympians who called themselves gods that annoyed Zeus or whether Zeus and Dionysos had quarreled over Semele. Dionysos would not hear a word against his mother, placing all the blame for her "death" on Zeus. Zeus grew cold when Semele was mentioned. He might not utter any direct criticism, but his inner sneer was all too plain and he often said he pitied Hades who was now forced to deal with her.

Whatever was the cause, Hekate realized there must have been a confrontation in which Zeus came out second best. Zeus twitched whenever Dionysos was mentioned, and although Dionysos remained respectful of his father, there was a new sadness in him, a tinge of hopelessness. He left his apartment in the palace for another of the empty houses that had once belonged to a Titan. This one was not in such perfect repair as Gration's house, but Zeus arranged for it to be refurbished and refurnished. Clearly Zeus would do anything to be rid of Dionysos.

None of these events made much impression on Hekate while they were taking place because all her attention was focused on the possibility of actually finding a permanent draining spell she could use against her father. The draining spell itself, although a temporary one, Hekate had found on the voyage back to Olympus after their ship made its way into the harbor of Lysamachia.

Lysamachia was a busy enough port, but Hekate and her companions discovered that all the ships there were either beginning a trading run south along the well populated coasts of Mysia, Ilyria, Caria, and so on, or had completed their trading runs–like the ship on which they had arrived–and were now turning around to sail home to a southern port. A ship going north along the more barren coast of Thrace to Greece was rare.

Hekate was sorry they had not waited in a port

like Miletus for a vessel that would island-hop across the Mare Aegaeum to Euboea and Greece. But those ships were less frequent than the coastal vessels plying northward toward Thrace, north was the direction in which they wanted to go, the captain of the ship they had selected was charming and knowledgeable . . . and they had made a mistake.

Now, having visited every factor in the port and made their wants known to almost every person who made a living in any way at all from the sea, the three had time on their hands. Dionysos promptly disappeared into the interior, seeking farmers with suitable hillsides for grape vines. Hekate and her black dog felt and smelled for magic.

The Talented were not officially persecuted in Thrace, although it was not unknown for the guards or officals of a town to look the other way when a magic worker was beaten or even killed. They did exist in Lysamachia, however, and, sought discreetly, were willing to sell or exchange spells with Hekate. None were even near her in power or ability, but Hekate concealed that fact and was eager just to talk about sorcery. She had found that there were often new bits and pieces attached to the most common spells that were useful–and she still never forgot a spell.

In the course of her talks, the name of one man was mentioned by several others as a source of interesting and esoteric spells. None had much good to say of Baltaseros, except that he had once been the strongest sorcerer in all Lysamachia, possibly in all of Thrace. The first time she heard this Hekate paid little attention, but after a while what she was hearing penetrated. "Had been" strongest was the key that drew her attention.

Finally she asked a moderately powerful witch, whom she judged not too clever–a nice woman, who concentrated on finding—where the sorcerer called Baltaseros lived and whether he would be willing to sell or trade as others were.

"Sell." Samira binte Kardel laughed. "Since he lost his power, that's the way he makes his living. We've all bought spells from him. But because he has no power his spells are costly. He demands trade metal for them."

"Lost his power?" Hekate repeated. "And it never came back? How could such a thing happen?"

Samira shook her head. "*He* says—" her expression implied disbelief "—that it was drained from him by an evil witch. To tell the truth, I think he burnt himself out. He is a disgusting person, sly and mean and greedy, the worst drinker and womanizer in the city, and he took every new drug that passed through the port. He abducted young girls, too, and misused them horribly. He was caught once and beaten within an inch of his life."

"And none of his spells could protect him?"

"Not against all of us. Together we were able to seal his power."

"How come he wasn't killed if you sealed his power?"

Samira shrugged. "We all got together and made sure he didn't die." She grimaced. "That would have set a dangerous precedent, letting the unTalented know that a few blows would kill us as quickly as one of them. As it was—" her lips twitched "—we prolonged his suffering considerably, but no fatal harm was done him no matter how many blows were landed on his less than worthy carcass."

"And he took no revenge?"

"First we were all on the watch for him; he knew that. Later . . . perhaps the beating did some damage we didn't foresee." Samira frowned. "He deserved it, but if that caused his loss of power . . . Still, we heard he had used magic afterward in dealing with clients. Then he disappeared the way he always did when he stole a woman, but no woman was missing in the town—and about a tenday later he crept out of his house crying that his power had been raped from him."

"Did he say by whom?"

"A witch, he said, an evil witch . . . Eurydice. We didn't believe him. No one had seen a strange witch, but his power *was* gone. From that day to this, no spell will work for him. He can teach spells . . . he taught me a spell for scrying, which doesn't come naturally to me, and when I did it, it worked perfectly, but nothing works for him."

Hekate's heart leapt when she heard Baltaseros' accusation about his loss of power but she didn't dare show how interested she was in the idea that power could be drained permanently. No Talented person would want to believe that and none would be willing to help her learn how to do it. Without saying so to Samira, she dismissed debauchery as the cause of Baltaseros' decline. More likely, she thought, it was a result of his anguish and frustration. Now she had to find the man without implying it was his loss of power in which she was interested.

"So you and others learned spells from him. I wonder if he would have any that would interest me?"

"He might. He has some strange spells." The finder wrinkled her nose. "But I wouldn't go there for anything any more. He's . . . you wouldn't believe me if I told you." Then she shrugged. "And he won't barter spells with any of us except for metal—and sex." She shuddered. "He says he doesn't need our spells. After all, he taught most of us the spells we know. Perhaps with you . . . You might know something that would be new to him. But he needs metal to live."

Hekate shook her head as if she didn't like that. She had trade metal in plenty with her, mostly silver and even some gold, but she preferred not to admit it, because that might lead to attempts at robbery. She would gladly pay every piece of metal she had for the draining spell, but there was no reason to tell Samira that.

"Well . . ." Hekate drew out the word. "I might speak with him anyway." She shook her head. "I have no idea how long we'll be fixed in Lysamachia waiting for a ship toward Thessaly. If I find I'm bored enough, perhaps I will look for Baltaseros. Where would I find him?"

She was given directions toward the least savory part of the city and then a description of the house in which he had lodging. She had to fight to stay relaxed in her seat instead of leaping to her feet and running out. It was as well, she thought, that Kabeiros had not come with her, for he would have sensed her excitement and discomfort and the dog's body might have responded with raised hackles or restlessness even though the man understood her need for secrecy.

Kabeiros was something to think about while she made inane conversation with the obliging witch preparatory to leaving. After an initial period of reserve on Dionysos' part and caution on Kabeiros', both feeling out the other's relationship with Hekate, Dionysos had asked Kabeiros to accompany him one day and see what he was doing. By then Dionysos could communicate with the dog—Hekate had insisted that they learn to mind-speak with each other because she had no intention of being the middle of a "he said" and "he answered" conversation.

Dionysos' invitation was accepted and he and the

hound went off together. The expedition had worked very well. Not only had they planted grape vines and imparted "dream" instructions about how to care for the vines and make wine from the fruit, but they had found a herd of wild goats—at least Hekate had hoped the goats were wild—and hunted together. They came home fast friends and the carcass they brought defrayed the cost of lodging and meals for several days, so Hekate was pleased.

From then on, unless he felt that Hekate might be in some danger, Kabeiros often accompanied Dionysos. Hekate sighed. She could not understand Kabeiros' behavior and he would not explain. In the caves, unless he went hunting with Dionysos, he was mostly occupied with restoring order in the caverns used for offerings. He slept with her every night and proved himself a passionate and demanding lover, but he never spoke of love or of permanence.

After they left the caves and he became a dog again, Kabeiros remained much more cheerful all the while they returned to Byblos and took a ship. Most of his good humor and seeming hopefulness persisted over the whole journey. He always came with her when she chose a spot as a "home place" to which she could leap on the way back to the caves. He would smell the whole area to make sure there were no other taints of magic that might disrupt her spell and he would examine it carefully with all his other senses so he could remind her of the appearance of the place if necessary.

Aboard ship or on the brief land journeys between ports, he showed the man within and above the dog, even made the mouth move as if the man were talking . . . but he would not share her cabin on the ship or her blanket by the campfire. Hekate sighed again. In the caves it was clear he found her body exciting–but he seemed to take special pleasure when she changed.

Did that mean that he was dissatisfied in being confined to one woman? If he could have left the caves as a man, would he have gone to the city to seek out other women even if she were waiting for him? So, was his withdrawal now that he was again a dog a sign that it was only her search for a spell to free him that kept him with her?

She came alert suddenly to a question that had obviously been repeated and apologized to Samira. Her mind was wandering, she admitted. She had been worried about her dog, who was with her young companion, who she was not sure could control him. And she had better go and see what they were about, since she didn't want to be fined if the dog–great clumsy brute that he was–did some damage. With that excuse she was able to leave.

Although she would have loved to rush off and find Baltaseros, Hekate went to her lodging. Samira did not seem very perceptive, but there was no sense sparking any doubt in her about an interest in the "special" spell. Besides, Hekate was not as certain as Samira that Baltaseros had not recovered any of his power. If he were indeed addicted to evil, how convenient it would be to pretend he had lost his power. Who then could accuse him of the thievery or death of his victims? It would be best to have Kabeiros with her to sniff for magic when she met Baltaseros.

She was glad to have the black dog accompany her for other reasons when she went the next day to find the man. She suspected that if not for Kaberios' huge size and ready snarls she might have had to use magic to deter some of the men in the area from trying to seize her. She wondered if she should have been the crone, but looking around convinced her that the inhabitants would probably just have tried to rob the old woman instead of trying to play with the maiden.

The really terrible conditions through which she passed had raised doubts in Hekate about Baltaseros' retention of power. Surely if he had any magic, he would have found a better place to live. The house, when they found it, added to Hekate's hope that Baltaseros' power had, indeed, been reft from him, and the man, when they managed to rouse him from his drugged stupor to let them in, confirmed how low he had sunk.

His eyes looked like dead horseflies drowned in yellow mucus; his beard was matted with spittle and spilled food, his hair tangled with unmentionable substances clinging to it, his clothing unspeakable. The room into which the outer door opened was filthy and cluttered with rags that might once have been pillows; gelatinous patches marked the splintery floor, and battered and chipped cups and platters stained with dried who-knew-what lay here and there.

Kabeiros sneezed violently and gagged as the stench hit him. Hekate managed to swallow the bile that rose in her throat and control the impulse to back away from the creature who had opened the door. It wasn't necessary because he staggered away to a foul nest near the far wall, leaving her to close the door. Considering the glaze in Baltaseros' eyes, there was no sense in trying to be subtle.

"I want to buy a spell," she said.

The dead horseflies moved enough to show Baltaseros was looking at her. A dull expression of lust made his face even more repulsive as he took in her appearance. "Why not?" The words were slurred, the voice thick and phlegmy. "But there's a little ritual we need to do in my bed before I give you a spell." He reached toward her and Kabeiros growled and showed his teeth. "Put that dog outside," he mumbled. "No ritual of protection, no spell."

Hekate took a twist of gold wire out of her purse and held it where Baltaseros could see it but not reach it. For a moment she couldn't speak because her gorge had risen at the thought of any physical contact with the creature, never mind coupling with him.

When she had control and his eyes had fixed on the gold, she said, "No ritual. The dog stays. I have heard what you do with women whom you can overpower. However, I have trade metal. I will pay in silver and in gold for the spell I want."

He didn't answer at first, staring at her, licking his lips and dropping a hand into his lap to stroke his rising phallus slowly then faster and faster. Hekate had to grab Kabeiros by the loose skin between his shoulders to keep him from leaping on Baltaseros and killing him. She felt almost sick enough to abandon her quest and leave—almost but not quite—because he was finished so fast. And as soon as he had uttered a strangled cry and a stain appeared wet against the many other stains on the rag that covered him, his dead horsefly eyes moved to the gold wire that still dangled from Hekate's fingers.

"What spell?"

He sounded more dazed now, barely able to speak. Hekate wondered if the effect of whatever drug he had taken was increased by physical excitement. She spoke slowly and clearly.

"The draining spell."

There was a silence. Some kind of emotion worked behind the dead eyes and filth. Finally, Baltaseros giggled. "It won't do what you want," he said. "It won't wipe out any other sorcerer the way it wiped me out."

"Why not?" Hekate asked.

He giggled again. "It takes a *real* witch to do that, a hot witch who's willing to futter a man out of his wits, so he can't spell her or put up shields. A frigid bitch like you wouldn't have a chance. But I'll sell the spell to you—for a mina of gold."

"I don't have a mina of gold," Hekate said, "but I have many spells that I could add in barter to what gold I do have. You could sell those to others. I have ways of making a spell last forever, of binding spells together. Many would pay well for those."

His eyes closed and he swayed. "I'm not interested in your spells. There's only one other payment I'll take for the draining spell—under me in bed until I get tired of you. I've got plenty of spells."

The words were so garbled together that Hekate needed to think a while to understand them. Baltaseros began to giggle weakly again and his hand drifted toward his body. Hekate stiffened and looked away, thinking he was going to begin to masturbate again. She wanted to leave, but she was not sure she could force herself to come again, even for the draining spell. Suddenly Kabeiros' ears rose to alert.

Magic, he said. *This place stank so much physically that I couldn't sense it at first.*

He still has magic? Hekate asked, raising shields.

No. Kabeiros' mental voice laughed. *He's got a grimoire!*

So he had. In fact when Hekate looked at him again, he was holding it open against his chest with one hand, the other was again stroking his phallus. His eyes were still closed. She should have guessed a wreck like Baltaseros would have a grimoire. Many sorcerers kept grimoires or bought them or stole them. Perses had many. Hekate had never bothered because she never forgot a spell; probably she wouldn't be able to forget one even if she wanted to.

"Come here," Baltaseros said. "Come close enough and you can read the spell for yourself."

Hekate cast the freezing spell at him, but the hand rubbing himself never faltered. She looked at Kabeiros.

*He's got no shields, but the spell's gone as if something in him ate the magic . . . * There was a tremor of uncertainty in Kabeiros' mental voice. *Like something inside me eats my magic. He can't do magic, but no magic can affect him either.*

"Come here. Come here to me," Baltaseros chanted. "I will let you read the spell, even two spells." In horrible contrast to the depraved and disgusting physical creature, the voice had lost its phlegmy quality and was smooth and seductive.

Hekate dismissed her shields and invoked a seeing spell. Everything sprang into incredible clarily. She could see a louse crawling through the hair on the back of Baltaseros' hand and the minute cracks in some liquid that had spilled and dried on the rag that covered him. Only the words on the page of the grimoire were still blurred.

That did it! The last shred of sympathy that Hekate had felt for a man deprived of his power evaporated. She knew that his promise that she would be allowed to read spells from the grimoire was false. No matter how close or how far from the book, the words in it would remain unintelligible until some magic condition was fulfilled. Not that Baltaseros would ever admit that; he would blame her, saying that the book refused to accept her or that her magic was insufficient for her to understand it.

Hekate's teeth set. She meant to have that spell. If Baltaseros would not set reasonable terms for a sale, she would simply take the grimoire and work out the spell for herself. She looked around, saw a fairly large copper pot; it had a crack in the bottom, but that wouldn't interfere with what she wanted it for. Gripping it firmly by its handle, she walked up to Baltaseros.

The floor creaked loudly. He heard her coming. His eyes opened a slit. Quick as a snake, his right hand left off stroking his phallus and grabbed for her. Quick as he was, Hekate was quicker. She raised the pot and brought it down with all the strength of her arm on the top of his head. With her other hand, she snatched the grimoire from him. Kabeiros, who had been standing ready to tear out Baltaseros' throat if Hekate's assault failed, and had been shuddering with horror at the idea of what he would have to take into his mouth, lolled out his tongue in relief and laughter.

Magic is good, but a strong right arm is often better, he said. *Come, let's go. You can study that thing just as well where it doesn't smell so bad.*

Hekate removed her purse and dropped it on the floor by Baltaseros' hand. Then she reached inside her tunic and pulled out the twisted cloth that held the bulk of her trade metal. She picked out all the gold except two pieces and put that directly in his hand. Kabeiros pulled at her skirt, growling, and she put away the rest of the metal and followed him.

However, outside the door, she stopped uncertainly. *It's his grimoire,* she said. *It's all he has. What will he do when the gold and silver I've left him is gone?*

He won't last that long, Kabeiros said, yanking on her skirt again. *He'll be able to buy enough drugs with what you left him to drift off into the underworld in a haze of joy. Or someone will discover what he has and send him off more abruptly and less pleasantly. Come away before he wakes up and begins screaming.*

Still she hesitated. Kabeiros sighed impatiently and pulled her toward the rickety stair, but Hekate resisted long enough to touch the door and the door frame and speak a spell. Now Baltaseros could come out of the door, but no one could enter. Kabeiros' remark about what would happen to Baltaseros if someone discovered he had gold had reminded her that the door had been locked when they arrived and they could not relock it. In this area, doubtless an unlocked door was an invitation to theft and murder. Until Baltaseros woke and could hide her purse and the gold, he would be safe.

Then she hurried down the stair, knowing that although they would not care what happened to him, Baltaseros' screaming that he had been robbed would be a perfect excuse for the hopeless denizens of the area to fall upon those who seemed better off. She could use the look-by-me spell to escape, but Kabeiros could not. He had strength and ferocity; nonetheless, if there were too many, he would be hurt. But she could not be glad of what she had done, and the grimoire tucked into the bosom of her robe, over the crossed girdle, seemed to weigh a thousand mina.

When they were out of the district, Kabeiros looked up at her face and sighed. *It's not the end of the world, Hekate. You can bring it back to him when you have what you want out of it.*

So I can, she said, feeling as if Atlas had returned and taken up the burden of the world again.

✧ ✧ ✧

It took Hekate three days to find the key to unlocking the grimoire's secrets. It was a good grimoire, and had not originally belonged to Baltaseros. Hekate wondered how he had obtained it, and then put the matter out of her mind. A grimoire generally did not leave the hand of its maker until that mage was dead. She did, however, read every spell in the book very carefully.

Most of the spells were harmless or, at least, no worse than those well-known by many sorcerers. Only the draining spell was truly dangerous, and even that was less dire than it might have been. Having learned the spell, Hekate understood what Baltaseros had said. It was not a spell that could be cast from a distance or infused into a lifeless carrier like an amulet. The spell-caster had to hold his victim until the draining was done . . . and nowhere was there any implication that the spell was permanent. It could be used to drain the life-force to nothing, but then the victim died.

Hekate laid her head down on the book and struggled against tears. She would never dare use the spell unless it was permanent. To drain Perses dry would be murder and the Kindly Ones didn't approve of daughters murdering fathers, no matter what kind of a father. In fact, she doubted she would dare use the spell in any case; she shuddered at the thought of needing to embrace Perses.

Poor Asterie . . . The thought of her mother let her spirits rise for a moment when she thought she might teach Asterie the spell. Then her mother could do to her father what he had done to her for so many years. But that hope died as quickly as it formed. After so many years of complete subjugation, Asterie might not be able to use the spell against Perses' will. Worse yet, since Asterie would have to touch Perses for the spell to work, he could easily overpower her physically.

She was so absorbed in her misery that she didn't hear Dionysos come in and wasn't aware of him until he rushed to kneel beside her and beg her to tell him what had made her so sad. She could sense something rising in him, something so deadly that it frightened her. She hurried to explain that no person had offended or saddened her, only what was growing, the more she studied it, into an insoluble problem.

"Nonsense." Dionysos sat back on his heels and grinned at her, the red and black roiling inside him gone as quickly as it had developed. "With you and me and Kabeiros working on it, nothing is insoluble."

Hekate couldn't help laughing at his youthful confidence, but it cheered her all the same so she went on to discuss with him whether to return the grimoire. It made her very anxious, she admitted, to have a draining spell in the hands of a man like Baltaseros. On the other hand, she simply could not live with the knowledge that she had taken from him his last resource.

"Then take out that page and give the rest of the book back," Dionysos said, looking puzzled.

"It's not so easy to remove anything from a grimoire," Hekate pointed out.

Dionysos cocked his head. "For you?"

Don't encourage her! Kabeiros protested. *Grimoires are often protected by dangerous spells.*

Hekate acknowledged that Kabeiros could be right, but gentle probes of this grimoire produced no reaction, and eventually she was able to remove the page on which the draining spell was indited. The next day, Hekate and Kabeiros returned to Baltaseros' rooms.

They climbed the shrieking steps and found the door to Baltaseros' place slightly ajar. Hekate touched the door and frame and found that the spells she had set were still active, although weaker. She dismissed them and pushed open the door, half expecting to see Baltaseros' corpse. For a moment she thought the still form in the foul nest was dead, but then it murmured a low litany of pleasure and she realized that Kabeiros had guessed half right. The creature was awash in drugs.

She was about to go out again, still carrying the grimoire. At the rate he was going, Baltaseros would soon be dead and the grimoire might be lost or taken by someone unfit to use it. The thought made her grimace. Who could be more unfit than Baltaseros? She shrugged. That was not for her to judge; the book was his . . .

He opened his eyes. "I have no spells to sell. A thief . . ." he began, then saw who it was and began to gargle with rage.

"I have come to bring back your grimoire," Hekate said. "So do not call me a thief. I paid well for a look at it. You have no reason to complain against me. However, there is one thing more I want to know. Who was the witch who drained you? Does she live here in Lysamachia?"

"Why should I tell you anything?" he asked.

He seemed to have forgotten his spurt of anger. His objection was like that of a two-year-old–for the sake of being obstructive without any particular reason. The resistance seemed to make him happy; he began to hum a little tune, grinning like an idiot and drooling.

"You should tell me because your grimoire is in my hands," Hekate said dryly. "Because you are too drugged to try to take it back from me, and because if you don't answer, I'll just walk out and keep the book."

Baltaseros' look of complacent idiocy changed to a tragic mask. Tears ran from his eyes and he began to sob. "No. No. Don't keep my grimoire. It's mine. Please give it back to me. He was my master. He left it to me. Don't take it away."

"Then tell me who drained you and where she lives."

Baltaseros sniffled and wiped his nose on the back of his hand. "Will you avenge me?" he asked.

"I have no idea," Hekate replied. "It depends on the woman, on why she drained you, on many things. Don't try my patience. The smell in this place doesn't encourage long visits. Tell me the name of the witch. Now."

The voice of command pierced the drug haze. "Eurydice," Baltaseros said. "Eurydice. That was her name."

He began to curse the woman in the foulest language and to weep with self-pity. Hekate was almost in sympathy with him before his drug-loosened tongue slipped and made clear what rankled him most. Apparently he had found one he considered an innocent girl in a small village outside the port, sensed her Talent, and brought her to Lysamachia for the sole purpose of draining that Talent from her. He had been sipping her strength for about a week, when she found his grimoire, discovered the key to make it legible, and drained him dry.

That was interesting and Hekate resolved to remember what Baltaseros said for when she found Eurydice. More important right now was that Samira binte Kardel, the finder who had told her how to reach Baltaseros, had also called the witch Eurydice, which meant that, at least in naming the witch, Baltaseros had told the truth.

"And where can I find Eurydice—in case I should want to avenge you?" Hekate asked.

The violent emotions he was experiencing—now Baltaseros was weeping copiously—seemed to have focused his mind. His speech was almost clear when he said, "I don't know. On my master's grave, on the grimoire he gave me, I swear I don't know. She left me so weak, I couldn't rise from my bed for near a ten-day. Do you think that if I knew where she'd gone I wouldn't have pursued her? And every sorcerer and witch in Lysamachia would have helped me."

"Oh?" The word was replete with sarcasm. "Were you so greatly beloved of the other mages in the city?"

Rage and spite temporarily cleared the drug haze. "Whether I was beloved or not," he spat, "the others wouldn't have wanted a strange, foreign witch to run loose holding that draining spell. They would have killed her for me. But she was gone. No one knew I had brought her to Lysamachia and she had just slipped away."

"But they didn't kill you for having the draining spell."

"No one knew I had it then. I was careful how I used it." He began to weep again. "Everyone would have thought that accursed Eurydice brought the spell with her and she would be dead and my power would have come back . . . Oh, I know it would have come back. Instead they laughed at me for blaming someone who didn't exist. They all blamed me for my own misery. Some said I had cast a spell wrong and it backlashed and burned me out; others insisted I tried to work such a mighty and evil magic that it drained me out. No one would believe me." He held out a hand which shook pathetically. "Please. Please give me back my master's grimoire."

Hekate was about to hand it to him, but Kabeiros blocked her way. *Don't trust him. Don't go near him. Remember how he tried to grab you, and you don't want his filthy hands on you. Give the book to me.*

The dog's skin shivered with revulsion and Hekate was about to protest that, considering his sense of smell, it was worse for him than for her. But then she thought of Baltaseros touching her, perhaps pulling her off balance—he was grossly heavy and because he was lying down would have his weight to use—so that she fell into the filth he lay in. She let Kabeiros take the grimoire in his mouth and drop it in Baltaseros' hand.

The precautions had probably been unnecessary, Hekate thought. The small period of clarity was fading fast as whatever drugs he had taken damped out his burst of rage and grief. His hand closed over the grimoire, but his eyes were already glazing over and he began to giggle as he tried to conceal the book in his rags and it kept getting caught. Hekate and Kabeiros exchanged glances, agreeing wordlessly that there was nothing more worth trying to pry from him. Without more ado, they left the room, closing the door behind them; Hekate renewed the spells she had set with a touch and a word and they returned to their lodging.

Although Hekate did ask questions in the town about Eurydice, it seemed that Baltaseros had told the truth about that, too. Most did not recognize the name at all. The few who did, associated it, as had Samira binte Kardel, with Baltaseros' story about a strange foreign witch. And several said that if there had been a Eurydice and she had done what Baltaseros had accused her of, she had surely taken a ship and fled Lysamachia as soon as she could.

Little as she liked to acknowledge that it was highly unlikely that she would find Eurydice in the area, Hekate had to accept the logic of her informants.

Her frustration was a little assuaged because Dionysos said he would ask for Eurydice everywhere he went. He had bought a horse and was ranging farther and farther abroad, staying away several days at a time, as the season waned to autumn. Autumn was the best time for planting, giving the vines a chance to root well before the burst of growth in the spring. It was also the worst time for sailing so there was little fear that Dionysos' absence would make them miss a ship.

Kabeiros no longer traveled with Dionysos. He told Hekate he was quite sure the young mage could protect himself and he was reluctant to leave her for so long at a stretch, specially when she had taken up healing again. Partly that came about by accident–Samira had taken a putrid fever and Hekate found her half dead one day when she visited; she had cured Samira, and Samira had recommended her to everyone who even had a sniffle. Since Hekate's store of trade metal was now very low, she gladly accepted the clients and began to repair her finances.

Dionysos did not find Eurydice nor any hint of where she came from or where she had gone. The autumn passed. Hekate did a good business in healing over the winter and could now afford to consider retracing their journey back to Miletus to find a ship that would go to Greece when a factor arrived with goods scheduled for Myrcinos in Thrace.

Alerted by one of the chandlers they had plagued for news of a ship in that direction, Hekate hurried to speak to the factor. He assured her that–barring a tragedy–a ship would arrive by April or May to take his goods. Since that was early enough in the spring for them to follow their first plan if the Greek ship didn't arrive, they decided to wait. The ship came in the beginning of May and willingly accepted them as passengers, but the captain explained it would make a very long coastal voyage. Hekate didn't mind because she would be able to mark several places outside ports to which to leap, Kabeiros didn't care, and Dionysos was delighted. Each stop gave him more places in which he could introduce his vines. However, they did not arrive in Olympus until late summer.

CHAPTER 24

They had a far pleasanter homecoming than Hekate expected. Gration's house was in perfect order, ready to receive them, and the servants were overjoyed to see Hekate return. Although the Olympians had been reasonably faithful about supplying them with food, they had been growing uneasy about how long that would continue in their mistress' absence.

To Hekate's surprise, the Olympians also seemed glad to welcome her home, most of them because they had tasted the joys of using magic and wanted new spells. Hekate told each she would be glad to supply them but must first obtain the approval of Zeus, which also gave her the opportunity to introduce Dionysos. That went very well. Zeus seemed much taken with this new son. He was less pleased with Hekate's request for permission to sell more spells; he knew it was a wedge in the door to let in a greater and greater use of magic, but he was in a cleft stick, not wanting to be blamed and suspected of unfairly restraining the power of his people, and he gave his approval.

The spells, Hekate pointed out, seemed relatively harmless. Hestia's worshipers were forever appealing to her priestesses to help them find small items they had lost; Hekate gave her a finding spell that she could use herself or bud off onto favored priestesses. She also wanted to give Hephaestus a finding spell—he had not asked, but Hekate felt she had a debt to him; he was forever mislaying his tools. Hebe wanted a spell for attracting birds; she loved the little creatures, but they wouldn't come to her. Hekate was delighted to devise that one. It lightened her heart as much as Hebe's.

About one request she seriously asked Zeus' advice. Artemis wanted a spell for testing chastity; she suspected one of her women of taking a lover. Hekate was afraid that Artemis' punishment would be too severe if the woman had slipped. Zeus frowned and agreed that that might be so, but said that the woman knew what she was swearing to when she took service with Artemis and should have gone to her mistress and begged for her freedom rather than cheat. A vow was a vow.

Those words pricked Hekate's conscience. Dionysos seemed well set for the present, although Hekate could still feel the binding to him. That surprised her; she had thought she would be released when she brought him to Olympus and he was so well received. For now, however, that was barely a thread that connected them. Even when autumn and winter passed and she realized he had quarreled with Zeus and was living on his own, there was no tugging at the bond. He had found friends, Bacchus and Silenos, and seemed content.

Another year passed; Dionysos' vines had taken hold; the grapes had been trampled, and their juice was in tuns fermenting. More years passed and grape wine became the favorite and then the staple drink for all. Temples to Dionysos sprang up all over the known world. He leapt from country to country blessing the vines and the wine they produced. The vintners grew rich and offered a good tithe of their profits and produce to the young god. Hekate put her doubts aside.

Over the passing years, the binding to Kabeiros was lighter, too, although it was more demanding than that to Dionysos. Hekate understood the twinges that binding caused her for she was deliberately trying to evade it. She no longer pestered Hephaestos to study Kabeiros' problem, no longer presented Kabeiros to this and that Olympian to find one who might be able to help him. She knew Kabeiros still wanted his power to change under his own control, but she was afraid that when he held it, he would leave her.

It was his right, but Hekate's throat closed with grief when she thought of losing Kabeiros. There were men among the Olympians who found her attractive, but she could warm to none of them, even as a casual lover. As a companion, to share her concerns, to give her advice, to laugh with . . . she shuddered at the thought. Among themselves they were like all people, good and bad, selfish and generous, kind and cruel, but they had no regard for others. They would help, harm, use, or cast aside any native as whim directed.

For her there was only Kabeiros, and since *he* no longer urged her to find a cure, she ignored the occasional tightening of her bond. When it grew painful or when she sensed his desire to be a man was growing, she managed to find some excuse to leap them back to the caves of the dead, where he could be a man and they could be lovers.

Fortunately—or unfortunately—finding an excuse to leap to Ka'anan grew easier as the years passed.

Fortunately because staying in the caves of the dead permitted the renewal of Kabeiros' role as a lover. Unfortunately for two reasons: the one that touched Hekate personally was that Kabeiros always seemed reluctant to make love to her. He always did and was as passionate and yet gentle and tender a lover as any woman could desire, but he never said he loved her, he never said he wished to be with her forever, and their coupling seemed to be profoundly disturbing to him.

The second reason was that Perses had managed, even without Hekate's cooperation, to seize the reins of power in Byblos. The seizure had taken longer, but he had succeeded at last. At first it made little difference to Byblos, even when the old king and queen died and Perses had tightened his grip on the new puppet rulers. The new king and queen were a little less rich and Perses a little more, but the cost to the people was small. A few extra men and women disappeared from the most wretched parts of the city, but such disappearances had been common enough before Perses established his hold.

Though Perses had done nothing really horrible yet, Hekate felt uneasy. The vow that bound her to her father's destruction pinched and pulled, but the draining spell she had learned was all but useless. Unless she could discover what Eurydice had done to make it permanent, Perses would recover his power. Wary and hating, she would have no second chance; she would fail and die, or worse, fall into his power.

Still, she could think of no other way to destroy Perses without killing him. She began a serious search for Eurydice, often leaping with Dionysos to his shrines and wandering the roads, towns, and cities asking for a witch of that name. She was cautious about lodging in any populated place—

because of the way witches were hated and feared—and often set up a campsite warded by magic at a crossroad. Sometimes as rumors of her presence traveled the land, she found suppliants waiting for her. Often she just slipped away, but the sick and the wounded drew her, so she healed while she searched. And, where she found the Talented in danger, she taught magic so they could protect themselves.

For a very long time, Hekate continued to search but she could discover no trace of Eurydice. She began to believe as the mages of Lysamachia did that Baltaseros had imagined a powerful witch to cover his own evil or ineptitude. And still Perses did nothing that could drive her to confrontation. Over the years, rulers changed in Byblos, but he held his power. Perhaps, Hekate thought, power was all he wanted. If that was so, all she need do was watch and wait; Perses was showing signs of ageing. A small hope flickered to life. She had not aged at all, but perhaps Perses could die.

Then she was distracted by a crisis in Dionysos' life. Temples had been founded to him in Crete and in one of those temples was a priestess who could interpret the Visions, which still came to him from time to time, and could give him peace in other ways. Then she was gone.

For a time, while Dionysos believed she had deliberately abandoned him, he ran berserk and fructified his precious vineyards with rampant lust and wanton spilling of blood. Hekate, Kabeiros, Aphrodite, Eros, and Hermes did what they could to assuage his hurt and grief. Sometimes one traveled with him and tried to control the madness of lust and fury that he induced in his followers because that only hurt him more—he feared he was going mad.

None of them thought to go to Crete; Hermes, Aphrodite, and Eros because they didn't care about the native people and getting to the island would be a lot of trouble. Hekate didn't go because she was so angry she knew she would have killed the priestess and destroyed the temple. However, when Dionysos' suffering made that punishment seem reasonable, Hekate did go. There she discovered that the priestess had not abandoned her god for another one or for a native man. She was old; she had died.

Dionysos was almost as outraged by the priestess' death as by her imagined defection, but he understood that native people had much shorter lives than Olympians and the violence of his "blessings" diminished. He was changed, however. The rage and panic he could loose upon others was much nearer the surface and he seemed to have less control over them. The Olympians grew wary of him; they made haste to accede to any request he made so long as he would go and leave them in peace.

Hekate could do nothing about that. She offered what comfort Dionysos would accept, but her inability to understand and interpret his Visions, which were growing more and more complex and disturbing and plagued him unmercifully, made her sympathy virtually useless. However, in those years a great joy came to Olympus. Eros, who had lost his soul through the evil he had done in the reign of Kronos, regained it in the love of a native woman called Psyche. And even Zeus, who had decreed the punishment, rejoiced at the reunion of beauty and the soul.

In the general aura of good feeling that enriched Hekate's circle of more-than-acquaintances if not quite friends, the loosening of her bond to Dionysos was hardly apparent. Until, as the years slid by, a new priestess named Ariadne was consecrated in Crete.

She, like the first Ariadne, could interpret Dionysos' Visions and bring him peace.

Joyfully Dionysos reported that the Mother had taken pity on him and returned to him all that he had lost and more, that this Ariadne was Mother-blessed and could draw the Mother down with her dancing. Unnoticed, Hekate's bond to Dionysos thinned to nothing and fell away.

Partly she didn't notice that she had been freed of her first binding because the situation in Ka'anan dominated her attention. Perses was old now, but no weaker, and Hekate knew it was blood magic that was sustaining him. More and more people were disappearing in Byblos, and not only the criminals and others who would not be missed. As his need grew, Perses was even taking daughters and sons of well-to-do established merchants, sometimes even scions of the lower nobility.

The second binding was tightening around Hekate's heart. She knew that she would have to act against Perses, but every time she tried to think of what to do she became faint with fear. Kabeiros repeatedly offered to kill Perses for her, claiming that he was invulnerable to magic; however, Hekate remembered that Medea had pierced that invulnerability and knew Perses had been attacked many times even by otherplanar beings and it was always the attacker who died . . . if worse did not befall him. Dionysos also offered his Gifts in whatever way Hekate thought they would work best, but not only would Dionysos be vulnerable to Perses' magic, all she could envision was the rage and panic causing her father to let loose all his most destructive spells at once.

Hekate worked desperately to make her shields impervious and studied spells of destruction. She hoped she still had a little time. Perses did not seem ready to act; he had taken an apprentice–something utterly unprecedented–and it would take him some time to teach the young man. Only Hekate soon discovered that Perses wasn't attempting to teach his apprentice anything, that the apprentice had very little Talent, only enough to make him particularly open and vulnerable to a stronger mage. She was bewildered until another piece of the puzzle suddenly fell into place.

The king of Byblos was slowly dying, whether of natural causes or not Hekate didn't know and didn't much care; the present king of Byblos, corrupted almost from birth by Perses, would be no loss to humanity. Hekate paid little attention until she learned of the plans for the king's funeral. Perses intended to replace with real people the hundreds of terra cotta figurines of attendants and servants that were customarily buried with the dead to serve them in the afterlife those people who would be sacrificed, ostensibly to honor the king, but in reality so that Perses could drink their life-force to perform some great act of magic.

Careful spying–the whole court was utterly corrupt and it was easy to buy information–informed Hekate that Perses' apprentice would play a large role in the funeral rites. Little by little that role became clear. At first Hekate could not believe the implications, but in the end she was unable to deny what Perses intended. He was planning to steal the young man's body, transferring his mind and will to it while sending the apprentice's mind and soul into his outworn husk, which would immediately die of the strain.

Then Hekate knew she would have to confront Perses alone. Caution bade her take him right after the transfer, but she couldn't bear to see so many die just for the hope of catching Perses in a weakened condition. Besides, who knew whether he would be weakened. Perhaps enough of that blood-force would have been generated to make him stronger than ever. And perhaps he would be weaker as an old man; perhaps he had waited too long to start his evil procedure.

Even so, Hekate did not really expect to survive. She now regretted the wasted years while she sought Eurydice. She should have been trying to free Kabeiros from his curse because if she died or was enslaved, his future was bleak. There was only one strong hope—one to which she had, deliberately, she feared, turned a blind eye in the past.

Had she not always managed to be elsewhere in the spring when Persephone came to Olympus to help her mother Demeter fructify the fields? In the caves of the dead, Kabeiros was a man. Hades' power negated the draining spell that afflicted the dog. Might not Hades have the answer to Kabeiros' problem? She should have spoken to Persephone, asked her help.

Now she couldn't wait for spring. If the king of Byblos died sooner than she expected she would need to try her strength against Perses before then. She would have to ask for an audience with Hades directly. She went to Zeus, lashed by guilt but still hoping he would say what she wanted was impossible. The hope was vain. It was much easier than Hekate expected to be invited to visit the underworld. As soon as she mentioned the effect of the caves of the dead in Ka'anan on Kabeiros, Zeus said he would arrange a visit. However, when she said she hoped Hades would be able to help Kabeiros regain his shifting power, Zeus shook his head.

"Hades doesn't know magic at all, as far as I know. His Gifts are working with rock and stone, but he uses no spells. Persephone . . . you need to meet Persephone to believe her. She has unlimited power, but no Talent for magic. However, I'll gladly tell Hades you are coming, and I'm sure Hermes will take you."

Hermes was not at home that afternoon, but they went the next day at a time when Hermes knew that Hades and Persephone held court. Hermes gripped Hekate firmly around the waist with one arm and fixed his other hand onto the loose skin between Kabeiros' shoulders. One moment they were in Hermes' reception room, the next Hermes was crying out in surprise as his hand slipped away from the man Kabeiros' shoulders, and Kabeiros, naked as the day he was born, dropped face forward to the ground.

"Gracious Mother!" Hades exclaimed mildly, rising and holding out his hand. "Cloak," he said over his shoulder, and a handsome cloak was dropped into his hand.

He went down the step of the low dais and tried to give the cloak to Kabeiros, but Kabeiros could not take it because he was struggling not to fall flat. When they leapt to the caves of the dead in Ka'anan, he was prepared for the change. This one had taken him unaware, leaving him dizzied and nauseated, unable for the moment to get his balance.

Hermes was staring with open mouth. He had never seen Kabeiros in man form. Hekate, somewhat stunned by Hades' appearance–for he looked as she had imagined the Titans would, huge and hard and black-bearded–and by Persephone's beauty, was also a trifle slow to respond. It was Hades who lifted Kabeiros upright, swirled the cloak around him, and steadied him on his feet.

"Kabeiros," Hermes breathed.

"Ah," Hades said. "The black dog. There are many

of your ilk among us. Will it help you to sit down, Kabeiros, or do you need to stand and walk?"

Hekate had hurried to Kabeiros' side. "I didn't know," she said. "I thought it was only the caves of the dead in Ka'anan that could free him–"

"Free him?"

The voice was soft, pleasant. Hekate turned to look at Persephone and gasped. Under the skin of an exquisitely beautiful Olympian woman was a well of power that Hekate suspected could no more be drained than could the Mother's power. Hekate bowed.

"You are a true avatar of the Mother, Queen," she said. "I beg you both to help Kabeiros."

"Help him how?" Hades asked.

As Kabeiros could now speak for himself, he did, starting with the simple fact that he was frozen into the form of the dog everywhere except the caves of the dead. In answering startled and sympathetic questions, he described when and as much as he knew about how the power to shift at will had been lost to him. Listening, with the knowledge of what Perses intended to do with the mass immolation at the king of Byblos' funeral in her mind, Hekate became aware that the scene Kabeiros described–the young and old sorcerers handfast together, the old one dying, the young one rising to punish Kabeiros–had also probably been an exchange of bodies.

Perses. It had been Perses who had renewed his youth in that disgusting way. It was Perses who had tried to drain Kabeiros, failed because he was too much weakened by the dreadful magic he had performed, and condemned Kabeiros to years of suffering. And Perses would change bodies again and again. Likely each change would require more power and more would have to die to provide it. If she didn't stop him, hundreds, perhaps thousands, would die so that Perses' evil life could continue.

His tale told, Kabeiros offered all he had or was if Hades could free him from his curse. Tears rose to Hekate's eyes. The passion with which Kabeiros spoke seemed like a knell of doom to her, a confirmation of his desire to be free. Nonetheless, she added her pleas to those of Kabeiros, pledging anything she had or could devise if Hades would free Kabeiros from the spell that was eating his power.

"I wish I could." The face that had at first looked as if it were carven of granite, twisted in dismay. "I have my Gifts and those can perform magic, but I can't even see what you say Hephaestos perceives in Kabeiros. I can light this cavern. I can walk through stone and mold it in my hands, but I know no spell that could free Kabeiros."

"Then why is he free in the caves of the dead?" Hekate whispered.

"I can't tell you that either," Hades admitted with a sigh. "All I can tell you is that in the distant past, in the time of my father Kronos, another people, the Titans, lived in Olympus. They were very skilled in magic and grew more so as time passed."

Hekate nodded. "I am living in the house of one of the Titans. It's as firm and fresh as in those ancient days. There was a stasis spell on it, as good a spell as I have ever seen."

"Yes, they could devise all sorts of spells and never seemed to lack power. This wasn't pleasing to Kronos, who feared they would grow so strong they would dominate or cast out his people. He was wrong. The Titans had no such plans, but Kronos began to torment and oppress the most powerful among them. Some stayed and resisted him–to their destruction–but others slipped away. And some must have come to the caves of the dead."

"Why?" That was Hermes, his eyes alight with curiosity.

"I think because they didn't wish to go far from Olympus. Some leaders, my poor Koios and others, felt they could come to an understanding with Kronos. I suppose those who took to the caves hoped they could return if Koios made peace."

"A triumph of hope over good sense," Hermes said, shaking his head, "considering what I've heard about Kronos. Surely they should have taken the measure of Kronos by then. Hadn't they traveled with him from the north?"

"Perhaps that was why. He was a hero to them, having stood against Uranos, and he had married a Titan."

"Your mother Rhea was a Titan?" Hermes seemed amazed. "Zeus never mentioned that."

Hades shrugged. "I'm sure he wasn't hiding it deliberately. He loved her. She was with him the longest, and in the end she died to protect him. But she had no Talent, I believe, or very little. I suspect it was the greatly Talented that took refuge in the caves, daring to remain close to Olympus in the hope they could regain their homes. But because they feared Kronos, I *think* they cast spells that negated magic."

"Not all magic," Persephone remarked.

"Perhaps only evil magic, although how a spell could determine what is evil, I have no idea. I know that when I fled Kronos, even before I discovered my Gifts, I was safe here. Mostly he could not find me, and once when he did his Gift seemed weak and I was able to slip away from him before he could draw out my warmth."

"That must be true," Persephone said, her eyes lighting as something that had puzzled her suddenly made sense. "You know that not all of those sacrificed to you are innocent of wrongdoing. There must be some who have spell-cast death or destruction. Yet no one—not one as far as I know—has cast an evil spell in our caves."

Hermes' brows lifted. "You say the dead are all good?"

Hades and Persephone laughed in chorus. "Not at all. There are many, many among us that pray at your shrines, O maker of mischief," Persephone said.

"And rape and murder and adultery . . . alas, I have meted out punishments enough for those." Hades shook his head. "But that is a fascinating idea, a spell with a conscience. Too bad we have no truly great mages among us who could probe this wonder."

"Perhaps Eurydice?" Persephone asked.

"Eurydice?" Hekate echoed. "Do you have a witch called Eurydice among the dead? Oh please, please, may I speak to her?"

"Of course!" Hades exclaimed. "What a fool I was not to think of her at once. Perhaps Eurydice could heal Kabeiros. She is a healer and finder of great power and excellence." He looked over his shoulder. "Acteon, do you know where Lady Eurydice is?"

A horribly scarred man stepped forward. He looked as if half his face had been torn away, and deep bite marks showed on his shoulder and down one arm. Hekate shivered slightly as she took in how many of those in Hades' Court were scarred or broken and twisted. She had a flash of memory of Kabeiros wanting to be invisible so he could protect those being sacrificed to the king of the dead.

"Likely with Orpheus in the cave of the children," Acteon replied. "I'll fetch her out."

While they waited, Hades, Persephone, and Hermes discussed the fascinating possibility of a spell that could determine evil intent, or, if not, how the spell of the ancient Titans worked and why it had not faded. Hekate knew the answer to the last; the caves of the dead were awash with earth-blood power and doubtless the spell was bound to that power, but she said nothing. She was watching for the coming of Eurydice, wondering what kind of woman she was and how to approach her to ask for a spell that must be considered evil.

In following Acteon's path, she had become aware of the immense cavern to which Hermes' leap had brought them. It was so high, she could see nothing but darkness above, but they were not in the dark. The cavern was supported by rows of immense white stone columns, and each of those columms was circled by quite ordinary torches, burning a bright, cheerful yellow that was reflected from the smoothly polished stone and gave a warm sunlit glow to the chamber. Behind them the cavern went back and back until, Hekate thought, there was a stone stair leading upward. There were people, too. Those close to them were listening to the talk, but farther away they seemed to be moving about on their own affairs or talking in groups.

Acteon still had not returned and Hekate felt a sudden qualm. Had the witch detected what she wanted and refused to come? No, that was foolish. More likely, considering the size of this cavern, Acteon had a long way to go. Hekate looked toward her guide and hosts, noticing for the first time the immense chair . . . throne . . . in which Hades sat. Beside it was another, obviously Persephone's, very slightly smaller but even more decorated with carving and jewels.

Behind the thrones were a pair of enormous bronze gates, one side of which was standing open and showing beyond a wide, square corridor in which Hekate could barely make out doorways. That corridor also opened on the side she could see into a passageway with a number of closed doors. One was open; light streamed from it and, faintly, the sound of women's voices.

"Ah, here she is," Persephone said.

Hekate turned quickly in the direction where Acteon had disappeared. Coming toward her was a small girl, quick and light as a bird in her movement. She had curly hair, cut quite short, and large, luminous, dark eyes. Smiling, she came right to the foot of the dais and asked how she could help Hades and Persephone.

"We have a strange problem here, Eurydice," Hades said. "This young man—" he gestured at Kabeiros "—is a shape-shifter, but outside of these caves he is locked into the form of a black dog."

"Locked in?" Eurydice's voice was light as her step, soothing and pleasant. She turned and took Kabeiros' hand. "I never heard of such a thing, but then, I never met a shape-shifter until I came into the underworld." She stared earnestly into Kabeiros' eyes and then shook her head. "I can feel nothing wrong. Your body is sound."

"It is not my body but my organ of power that is affected," Kabeiros said.

Eurydice closed her eyes. After a moment she said, "Yes. Yes. I . . . there is a film, a web . . ." She shuddered and opened her eyes, then suddenly, with a little gasp, let go of Kabeiros' hand and stepped back.

"You know what spell is crippling him, don't you?" Hekate asked softly. "Can you remove it?"

"It shouldn't need to be removed." Eurydice's voice was high and frightened. "It should die of itself. It should never have attached itself to his power." She swallowed. "I have no idea how such a thing happened."

Hekate's heart fluttered. She was torn between hoping that Eurydice was lying about not knowing how the spell could be bound to the power source within a person and knowing that if she was lying she would deny having such a spell. Her only hope of convincing Eurydice to open up to her was to deal with the matter in private. She must convince Eurydice of her need for the spell and the need for Eurydice to remove the spell from Kabeiros, neither of which would be possible if she exposed Eurydice as knowing a draining spell. That knowledge wouldn't be welcome, even in the caves of the dead where the spell probably wouldn't work.

"Eurydice," Hekate said gently, "Kabeiros needs his freedom. He has lived bound to me and to the form of a dog for a very long time. Won't you examine his problem and see if you can devise a spell that will remove this curse from him?"

"I never devised a spell in my life," Eurydice breathed, large eyes even larger with fright. "My finding and my healing, those are Gifts. And I have the power to work magic spells also, but I can only use those I have learned. I . . . I don't know *how* to devise a spell."

Hekate smiled. "That I can teach you, if you are willing to learn. Will you come aside with me and Kabeiros? I fear we have already taken far too much of Lord Hades' and Lady Persephone's time. I can see their people are growing impatient for their attention."

"Not impatient," Hades said. "The dead are very patient, but they have their problems, as do those of the upper world and to each his own problem is the most important. Eurydice, you know you are free here to do as you please. Are you willing to go aside with Hekate and Kabeiros?"

"Oh, yes," Eurydice said, her voice stronger. "If I can help, of course I must."

"And if you need power, child, you only need to tell me," Persephone said, "and I will feed you."

Hekate wondered who could need power when the whole cavern was nearly drowned in it, but she said nothing. She remembered how surprised Kabeiros had been when she saw the veins of earth-blood in the other caverns so long ago, and remembered also that the Olympians didn't seem aware of the sea of earth-blood in which they lived. Perhaps it was just as well. She shuddered to think what Olympians would do with unlimited power. Then she remembered something else, that Hermes had brought them and might well be growing impatient, not being one of the dead.

She looked around for him and saw him talking earnestly to Acteon. "I'm sorry to keep you so long, Hermes," she said, coming close and touching his arm. "Can I use your spell to leap home from here? If so, you need not wait for me and Kabeiros. We will be a while longer, I fear."

"It doesn't matter," Hermes said. "Acteon tells me that a saurima has been bedeviling the moss gatherers in one of the upper caverns, so a-hunting we will go. If you get hungry or thirsty, Hades will arrange for food and drink from the upper world to be brought to you. They have a store of such things for invited guests."

Hekate nodded, thanked him, and said that when he wanted her he would find her in Eurydice's quarters. Then she went back to where Eurydice and Kabeiros waited. He was assuring her that he didn't blame her for his plight.

"It was a man who cast the spell on me," he said, "and Hekate thinks that he may have done something even more foul. He may have stolen the body of a younger man and sent that man's spirit to perish in his outworn flesh."

"That is terrible, terrible," Eurydice whispered. "Oh, sometimes I understand why the Greeks hate magic so. It must seem to them that the only safety lies in extirpating the ability completely."

"Throwing out the baby with the bath water?" Hekate suggested, smiling. "By destroying all magic, they also destroy healing, which does much good."

She won a small smile from Eurydice, who then led them to the right and back behind the dais to enter the open side of the bronze gate. To the right was that gleam of brighter light that betokened an open door; women's voices and laughter came from there. Hekate's head turned in that direction, but Eurydice touched her arm and led her to the left.

"Arachne and her weavers are in those rooms. They seldom close the door when Hades holds court." Eurydice smiled a small, mischievous grin. "I think they have a few very keen-eared women and they listen to what goes on."

"It hardly seems worthwhile," Hekate said. "The court is open. Why not attend it if they're curious?"

Eurydice shrugged and grinned. "Perhaps it makes them seem more mysterious . . . you know, shut away weaving but they still know everything." Hekate laughed and Eurydice smiled again. Pointing to the door to the corner room, she added, "Koios' chamber. It is closest to Hades' own rooms, which are down the square corridor we passed. He is so crippled, poor Koios. Sisyphus is next, but he is rarely here."

"Sisyphus." Hekate frowned. "I've heard that name."

"Oh, yes. He got into a terrible quarrel with Zeus and . . ." She stopped, folded her lips, went on. "He's much better off here. He's the chief miner, and aside from Hades telling him what ores are in greatest demand he does pretty much as he pleases. Mostly he lives near the mines. Orpheus and I are at the far end so Orpheus can practice. In the beginning, we were out in the general living quarters, although near the great hall so I could be summoned for healing, but everyone stopped what they were doing to listen every time Orpheus began to play, so Hades moved us in here."

She opened the door as she spoke. Hekate stepped in and then aside, Eurydice followed, touching a column of stone near the door that immediately came alight. Last came Kabeiros who shut the door behind them. Eurydice spoke a soft word, and a myriad of tiny sparks lit the ceiling. The room was now bright as day.

"How lovely," Hekate said.

"Hades sets the spell, but I don't know what kind of spell–there don't seem to be any special commands or symbols–and then a key word is all one needs to cause the lights to come awake."

"That's the way it is for all magic that comes from a Gift," Hekate said.

Eurydice smiled again, gesturing toward a small table with a polished top that had four stools around it, and said, "Sit, please."

On the other side of the small room two comfortable chairs with leather seats and backs faced each other, but there were only two, and Hekate understood why Eurydice had chosen the stools around the table. She went to one. Eurydice sat next, and Kabeiros sat next to her, across from Hekate.

"I know the draining spell too," Hekate said softly.

Eurydice drew a sharp breath and hugged her arms around herself. "I never told anyone. And I never used it, except that once. Never."

Hekate nodded acknowledgement and acceptance.

"I believe you, or you wouldn't be so beloved of Hades and Persephone. I have never used it either. But I also got the spell from Baltaseros or, I should say, from his grimoire."

"Then you know everything about the spell that I do, Lady Hekate." Eurydice shivered. "He was draining me. You don't know how terrible that is."

Only Hekate did know. She had seen it happen to her mother, seen her life drawn out of her drop by drop until poor Asterie was no longer really a person. But she didn't speak, not wanting to distract Eurydice.

"He found me in a village not far from Lysamachia," the girl continued, eyes fixed on her knotted hands on the table. "And he told me he would make me his apprentice and teach me much magic that I didn't know. I went with him, like a fool, all unwarded. And he put a compulsion on me so that I couldn't leave and whenever he needed more power, he drained me. He–" she lifted her dark eyes and they glittered with rage and revulsion "–he forced me into his bed too."

Hekate covered Eurydice's hands with her own and Kabeiros leaned forward and patted her shoulder.

"I pretended to be completely broken, following him about and pressing attention and service on him. He liked . . . No, I don't think I need tell you that–"

"I don't think we need to hear it. We met Baltaseros, Kabeiros and I, and know what kind of creature he is."

Eurydice sighed. "He grew accustomed, contemptuous of me, and he was often drunk or drugged and careless. I found the grimoire." She hesitated, almost smiled. "It had some very good spells in it–a freezing spell that I have often used. It is wonderful if one must set a bone or cut out a putrid place. The victim never feels any pain. And a look-by-me spell . . . And then I found the draining spell."

She fell silent, her face white, her lips dry.

"And you had to get away. And you used it on him. I don't blame you, Eurydice, but I need to know–I will tell you why before you tell me. I need to know how you made the draining spell permanent. All these years–ten? twenty?–and Baltaseros still has no more power than the totally unTalented. He knows the spells, but he cannot even light a candle with magic."

"No," Eurydice cried, shaking her head. "I didn't. I swear I didn't. I used the spell just as it was in the grimoire . . . oh, I think I did. I was so frightened and in such pain. He was mounted behind me, hurting me dreadfully, making me grip him so he could thrust harder . . . and I just said it. I said it twice . . ." Her voice broke and she began to sob. "Oh, poor Baltaseros. He was disgusting, horrible, but I never meant to punish him so dreadfully as that. I just meant to drain him so deeply that he would be unable to pursue me for a few days, and then I ran south, into the Cheresonesos and there I met Orpheus and found a new life."

"Do you remember the spell you spoke, Eurydice?"

The girl looked at her with haunted eyes. "How could I forget?" she whispered.

Hekate sighed. "I know the spell from the grimoire and I know it exactly. I . . . There is a compulsion on me that prevents me from ever forgetting a spell. Tell me the spell you used so I can see in what way the spells differ or if it was the double casting that made the difference . . ."

Eurydice withdrew her hand from Hekate's clasp and cast an angry glance at Kabeiros. "No! It is bad enough to drain the power from a person, but to do so forever . . . No. I won't help you do that!"

"It's nothing to do with Kabeiros," Hekate said hastily. "We aren't seeking revenge for the hurt done him, I swear it."

"Then why is he here?" Eurydice asked coldly.

Hekate blinked. "He is here because we are always together." She had to stop for a moment and swallow as the thought came that free, he would leave her. "And because I knew you had the spell and thought you might know a way to remove it as well as cast it."

"I told you," Eurydice said. "I only know spells I have been taught. There was no removal spell in the grimoire, and why should there be? The draining only lasts as long as one embraces the victim. When caster and victim part, the victim slowly recovers . . ." She looked stricken. "Or so I thought." She closed her eyes, drew a deep breath. "I always recovered when he left me."

"So it seemed to me it would be from reading the spell and from studying its parts. Naturally I haven't cast it. But I need a spell that . . . from which the victim will never recover."

"No!" Eurydice said, leaning away from them.

"It's not for myself. I don't want the power!" Hekate shuddered and swallowed sickly. "It's blood-magic power. I couldn't bear it."

"Hekate," Kabeiros said. "Begin at the beginning and tell her."

She looked at him, face pallid.

"No child is responsible for its parents," he said with a half smile.

"There is a very, very strong and very, very evil sorcerer in a land called Ka'anan. That man was my father . . . *is* my father . . ." Hekate began.

She told Eurydice how Perses had drained her

mother, what he had planned to do to her so that she had been forced to flee and take sanctuary in the caves of the dead where she had met Kabeiros and why many years later they had returned to the caves of the dead, what she discovered Perses had done to seize power in Byblos, and for a long time how he had seemed to be satisfied but that he now planned to slaughter at least a hundred people to drink their life-force so he could prolong his own life in the stolen body of an innocent.

"I cannot permit that. I cannot! Still, he is my father," Hekate concluded. "I cannot simply kill him, nor can Kabeiros kill him for me—the Kindly Ones are too clever to be deceived by such a ruse. All I can do is take away his power and any ability that he might in the future regain his power, which will render him harmless. I beg you to help me, Eurydice. I swear on my poor mother's soul, on my favor from the Mother of us all, on whatever you wish me to swear on, that I will never use the spell on any other person or being, or that, if a case equally monstrous arises that would necessitate its use, that I will come here and explain to you and gain your permission before I use the spell."

In the beginning Eurydice had listened almost in silence, except for a brief expression of dismay now and again. However, toward the end of the tale, she had begun to look very thoughtful.

"You say that now this Perses plans to slaughter hundreds to prolong his life and you cannot bear it, but he has already done so one or two at a time and you . . . looked the other way. Why is this different?"

Hekate stared at the seemingly young woman, her short curly hair and soft mouth childlike, her luminous eyes sad . . . old . . . but she didn't speak. Only what little color had been in her face as she told her story drained away. The hand lying on the table trembled; Kabeiros put his over it firmly.

"You are a very powerful mage," Eurydice added softly. "You know more magic and in some ways have more power than the gods of Olympus. Zeus himself does your bidding without argument and has made no attempt to drive you out, although I know that Zeus does not love magic. So why have you watched your father torture and destroy . . . hundreds . . . over the years and done nothing? Because they were themselves evil? Did their crimes make his less? But many were not evil. Many were only poor and helpless–"

"Stop," Kabeiros said, getting up and going to where he could stand beside Hekate and put an arm around her. His eyes were very bright, fixed on Eurydice, his lips drawn back, and his voice carried a touch of the snarl of an angry dog. "She has helped as many as he has hurt. And it was only a little time ago that we found the spell for which she had searched since she fled Perses."

Eurydice blinked at him. "I don't hurt unless I must to heal," she said. "I cause pain when I treat a wound or set a broken limb. But my purpose is to help."

"Because I am afraid," Hekate said. She clutched Kabeiros' arm tighter around her, shivering. "Don't tell me it's ridiculous. Do you think I don't know it? I know how strong I have grown both in power and knowledge. And you are right, Eurydice. I don't fear Zeus or any of the other Olympians. Oh, I know that if they combined they could overwhelm me, but I also know that if I give them no reason to hate me, they will leave me in peace. Perses would not."

"No, but there is only one of him," Eurydice said.

"And I will be there, Hekate," Kabeiros promised, leaning down as if he would enfold her with his body. "I will savage him, distract him. And Dionysos will cloud his mind with panic."

"You are speaking reason," Hekate cried, pushing back the stool and getting to her feet, turning and trying to shrink more deeply into Kabeiros embrace. "In this there is no reason." Her wild cry sank to a whisper as she admitted, "I am afraid! I am afraid! And if I fear, my spells will fail . . . I will forget them . . . I will misspeak them so they lash back at me." She turned in Kabeiros' arms to face Eurydice again, screaming, "Don't you understand? *I am afraid.*"

"Yes," Eurydice said softly. "I do understand. Some healings take me too deep and I fear I will lose myself, so I understand. But now it is too late for you to find other reasons to avoid a confrontation. You must face that fear and master it." She paused and looked down at her own hands, knotting and unknotting on the table. Then she said, "Some day you will. Sit down, and I will give you the spell that I used against Baltaseros."

CHAPTER 25

With considerable mental agility Hekate managed to avoid thinking about what Eurydice had forced her to expose. She had always admitted that she was afraid of her father; she had said so to Kabeiros several times over the years. Perses was a great mage and only the worst kind of fool would not fear him. She had admitted being afraid of Medea and cautious about Aietes and the Olympians. What she had not admitted was that the fear of Perses went much deeper. It was like a black fungus growing in every hidden corner of her soul.

Some day she would have to confront him . . . Yes, but that day wasn't yet and she filled her mind with peripheral matters–not so far from the confrontation with Perses as to rack her with guilt, but far enough away that the dread moment still seemed quite distant.

First, of course, was the spell itself. Hekate compared what Eurydice had told her line for line with what came from Baltaseros' grimoire. The words were the same. The symbols were the same. The only difference Hekate could find was that owing to pain and fear Eurydice had three times broken the spell by hesitations almost long enough to spoil it and make it backlash. And, of course, she had repeated it twice, the second time without pause because Baltaseros was already feeling the effects and his rape had stopped.

Hekate racked her brains for a way to test her ideas. Obviously, one couldn't find a human subject for such an experiment, not even an animal subject—if animals cast spells. She conceived of the notion of setting the spell she had for gathering energy into a figurine, allowing a pool of power to infuse the figure, and then draining it. It was not a difficult idea to conceive of; making it work was considerably more complicated and took several ten-days.

She had just about solved that problem—with several refinements, too . . . not that she was wasting time, not at all. How could she know what she would need to be prepared against? It was nearly time to begin actually testing the draining spell when Dionysos came to her with a very complex problem.

Ariadne, his high priestess and the woman he loved, was a true Mouth for his Visions and was able to control him when he was about to loose rage and panic. He needed to have Ariadne live with him in Olympus, but she had a half brother who was, poor creature, a feeble-minded monster with a bull's head welded to a man's body. This creature had run amok and killed several people, and his father and mother wished to confine him so he could do no more harm.

The trouble was that Ariadne had a most tender heart and having cared for the Minotaur all his life could not agree with her father who had been ready to bury the bull-head in an underground prison. A servant of her father's had proposed to build instead a maze, where the Minotaur would be able to walk free, see the sky, and enjoy little gardens. However, no merely physical maze would be enough; the creature was not only incredibly strong, but already enormous and might grow more. The maze would have to be magical and also be sealed so the Minotaur could not escape.

Could Hekate add magical twists and turns? magical strength to the walls? seal it? Could she lock those magical ways, strength, and seals into some unlimited power, as she had the illusion in the valley of the Nymphae, so the spells wouldn't need renewal? If she could do that for him, Dionysos said, Ariadne would agree to come to Olympus and the excesses of his "blessing of the vineyards" would be over.

It was then that Hekate truly realized that her bond to Dionysos was gone. The binding was broken. She was free . . . but so was he! He was a man, not a boy, and Ariadne was now the balance wheel that would keep him steady. She would lose him, too, she thought. Who or what was this Ariadne? But she didn't want to know. If the woman could give him peace, she must let Dionysos go. She had never been able to give him peace.

She pulled her mind away from the black emptiness that loomed ahead of her. "It isn't a question of my strength," she said slowly. "It's a question of how much earth-blood I can reach to power the spells. And the illusions, which must shift and change . . . This is no small project you are proposing to me."

Dionysos grinned at her. "*I* was no small project and you have brought me nearly to completion now. Think how bored you will be when I am not running wild and causing riots and bloodshed. A nice quiet maze with a monster in it should be just a light amusement for you."

Hekate couldn't help laughing. "I will go and look over the ground and see whether it is possible at all."

"Come and meet Ariadne. She will be able to explain better–"

"No," Hekate interrupted, concealing panic. "I must see for myself without any shadows in my mind."

Dionysos shrugged. "You know best. And, besides, we have that business with your father to settle." The good humor left his expression and his eyes brightened dangerously. "I am looking forward to that. The sooner the better. He has caused you much pain, Hekate . . . and you are dear to me."

He took her hand, squeezed it, put it to his lips, and was gone from the chamber. Hekate stood up, staring after him. He had never done anything like that before, never shown the least sign that he was aware of the burden he was to her or that he had any special affection for her.

He is growing up, the black dog said, lifting his head from his paws where he lay beside her chair.

"He mustn't come." Hekate's voice was choked with panic. "He has no real wards against magic. Perses could harm him, kill him. He is just beginning his real life."

Will you make him carry his debt to you through that whole life?

Hekate felt as if a knife had lodged in her throat. Was that how Kabeiros felt? Crushed beneath a weight of debt? No wonder he wished to be free of her. She must test her spell and go to face her father in Ka'anan. If she died or was destroyed in mind if not in body, at least Kabeiros would be free. And truly free. He need not live alone in the caves of the dead in Ka'anan to remain a man. He could live with Hades and

Persephone. He could have friends, hunt, use his magic . . . find a woman to love.

A woman to love among the dead? Hekate wondered at the thought and then sighed. There could be a woman. The dwellers in the underworld were only dead to the upper world. Eurydice's hand had been as warm and firm as her own. She remembered Hermes' arm resting on Acteon's scarred shoulder. That was no wraith but solid flesh. Those sacrificed to the king of the dead were living and could be hurt, which was why Kabeiros had wanted to protect them. And she could not imagine the sacrifices being killed by any order of Lord Hades, whose kindness was palpable. So they were alive and she must stop using Kabeiros' need of her as an excuse to avoid confronting Perses.

She began to work on the draining spell again, testing the figure that was drawing power, drawing power from it in small amounts using the spell as it was written, then checking to see that the power was building up again in the figurine. That went well, but when it came to trying the spell in its most dire form . . . she couldn't. She stumbled over the timing, stumbled over the words–she who had never stumbled over a spell in her life. The servants cowered in their quarters as the house rang with thunderclaps of power gone awry, and more than once Hekate took to her bed suffering the pain and debility of backlash.

Eventually Kabeiros stopped her. *What a fool you are!* he snapped, snapped literally because his jaws opened and closed within a hairsbreadth of her arm while he thought at her. *First you idle away weeks refining a spell that doesn't need embellishment, then you fix so hard on polishing this stupid spell, which I am sure will pour out of you perfectly when you need it, that you make yourself stale. Enough.

If you aren't ready yet to do what you must, let's go look at Crete and see if you can create what will be necessary to hold this Minotaur.*

Hekate agreed meekly. She had met Ariadne briefly when she came for a visit to Olympus, and in her presence Dionysos was a different person. His eyes did not stare, violence did not seethe behind his smile. Her servants, accustomed to her calm, always reacted badly to Dionysos. With Ariadne beside him, they didn't tremble and wince away, extending a tray at arm's length when summoned to bring wine and cakes. The madness that had shimmered around him more and more was gone. It was time, Hekate knew, for Ariadne to take up permanent residence in Dionysos' house, so the Minotaur had to be contained.

Hermes took her to the great palace at Knossos so she could see the maze Daidalos was creating. The first step was complete when she found more than enough earth-blood pulsing through thick arteries in the ground. The danger here was that the earth would rise and shake and the spells would be broken free. But since that violent a shaking—and Hekate saw that such had happened in the past—would almost surely kill everyone, the monster included, she set the worry aside.

Marking the real walls, she planned those that would be illusion. Kabeiros seemed to enjoy the temporary illusions Hekate created for the Minotaur's maze. He tested the magical pathways by sight and sound and scent. He was so plainly having a good time that Hekate allowed herself to take pleasure in her work. She set the spells and polished her plans so that when Daidalos' work was done she would only need a few hours to complete her part. Dionysos could carry the spell to dismiss and invoke the maze to Ariadne and she could transfer it to whoever else was necessary.

She and Kabeiros, perhaps closer than they had been since outside threats were gone and they settled into safe and comfortable residence in Olympus, were head-bent together over a chart of the maze. "The hardest part," she was saying, "will be to make the spell sense when the beast needs a change and open a new pathway. I will need—"

Her voice broke off as hurried steps sounded in the entrance corridor and Dionysos burst through the archway. "The king of Byblos is dead!" he cried. "Seventy days for drying the corpse. That's all we have, and you cannot carry both me and Kabeiros if you leap to Ka'anan. We must leave at once, Hekate."

"Yes," she said, standing up, one hand on the table to steady her. "We must leave at once. You can leap to Memphis, can't you, Dionysos? Or will Hermes take you? I can carry Kabeiros that far. There we can take ship for Byblos."

"I'll get Hermes," Dionysos said, dashing out again.

The black dog looked up at Hekate. *How did he know the king was newly dead and that we had all seventy days to travel?*

I would imagine the news was passed from one of his temples in Ka'anan on to some priestess whom Bacchus was able to scry. He's not good for much, that Bacchus, but he is a powerful scryer. He can even bring aloud what is said, if he tries hard.

Her thought was intent, as if what she said was of utmost importance instead of just babble to fill a silence into which shrieks of terror might erupt. Kabeiros gave her no time to think longer. *Trade metal,* he said, *and the little figure. We should take that, too. Will you need clothing?*

No. I'll dress as an Egyptian. Egyptian women take part in trade and are much freer than those of Ka'anan. If I take trade metal I can buy what I need in Memphis.

Except a dark skin.

You want me to have more to worry about?

Yes, Kabeiros said, lolling out his tongue. *Real worries you can solve will benefit you.*

He needed to say no more to distract her because Hermes and Dionysos appeared in the middle of the reception room floor. A flurry of activity followed—Dionysos rushing home to get trade metal for himself; Hermes flashing back to his house for the mask of Anubis when he realized they were going to Egypt; Hekate packing the figurine that pulsed with power again after its last draining. Then they were all assembled. Hekate slipped her pack over her shoulders, grasped Kabeiros, and laid her free hand on Hermes' shoulder. He extended a hand to Dionysos . . . They touched utter lightlessness, utter cold, and all stood together in the inner chamber of a deserted house in Memphis.

As soon as they were all steady on their feet, Hermes raised a hand in farewell and slipped out into the empty courtyard, his black jackal head silhouetted for one moment against a pale garden wall. Then he was gone. Hekate stared into the empty courtyard for a long moment.

"I wouldn't have let him come with us in any case," she said, "but that Hermes of himself could resist sticking his nose into someone else's affair is very strange. Do you think in his travels Hermes could have heard rumors of how powerful and dangerous . . . 'he' . . . is?"

Hekate didn't think the words "Perses" or "father." They weren't close but there were no shields on the building in which they arrived and she feared such personal references might resonate into some otherplanar place and draw attention.

"Not from me," Dionysos said, a shade defensively. He wasn't very good at keeping secrets.

Kabeiros laughed into their minds. *Oh, no. It was Hekate herself who convinced Hermes that this business is no jest and might end ill for anyone connected with it.*

"Me?" She was astonished. "I never said a word to Hermes about . . . 'him.' "

There was no need for words. Kabeiros laughed harder. *All Olympus keeps track of what you do and everything you say, and your feeling about . . . that one . . . is known. Since even Zeus fears you—*

"I've given him nor anyone else any reason to fear me!" Hekate snapped.

No, you're right. It isn't fear. Perhaps it would be better to say they are in awe of you and what you do, the dog continued. *To Hermes' mind, anything you fear is too big a mouthful for him to chew . . . And in a place where he has no near homepoints to leap to, he might well be caught and mangled.*

Hekate shook her head and sighed. "Well, I'm glad he's gone. That's one less I have to worry about. Dionysos, have you been practicing those shields I taught you?"

"Oh, yes. I'll be able to raise them when I need them, but now is too soon, and I'm hungry. Let's stop standing in this empty room."

He's not so grown up, Hekate thought, that he doesn't need to eat all the time. The thought made her swallow and wonder if she had done right in listening to Kabeiros. Perhaps it would have been better to leave Dionysos with his burden and keep him safe. But she said nothing. It was too late; she only agreed that they should find a place to eat and to stay while they arranged passage to Byblos.

That was not difficult. All the goods traders had gathered over the winter was ready to be shipped north along the coast in exchange for lumber and copper. Although the ships didn't leave every day, the travelers actually had a choice of vessels and chose a sturdy ship with a clever captain scheduled to arrive in Byblos a ten-day before the summer solstice–and fifteen days before the funeral of the king.

Indeed, at first the captain of the ship had believed they were traveling to attend the funeral. Before she thought, Hekate denied it emphatically, asking, "Whose funeral?" in an attempt to conceal her purpose of interfering with the rite. Then she was annoyed with herself because to have agreed would have provided a reason for their journey. However, the captain was too polite to ask her business and her instinctive desire to separate herself from the funeral turned into a marked benefit. Assuming them ignorant, the captain was delighted to discuss the topic at great length.

The king had died, he told them, and good riddance for he was cruel, corrupt, and unjust. He had been that way from childhood, as had been his father, both ruined by an evil advisor. Hekate nearly held her breath to hear the man so casually blame Perses for Byblos' ills. And then the reason followed for the captain's freedom of speech. The advisor, accordng to the captain, was gone–he hoped dead.

The advisor had been ancient, the captain explained, old in the king's father's time. When this king sickened, it seemed the advisor had at last felt the weight of his years. He had taken a young apprentice, and more and more it was the apprentice who fulfilled the advisor's duties. And when all hope of the king's recovery had been abandoned, the advisor had announced that he was exhausted by his efforts to save the king. He would leave the funeral arrangements in the hands of his apprentice while he rested and restored his strength in his residence at Ur-Kabos.

To say the least, Hekate, Kabeiros, and Dionysos had been amazed at this information. None of them really believed it, but the tale was consistent no matter to whom they spoke. Kabeiros also picked up some extra information deemed unsuitable to be disclosed to foreigners by developing a fondness for the captain's company and sitting at his feet whenever he was off duty and relaxing with Ka'ananite passengers or the other ship's officers.

Among many private matters, which he ignored, and some financial ones that he stored in his mind to tell Dionysos for Hermes, Kabeiros learned that aside from feeling the funeral celebration was too extravagant, the Ka'ananites were not afraid. They suspected nothing of Perses' plans; one even had a relative who would go into the tomb and showed no concern. They complained of the expense, nothing else.

The blame for the costly plans was fixed on the advisor. All also agreed that the advisor's plan should have been abandoned now that he was gone. That it had not been was the fault, except that it was mentioned with a kind of affectionate tolerance, of the young prince and attributed to his foolish sentiment and lack of experience. Plainly the Ka'ananites had high hopes for the young prince, who, according to the bits and pieces they told each other, had been totally ignored by the king and his advisor and had grown up in the care of servants relatively untainted by the viciousness of the older men.

In the privacy of a tent-like draping of blankets

in their corner of the deck, Hekate mentally insisted that she couldn't believe it. It was incredible to her that *he* would fail to seal the prince to his own purposes. Utterly ridiculous. If he was planning to renew his life by stealing the apprentice's body, he would need to control the next king. Dionysos suggested cheerfully that *he*, wishing to deny he was ageing, might have waited too long. Perhaps the "old man" was simply failing. For a little while a hope rose in Hekate, but she suppressed it because it was dangerous to have a hope that permitted underestimation of her opponent.

There was little sense in dwelling on facts that would only become clear when they arrived in Byblos, so mostly they talked about what to do there. First, Hekate would establish herself as an Egyptian dealer in medicinal herbs and spices. Under that guise it would be easy enough to inquire about the death of the king, the preservation of the body, the rites to be observed at his obsequies. Meanwhile Kabeiros and Dionysos, neither of whose auras Perses could possibly know, could try to determine where he really was.

The ship set them safely on the dock in Byblos well within the promised dates, twelve days before the summer solstice and seventeen days before the funeral rites would begin. The first part of Hekate's plan was easily implemented and, to her amazement, what they had learned aboard ship seemed to be the truth. Screwing her courage to the sticking point, Hekate actually approached the advisor's palace. It was still shielded too well for her to feel passively any magic within, although the shields were wearing thin. She could not bring herself to probe the place actively; those shields had been constructed by Perses, but it was too dangerous to try to discover whether he was hiding behind them.

Still, they had to know. After much argument, Hekate was forced to agree that Kabeiros should try to get inside. If he smelled Perses, he would escape immediately; if the sorcerer truly wasn't in the palace, he would try to gauge the quality of the apprentice.

Following close on the heels of a butcher delivering meat, Kabeiros gained entrance without the slightest difficulty. He was shocked at the laxity and dullness of the servants. They did smell of a foul magic but the smell was old, and they were like ill-controlled automata. Even when one looked directly at him, he showed neither emotion or curiosity about the huge black dog that had appeared in the kitchen quarters, and allowed Kabeiros to escape into the main house without outcry. After that, Kabeiros went on with some confidence that all the rumors were true and Perses had left Byblos or lost his power. The man Hekate feared so much wouldn't have barely functioning servants.

He investigated the whole house, smelling for magic and found only old traces, like those of the compulsion on the servants. Fresh magic only wafted from one room–and that room was neither locked nor bespelled. Work with jaw and paw on the latch let Kabeiros enter what had obviously been a sorcerer's workroom, although little sign of real magical apparatus remained. The spell smell was concentrated on a single medium-size amphora, both capped with wax and sealed with magic. There was also a hidden power source.

Then, as he was about to slip out of the door and leave, the apprentice entered the room. Unable to escape, Kabeiros abased himself, wagging his tail and fawning on the young man, who greeted him with about equal surprise and delight. Kabeiros' suprise and delight were much stronger; he had known that the apprentice had little Talent, but he hadn't known that the boy was a total blockhead. Even a stupid apprentice should be alarmed by discovering a large dog in his workroom. Kabeiros could only conclude that the boy had been selected for his perfection of Ka'ananite beauty, not Talent or brains.

Of course, whatever wits the boy had had might have been addled by the powerful compulsion spell he carried–and that, unlike the servants' spells, was working perfectly. The apprentice stank of magic, but not his own, and the compulsion spell might have made him even duller than he was naturally. Fortunately, the compulsion did not seem to cover the appearance of nonhuman creatures in the workroom.

Fawning on the boy gave Kabeiros license to stay close to his "new master." In the three days he remained in the palace he learned the entire progression of the rites and who would do what when. Court functionaries came and went–perhaps fifteen all together–and every one of them was also bound by a compulsion spell. No wonder Perses could leave his apprentice alone to carry out his orders. Moreover, when giving those orders, the apprentice seemed to come alive, to speak in a different, richer voice. Internally Kabeiros shrank into a hard protective ball. The apprentice was, at those times, seemingly under the direct control of Perses.

The compulsion, or whatever spell it was that controlled the apprentice, was incredibly detailed and seemed to have an answer for every contingency. Kabeiros panted a little with anxiety; this spell, as intricate as anything Hekate herself had devised, was evidence of the mage Hekate feared. About the only thing Perses had not foreseen was the advent of a large black dog carrying a man's mind.

After the apprentice was asleep on the third night,

Kabeiros crept away, waited until a servant needed to use the privy, and escaped into the night. He felt a little sorry for the apprentice, who was plainly very lonely and had showered him with affection, but since it was partly on his account they were thrusting themselves into danger, he went without reluctance. However, had he known how he would be greeted on his return to Hekate's lodging, he might have stayed the night.

When Kabeiros did not return the night of the day he went to the advisor's palace, Hekate went half out of her mind with fear and regret. Before he could even have reached the advisor's palace, she had begun to lash herself for Kabeiros' imagined suffering and death because she let him go. Free of guilt, Dionysos pointed this out, laughing at her and assuring her that Kabeiros was strong and clever and well able to fend for himself.

When night fell Hekate cried she couldn't bear waiting any longer and readied herself to go after him. Again Dionysos held her back, reminding her that Kabeiros had said he might not find any opportunity to get into the place during the day. Hekate had cast an angry glance at Dionysos, but she hung up the thin black cloak she had removed from its hook and sat down where she could look out of the window. Knowing how she felt, Kabeiros had extracted a promise from her not to interfere within a reasonable time.

In case he could not get past servants or guards during the day, Kabeiros had said, he would wait for night and try to squeeze past someone going to the privy, enter with someone returning, or slip in while doors and windows were checked for security. Since he didn't expect to learn much with everyone asleep, he would probably stay the following day.

"And you know, he could even get locked in a second night," Dionysos warned. "For the Mother's sake, Hekate, you will put him in more danger by going there. When Kabeiros traveled with me and we got into trouble, it was more often Kabeiros who found a way out than I. He's very clever. Don't . . . don't treat him as if he *were* a dog."

That silenced Hekate. She knew how hurt Kabeiros felt when she tried to protect him, as if he were less than a man because he wore the form of a dog. And although she grew more and more frightened as the hours of the second day passed and she saw that Dionysos was also growing uneasy, she still did nothing. It was too late to do anything about Kabeiros anyway. Either he was free and trying to learn as much as he could and would be furious if she interfered, or he had been caught by Perses that first day and was dead or in Perses' power.

Grief and terror distilled themselves all through that day and the sleepless night that followed into a rage so white-hot that on the morning of the third day she seemed to have found an icy calm. Only Dionysos who knew her so long realized she was no longer rational. He wasn't wise in magic, but he knew that was no way to confront a clever sorcerer and he managed to get across to her the fact that the only one who would benefit if she attacked Perses unprepared was Perses. Nor could it do Kabeiros any good if she were dead or also bound to Perses' will.

"We have planned what to do when there were three of us," he said. "Now you must think of how to manage when there are only two. I can threaten you-know-who physically at the same time that I try to confuse his mind, but my threat will not be as startling as that of a huge black dog. Think, Hekate, how to make me more fearsome. An illusion?"

"I have lost Kabeiros." Hekate's voice was flat, as if terror and grief and rage had battled within her until she was emotionless. "I could not bear to lose you also. No, Dionysos, I will go alone."

"To what purpose?" Dionysos asked, cocking his head as if in curious inquiry. "If you just want to be dead, you could jump into the ocean or step in front of a heavy cart. If you want revenge on 'that one,' you must leave him as you told me Baltaseros was. I think if I can distract him long enough for you to lay a hand on him and start the spell, I will be quite safe. I think you said it works very fast."

"The spell!" Hekate stood up like a sleepwalker. "To make him like Baltaseros," she breathed. "Oh, yes. But I need to be able to compress the invocation." She looked at Dionysos and for a moment her grief showed on her face so that she almost took on the appearance of the crone without shifting. "It is too late to save Kabeiros so another few hours cannot matter. You are very right, Dionysos. I need to prepare a few spells and try once again to make the draining spell work the way I want it to work."

At two or three candlemarks after dark, Hekate came out of the inner room and showed Dionysos the little figurine. He hesitated to touch it; in the past it had been so strong a repository of power that it made his fingers tingle. Hekate smiled at him and urged him to take it. It was dead.

"And I cannot make it accept power again, no matter whether I draw from high or low." She smiled. Dionysos shuddered at her expression, which made her laugh. "Come. I'm ready to go now."

"How will we get in at this time of night?"

"I will blast down the door. That should bring 'him' quickly enough—"

"And warn 'him' of attack by an enemy."

Hekate smiled again. "All to the good. He will

think of those enemies who would naturally use violence. He wouldn't expect it of me."

Dionysos shrugged and went to get the two black cloaks. "You know best," he said.

And a dog scratched on the door. The cloaks slipped from Dionysos' nerveless hand and he spun to face the sound. Hekate choked on a sob and rushed toward the door. Dionysos caught her.

"Do you think that is truly Kabeiros?" he whispered.

Tears were now pouring down Hekate's face. "No," she sobbed, "no. But we must let it in to destroy it."

CHAPTER 26

The door was opened. Kabeiros stepped through. If he had come as a man, he would have been dead. The dog's senses were sharp enough to catch a gleam of metal and sense a violent overhand blow directed at him. He leapt forward and sideways, which put him just out of the direct line of Hekate's pointed finger. The spell of dissolution brushed him and he howled. Although he was invulnerable to magic, that spell burned.

What the hell are you doing? he bellowed mentally. *Are you both mad?*

Dionysos, charging forward with his left arm wrapped in the cloaks he had hastily scooped up and his right holding his long knife, tripped over his own feet and fell sprawling as the soundless voice roared into his mind. Hekate had barely time enough to avert her pointing finger. A large hole appeared in the wall above Kabeiros' head.

After the crash of splintering supports and the whoosh of falling remains of mud and withies, a dead silence fell. Kabeiros stood with mouth agape and raised hackles. Dionysos stared up at the dog that could easily have leapt on him and torn out his throat if it were inimical. Hekate sank to her knees, hope and terror making her breath come fast.

"Kabeiros?" she whispered.

How many other black dogs of my size with white eyes have you come across recently? he asked irritably. *Who did you expect?*

I thought . . . he . . . had taken you and sent something in disguse . . . Oh, Kabeiros, is it really you?

For answer, the image of the man with whom both Hekate and Dionysos were familiar rose above the dog. Dionysos climbed to his feet, sheathed his knife, hung up the cloaks again, and seated himself at the table. Hekate burst into tears and crossed the floor on her knees to fling her arms around Kabeiros.

"I thought you were dead," she sobbed. "I thought you were bound in torment."

You don't have much faith in me, do you?

You know that's not true. She sat upright and sniffed. *You know how I feel about . . . him.*

The dog shook himself. *I don't know whether to say you are completely wrong or that you're completely right. I wasn't in that house three days for nothing. One thing is sure, *he* isn't there. I covered the place from the roof to every outhouse. The only ones there are the apprentice and eight servants. And no one has done any magic there for some time, although a source of power exists.*

"Just power? No new spells? And *he* wasn't there!" She shrugged. "Are you hungry, thirsty?"

No. I was fed and overfed. The apprentice fell in love with me . . . poor boy.

"Poor boy! He apprenticed himself to *him*, didn't he?"

I doubt it, Kabeiros said, and went on to tell

them everything, ending, "There's one more very strange thing. Whenever he receives a court official, the apprentice wears a mask.*

"A mask?" Hekate echoed the mental statement aloud.

"What kind of mask?" Dionysos asked. "Is it blank? Is it painted to create awe? Is it terrifying?"

"It's tinted and shaped to the boy's face, but there's no attempt to hide the fact that it is a mask. Nor is there any attempt to use it to frighten or awe. And I can't think why you-know-who should want to hide the boy's face; it's almost a classic Ka'ananite portrait."

Hekate shrugged. "You said his voice when speaking to the officials was deeper and more mature. Perhaps the mask is just to hide how young the apprentice is."

Perhaps. But Kaberiros' mental voice was filled with doubt. *I can't see how it could make any difference. Every one of them is spelled to obey.*

Strong spells? Hekate asked.

Yes, but they're wearing thin. I doubt they'll hold another moon without renewal.

"They won't need to hold as long as that," Hekate said with a slight shiver. "And they won't need renewal. Didn't you say that all those officials are supposed to go into the tomb? If *his* plan works, they'll all die there."

She shivered again and then got to her feet. "Well, you may have been fed, but Dionysos and I are starving. Our appetites were not at their best while you were gone."

The dog lolled out his tongue. *Serves you right. If you were willing to give me the smallest credit for common sense if not for cleverness, you would have eaten and slept. Now, where are you going to get food at this time of night? Do you want me to hunt?*

"That would take hours. No, you don't have to hunt. The food is here."

Hekate left the table and went to a shelf along the wall from which she lifted down a large covered bowl and crock. Dionysos followed her and collected two more bowls and some earthenware plates, which he set on the table. As Hekate dismissed the stasis spell that had kept the food fresh and began to serve herself and Dionysos, she showed Kabeiros each dish. To keep them company, he selected some stew and two slices of fat mutton, which Hekate put on a plate down on the floor. For a while all three ate in silence.

When Hekate refilled their cups with well-watered wine, she said, "Let me see if I have the sequence of the rites clearly in mind. In eight days, the king's body will be placed in its sarcophagus. A procession of all those who will accompany it to the tomb will follow the body to the palace. You-know-who, together with the apprentice and the prince, who will be crowned king after the king's body is entombed, will meet the body and the procession in the great hall of the palace." She frowned. "What will they do there?"

No one mentioned that, Kabeiros said. *I suppose there will be prayers and eulogies.*

"I would think it would depend on the prince," Dionysos remarked indifferently.

"Holy Mother," Hekate breathed, "I wonder if *he* intends to transfer all the spells he laid upon the king to the prince at once? That could be why he didn't bother with the prince before." She blinked. "Is that possible? Would the spells have held after the old man died?"

"You're asking *me*?" Dionysos said, with a laugh. "Kabeiros may know something about magic, but I don't."

I don't know that, Kabeiros said, *but it seems a crazy thing to do before he's in the apprentice's body.*

Hekate sighed. "Yes. We must examine the whole process. To go on: In the great hall, four of the selected attendants will stand vigil a candlemark at a time, until all have served, going to wait with their fellows in a specially prepared chamber. When the last four leave the sarcophagus, it will be carried to the tomb. The funeral goods will then be carried in and placed around the sarcophagus. Finally, the attendants will enter. Each will carry into the tomb a figurine of themselves–"

"So that's why they're all so willing to participate," Dionysos said. "They think they'll leave the figurines in the tomb to attend the dead king in the afterlife."

It must be then that the mass killing will take place, Kabeiros pointed out. *Do you think the figurines are bespelled to kill?*

"I doubt it," Hekate said thoughtfully. "No matter what orders *he* gives–unless all the attendants are under compulsion, and I think that would be too much, even for *him*–there will be some disorder once the attendants enter the tomb. The bolder and more ambitious will probably enter the actual burial chamber to place their figurines on or near the sarcophagus . . . to be first in attendance when the king rises. No, I think it's that golden cup of sacramental wine you mentioned. You said there would be a loud fanfare of horns and they will all drink together. They'll almost certainly do that as ordered– and if we don't stop *him*, they'll all die nearly at once–"

You're right. Kabeiros stood and circled nervously before he sat down again. *That's what must be in that amphora I noticed in the workroom, the one that was sealed with a spell. What a shame I didn't knock it over and break it.*

Hekate shrugged. "If it was that important and the apprentice is as much of an idiot as you think, you wouldn't have been able to knock it over. The spell could have fixed it in place as well as sealing it." She hesitated. "Are you *sure* he isn't there, Kabeiros?"

I am sure he wasn't there until the moment I left the house.

"Then I think I better get in there tomorrow and see if I can make the contents of that amphora harmless. Then, even if . . . if I fail to control him, the spell of transferance will fail. Maybe he'll die . . ."

She thought Kabeiros would object, but he said, *That's a good idea. The servants are little more than bad automata and I think the apprentice will be so glad to see me that I will be able to keep him away from the workroom. Unless what you do to the amphora sets off some alarm . . .*

"That wouldn't matter if *he* is at Ur-Kabos. It's at least a candlemark away, even if *he* gallops a horse all the way."

"But *why* should he go to Ur-Kabos?" Dionysos asked. "It seems mad to go so far from a complicated work-in-progress. Does it occur to you that there is a much more logical place for him to be? The palace itself."

"Oh, dear Mother," Hekate sighed. "How could I be so stupid? He *must* be at the palace. He must be ensorcelling the prince!"

That's all too likely, Kabeiros said, *but there's nothing we can do in the middle of the night. I suppose we should have found an excuse to get inside so you could establish a leaping spot, but we didn't, and truthfully I'm so tired now, I'd be no use.

I'm going to sleep for a while and think about this tomorrow.*

Hekate was herself so exhausted that she found nothing peculiar in Kabeiros' statement or that Dionysos agreed with him at once and went off to his own chamber. She, too, went to bed and was delighted and gratified when the dog leapt up and snuggled down beside her. Soothed and comforted, she drifted asleep, deeper and more quietly asleep than she had slept since working on the Minotaur's maze.

She hadn't known how tired she was, how much she needed sleep, until past noon she was wakened by Kabeiros pulling the blanket off her and poking her with his cold, wet nose.

"What?" she mumbled sleepily.

I know why the apprentice wears a mask, Kabeiros almost shouted into her mind.

"So?" Hekate sat up, yawning, and pulled the blanket back over her. "I'm glad one puzzle is solved."

You won't be when you learn the answer, Kabeiros snapped. *That blockhead with near no Talent was chosen because he's the living image of the prince. I got into the palace early this morning–*

"You did what?" Hekate shrieked.

Be still, Kabeiros said sharply. *I am a man grown and no fool. And if you want to know why I went without telling you, I'm tired of you behaving as if I were a witless dog and trying to stop me from doing what I am peculiarly suited to do by this curse I carry.*

"But–"

But me no buts. There was no danger for me. The worst that could have befallen was that I would be driven out before I learned what I wanted to know, but that didn't happen. I went in before dawn under a delivery wagon. If anyone saw me, they didn't think me important enough to mention. For at least four candlemarks I had the place to myself except for a sleepy guard or two. It's a big palace, but I can smell my own trail so I don't retrace my steps. There's no new magic in the whole mess of buildings.

"No new magic? How can that be?"

The only way I know it can be is that you-know-who isn't there. If he were ensorcelling the prince, I would certainly have smelled that–and I saw the prince. I got quite close to him by sneaking behind the throne. He didn't smell of magic.

*And you're sure there's no magic workroom . . . *

There may be a hidden cellar somewhere. I was down the main cellars with someone fetching wine for fast breaking. I was down the dungeons, which, believe it or not, are totally empty.

Oh, I believe it, Hekate thought back bitterly. *I'm sure within hours of being taken prisoner, no matter how minor the crime, any man, woman, or child ended up yielding up life-force to *him*.*

The dog shivered his skin as if ridding it of pests. *I forgot that.* Kabeiros sighed gustily. *Well, as I said, there may be some hidden place, but I did cover the palace thoroughly and there wasn't a smell of magic except some remnants in the king's apartment. The prince hasn't moved in there yet.*

"No magic," Hekate muttered. "No workroom. Not at his house nor at the palace. Where is he? What is he doing?"

Preparing to change bodies, Kabeiros said. *Don't you see what the prince and the apprentice having virtually one face means?*

"What?" Hekate cried, jerking more upright so that the blanket she had drawn back over her when she sat up fell away from her naked breasts.

Kabeiros looked away. *What do you mean 'what'? It was the first thing I told you when I woke you.*

"Maybe my body was awake, but my mind was still asleep. Anyway I was so shocked at hearing that you went to the palace that everything else went right out of my head. I didn't properly understand . . ."

Her voice faded. Slowly she got out of bed and began her morning activities. She chewed a green twig of lemon and brushed her teeth; she washed her mouth with wine; she washed her face and hands—later on an ordinary day she would have gone to the bathhouse; she drew on an Egyptian robe of thin linen and belted it around her; she combed her hair. Automatically she got the little remaining food from the shelf and ate some hard bread with cheese and olives.

After she had swallowed the last bite, she turned to Kabeiros and said, "Of course there was no need to ensorcel the prince. The prince will die in the tomb with all the others. You-know-who will seize the body of the apprentice using the tremendous outpouring of life-force that the deaths will provide. The old body, the advisor, will also die and will take with it the hatreds that *he* has generated in all these years of evil. The apprentice, wearing the prince's face and clothing and carrying *his* mind and will is the only one who will emerge from the tomb."

I thought so too, Kabeiros agreed, *although I'm not sure exactly how he will explain how he survived.*

"I wouldn't," Hekate said with twisted lips. "I would say something like 'A great force struck me and then I felt a warmth and a pulling and I followed a soft and beautiful light and when I opened my eyes all the others were dead . . .' And maybe some 'oh, woe is me, that I live when all my friends and advisors are gone.' Maybe someone else will come up with an explanation, and what odds do you want to lay that the dead prince's face under the apprentice's mask will have suffered some severe damage."

No odds on a sure thing. Kabeiros shivered his skin again. *Well, at least none of it will happen. Let's wake Dionysos and get to the advisor's house so you can change or destroy whatever is in that amphora.*

"We won't need Dionysos. If *he* isn't there, I don't have to worry about anyone detecting my aura, so no one's mind needs to be clouded. I'll just go in wearing the look-by-me spell. You can stay with the apprentice. Don't try to keep him away from the workroom, just bark when you're outside the door so I know he's coming in and can get out of the way. I'd be interested to see what, if anything, he does with that amphora."

Getting in with the look-by-me spell was easier said than done, however. When she came to the door, Hekate found it blocked. Kabeiros had already trotted through and he stopped halfway across the kitchen to look back at her.

What is it? he asked, coming back to the door.

Warded against magic, she said.

Can't be, Kabeiros said. *All the servants are under compulsion spells and all the officials, too.*

He must have tagged his own spells so the ward recognizes them. I don't have time to try to find the tag and duplicate it. Tell me when the kitchen is clear of servants. I'll just walk in and reinvoke the look-by-me.

It wasn't a long wait, but even after she dismissed the spell that concealed her, Hekate couldn't enter. *Worse,* she said to Kabeiros. *It's warded against those with power. Maybe, if the apprentice's Talent is so weak, against power of a certain level—to keep out other mages, I guess.* She sighed. *I'll have to undo the spell and hope there's no alarm to warn *him*.*

*Can you undo it and then redo it quickly? If you are quick enough, even if there is an alarm, it will appear and disappear so fast *he* might not notice.*

A good thought. I'll try.

Still, it took time to examine the ward, make another as close to the first as possible, dispell the ward, step into the empty kitchen, and reestablish the ward. She could only pray that Perses would not come to this house again, or that he wouldn't bother to check the wards and thus possibly recognize the replaced ward as her work.

Midmorning Hekate finally dimissed Perses' ward, stepped into the kitchen, reinvoked the ward, and then reinvoked the look-by-me spell. She was not quite in time. A dull-eyed servant was in the doorway of the kitchen when her spell took hold. He looked at the empty space beside her for as much as ten heartbeats. Hekate waited for him to cry out, but his gaze slid away to the top of the table, on which he laid the platter he had gone out to get.

Letting her breath trickle out softly, Hekate followed Kabeiros, who had been waiting in the shadowed passageway, to the workroom. For the next few candlemarks, during which she was only trying to understand what spell had been used, she was nearly uninterrupted. The apprentice came to the workroom only once; Kabeiros barked; Hekate dismissed the spells she had been using and backed into an empty corner.

The apprentice entered and to Hekate's and Kabeiros' surprise shut the dog out. He then unlocked a concealed cabinet with a key from around his neck and took from it a short black rod that radiated power. Hekate nodded. The power source Kabeiros had sensed. The apprentice approached the amphora, touched it, and whispered a word Hekate could not catch. Then he whispered again, held the rod against his forehead for a count of ten. Finally he replaced it in the cabinet, relocked it and, smiling, went out to join the dog.

First Hekate had to restrain a sigh of relief when she saw why the spells on the apprentice and the amphora were fresh and strong; her father didn't need to be near to renew them. Then a too-familiar chill ran over her. Her father also had the ability to feed power into an inanimate article and let someone else use that power source. If he knew that, what else . . . She buried that idea, which could only increase her fear, and went back to the amphora.

The spells on it reduced her anxiety again by being very simple. So simple, in fact, that she became acutely anxious and spent several candlemarks studying what scarcely needed half a candlemark's attention. The magical seal was just that, a seal that would prevent anyone from touching the contents of the jar, plus, as Hekate had suspected, a spell for stability, so the jar couldn't be tipped over or moved from where it stood. She could hardly believe that Perses would not take greater precautions.

Then she felt foolish for her doubts. What need was there for greater precaution? No one entered that house except those already under compulsion spells. There was nothing to attract a casual thief to the workroom or the amphora and probably most were too afraid to try to steal from Perses' house anyway. And as for other mages, there were the wards against them, but Hekate suspected they had seldom been tested. The other mages might fear Perses even more than thieves.

The simplicity was deceptive, too, she found. The two spells were twined together. She spent several more candlemarks finding a way to alter the seal spell without touching the stability spell so she could withdraw a sample of the liquid in the amphora. She then carefully smoothed over the breach she had made, hoping, since the spell that held the vessel steady had not been touched, that Perses would simply dismiss both spells together when he came to use the amphora . . . if he survived and she didn't. Hekate took a short, deep breath, held it for a moment and then sent to Kabeiros that she had what she wanted and was leaving.

Go, and quickly, he responded. *Some officials are coming and if we don't need to take the chance they will see us, so much the better. They are compelled to follow *his* plans, but most can still think. I will slip away as soon as they arrive. The apprentice will be too busy until they are gone to miss me. I'll follow you home soon.*

When he arrived, he found Hekate sitting at their table regarding the innocent-looking wine she had brought from Perses' workroom with some puzzlement. The remains of the evening meal she had shared with Dionysos were pushed carefully away to the other end of the table, as far as possible from the small cup she had taken from Perses' house. Dionysos made some sharp remark to Kabeiros about being left out of the "fun" when he let him in, but Hekate didn't look up.

"It's laced with a very virulent poison," she muttered as much to herself as to her companions, although plainly she had been waiting for Kabeiros, "as I suspected it would be, but there's a spell on it too."

"What kind of spell?" Dionysos asked, sitting down at the far end of the table again.

Kabeiros came to sit beside Hekate, but she waved him away. "Just in case it spills or splashes. I think it would work through the skin as well as if swallowed."

"Is it the spell that makes that possible?" Dionysos asked.

That Hermes! Hekate thought. He was infecting her innocent Dionysos with his own insatiable curiosity. On his own, Dionysos had little interest in magic, being content with his own Gifts and the simplest of spells, like making fire and preserving offerings made to him with stasis. She had to grin, suspecting that when they returned to Olympus—a little shiver of fear that she would not see Olympus again ran down her spine, but she ignored it—Hermes would be their first visitor, demanding the tale of their adventures in the greatest detail.

"No, not the spell," she said. "The virulence is the nature of the poison itself. As to the spell . . . it seems to be some kind of youth-preserving spell. What that can have to do with such a poison . . ." She bit her lip, then said, "Catch me a rat, Kabeiros. I want it alive."

Yech! Kabeiros exclaimed, *I hate to catch rats and having one squirming around in my mouth isn't my favorite pastime.* But he rose obediently and Dionysos let him out.

Rats were common enough in the alleys of Byblos and it didn't take long for Kabeiros to find what he wanted. When he returned, the food was cleared from the table and the cup of poison stood alone near Hekate's chair.

Where do you want it? he asked, leaping onto the chair that Dionysos had used so the rat in his mouth was well above the table level.

"There." Hekate pointed almost directly below where he was. "Lift your head high. There are wards." Kabeiros put his front paws on the table and stretched up. "Yes, right there. Drop it."

The rat fell to the table top and lay panting. Its fur was matted and mangy. It had lost an ear and part of its tail. There was an ulcer that had eaten away part of one cheek and other sores on its body.

Dionysos came over and peered down at it. "That's the worst looking rat I ever saw in my life," he said. "And I've seen plenty of them in the storage sheds and vineyards. Actually, they're kind of nice creatures, not vicious if they aren't cornered. I like their beady little eyes and clever ways. If only they weren't so destructive . . ."

Kabeiros was pawing at his mouth. He jumped down and went to his water bowl to lap water and let it run out of his mouth again. *It's the worst tasting one too, but I looked for something that wouldn't mind dying, since I assume Hekate plans to poison it.*

"Yes." She couldn't help smiling at Kabeiros. "If the poison works as swiftly as it should, you will have given the poor creature a 'grace' it surely needs. I hope it has life enough in it to eat."

That's what it was doing when I caught it.

It was, indeed, enough alive to eat and struggled upright when Hekate put into its invisible cage a piece of bread with a few drops of the poisoned wine on it. In fact, despite its dilapidated appearance, the creature had a very healthy appetite. The bread disappeared in a few heartbeats' time. In less time than it took to eat, the rat let out a thin, high screech and began to convulse.

Dionysos stepped back from the table with a look of distress. Hekate was surprised. She had seen him take part in tearing apart alive a human sacrifice–but that was in an orgiastic frenzy, and he had later hated what he had done. Kabeiros lifted his head and shook the remaining water out of his mouth.

"It will be dead in a moment," Hekate assured them.

Only it wasn't dead in a moment. The keening continued. The convulsions intensified until it was clear that the poor rat's bones were snapping in their violence.

Kill it! Kabeiros roared. *Kill it at once!*

Dionysos had already drawn his knife. Shuddering, Hekate dismissed the wards that had confined the rat, and Dionysos cut off its head. In the silence that followed, all three stared at each other with dilated eyes.

"That was what *he* planned for the attendants and officals?" Dionysos breathed. He drew in on himself with horror. "How long . . . ?"

"I don't know," Hekate whispered. Her eyes were full of tears. "That's what the spell did . . . it didn't let the rat die."

What are you going to do?

For a little while, Hekate just stood, staring down into the cup of poison and shivering. Then the shivering stopped. She cocked her head to the side, nibbled softly on her lower lip. Suddenly her eyes lit up and she grinned. "If the poison were destroyed and the spell left intact, what do you think would happen?" she asked.

The dog lolled out his tongue to laugh. *I suppose all those intended victims would live long and healthy lives.*

Dionysos chuckled. "A fitting solution."

"Yes, but I'll need two more rats," Hekate said, her expression alight with mischief. "Only this time, get me two young healthy ones—only be sure they are of the same sex. Mother knows, I wouldn't want those breeding if this spell should happen to be a long-lasting one."

"Why two?" Dionysos wanted to know.

"Well, if I don't get the amount of antidote right or if my memory is at fault about the antidote . . . or if the antidote doesn't work, one might die, but I won't let it suffer. If it shrieks, I'll kill it instantly."

You don't sound very sure about this antidote.

Hekate shrugged. "The poison usually works so fast there's no time to administer an antidote. However, it did work in cases where a person got so tiny a dose that the poison wasn't instantly fatal. It *is* only a rat, after all."

Yes–" the dog managed a comical grimace "–but I have to catch them and bring them back alive.

Two nice, healthy, sleek young rats were soon settled into warded spots on the table–which Dionysos remarked with a wrinkled nose would have to be thoroughly cleaned before they could eat on it again. By the time the second one was imprisoned, Hekate had rummaged through the things she had purchased in her guise as an Egyptian trader in medicinals. There were herbs, there were amulets, there were well-stoppered flasks of many-colored liquids, there were packets of fine-ground solids, some of which looked like sand but smelled quite different. A selection of these now sat on the table not far from Perses' cup of poisoned wine. Hekate sighed with relief.

"I have all that I need," she said. "There's no sense in you both sitting up and watching me prepare the antidote. Probably it will take me all night. Go to bed."

For once neither Dionysos nor Kabeiros argued. They knew they would be of no help and that watching Hekate grind, boil, filter, and mix would be of little interest since neither had the least notion of what she was doing. Dionysos did leave his door open so that he would hear if Hekate called him; Kabeiros merely stretched out on her bed. Once both stirred because of a high-pitched squeal, but the sound stopped so quickly that neither really woke.

In the morning, the poisoned wine was gone from the cup and a slender flask that could be easily concealed within the flowing robes of an Egyptian woman stood beside the empty cup on the table. At the other end, two wonderfully handsome rats groomed their shining fur and wiggled their little pink noses. As Dionysos and Kabeiros approached the table, the rats tensed and ran to hide but the wards confined them, and in a remarkably short time their efforts to escape ended.

"I see you succeeded," Dionysos said, "but are those the same rats? They are elegant, and more than usually clever."

Hekate laughed aloud. "Oh, yes, they're the same. I nearly lost one of them. I hadn't put enough antidote in the wine and the poison started to work, but enough of it had been countered by the antidote that I was able to give more antidote to the rat directly and from that determine how much to put into the amphora. I gave a double dose of the treated wine to the second rat, and he had no ill effects at all."

Good, Kabeiros said. *We should go and put that antidote into the amphora at once. I dreamed all night of that first rat's death throes.*

"I agree," Dionysos said. "And when you return, I think we must make ready to go to Ur-Kabos and see if the one we want is there—although I still don't see why he should be."

"I think I know that," Hekate said, sighing with weariness. "*He* had to bring all his sorcerous equipment back to his old workroom in Ur-Kabos."

Then she explained, reiterating the events she and Kabeiros had deduced Perses had planned for the funeral. An essential part of the plan was that the body of the old advisor, who was greatly hated, would be found as well as that of his apprentice. Seemingly then the taint of evil magic would be gone from Byblos because only the innocent prince would appear to have survived. Perses, Hekate pointed out, would want to keep the king free of any sorcerous taint because he would then be able to say he hated sorcery and be free to rid Byblos of other sorcerers, even to make war on any neighbor that tolerated magic.

To protests from Kabeiros, she replied that Perses would need no magic with which to influence the king because he would now himself *be* king. Even so Hekate agreed that she could not believe Perses would give up the power of sorcery; thus, he would need a place to work. Ur-Kabos, she pointed out, was ideal. Far enough so that the doings of that less-important place were of little interest in Byblos and close enough, less than two candlemarks ride on a good horse, for Perses to travel back and forth frequently.

"Then it is likely he is there," Dionysos said. "Good. If you are still unwilling to face him, Hekate, I will go alone." His generous lips thinned as a red light behind his blue eyes seemed to make them glow purple. "I am tired of your father. He has hurt you long enough. Not to mention that a person who would inflict such suffering on near a hundred innocents to better drain the last dregs of their life-force is better gone from this world."

"No, Dionysos!" Hekate cried.

The blue eyes glared, but his voice remained soft when he spoke to her. "You need not worry," he assured her. "I'll not risk myself. The whole city of Ur-Kabos will be roused to fall upon him and tear him to pieces."

Hekate was aware of a whole mix of emotions. There was pride and relief because the wild, half-mad boy was now a man. No longer a victim of his enormous powers, he was able to leash them and free them deliberately as he needed them. She felt relief, too, that Dionysos had sense enough not to wish to expose himself to Perses. And she felt a kind of resigned amusement because she was aware that many more than a hundred innocents might suffer when he sent a whole city into a frenzy of rage and terror. To that, Dionysos seemed unaware or indifferent. But above and beyond all the other emotions was her awareness that even if the whole city razed the house in Ur-Kabos, they might not find Perses if he sheltered in the buried workroom.

Hekate went to Dionysos and touched his cheek. "No, love," she said gently. "I am ready now—at least I will be as soon as the amphora is fixed. I'll not risk the chance that—" she took a breath and then said deliberately "—that Perses will win and doom those people."

Rendering the contents of the amphora harmless, even beneficial, was more easily accomplished than Hekate had expected. She already had the means to dismiss and reinvoke the door wards, and she was uninterrupted both in entering and while working. Either Kabeiros had successfully distracted the apprentice or the power source was only used for renewal of the spells at intervals.

She carried with her not only the flask of antidote—to be safe she had doubled the amount she thought she would need—but a rather scruffy mouse. Kabeiros had had a terrible time catching such small prey, but Hekate refused to carry a rat.

When she had again made a penetration of the sealing spell, she first drew out the same amount of liquid that she intended to add and neutralized it. Then she mixed the antidote thoroughly into the contents of the amphora. After waiting a few moments to be sure the antidote had destroyed the poison, she took the mouse and a piece of bread from her pocket, added a few drops of the liquid in the amphora to it, and put it and the mouse under a dark ward.

The mouse ate the wine-soaked bread, took a few tentative steps, and fell over. Hekate drew a frightened breath, thinking for a moment that her antidote had failed. But the mouse didn't squeak, didn't twitch, didn't seem uncomfortable. Hekate leaned closer. It was breathing well, softly and for a mouse deeply. It uttered a tiny, contented snore.

Hekate clapped a hand to her mouth to suppress her giggles. She had put too much wine on the bread. The mouse was drunk. Still smiling she removed the wards that imprisoned the mouse, sent her mind voice to Kabeiros to warn him that she was leaving, and went out of the house with no more difficulty than she had entered it.

Now one part of her screamed to set out for Ur-Kabos at once, to end, one way or the other, the fear that had eaten away at her all her life. Perhaps if that were gone, she wouldn't cling to Kabeiros so tightly that he was half smothered. Perhaps if she weren't afraid, she would manage to survive if Kabeiros left her . . . if either of them were alive . . . if either of them were sane . . . if either of them were not helpless slaves.

She stumbled, needing to catch herself against the wall of a house to keep from falling and realized how very tired she was. Could she walk the distance to Ur-Kabos? Did she have the strength . . . She stumbled again and went to her knees. One passerby looked at her with disgust, apparently thinking she was drunk; another came to help her up and, seeing her close, made a lewd suggestion. Hekate tried to pull away. He gripped her arm . . . and the black dog was there, snarling at the man who retreated in haste, offering his sturdy shoulder for support.

Hekate steadied herself and pushed away the desire to finish, to escape immediately from the fear that oppressed her. She was too weary, having been up all night, to do more that day, and it was the ultimate stupidity to set out for Ur-Kabos exhausted. If she were anything but completely ready, completely at the top of her powers, the worst would not only befall her but likely Kabeiros and Dionysos. And even if they escaped, Perses would be free to play his evil games again.

CHAPTER 27

Hekate slept all the rest of the day, ate heartily of a meal Dionysos brought in from a cookshop, and then slept all night with Kabeiros pressed against her in the bed. She woke early, refreshed, almost happy, and slipped out of the house to visit an old shrine of the Mother. She felt no special greeting, but was comfortably aware of the swirling above her of the high power and the thin threads of earth-blood below. Byblos was not rich in earth-blood. Was that why Perses had turned to blood magic? No, she wouldn't excuse him. He used blood magic because he enjoyed the suffering of his victims.

Kabeiros and Dionysos were breaking their fasts when she returned and she joined them.

"What do we need to take?" Dionysos asked.

"Some food for a noon meal along the way. There are some farms, I suppose, but I prefer not to involve any other people in this. Perses might just be able to detect my aura and punish the folk for helping me."

So that was how they went, carrying nothing but

the makings of a good meal and a flask of wine and another of water. They kept a good pace, but not a hurried one. At midday they stopped and ate. Hekate described her father's house as it had been when she had left it, hesitating as she realized for the first time how many years had passed. But she was sure there would be few changes in the workroom . . . except for the way in, which seemed to have changed each time she was forced to use it. So she warned her companions of the way Perses could change the passage.

"It was straight when I Saw it," Dionysos reminded her.

She looked at him in surprise. "How can you remember so long ago?"

"I never really forget a Vision," Dionysos said, his eyes shadowed with old sadness. "After I know what they mean, I don't think about them anymore. But if I need to See one again, I only need to—" he shrugged "—call it up from inside me. It's always there."

"If I took you to the entrance to the passage," Hekate said, "could you remember the way you went?"

"I think so," he said, "but I can't be sure. Why is it important?"

"Because if he senses our coming, which I expect he will, he might turn that passage into a maze. If I know which walls are false, I can try to break the spells on them. I don't want to waste the time or the power trying to dissolve real walls."

I can help with that, Kabeiros said. *Real walls will smell of wood or stone; wards and illusions will smell of magic.*

"Will you have power enough for breaking the illusions and dealing with him?" Dionysos sounded grim, as if he had suddenly realized what they would face.

"Yes. There's little earth-blood, if any, in his workroom, but the higher power should be there."

She didn't say any more just in case her father's scrying had become cleverer and less heavy-handed than it used to be, but she thought to herself that the draining spell didn't take much power. Once initiated it supplied far more power than the mage expended in maintaining it.

Thoughtful but silent, Dionysos gathered up the remains of their meal. He looked at the chunks of bread and cheese, the slices of meat and his expression grew grim and very determined. Then he rewrapped the leftovers and put them back in the pack. Plainly Dionysos had decided they would need the supplies for the return journey. Hekate prayed he was right as she watched him carefully stopper the wine and water, tie the flasks together, and sling them over his shoulder. Kabeiros got up and shook himself.

They set out on the road again. The day was hot but not unbearable and there was shade by the side of the road, but no one suggested resting in it. All were now determined to reach their goal as quickly as was consonant with their strength and readiness. Dionysos was grim. Kabeiros was silent and withdrawn. Hekate, after so many, many years of denial, of excuses, of shameful fear, was very nearly merry although she didn't impose her mood on the others. Better for them to be anxious and wary.

About three candlemarks after noon, they drew close enough to glimpse Ur-Kabos on its plateau and Hekate began to worry about recognizing the right lane. So many years had passed . . . fifty? seventy? The problem didn't materialize; on their own her feet turned into the path that, shockingly, seemed as familar to her now as it ever had been. She did think as she turned in that the hedge bordering the garden looked a trifle unkempt, but she passed through the opening only to stop dead and stare.

The garden itself was the real shock. Gone was its ordered perfection. What was not overgrown with drought-tolerant weeds was brown and withered with lack of care. Hekate hurried up the path, Dionysos hard on her heels, Kabeiros a man-length to the fore. They mounted the three broad steps. Kabeiros was waiting at the closed door.

Hekate expected the door to be locked and as she climbed the steps was thinking about whether it would be better to try to manipulate the lock by magic or blast the door open. Both would warn Perses that an enemy had arrived, but the blast might direct his attention to the wrong enemy. She warned Kabeiros and Dionysos to stand away from the door, turned to face it to begin the spell . . . and the door opened.

Within it was a doorkeeper, what looked like an old man chained by the neck. Hekate's lips parted to invoke stasis on him, but the spell remained unuttered. This wasn't the creature she remembered. There was recognition in the eyes of the old man.

"Hekate," he mumbled. "You used to give me sugared dates."

"Mahound," she whispered as she made out the remnants of the features of one of the little page boys who had run errands while she lived in the house. "What happened?"

"We tried to run away. Farran was lucky. He died."

"I'll set you free—"

But his eyes had gone blank and he shook his head. "If you are summoned, you know where to go."

"Later." Dionysos took her arm and hurried her

through the doorkeeper's chamber. "When you are done, you can come back and free him."

For a heartbeat, Hekate resisted, then went forward into the courtyard. If she lost the battle, she thought, the doorkeeper would be recaught and punished or killed; if she won, she would have time enough to try to restore him.

The courtyard was another shock. The stone paving was broken and unswept. The flowers were gone, their containers filled with cracked, dusty soil; the bushes that had been so luxuriant were dried skeletons of bare twigs. Opposite the open arch that led to the reception chamber was what looked like a solid garden wall. Hekate approached that, running her fingers lightly along the surface. Dionysos and Kabeiros waited, silent. At about the two-thirds point, Hekate paused, pushed, prodded, and a narrow door, plastered and painted to match the surrounding stones, clicked open. Kabeiros slipped through, then stood waiting.

A very short passage terminated in a second passage, like the leg and head of a T. To the right was a closed door and a stone wall. To the left, the door was open. Hekate cast her mind back and remembered that the way through the right-hand door was much longer than the way from the left.

"That's right," Dionysos said, looking toward the door on the left. "I only came out this way, but I know the left-hand door is the way in."

It was. As soon as they passed through the door, they were at the head of the stairs Hekate remembered all too well. Below was only darkness. Hekate said the word she had heard her father use so often and wondered what would happen. Would the mage lights be as decayed as everything else? No. They came up bright and clear, illuminating the steep, dangerous stair that had been hacked out along the curving wall of a natural sinkhole. Naturally, Hekate thought, starting down. Perses uses this stair. Naturally he would keep it well lit.

Dionysos followed, pausing only once to pick up a pebble and cast it down. At first nothing came up except the faint indeterminable noise that Hekate had never been able to decide was moving water or echoes. Eventually there was a ping of stone against stone and finally a very faint splash. Hekate could hear the black dog panting. She was aware suddenly that dogs didn't manage steep downward stairs well.

Be careful, Kabeiros, she whispered.

Don't worry, Dionysos said, for once using mental speech. *That's why I went ahead. If he slips, he'll run into me and I'll grab him.*

Both Kabeiros and Hekate thanked Dionysos, but Hekate was more frightened rather than less. Dionysos was no weakling, but she had her doubts about his ability to hold Kabeiros' weight on the curved, narrow stair. If they went down together . . . Frantically she sought a spell that could catch them. She had little confidence any spell could do so, but she had to do something . . . and trying to increase the power of the spell filled her mind so that she was unaware of the descent and was suddenly at the end of the stair.

The mage light showed only the black maw of the corridor, nothing within it. Recalling how often she had bumped painfully into walls and corners and that Dionysos had Seen the corridor as straight, Hekate prepared a spell of dissolution of magic, called for a mage light, and stepped forward . . . into a short straight corridor closed with a plain wooden door.

She put her hand out but could not grasp the doorlatch for a moment. Her breath stopped and she could not draw it in. Magic? No, she told herself, cowardice . . . panic. She forced her hand forward, lifted the latch, shoved the door open–and breathed. And stopped breathing!

She had intended to rush forward and seize Perses in her arms before his surprise at her arrival permitted him to act in any way, but shock froze her in place for an instant. The workroom had not changed. The creatures in agonized stasis still hung from walls and ceilings. The alembics, the jars with their strange contents, the little skeletons, all the apparatus were on the tables and the shelves that lined the walls. But Perses had changed. He was old, old as the crone. A few strands of yellow-white hair straggled over his scalp, his mouth was sunken so that his nose almost touched his chin. His back was bent, his hands crooked and mottled. Open-mouthed, Hekate stared.

The sunken lips stretched into a travesty of a toothless smile. "Come in, Hekate," Perses said. "I've been expecting you."

With the words, his will lashed out at her. That wasn't old. It was as strong as it had ever been. Change flooded over her, and it was the crone that hobbled forward helplessly in response to his imperious demand.

Seeing the change, Dionysos believed Perses had sucked most of the life out of Hekate. His pain and fury knew no bounds, and he flung at Perses the full power of his Gift, willing him to panic and madness.

That was not the first time one of Perses' victims had fought back. He was shielded, armored against magical attacks, but he had never been touched by any as powerful as Dionysos'. Terror racked him; confusion caused chaos in his mind. But he was even prepared for that. Almost lost to himself, a mindless, prepared response took over.

Words, now without meaning to him, began to pour from his mouth.

Dionysos gasped and staggered back under a violent blow. His mouth opened as if to cry out, but no sound emerged. He was mute. Instinctively, he tried to move forward but ran into . . . nothing, as hard as a rock wall. Checked, his blue eyes bulged as if they would leap from his head at his enemy. Perses uttered two more words and his right hand began to rise to trace in the air the symbols that would complete a second spell . . . and a huge black dog leapt up, seized the arm, and began to close its jaws.

Flesh tore, bone cracked. The dog whined between set teeth as a guarding spell flowed over, burning him. Perses howled with pain, the spell he was about to cast aborted. He howled again, as the gathered power was released and lashed back at him. In the far corner of the room, beneath a frozen form, part serpent and part horse, contorted in agony, a bundle of rags stirred. No one noticed. The hobbling crone reached Perses and threw her arms around his neck.

Hekate had been overpowered for a moment, but only for a moment. Then she yielded willingly, knowingly, to the will demanding that she come within Perses' reach. How to come near enough to touch him had actually been a problem she had not solved. She had hoped to bypass it by an initial rush that would carry her to him before he could ward her away, but she had lost that opportunity. So when his will pulled her toward him, she had not raised shields to lock out the will; she had yielded to it.

Kabeiros' violent pull on Perses' right arm nearly broke Hekate's grip. Perses screamed again as the black dog's teeth tore more deeply into the flesh. His left hand scrabbled at his waist for the knife in his belt as another spell poured from his mouth. Tears ran from the black dog's eyes but his jaws only locked tighter and he wrenched his head from side to side. Perses' right hand was already hanging loose, one edge of the broken bone showing, blood pouring down to stain the hound's jaws and add to the stains on the floor.

The knife Perses had drawn struck wildly at the dog, but the blow had missed the throat and only a thin line of blood showed on the shoulder. A high whine shrilled from the hound, but it came from between the set teeth; the jaws didn't loosen and the big head twisted savagely. More flesh tore. Perses shrieked and the knife fell from his hand.

Panic pounded in Perses' mind. Madness denied him his spells. Escape was his only hope. He twisted violently, trying to turn and run. The bundle of rags had come upright. The rags heaved and shifted and a glint of a knife honed nearly to a thread showed in the mage light.

Hekate was shoved brutally away from the body-to-body contact she had been seeking, but she would not let go completely. The crone's skinny arms clung like tough, dried vines around Perses' neck. Another frenzied shove pushed her sideways, but her grip still held and she ended up clinging to Perses' back.

She had a vivid memory of what Eurydice said Baltaseros was doing when she drained him. Face to face wasn't necessary. Hekate tightened her grip, took a breath, and began the draining spell. A trickle of power began to flow into her and she had to fight against gagging and being unable to complete the spell. Her mind was flooded with the stench of blood and fear and a hot tingling of the sorcerer's excitement that had somehow got caught up and worked into the power. If she hadn't failed so often while she was trying the spell against the figurine, she would have lost the words, and the symbols in her mind would have been distorted and buried under horror and disgust.

As it was the spell poured out of her automatically. She even paused for breath at the right time and place. Out of the corner of her eye, she caught movement, a sort of flutter as of an edge or a strip of cloth. She dared not shout a warning to Dionysos. To interrupt the spell she was speaking would be fatal, and Kabeiros, who might otherwise have been aware, was tearing at the last tough tendons that held Perses' arm together. The dog's eyes were closed against the desperate pounding and clawing Perses' left hand was inflicting on his head. Dionysos had fallen to his knees, his chest heaving as he fought for breath against Perses' spell, but his eyes were still wide and staring, still fixed on the screaming, writhing sorcerer.

The second part of the spell was welling into Hekate's mind and she began to speak and to build the symbols in her head. More power flowed into her, more grief and agony, more fear and sick relishing of the misery. Tears poured down Hekate's face; her body shook so hard her knees banged into the back of Perses' leg. He began to sag sideways. Hekate braced herself against his weight, gasping for breath . . . in just the right place for the second pause before the third part of the spell.

Blind instinct wrung the last words out of her, painted the figures she was supposed to see behind her closed eyes. The river of power flowing out of Perses turned into a flood. Hekate was drowning in a sea of pain, wrenched by one torment after another, sunk in unrelenting terror, repeatedly scalded by the hot, disgusting, near sexual delight of the original power-drinker in the power and the pain.

Kabeiros gave one last great pull on Perses' arm. His weight added to that of Perses overwhelmed the support the frail crone was able to give. Perses fell, the crone going down with him. The screaming, thrashing weight knocked the breath out of Hekate. She gasped for air, knowing she must begin the second casting of the spell because without it, Perses would not be bound into unending powerlessness.

Crushed under Perses' weight, she began. The first words released such a torrent of power—not only from Perses himself but from all the artifacts and all the tortured creatures in stasis in which he had stored it—that Hekate knew she would never be able to absorb it. She could feel the lines and organ of power within her begin to swell and then to burn. Because to stop would be instant death from the backlash of such enormous energy, she went on with the spell, knowing she had won . . . and lost. Before Perses was drained, she would be a witless idiot or literally burned, and dead.

CHAPTER 28

Hekate's eyes saw and did not see what seemed a stack of rags supported by a short stick that had wavered close and was about to fall on her. Dionysos shouted. Kabeiros was trying desperately to fling away the arm that was caught in his teeth.

It was too late. Out of the heap of rags came a long thin knife. Unable to stop, Hekate said two more words of the spell, three . . . insanely wondering whether the knife or the burning of the power would kill her first. The knife flashed down, missing her arm by a fingerwidth, to plunge into the base of Perses' throat, to be drawn viciously right and left to an accompaniment of thin, high shrieks.

Another shriek echoed, this one deeper, a man's, somewhat muffled as if his mouth was full. Hekate fought a terrible pain in her throat to complete the spell, but the intolerable flood of power into her had already stopped. The bundle of rags collapsed. Hekate frantically pulled her arms away from the blood that poured from Perses' slit throat.

Dionysos got unsteadily to his feet and staggered

toward the pile—Hekate on the bottom, Perses atop her, and then the heap of rags. He picked up whatever it was the rags covered and tossed it aside, crying, "Hekate. Hekate. Are you all right?"

But Hekate could not have answered even if the bodies atop her had not deprived her of breath to speak. When she originally grasped Perses around the neck, she had turned her head to the right so her mouth would not accidentally take in the few strands of Perses' rank hair as she spoke the spell. At the moment the knife had ended Perses' life and the thin shrieks had issued from the heap of rags, she had seen the man Kabeiros appear on his hands and knees with Perses' arm in his mouth. A shock of joy mingled with an agony of loss deprived her of any ability to respond to Dionysos.

A moment later, Kabeiros had used a hand to free himself and flung the arm away, retching once and then swallowing down his bile to crawl—not trusting his balance—to Hekate. Dionysos was already pulling Perses' body off her; Kabeiros helped by shoving from his side and then lifting the crone to a sitting position. She shifted form in his arms, and he nearly dropped her because of the change in weight. Their gazes locked, tears filling both pairs of eyes.

Oblivious of the emotions racking them, Dionysos squatted on his heels beside them. He blew out a deep breath. "I'm so glad you are you again, Hekate. I thought your father had sucked out your life and made you old. I forgot all my good resolutions and threw everything I had at him." Past shock was mirrored anew in his eyes. "He should have died. . . ."

Hekate turned her head and put out a hand, which he took. "It's just as well you acted on instinct, Dionysos," she said. "I nearly killed us all by my hesitation."

"You were afraid," Kabeiros murmured, clutching her tighter to him.

"No," Hekate said quickly, then paused to think, and said much more surely, "No. I wasn't afraid. I was so surprised to see an old, old man that everything I planned went out of my head. But he wasn't old inside. He was as tough and strong as ever."

Dionysos nodded tiredly. "That was quite a fight," he said, "and it took all three of us to bring him down." He sighed. "I took him by surprise with my first blast, but when he started to fight back, I couldn't have held him if Kabeiros hadn't grabbed his arm. Even so, it's lucky I wasn't using magic. I couldn't have said a word after that first spell hit me. It went right through my shields; I could hardly breathe." He shook his head. "And despite all my power, even with the dog ripping off his hand, he still had me walled out from some deep inner part of himself. But then I felt him begin to weaken. That was when you began the draining spell, Hekate." He hesitated and then said softly. "That wouldn't have finished him, would it?"

"No," Hekate whispered. "It would have finished me. His power would have burned me out, killed me." She shuddered. "He had so much power, so much, all wrenched out of the dying agonies of so many, and it was all pouring into me." She closed her eyes. "Blood magic. All blood magic. All that pain. All that fear. All those lives . . ." She shuddered again. "I don't know how I will ever cleanse myself of the filth that poured into me." She buried her face in Kabieros' naked breast and wept helplessly.

"You will take it to the Mother," Kabeiros said softly, stroking her hair. "You will offer it up to Her. She will make you clean." Then a tension came into the arm that was holding her and Kabeiros' other hand froze on her hair. "Who killed him?" he asked, looking over Hekate's head at Dionysos and then beyond him to the pile of rags on the floor.

"It looked to me like an animated heap of rags," Dionysos said, turning around to look. "It still looks like that. Do you think there's anything underneath?"

"Wait, let me," Hekate said. "If it's some trap spell set to catch Perses when he was already distracted, I can probably disarm it."

Shakily Hekate and Kabeiros climbed to their feet, leaning on each other. Dionysos came to steady them both, although he, too, was trembling in the aftermath of his struggle with Perses. They stepped around the body, which had a strange, flaccid look, and turned their eyes to the limp pile of rags. Cautiously, Hekate bent down and touched a finger to them.

"No magic," she said, and sank to her knees to pull away what might have been veils at the top of the heap.

Then she stared at what she had exposed. A face so worn and wizened that the features were unrecognizable. She pulled the rags aside further to see better, and gasped. On the neck was a gaping wound with cuts to either side . . . Hekate's head whipped around to look at Perses. The wounds were identical . . . but no one had touched the creature festooned in rags and no blood had flowed from these wounds.

"Bespelled. Whoever that was was bespelled so that whatever happened to Perses also happend to him . . . her."

Suddenly Hekate remembered the pain in her own throat. She, too, had once been bespelled to suffer what Perses suffered. She raised a hand to feel her neck, but there was no wound in it. She had not inflicted the wound; perhaps that was what saved her. No, more likely when she freed herself from the compulsion against doing magic she had severely weakened the spell of concurrence. She bent lower to look again at the still face surrounded by rags and slowly her eyes widened in horror.

"Asterie?" she whispered. "Mama?"

"Oh dear Mother," Kabeiros breathed, kneeling down beside her. "Oh, Hekate, poor Hekate." He put one arm around her and with his other hand drew her head aside so she was not looking at the dead face.

Hekate didn't resist, but she stared into nothing. "I should have come back sooner. Perhaps if I had, I could have saved her."

"How much sooner?" Dionysos asked harshly. "This didn't happen in a year or two, and if you had come back without the draining spell what good would you have done? I asked you when you wanted to chase after Kabeiros how it would have benefited him if you were dead or enslaved. I ask you that again. In what way would your mother have benefited if you had confronted Perses without a weapon and died or been enslaved?"

"Hekate, she was lost already, long, long before," Kabeiros added. "You told me in the caves of the dead that when you left your father's house your mother was dead to you, had been for several years."

"But she gathered enough of herself to send me a warning," Hekate whispered.

"Yes, and she saved enough of herself to find that knife and hone it and, in the end, use it. But do you think there was really a thinking, feeling person under those rags?"

Hekate freed herself from Kabeiros' restraining hand and looked at the old woman again. "She's smiling," Hekate said, and began to sob heavily.

Kabeiros sighed. "Perhaps there was enough mind, enough person to be glad she had acted and was free. When I was slipping away into the dog, a stimulus could bring back the man for a moment or two. But then I was a dog again and forgot I had ever been a man."

"But you were saved, made a man again by entering the caves of the dead. If I had acted sooner, I might have saved her."

"No, Hekate. If I had stayed a dog any longer I would have been a dog in a man's body when I reached the caves of the dead. I almost was. It took me months, years, to escape from the dog . . . and I'm not sure I've completely escaped. I . . . even now I yearn for the dog." He gritted his teeth.

"Hekate, you're being a fool." Dionysos' voice was sharp. "Say there was some of your mother left in the body Perses so misused. Think of the effort she made to warn you you must run. Think what she would have felt if you returned to save her and lost yourself. Was that what she would have wanted? Do you think it would have added comfort to her remaining years with Perses to know you had died or were enslaved for her sake?"

Hekate covered the face she could barely recognize and stood up. Her lips quivered toward a smile. "My little Dionysos, you're quite right. To return before I was ready would have rendered worthless all my mother's sacrifice. Let me hold to my heart the look of peace and pleasure on her face. But you, who made you so wise?"

"Oh, Ariadne. She and you should be friends of the heart. She, like you, is always beating herself for not being wiser, quicker, not sacrificing herself more completely whether for a useful purpose or not. I think I have learned and used every argument there is to counter self-blame."

Hekate was about to reply when Kabeiros pulled at her. "We need to leave here," he said. "I may not be a dog any longer, but even my man's nose can no longer bear the stench here."

Awakened to an uncomfortable reality, Hekate looked around. The contorted creatures had mostly fallen as the spells fixing them in place had been drawn out. The stasis that had preserved them had also vanished, and they had begun to rot at an accelerated rate. Perses, too, had been in a sense preserved by magic, which was now gone. He was also rotting, his body liquefying and leaking an incredibly foul ooze.

"What can we do?" Hekate asked, swallowing sickly.

"Burn them," Dionysos said. "Burn it all. I can't imagine that there's anything here you want to keep. There must be oil in the kitchen or somewhere. If not, I'll go out and buy some. There's furniture up above. Fetch down what you can carry, Kabeiros, and clothes and hangings. We'll soak them in oil, and let it all burn."

Some frantic hours ensued. Still feeling soiled beyond bearing, Hekate left the men to the cleansing of the hidden workroom while she fled to the shrine in the forest. There she wept for her mother and accepted what she had known since she left Perses' house so many years before—that Asterie was beyond saving and lost to her.

Then she begged to be purified . . . and fell fast asleep. She never knew whether that sleep was the Mother's doing or whether it was a natural result of the terror, exhaustion, and grief she had suffered; however, when she woke not much later by the sun's decline, she knew exactly what to do with Perses' power, which now seemed to be in a tight ball separate from her power and her being. There was a remaining weight hanging about her, another sorrow to accept, but for now she must put that aside and attend to smaller but more immediate problems.

She returned to the house through the long rays of the sun gilding the fields, and went through it seeking servants or anyone else in the place. She released the doorman both physically and then from the compulsion spell that bound him and the five other servants. She told them that Perses was dead, that she was his daughter and now the mistress of the property–which Mahound, the doorman, confirmed. She told them also that they were free, but even after being relieved of their compulsion spells they could not imagine doing anything except living in that house and caring for it. They were more terrified of freedom than they were of slavery.

Most of all they feared she would blame them for the condition of the house. The master had ordered it, they said. He had not told them why, but he had told them he wanted the house to look abandoned. They were not to water the plants in the courtyard or care for the garden or dust or sweep the rooms, only to cook for him and prepare baths when he ordered them and keep his clothing clean and repaired.

Hekate understood, even if they did not. He had intended to work sorcery in his workroom, but wished to keep that a secret, and the best way was to make it seem that no one lived in the house. As to his discomfort, it would be brief and minimal, since most of the time he intended to live in royal luxury as the king of Byblos.

Then Dionysos came to fetch her, and she went down to the workroom, thankful that the mage lights on the walls were set spells that needed renewing occasionally but did not draw their power from Perses. She opened the door, which the men had closed to hold down the stench; she had to hold her breath, but she saw that one of them had brought down a divan and lifted her mother's body to that. She whispered, "Mother take you and reward you, Mama." And then. "Burn!" Drawing out and willing fire with all the blood-magic power that Perses had gathered. "Burn! Burn!"

Dionysos pulled her back from the inferno she had created and slammed the outer door of the passage shut. He sighed. "At least we don't have to worry about the fire spreading. It doesn't even matter if it burns through the door. It isn't going anywhere." He looked up the long flight of stairs and sighed again. "I'm tired," he admitted, as they started to climb up. "Do we have to go back to Byblos tonight?"

"No," Hekate said. "I hope you and Kabeiros didn't burn all the beds and the bedding, but if you did we can get some from the servants, I suppose. And the servants will be delighted to provide us with a meal." She frowned. "I told them they were free, but they wept and pleaded not to go. They want to stay here and go on being servants."

"Then let them serve," Dionysos said, shrugging. "Fix a homeplace for a leaping spell here. If you come once or twice a year to collect rents and the yield of the farms, the servants will be happy, you can keep an eye on the young king in Byblos, and you can have me and Ariadne as guests. There's lots of wine-making around here." He hesitated and then said, "Unless you can't bear to be here?"

Hekate thought that over for a few moments and then shook her head. "No. There was enough good in the early years when my mother was teaching me in the shrine in the forest. I liked the house then, and I always liked the garden and the forest. My father didn't bother with me much when I was young—except to teach me to speak mind-to-mind and–" her lips thinned "–to put his compulsion spells on me. But I didn't know about those until long after I left the house." She shrugged. "I wouldn't want to live here all the time, but for a few nights now and again to see to the farms and the servants, it will be fine. Actually it would be best if you could consider the house yours, Dionysos. I'll come as the guest. I can fix a spell for you that will give you a homeplace here. We can pay Hermes later."

He grinned. "I hoped you'd say that. This is close enough for me to visit my aunt–" his grin broadened "–that'll give her a shock. I'd like to see the Nymphae, too, and to visit my temples here and show them to Ariadne. Yes, I'll be here often enough to let you know if anything is going wrong that you have to look to."

They had reached the top of the stair by then. Hekate went through the door, turned to face it, murmured a sealing spell, and lifted her hand to complete it with a gesture. She stopped suddenly and dismissed the spell. "Sweet Hades," she said, "I almost sealed Kabeiros . . ." Her voice checked and she swallowed. "Kabeiros isn't a dog any more." She swallowed again. "Where is Kabeiros, Dionysos?"

"I don't know." Dionysos frowned. "He insisted on carrying down that divan–it's a miracle that we both didn't end up at the bottom of the hole–and laying your mother on it. He said you wouldn't want her on the floor with the other decaying monsters. And he said to tell you that she . . . her body wasn't rotting like the others. But when we came up, he went out. Maybe he went to wash the stink off him. Even as a man his nose is more sensitive than mine, I think."

She managed to say, "Thank you, Dionysos. Would you do another favor for me and tell the servants to clean rooms for us and prepare a meal? I'll set them to restoring the courtyard and garden tomorrow."

He agreed easily and turned in the direction she pointed out as where the kitchen was. She even managed a brief smile before she ran out the door. Inside, her heart was like a lead weight in her chest. He's gone, she thought. He couldn't even bear to wait to bid me farewell. But I must take some leave of him, I must. I must see him once more, at least once more . . .

Outside she stopped, shaking. It was growing dark. I'll never find him in the dark, she thought, but I must. Deep within she wailed *Kabeiros. Kabeiros.*

I am here, he replied.

Hekate stopped so suddenly that she almost fell. The mental voice was so close . . . She looked frantically down the path and from side to side, terrified she would not see him in the dim light. But he was there, along one of the side paths in the devastated garden, sitting on a bench that had once been sheltered by a magnificent flowering oleander. She started toward him. He had on a worn tunic that was far too short, barely covering his buttocks and genitals.

She wanted to fling herself down on her knees and plead with him to stay with her. She knew he would stay if she begged him, but that would be terribly unjust, terribly cruel, so she tried for a normal sort of remark.

"Did you burn *all* of my father's clothing?" she asked. "You were naked. Why didn't you take some things to wear?"

"I thought you wouldn't want to look at anything of his."

She had come up to the bench. He didn't raise

his head to look at her but kept his eyes fixed on his long, elegant hands. "May I sit with you?" she asked.

"You may do anything you want with me. I owe you my life, my sanity, all my being . . ."

She had started to sit, but jerked upright. "You owe me nothing!" she said, her voice low but so intense it might have been a scream. "You helped me, supported me, sustained me . . ." Tears filled her eyes and she swallowed. "You even loved me when I needed it, even though you could hardly bear to touch me."

His head came up. In the very last of the light, she saw the golden eyes of a dog widen. "Hardly bear to touch you? Are you mad? I could hardly bear to keep my hands off you. Wasn't it wrong to take that, too? How could I ask you to lie with a creature that was more beast than man? You think I don't know why you never accepted the invitations of any man in Olympus? Even that natural pleasure you sacrificed to me. You knew how it would hurt me, and you denied yourself–"

"I denied myself nothing!" She leaned forward and took Kabeiros' head in her hands. "Kabeiros, don't you want to be free of me? You have been bound to me by necessity for so long. I was your anchor to humanity. Do you mean to say that you didn't resent that? That–" her voice started to rise into a protesting wail "–that I have been torturing myself uselessly with the fear that you would leave me as soon as you were free of the curse that bound you?"

"Leave you? I would never leave you of my own will. I love you so much, Hekate. I thought you would cast me out, shake off the burden I was to you as a dog sheds water, as soon as you were free of your binding."

"Free of my binding?" Hekate echoed, seeking within her. "But I'm not free of my binding. You are still here." She touched her breast. "Wound around my heart . . ." Her eyes fixed on him with urgent anxiety. "Dear Mother, don't tell me that now you *can't* change into a dog!" And after an infinitesimal pause, her voice grew light and cheerful. "We will have to begin all over again. You must not lose the dog. You love him—and so do I."

"You love the dog? It doesn't trouble you when I kiss you, when we couple, that part of me is a dog?"

"Oh, no. Not at all. When we have found the cure and you can shift man to dog and back again any time you wish, I would be delighted if you were a dog all day . . . and a man all night." She knelt down before him. "I love you, Kabeiros, dog or man. Won't you stay with me? I will let you go if you feel imprisoned, but if you will live with me, I swear I will not try to bind you in any way. I will let you come and go . . ."

He rose from the bench and pulled her up with him. "Hekate," he said, his lips beginning to twitch, "you are begging me to stay with you. I have been dying with fear that you were tired of the burden and would drive me away. Now I must ask you whether it is the burden you love or me?"

"The burden? What do you mean?"

"You love magic, Hekate. Your greatest pleasure is to work with spells, to do things no other can do with spells and to spells. What if I am not frozen into the form of a man? What if I can change from man to dog and do not need to be cured? Will you still let me stay with you?"

There was a long pause while Hekate examined Kabeiros' face as well as she could. Then she sighed gustily.

"You never intended to leave me," she said, and shook her head. "How could I be so stupid? How could I misunderstand you so completely? When you wouldn't lie beside me or you ran away when I changed my clothing . . . that was because the man desired what the dog did not and the pain was too great for you."

She took his face in her hands and kissed him gently. "And you have always put me first, not in things that endangered me—you might have done that because you needed me—but in consideration of my feelings. You endangered your own life and that of Dionysos to give my poor mother some dignity in her death, you were willing to wear a servant's cast-off so I would not need to see my father's clothing." She paused and sighed. "Have we both been tormenting ourselves for nothing?"

"Yes," he said succinctly. "And now that we've stopped . . ." He put both arms around her and pulled her hard against his body. "I'm very hungry."

"Direct as a dog," she said, laughing and wriggling her hips against him. Then her body stilled and she frowned. "You say you can change at will?"

Kabeiros dropped his arms, and the black dog stood before her, his white eyes fixed on her face. *Here I am, a dog. Why do you question me?*

Because I still feel the binding to you around my heart. Not that I mind it. I would be empty without it, but I fear something is wrong.

"No, love." He was standing before her, a man, his arms around her again. "Nothing is wrong. It could not be more right. What you feel I feel also. It is not a binding, but a bonding. We are life-bonded, my love."

"Life-bonded." She sighed with satisfaction and dropped her head to his chest. "We will have a wonderful time, Kabeiros. How would you like to go to fabled Chin and India?"

"Why not?" He laughed aloud. "You are free of your bindings and we are two together. We can go anywhere."